TEXAS JADE

Holly Harte

Zebra Books
Kensington Publishing Corp.

http://www.zebrabooks.com

ZEBRA BOOKS are published by

Kensington Publishing Corp.
850 Third Avenue
New York, NY 10022

First Printing: July, 1998
10 9 8 7 6 5 4 3 2 1

Printed in the United States of America

TEXAS PASSION

As Eli started to pitch forward, Jade grabbed his arms and braced herself to break his fall if she couldn't steady him. Several tense seconds passed before his swaying stopped, allowing Jade to relax.

"Do you want to sit down for a minute?" she said.

Eli slowly shook his head, never taking his gaze from her face.

"Then, I'll . . ." Jade licked her dry lips, bringing a rumble from Eli's chest. "I'll help you into—"

His mouth pressed to hers halted her words, making her forget everything except the taste of him. The kiss began as a soft and easy exploration of her lips, then quickly escalated into a fierce possession of not only her mouth, but of something much deeper as well. It was as if he had taken possession of the core of her being with the kiss. Moaning, she rose to her toes, then slid her hands up his arms and over his shoulders to lock behind his neck.

Eli's head spun, his senses in complete disarray. He shouldn't be kissing Jade, shouldn't be enjoying the kiss so much. He tried to end it, but Jade would have no part of it. Instead, she pressed more fully against his chest, tightening her hold on him . . .

Books by Holly Harte

Dancer's Angel

Texas Silver

Texas Jade

Published by Zebra Books

Special thanks to Park Ranger Mary L. Williams from the Fort Davis National Historic Site, for generously sharing her knowledge of Fort Davis and the surrounding areas of far West Texas.

Chapter 1

Far West Texas, April, 1871

Clang. Clang. Clangity-clang.

Eli Kinmont turned his head slightly at the sound, then wished he hadn't. Any movement at all made the pounding in his head even worse. *What the hell's that infernal racket?* Of all the sounds he might have heard in the middle of these West Texas mountains, he hadn't expected to hear the clanging of a bell. Maybe his head injury was worse than he thought. Willing to risk the pain to see what was making the irritating noise, he sucked in a deep breath, then carefully turned his head toward the sound.

Over the pounding in his temples, he heard the clanging again, closer this time, almost as if the bell were right above him. He waited for the pain to ease, then slowly opened his eyes to stare at a tuft of white hair less than a foot above his face. He blinked several times, bringing into focus an equally hairy chin from which the tuft sprouted.

"What the hell?" he said, trying to lever himself up to get away from whatever creature lurked over him.

A sharp, lancing pain shot through his head, threatening to drag him into the depths of unconsciousness. He had to take several deep breaths before he managed to stave off the encroaching blackness. When the pain subsided and his vision cleared, the identity of his unexpected visitor became apparent.

A long-haired, brown and white goat stood beside him, a large metal bell tied around its skinny neck, its bearded chin bobbing just inches above his face.

He blew out his breath in a short huff, squeezing his eyes closed. *Instead of the face of an angel, I'm seeing a damn goat! Guess that confirms what I've known all these years. A man like me wouldn't be sent to the place where angels—*

Another sound interrupted Eli's thoughts—this one he had no trouble recognizing, even though it had been years since he'd heard one so close: a woman speaking English.

"Don't be afraid of Trella, *señor*. She won't hurt you; she's just curious."

He opened his eyes again, then turned his head toward the sound, wincing at the movement. "Who—" Eli licked his dry lips, forcing the words through his equally dry throat. "Who the devil are you?"

The woman bent down beside him. "My name is Jade Tucker," she said, placing a palm on his forehead. "You don't seem to be feverish. That's a good sign. How long have you been lying here?"

Eli frowned, squinting against the glare of sun that haloed around the woman and prevented him from seeing her face. "What do you care?" Although he meant to sound gruff, his words came out even harsher than he'd intended.

To the woman's credit, the only reaction he detected to his rudeness was a slight catch in her breathing. She exhaled slowly, then said, "I care because you need medical assistance. Now, when did you get hurt?"

"I fell this morning, just after daybreak while I was

tracking a mountain lion. Not that it's any of your concern."

She ignored his sarcasm, then said, "Can you get to your feet? If not, I'll help you."

"I don't want your help."

"But—"

"Didn't you hear what I said?" His voice took on an even frostier tone, one which would have gotten him immediate results in another life—a life he'd left behind a long time ago. "I don't want or need your help. I can get up on my own when I'm damn good and ready, so go away."

Jade clamped her mouth shut, holding in the retort she longed to make. Instead, she straightened, turned to grab the reins of Luna, her pinto mare, then moved a few yards away. After tying the horse to a small piñon tree, she took a seat on one of the many rocks along the mountainside trail, prepared to wait him out. She'd dealt with stubborn men before and was all too familiar with male pride. Such a fragile ego—as delicate as one of the wild rose blossoms growing in the mountain pass to the north—required time to come to terms with what she already knew—this man needed her help.

As Jade waited, she studied the man she'd stumbled on while gathering Paloma's goats from a valley deeper in the mountains. He lay on his back a few yards away, arms at his sides, hands curled into fists. Hatless, his long light brown hair with its streaks of gold was tousled, one thick lock dropping onto his broad forehead. She wasn't sure of the color of his eyes, but based on the brief glimpse she'd gotten when he glanced up at her, she thought they were a deep blue. His closely cropped beard and tanned face bore the rugged look of a man accustomed to living outside. His cotton shirt and buckskin trousers revealed a lean but well-muscled build, and though judging his height was difficult from his prone position, she guessed him to be close to six feet.

She watched the man struggle to get up, inwardly wincing when he fell back onto the ground with a soft groan. Though she longed to go to him, she didn't move. She remained seated on the rock, back stiff and hands clenched tightly in her lap.

Eli bit back another groan, silently cursing his weakened state. For six years he'd gotten along just fine without needing anyone. So finding himself in a situation which might change his self-sufficient life as a trapper didn't sit well. Summoning the strength to try again, he pushed himself up onto one elbow, then to a sitting position. He shifted his legs in preparation for getting to his feet, but his spinning head and throbbing ankle told him he was fighting a battle he couldn't win. With a muffled curse, he dropped back onto the ground.

"All right, dammit," he said after a moment, his breathing harsh in the stillness of the mountains. "You win."

Jade ignored the satisfaction his words caused, unclenched her hands, then got to her feet. She moved closer to the man, whose face had changed from a healthy tan to a sickly gray. "Lie still and catch your breath. I want to look at the cut on your head, then check your ankle before we try to get you onto your feet."

"What are you, some kind of yarb woman?"

"Not exactly, though I do use herbs to treat those who need my services," she said, kneeling beside him again and leaning closer to get a better look at the dried blood caked along the hairline on the left side of his head.

"You're a *médica*, then?"

"No, not a formally trained doctor." She gently probed the crusted-over cut on his head. "I learned my healing skills from my mother and *Señora* Paloma Diaz."

As her probing fingers found a particularly sensitive spot, Eli winced. "Who's Paloma Diaz?"

"She's an *herbaria*, and also a highly skilled *partera*," she replied. "I was her apprentice for several years before she moved to this part of West Texas. Trella and the other goats belong to her."

"So, you're an herbalist and a midwife?"

"As I said, I use herbs in my healing, but no, I don't consider myself a *partera*, even though the *señora* has taught me much about bringing babies into the world. I don't want to be labeled as one type of healer. I want to be skilled in all areas of healing so that I can treat all patients, like a true medical doctor."

"A noble goal. But keep in mind, not all those claiming to be doctors received any formal training. Some just start practicing medicine without ever having stepped inside a medical school lecture hall. Take care not to pattern yourself after those quacks."

She shifted her gaze for a quick glimpse of his face, her brow furrowed at his warning. "I don't intend to."

Eli remained silent for a moment before saying, "You said you were an apprentice to *Señora* Diaz before she moved, so are you visiting her?"

"I have recently moved here from my family's home to the south. I now live in the town of Fort Davis. I visit *Señora* Diaz whenever I can and help her with her goats. She lives alone, near her son in a canyon just to the east of here."

"If she lives near her son, why doesn't he help with her goats?"

"He does, when he can. But he's busy working on his ranch and often goes to Del Norte across the Rio Grande for days at a time. I owe the *señora* a great deal for all she's taught me, and I care for her like she is part of my family. So I'm more than willing to help her in any way I can."

Eli made no comment, thinking about everything she'd told him. Her recent move to Fort Davis explained why he hadn't seen or heard of a healing woman on his previous visits to the military post and neighboring town bearing the same name. But then he'd only been this far north a couple of times in the six years since he arrived in West Texas, and he'd never spent more time than necessary when passing through. He stopped only long enough to buy supplies or sell some of his pelts, then immediately headed out of town. At last, he said, "Have you seen my horse and pack animals? A dun gelding and a pair of gray burros? I left them down the trail a ways, while I tracked the cat on foot."

"They were still there. That's how I found you." She didn't add that the visions she'd had revealed not only the horse and burros, but also a man needing her help. "I gave them water, then left them picketed in a small stand of piñon." She shifted positions to check his other injury.

When she squeezed his left ankle, he sucked in a sharp breath. "You don't have to check for broken bones. I twisted my ankle when I fell, severely stretching the ligaments, but nothing's broken. It's just badly sprained and needs rest to heal."

Her hands stilled on his leg. "How do you know that?"

"I . . . uh . . . I knew someone who got hurt like this, and that's . . . er . . . what the doctor said."

Jade considered his response for a moment, then removed her hands and sat back on her heels. "Lie still while I go get your animals."

She started to rise, but his fingers gripping her arm stopped her. "Wait."

"What is it, *señor*?"

Eli released his grip and dropped his hand back to his side, his breath lodged in his throat. The angle of the sun had changed enough for him to get his first real glimpse of her face. She didn't possess the features he'd always equated with the epitome of female beauty. Her eyes were a little too wide-set, her lips too full, chin too small and her complexion wasn't milky white, but the pale tan of a deer hide. But even so, her lack of classic beauty was made up tenfold by her hair—deep, rich mahogany waves shot with brilliant red highlights flowing down her back—and thickly lashed eyes of a color like none he'd ever seen—a clear, bright green with bits of silver swimming in their depths.

He swallowed hard, pushing aside his unwelcome reaction to this woman. "The name is Kinmont, Eli Kinmont."

Jade wondered at the return of his gruff tone, but made no comment. Instead, she left the man her visions foretold she'd meet and went to retrieve his horse and burros.

By the time she returned, Eli had managed to make it to a sitting position, though his labored breathing and sweat-dotted forehead told her what his efforts had cost him.

She waited until the pallor left his cheeks and his breathing eased before stepping closer to hand him his hat. "I found this tied to your saddle."

He reached up to take the hat, scowling at how his hand shook. "Thanks."

"Are you going to be able to ride?"

He settled the worn hat on his head, then gingerly tugged the brim down onto his forehead. "Yeah, I think so. Just give me a minute."

When he indicated he was ready, she helped him get to his feet, then supported his weight while he hopped on his good leg over to his gelding. By the time he'd finally managed to swing onto the horse's back, he was biting his lip to hold in a moan, his head reeled with dizziness and his ankle throbbed unmercifully.

As they started down the mountain trail, Eli didn't ask where they were headed. Speaking aloud would have required too much effort, and besides, at the moment he didn't care where they were going. All he wanted was to get some place where he could lie down and, if he was honest with himself, another chance to look into the incredible eyes of the woman riding not far from his side.

Jade kept glancing over at the man on the dun gelding, wishing they were closer to town. She wanted to pick up their pace, but she didn't dare. Noting how Eli had tangled his hands in the hair of his horse's mane, how his jaw muscles flexed with the jarring motion of the gelding's gait, she knew he already had all he could do to stay in the saddle without trying to increase their speed.

"We need to make a stop before we head into town. *Señora* Diaz is expecting me to return with her goats, and I'll have to go in and see her when we get to her house."

Eli flicked a brief glance in her direction. Unable to summon the strength to speak, he gave her a quick nod.

Though time seemed to stand still for Jade, only a few minutes had passed before she and Eli entered the canyon where Paloma Diaz lived. At the southern end of the meadow on the canyon's floor stood the house and out-buildings belonging to her son. On the northern edge of the meadow, a small *jacal-hut* had been built against the brown craggy rock wall of the canyon.

Jade pulled her mare to a halt, slipped to the ground, then moved to Eli's gelding. "I can help you dismount if you want to get off your horse."

"I'll stay where I'm at," he said, his voice low and laced with pain. "If I got off, I'd never get back up here."

She nodded, her heart cramping at his obvious discomfort. "I'll be back as quickly as I can."

Eli watched her lead the small herd of goats to a pen beside the tiny house, for the first time noticing more about her. She was dressed much like the Mexican women he'd seen in his travels below the Rio Grande: a full, ankle-length, dark green skirt which accented her narrow waist, and a scoop-necked, short-sleeved white blouse hinting of a full bosom. As her skirt swished about her legs, he caught a glimpse of tall, buckskin moccasins trimmed with what appeared to be brightly colored beads.

For a few minutes he forgot about his pounding head and throbbing ankle, content just to look at the gentle swaying of Jade Tucker's backside as she walked from the goat pen to the house. She sent a quick glance in his direction, then disappeared through the front door. He drew a deep breath and eased it out slowly. His gelding

snuffled then stamped one hoof, jarring Eli's entire body
and chasing his thoughts with a jolt.

"Dammit, Rex, stand still," he said, gritting his teeth
against the sudden nausea gripping his middle. He shot a
glare toward the closed door of the small house. *And you,
Jade Tucker, get those silver-flecked eyes of yours back out here so
we can get moving.*

"It is good to see you, *chica,*" Paloma Diaz said after
Jade gave the older woman a hug. Paloma's wrinkled brown
face broke into a grin, her steel-gray hair pulled into the
usual tight knot at the back of her head and black eyes
snapping with fire in spite of her failing eyesight. "I hope
Trella and the others didn't go too far this time."

In spite of Jade having recently celebrated her twenty-
first birthday, Paloma continued to use the nickname she'd
given her from the moment they met many years earlier.

"No, *maestra*—teacher," Jade said, returning the smile
of the woman she also considered a dear friend. "They
were grazing on a hillside in a valley I know they favor.
I'm sorry I didn't get here earlier, but I—"

"There is no need to explain. You finally found the man
in your vision, *sí?*"

Jade blinked. "How do you always know what—?" She
shook her head with a laugh, then said, "Never mind, I
know you won't tell me. Yes, I found him. He's an Anglo
trapper, and as the Spirits predicted, he needs my help. I
must get him into town right away, so I can treat his injuries.
I'm afraid I won't be able to stay."

"Está bien—it is all right. You know I enjoy our visits, but
today you have something more important to take care
of." She stared at Jade, squinting in an attempt to make
out the younger woman's expression. "His injuries, they
are not serious?"

"No, I don't think so. He said he fell while tracking a
mountain lion not far from here. He has a cut on his head

and a sprained ankle, but neither injury appears to be serious."

"*Bueno.* Then go see to the Anglo," Paloma said with another smile. "We will talk another day about your man."

Jade's mouth dropped open. *Her man!* What was Paloma hinting at?

Jade bent to give the woman another hug. "Take care, *maestra.* I promise I will stay longer next time I visit."

Paloma patted Jade's cheek with one gnarled hand. "I will be fine, *chica.* Now go."

At the door, Jade paused for a moment. From the shadow of the open doorway, she stared out at the man the Spirits had predicted she would meet. Her visions hadn't revealed that Eli Kinmont would become anything more than her patient, so she couldn't let the fanciful musings of Paloma influence her reaction to the man—no matter how attractive she found him.

Chapter 2

By the time Jade pulled Luna to a halt in front of her house at the edge of town, she feared the trip had been too hard on Eli. His posture told her he'd remained in the saddle by sheer determination, shoulders hunched forward, chin nearly resting on his chest and fingers still knotted in the black mane of his gelding.

For a moment, she doubted her decision to make the six-mile trip from *Señora* Diaz's house. Maybe she should have made camp where she'd found him and tended his injuries there. Glancing over at Eli again, she gave her head a shake. No, she'd made the right decision.

Her healing supplies were here at her home, along with a bed and plenty of food. Everything Eli needed to recover. She dismounted, then hurried over to his gelding.

At Jade's encouragement, Eli managed to get his right leg over his horse's back. Holding his breath against the pain he knew awaited him, he kicked his injured leg free of the stirrup and let himself slide to the ground. As soon as his feet touched the hard-packed earth, he gasped and his knees buckled. If not for Jade pressing her body against his left side and her right arm wrapped around his waist, he would have fallen in an awkward heap.

"The door is only a few steps away, *Señor* Kinmont. You can make it."

"I don't—"

The excited yip of a dog cut off Eli's reply. From around the house, a small cream-colored dog came bounding toward them, its curled tail wagging furiously in greeting.

"Zita, that's enough," Jade said. "Be a good girl and stay out of the way while I get my patient inside." The dog quieted, then moved a few feet away and lay down, her tail swishing back and forth over the dusty ground.

Jade smiled at her pet, then turned her attention back to Eli. "I've got you," she said, tightening her hold around his waist. "We'll take it real slow."

"You should have left me on the trail," he said, barely able to hear his own words over the pounding in his head. "I'm not worth the trouble."

Something inside Jade tightened at his words. "Don't ever say that," she said, her voice a fierce whisper. "You're not any trouble. And you're worth whatever it takes to heal your injuries."

Whatever it takes. The words echoed in Eli's head. Maybe she could heal him on the outside. But what about the injuries she couldn't see, the ones on the inside—the ones that would never heal? If she knew about those wounds, she wouldn't be so quick to offer her help.

A few minutes later, Jade had managed to get him through the front door of her house, across the main room, past a door leading to another room, probably the kitchen, and through a second doorway into what he immediately realized was her bedroom.

He halted his awkward hopping gait in mid-stride, biting back a curse when he put too much weight on his left foot and sent a sharp pain radiating up his leg. "No, not your bed! Isn't there—?"

"Shh, it's all right. I have only one bed, and you are more than welcome to use it."

"I'll take the floor. A no-account like me is used to sleeping on the ground, so it won't be any hardship."

Jade glanced up at his face, wondering why he had so little regard for himself. "I won't permit a patient of mine to lie on the floor when there's a perfectly good bed available. Now, stop arguing and help me."

He started to protest further, then snapped his mouth shut. The prospect of a real bed, his first in months, was too appealing. As he made the last few clumsy hops to the bed, he glanced around. The room was small but neat, bathed in a soft golden light from the late afternoon sun shining through the single window and filled with a scent he already associated with the woman pressed against his side—crisp mountain air laced with the spicy tang of wildflowers and the sweetness of fresh grass.

She removed his hat and tossed it aside, then reached down to flip back the blanket and top sheet. Following her whispered directions, he turned and sat on the edge of the bed, then lay down on his side. His head sank into the welcoming softness of the pillow, bringing a sigh to his lips. When she lifted one of his feet to remove the boot, he realized he couldn't help her with the task and silently cursed his weakness.

The right boot came off without much resistance, but the left wasn't so easily wrested from his foot. He tried not to make any noise, biting his lip against the urge to cry out. But her efforts to pull the boot over his painfully swollen ankle finally wrenched a howl of protest from deep in his chest.

With one final tug, the second boot came off, leaving him breathless, his head spinning and his leg hurting more than ever. Waiting for his dizziness to pass and the throbbing in his ankle to ease, he wondered if he'd actually made the piteous sound still echoing in his ears. But then he shouldn't wonder, not with the memory of the inhuman sounds he'd once been forced to listen to, screams of men experiencing unbearable pain, screams he knew were forever etched into his soul.

He shoved those troubling memories aside. That was the past, a past he'd buried long ago, a past he had no plans to unearth. Rolling onto his back and closing his eyes, he exhaled heavily then let the tension seep out of his muscles. In a matter of minutes, he had relaxed enough for sleep to tug him into the soothing depths of oblivion.

Jade worked quickly, taking advantage of Eli's slumber. She carefully cleaned his head wound with soap and water, then rubbed creosote bush salve on the cut. Next she applied a warm poultice of powdered ocotillo root wrapped in a length of clean cloth to his swollen ankle. Standing back to look at him, she knew there was little more she could do for the time being. Once he awoke, she could make him a tea if he experienced a lot of pain. But for now, he appeared to be in a sound sleep. Satisfied she had done all she could, she headed outside to take care of the animals.

After unsaddling the horses and removing the packs from the burros, she stowed the gear in the lean-to built against the rear wall of her house then turned Luna and the others loose in the small corral. She would have liked to give all four animals a much-deserved rubdown, but she only took enough time to make sure they had plenty of feed and water before picking up Eli's saddlebags and returning to the house. She let Zita inside with her, but made the dog stay in the main room while she checked on her patient.

Eli still slept, his face relaxed for the first time since she'd found him on the mountain trail. She stared down at him, wondering again why the Spirits had told her of this man in the visions they sent her. Whenever she'd had visions in the past, there had always been a reason for the Spirits to speak to her: foretelling danger, predicting the future or showing her the way to accomplish a task. But what was the reason for Eli Kinmont's appearance in her visions?

She pushed aside that question and others about this stubborn man, knowing she would have to wait for the Spirits to reveal the answers. Still staring at the man lying on her bed, she longed to run her fingers over his forehead, down his slightly crooked nose, across his wide mouth now slack with sleep, but she resisted the temptation. Instead, she contented herself with simply looking at his strong features and wondering about him. Where was he from? And why had he come to far West Texas? The slight southern drawl she'd detected in his speech was similar to many of the soldiers at Fort Davis, though Eli's accent was less pronounced, more cultured. But other than her suspicions about his southern roots and being well-educated, she knew only that he apparently made his living by hunting wild game, since the packs on his two burros contained an assortment of animal pelts, and that he knew at least some Spanish. All in all, she realized she knew next to nothing about the man she'd brought into her home.

Her eyes suddenly widened. What if he was one of the men she'd heard her father talk about—those who'd come to an area once labeled The Bad Lands by early map makers—desperadoes of every sort who came to this desolate part of Texas after the War Between the States? Surely the Spirits wouldn't have brought a man with such a background into her life. Would they?

As she contemplated those troubling questions, the man filling her thoughts stirred. He blinked several times then slowly turned his head to look around the room, his gaze finally landing on her.

Jade moved closer, dropping his saddlebags on the floor beside the bed. "How are you feeling? If you're in pain, I can get something for you."

He lifted a hand to gently probe along his hairline with his fingertips. "What the devil did you put on my cut?"

"A salve made from a healing plant."

His thick eyebrows snapped together. "Healing, ha! Nothing smelling that bad could be called a healing plant."

Jade chuckled. "Unfortunately, the creosote bush does have an unpleasant odor. That's why the Mexicans call it *yerba hedionda*—stink bush. In spite of its smell, the salve is excellent for cuts and scrapes."

He didn't reply, but merely grunted. Shifting positions, he winced when he moved his left leg. Looking down at his ankle, his brows knit even tighter. "Is that what's on my leg?"

"No, I used a poultice of powdered ocotillo root on your ankle. To reduce the swelling."

"Roots and foul-smelling salves," he said with a snort. "Asinine folk medicine."

"The plants do a good job of healing," Jade said, curling her hands into fists. "Or my mother's ancestors wouldn't have used them for generations."

"Your mother's ancestors?"

Jade braced herself for his reaction. "My mother is a *Nde* medicine woman."

"Ah, so you're half Indian," he said, figuring that explained her beaded moccasins.

"No, a quarter. My grandmother was full-blooded *Nde*. My grandfather is Spanish."

Eli didn't respond for a minute, then said, "*Nde?* Isn't that what the Mescalero Apache call themselves?"

"Yes, how do you know that?"

"Can't travel through these mountains or the ones down by the Rio Grande without crossing their path. I've run across a hunting party a time or two. Even shared a campfire with four of them one evening. They spoke excellent Spanish, which is how I came to know the word *Nde*."

"You're fortunate. Not all *Nde* are tolerant of white men in their homeland."

"Yes, I know, but I have no quarrel with them. Not like the Texas government saying the Mescalero no longer have a home inside the state's borders, then trying to force them onto the Bosque Redondo reservation in New Mexico Territory.''

"For a solitary trapper, you're awfully well-informed.''

He shrugged. "I figure it doesn't hurt to know what's going on around you. So, whenever I get to a town, I catch up on the news." When she didn't respond, he said, "Were your relatives among those that disappeared from the reservation back in '65?''

"No one should be forced to live in those conditions," Jade said, suddenly uncomfortable with the path their conversation had taken. Though Eli said he had no quarrel with the *Nde*, she wasn't ready to trust him. If she revealed that her cousin Night Wind lived with a band of *Nde* deeper in the Davis Mountains, she might be putting him and the others in grave danger. If the commander at Fort Davis found out a band of *Nde* was camped less than a day's ride . . . She repressed a shudder, unable to finish the thought. Determined to change the subject, she said, "You didn't tell me whether you're in pain. I'll make some herb tea. I promise it will help.''

"More folk medicine. You sound just like that fool—"

"I sound like who?''

"Nobody, it's not important," he replied, wincing when he tried to change his position.

Though Jade longed to tell him he could just lay there and suffer, she couldn't bring herself to say the words. She was a healer, and she'd never refused to help anyone, no matter how out of sorts they were or how much they stirred her anger. "You must be hungry. I'll fix you something to eat while the tea steeps.''

"I'm more thirsty than hungry. I could use some water, unless you've got something stronger." He wasn't a drinking man, but at the moment, a shot of whiskey to take the edge off the pain in his throbbing head and ankle sounded damn good.

"The strongest drink I have is peach brandy.''

"Brandy from the peach orchards owned by John Davis?"

"Yes. He lives on Alamito Creek not far from my parents' ranch. Do you know him?"

"Only by the reputation of his peach brandy. It's excellent."

Jade nodded, then said, "I'll be back in a few minutes with the tea and some food." When he started to speak, she gave him a pointed glare and added, "I know, you want something stronger. After you do what I tell you, then you can have some brandy."

Eli snapped his mouth closed, accepting defeat. Jade Tucker was a tough opponent, and there was no point in continuing an argument he couldn't win. Actually, now that he paid attention to his body's signals, he realized he was hungrier than he'd originally thought. With a wry twist of his lips, he figured he hadn't lost the verbal battle after all.

As soon as Eli finished the meal and the tea Jade insisted he drink, she kept her word and handed him a half-filled glass of peach brandy. He accepted the glass, his fingers brushing hers. A tingling sensation raced through her veins and a strange searing heat swept over her entire body. Wondering at her odd reaction to this man, she rubbed her hand against her skirt to rid herself of his touch.

"I have to leave you for a while."

He lifted his eyebrows but didn't respond.

"I need to go to the fort to let Dr. Chadbourne know I'll be late to work tomorrow."

"Work? You work at the fort?"

"Yes, I work at the post hospital."

"As what, a nurse, a matron, or maybe a laundress?"

"No, I'm Dr. Chadbourne's assistant."

Eli chuckled. "Really? A female civilian assistant. I find that hard to believe."

Jade's chin came up. "Dr. Chadbourne's last assistant surgeon was transferred some months ago and won't be replaced because the army has cut the post's budget. Which meant hiring a civilian was his only choice, and Dr. Chadbourne thought I was well-qualified."

"He didn't have any misgivings about hiring an assistant who's not only a woman, but also part Indian? Or didn't you tell him that bit of information?"

"Why should it matter that I'm a woman or that I have *Nde* blood? My healing abilities should be what's important."

"Should be, but a lot of folks—especially the army—might not agree." He took another sip of brandy, then said, "So, did you tell him, or not?"

"I ... well ... not in those exact words. I told him I learned my healing skills from my mother and that she was taught by her grandfather, a highly skilled medicine man. So I assumed he made the connection."

"Let's hope he did," Eli said in a low voice, then louder, he added, "how do you assist the good doctor? Change beds. Empty bedpans. Spoon-feed the sick."

The heat of a blush burning her cheeks, she was tempted to slap him for the sarcastic remark. Inhaling a deep breath, she crossed her arms over her chest to keep from giving in to temptation.

"If necessary, I'll do all those things," she said through tight lips. "But I'll also be assisting Dr. Chadbourne with the patients at the fort hospital."

"Is that right?" His forehead furrowed, he pinned her with a fierce stare. "Assisting how? Holding a patient's hand while the doctor lances a boil or stitches up a cut?"

"Why are you making such contrary remarks?" Jade said, her usually even temper rapidly reaching the boiling point.

Eli shrugged, then replied, "I just don't see how a yarb woman would—" Seeing the spark of anger in her eyes, he held up one hand to halt her retort. "Okay, I don't see how a yarb woman *and* midwife would be much help treating the soldiers garrisoned at the post."

"There are also civilians living at the fort who might need medical treatment, and I've already treated some of the people in town."

Eli shifted his gaze away from her. "How much do you know about treating a gunshot wound, or administering anesthesia or . . ." His voice dropped to a whisper. "Amputating a shattered leg."

Jade stared at him through narrowed eyes. "Not much, but I intend to learn. That's the main reason I applied for the job as Dr. Chadbourne's assistant, so I could add to my healing abilities by learning how medical doctors treat their patients." She paused for a moment to gather her thoughts. "I don't understand why you're saying these things to me. You . . . you sound like you know about gunshot wounds and anesthetic and—"

"So, you think Dr. Chadbourne is going to be your teacher?" he said, swivelling his head back to face her.

She nodded. "He said he would when his schedule permitted."

"So what has he taught you so far?"

"Actually, he hasn't had time to begin my lessons. He's away from the post a lot, visiting the troops guarding the mail stations or the garrison at Fort Quitman. So after I complete my duties at the hospital, I've been reading the medical journals in Dr. Chadbourne's off—" His chuckle turned her voice icy. "And just what's wrong with my desire to improve my healing skills?"

Eli drank the last of the peach brandy in one swallow, then held the empty glass towards her. "Nothing, *roja*. Now go. Go see your Dr. Chadbourne."

Ignoring his calling her *roja*—red—and the resulting sizzling warmth tumbling through her body, she pressed her lips into a thin line. *Stop it! Stop reacting to this man.* As much as she wanted to heed her own warning, another round of wildfire raced through her veins. She fought for control of her wayward body, willing her unwanted reaction to fade, but with little success.

She drew a shallow breath then released it slowly. Stiffening her spine, she uncrossed her arms then reached out and took the glass, careful to keep her fingers from touching his. Without another word or looking into eyes she now knew were an incredibly beautiful, deep shade of blue, she turned and left the bedroom.

Chapter 3

As Jade made the mile walk to the fort with Zita trotting along beside her, she couldn't get the conversation she'd just had with Eli out of her head. Why was he so cynical about her working for the post surgeon, or her desire to learn more about healing? Why was he so adverse to using herbs and plants to treat the sick and injured? And, unless her initial impressions of him were badly mistaken, where had he acquired his apparent knowledge of medicine? Picking up her pace, she made up her mind to find out everything she could about the man currently lying in her bed. A man whose arrogance easily infuriated her into an uncharacteristic display of temper, yet, being totally honest with herself, a man who just as easily stirred her desires as a woman.

As she entered the military post, she tucked away thoughts of Eli Kinmont for the time being and concentrated on her surroundings. Fort Davis, rebuilt four years earlier after sitting empty since the Confederacy closed the post during the War Between the States, was located at the mouth of Limpia Canyon in the Davis Mountains—

one of the most picturesque settings Jade had ever seen. Surrounded on three sides by sheer walls of dark reddish brown rock, the military reservation faced a flat open plain which stretched eastward as far as she could see.

Jade always enjoyed walking across the grounds of the fort, soaking in the beauty surrounding her, especially on such a pleasant spring evening. The wind had died, now just gently rustling the oak trees she passed. The post hospital consisted of a group of adobe brick buildings which were located midway up the canyon, behind a line of small stone houses known as officers' row.

At the door to the post surgeon's office, Jade told Zita to stay then entered the building to find Dr. Chadbourne checking the supplies in his medical bag.

"Ah, Miss Tucker, I'm glad you're here. Saves me sending you a message." Dr. Thomas Chadbourne was of medium height, whipcord thin, with kind hazel eyes behind his spectacles and sporting a thick moustache the same shade of dark brown as his collar-length hair.

Jade moved closer to his desk. "I came to tell you I may need to work shorter hours for the next few—" His actions and words finally registering, her heart sank. "Have you been called away again?"

He gave her a weak smile. "I'm afraid so. I'll be heading to Fort Stockton at dawn. Dr. Wheatley has taken ill, and I've been summoned to take his place until he regains his health."

"How long will you be gone?"

The post surgeon removed his spectacles, rubbed his eyes then pinched the bridge of his nose. "I wish I knew. I don't know the nature of Dr. Wheatley's illness, so until I get there I can't make a prediction on how long his recovery might take."

He put his glasses back on, then shut his medical bag. "At least I'm not leaving a filled infirmary. I released our last patient this afternoon, a situation I can only hope will continue during my absence."

"If it doesn't, you know I'll do my best to care for anyone who needs medical treatment."

"Yes, yes, I know that, Miss Tucker. I just pray nothing serious happens to any of the troops. Now what's this about you needing to shorten your hours? Is there something I can do to help before I leave?"

"No, I . . . I have a patient who shouldn't be left alone all day. So I came to ask if you'd allow me to take some time off in the morning and perhaps leave earlier in the afternoon for the next few days. But since you've been called away, I guess—"

"Don't worry, Miss Tucker. As long as you're here each morning to examine any men who reported sick at roll call, none of their complaints prove to be serious and, of course, barring any unforeseen rash of illness, I see no reason why you can't shorten your hours." He picked up his bag with one hand and reached for his hat with the other. "I'll send word when I know more about Dr. Wheatley's condition. Now if you'll excuse me, my wife's holding supper."

Jade stepped aside to let him pass, then watched him open the door and step into the fast-fading sunlight. Taking a deep breath, she looked around the sparsely furnished office. The notion that, for the next few days at least, this would be her office brought a smile to her lips. Then she remembered her reason for coming to see Dr. Chadbourne—the patient currently recuperating in her home—and her smile faded. What was she going to do with Eli Kinmont?

Answers having nothing to do with medicine flashed through her mind. Images of her lips pressed to his, her hands moving over the sleek hard muscles of his upper arms and chest. Images she found disturbing, yet also wildly exciting.

* * *

Eli shifted positions again, the fourth time in as many minutes. No matter how much he wiggled and squirmed, he couldn't find a position that was completely comfortable. He finally settled for lying on his side, facing the bedroom door which would hopefully allow him a view of Jade as soon as she returned.

Jade. The name rang in his head, adding to the pounding already going on inside his skull. Just his luck, having a yarb woman find him in the mountains then drag him back to her house, but worse, she worked at the nearby fort. He expelled his breath in a huff. Didn't she know what the men must think of her, a single woman working on a military post? And if her mixed blood became common knowledge, she was bound to learn about bigotry firsthand. *Dammit, why am I thinking such things? Jade Tucker and how she might be treated are none of my business. As soon as my ankle heals, I'll be heading out of here.* So why did the idea of leaving her to face such problems alone cause his stomach to twist into knots?

He closed his eyes, determined to stop allowing thoughts of Jade to worm their way into his mind. Worrying about how others might react to her served no purpose and kept him from getting the rest he needed. Releasing a long sigh, he willed himself to relax. As slumber once again lured him into its soothing darkness, his mind conjured up a picture of Jade with her beautiful silver-flecked green eyes and fire-filled mahogany hair. He barely knew her, yet he was mesmerized by the proud, fiery woman he'd called *roja.* A smile played about his lips. Yes, the name definitely suited her.

The squawk of a door brought Eli's eyes open with a start. Glancing around, he realized he couldn't have slept more than half an hour. The sun had apparently sunk below the mountains behind the house, deepening the room's shadows, but darkness had yet to claim the last of the day's light. Sounds from the other rooms filtered in to him, the soft swish of Jade's full skirt as she moved, the click of her dog's nails on the wooden floor, the slosh of water being poured, the scrape of something heavy being dragged across the room.

As he stared at the bedroom door, she appeared in the opening.

"I put water on to heat and pulled a metal tub close to the stove, if you'd like to take a bath."

Eli swallowed hard against his unwanted reaction to seeing Jade in the doorway, the idea of his taking a bath under her watchful gaze, of pulling her into the tub with him and—He forced his thoughts back to the present, cursing himself for allowing suggestive notions to invade his mind. Just as he had no business thinking about protecting her from slurs and prejudice, he also shouldn't be having sexual thoughts about her. Not since he'd discovered some years ago that, just as he'd cut himself off from his former life, he'd also left behind his ability to—Jade's voice jerked him from memories he hadn't wanted to examine.

"Are you all right?"

Eli glanced up, tightening his jaw against the concern he saw reflected on her face. "As well as can be expected for a man with my affliction."

Jade moved into the room, stopping beside the bed. "What do you mean, affliction? You're talking as though you've contracted a virulent disease. You have a cut on your head and a badly sprained ankle—neither of which can be considered serious, let alone fatal."

He squeezed his eyes closed for a moment, thankful she hadn't realized he was speaking of another kind of disorder, one he had no intention of discussing.

When he didn't respond, she said, "So what about a bath?"

He pulled himself together, then opened his eyes. "I could stand a long soak, but getting my clothes off and into a tub would be too much work, especially since I'm still suffering from vertigo."

"Vertigo?" Jade stared at him thoughtfully, her eyebrows pulled together in a frown. "Well then, I'll bring a basin of water in here so you can take a sponge bath. And since you're still bothered with dizziness, I'll help you." She reached for the buttons of his shirt.

Eli's eyes widened. "Hold it right there! You've put your damn herb salves and root poultices on me, but I draw the line at you giving me a sponge bath."

Jade straightened, her hands fisted on her hips. "I don't intend to bathe you, Mr. Kinmont. You're capable of washing yourself, in spite of your vertigo. I'm just trying to help you get undressed. Now, do you want my help or not?"

As much as Eli wanted to protest, to tell her to get out and let him fumble with removing his own clothes, he also realized her help would make the task much simpler. He blew out a breath, then said, "I'd be much obliged."

She nodded, then again reached for the buttons of his shirt. As she freed the last of the buttons and pushed the fabric open, she tried to keep her gaze off the muscular expanse of male chest with its dusting of dark brown hair. He was a patient, she reminded herself, whose physical attributes shouldn't affect her, yet her rapid pulse and increased breathing said otherwise.

Once she helped him shed his shirt, she tossed it to the foot of the bed, then removed the cloth wrapped around his ankle. Taking a deep breath, she shifted her attention to his trousers. He'd already unbuttoned the fly, the gaping fabric revealing his navel. Thankful he'd taken care of that chore, she drew another deep, steadying breath, then slipped her fingers beneath each side of the opened waistband.

Jade wasn't sure what happened next, but all at once Eli's hips bucked upward and a sharp burst of laughter filled the room. Lifting her gaze to his face, she moved her fingers again and watched another laugh work its way from his chest up to his lips. Her eyes went wide. "You're ticklish!"

"Yes," he managed to say in a choked voice. "Just get my damn trousers off, and be quick about it."

Jade smiled, intrigued by this new revelation. She wiggled her fingers again, a gentle brush over the smooth flesh just below his waist. He immediately jerked in reaction, his breath catching as he tried to stop another laugh from escaping. She giggled, delighted with her discovery. Unable to resist testing her newfound power, her fingers moved higher to skim over his ribs.

His laughter surrounded her, filling her with a happiness like none she'd ever known. How the laughter of this man, a man she barely knew, could make her feel so happy, so complete, went beyond her understanding. But whatever the reason, she planned to enjoy it for as long as possible. His laughs became infectious and her peals of laughter soon joined his.

"That's enough," Eli said, trying to pull her hands away. Each time his fingers wrapped around hers, she somehow managed to escape his grasp and continued her tortuous tickling. "Stop. *Roja,* please stop."

Something in his plea, maybe the breathless way he said *roja*, brought an abrupt halt to Jade's fun. Stilling her hands then carefully withdrawing them from his sides, she sat down on the edge of the mattress with a sigh. She moved her gaze upward, past the indentation of his navel with its whorl of hair, across the flat plain of his belly, over the rapid rising and falling of his broad chest, finally settling on his flushed face. Other than when she'd watched him sleep, for the first time since she'd found him on the mountain trail, he looked relaxed, not hiding behind the harsh facade he tried so hard to maintain.

"I'm sorry," she said in a soft voice. "Your being ticklish took me by surprise and I . . . I guess I got carried away."

Eli lifted a hand to wipe the moisture from his eyes, then drew a deep breath. "No harm done."

Jade smiled, relieved she hadn't received a stinging retort. Lowering her gaze to his trousers, she said, "We still haven't gotten your clothes off."

"Maybe we should just forget it."

"No, you'll feel better if you get cleaned up. Let's try again. I promise not to tickle this time." She offered him another smile and waited for his response.

He stared at her for a moment. When his breathing returned to normal, he said, "If you do, I swear I'll get even."

Jade repressed a shudder at the thought of *his* hands on *her* bare flesh. Refusing to allow herself to think more along those lines, she turned her attention to the task at hand. She grasped his trousers by the waistband, careful to keep her fingers on the outside of the buckskin, and began peeling them down his body. As he lifted his hips off the bed, she kept her gaze on his trousers, not on what was underneath, certain her face would flame a bright scarlet if he wasn't wearing drawers.

By the time she'd pulled the garment down his legs and over his feet, taking care not to jar his injured ankle, Eli had drawn the top sheet over his midsection. Frowning at seeing a sheet covering what she'd avoided looking at, she experienced an inexplicable moment of pique. She was shocked to realize, she did want to know what, if anything, he wore beneath the buckskin trousers.

She busied herself by folding his clothes into a neat pile, telling herself she had absolutely no right to be annoyed. But for reasons she didn't want to examine, her disappointment wasn't so easily appeased.

"I'll bring in a basin of water," she said, avoiding his gaze as she turned toward the door.

Eli didn't reply, but watched her leave the room, wondering at her high color. He frowned. Why would she be embarrassed when he was the one who'd been stripped naked? By fast thinking and a quick flick of his wrist, he'd barely managed to save his modesty. If he hadn't covered himself with the sheet, she would've had a real reason to blush.

Jade returned in a few minutes with a basin of water, several pieces of toweling, a bar of soap and a washcloth. Setting the basin on the bedside table, she arranged the other items beside it then met his gaze. "Are you sure you can do this yourself?"

For a brief moment, Eli contemplated telling her he wasn't up to the task and needed her help. Imagining the look on her face, he bit the inside of his cheek to suppress a smile. He shoved the image aside and said, "I'll manage. But I would appreciate your fetching my razor from my saddlebags. There's a clean set of clothes in there, too."

While she did as he asked, he slowly scooted himself toward the head of the bed until he could lean against the headboard in a half-reclining position. After taking the razor from her, he flashed her a grin. "If I get too weak to finish, I'll definitely call out."

Jade sucked in a surprised breath, her insides turning to mush by his first real smile. She had to clear her throat before she could speak. "You . . . uh . . . you let me know when you're finished, and I'll come get the basin."

Eli nodded, fighting hard to hide his amusement.

Jade spun around and marched out of the room, her back stiff. For the first time, she closed the door behind her.

As soon as the door clicked shut, the chuckle rumbling in Eli's chest broke free. In spite of the pain of his sprained ankle and still-throbbing head, he realized he hadn't felt this good in years.

All the while he gave himself a quick sponge bath, then lathered his face and carefully scraped off his beard, his mouth kept curving into what he knew could only be described as a foolish grin. That would have disturbed him a day earlier, and would probably disturb him in the days ahead, but for the time being, he didn't care if he was grinning like an idiot.

By the time Jade heard Eli's call through the closed bedroom door, she had regained her composure. At least she prayed she had. But once she stepped into the room and got her first view of him without his beard, her self-control promptly slipped a notch or two.

Though the skin revealed by the removal of his beard was a shade lighter than the rest of his tanned face, his square jaw and the small cleft in his chin made him even more devastatingly handsome. Her breathing suddenly erratic and a wild heat swirling in her belly, she fought down whatever inner demons made her react so strongly to this man.

She kept her gaze away from his clean-shaven face while retrieving the basin and other bathing paraphernalia, afraid her eyes would reveal something even she didn't understand. She retreated from the bedroom a second time, to take the basin to the kitchen then fetch a plate of the food she'd fixed while he bathed.

When she returned, she had herself under control again, more determined than ever to keep it that way.

"Would you mind if I ate my supper in here with you?" she said, after handing him his plate. Seeing his eyebrows arch in question, she lifted one shoulder in a small shrug. "It's just that I'm used to sitting down to eat with my family, and I still haven't gotten used to eating alone."

Eli waved one hand toward the foot of the bed. "Be my guest."

Jade gave him a tentative smile, then went to fetch her own plate.

After they'd eaten in silence for a few minutes, Eli said, "How long have you lived here?"

"Just a couple of months. After Dr. Chadbourne agreed

to hire me as his assistant, my father had this house built for me. I told him it wasn't necessary, but he insisted."

"I thought you said your parents live south of here, on Alamito Creek."

Jade nodded. "Papa has a contract to supply the fort with beef, and he often rides with his men when they deliver cattle. When I sent word to my parents that I would be working as the post surgeon's assistant, Papa insisted on coming here to make sure I had a decent place to live." She smiled. "I think he was afraid I'd end up living too close to Chihuahua."

"Chihuahua?"

"A section of town, east of the main road. Many of those living in Chihuahua moved here from Mexico. Most of them are good, hard-working people, like the ones I've treated. But Chihuahua is also where soldiers from Fort Davis spend their free time, drinking, betting on cockfights and whor—Uh . . . I mean, consorting with women."

"Consorting?" Eli chuckled. "Those pretty, black-eyed *señoritas* would be flattered by your polite way of describing what they do for a living."

Before Jade could stop the words, she said, "Just what do you know about black-eyed *señoritas* who sell their bodies?"

He set his empty plate on the bedside table before replying. "Enough. I spend the coldest months of each winter in Mexico." Sensing her irritation, he couldn't resist adding, "Where the weather, and the women working in the cantinas, are a whole lot hotter."

The sudden stab of pain his words caused caught Jade off guard. She inhaled slowly to ease the ache in her chest, shocked to realize the source of her discomfort. She barely knew this man, so there was no reason for her to be jealous. Absolutely none! Yet, she had no doubt that the thought of Eli Kinmont with another woman, even a Mexican prostitute, was responsible for the pain squeezing her heart.

Chapter 4

By the following morning, Jade had convinced herself that no matter what Eli said to her, she refused to experience another second of jealousy. She had no idea what the future held, and until the Spirits favored her with another vision which might reveal what lay ahead, she had no right to feel possessive about Eli Kinmont.

After letting Zita outside, she folded the blankets she'd used to make a pallet for herself on the floor in the main room of her house, then entered the bedroom. She moved quietly so as not to disturb Eli. But when she reached the side of the bed, he stirred, opening his eyes to meet her gaze.

She studied his face and eyes for a moment, then said, "You look flushed this morning." Her brow furrowing, she tested his forehead with her palm. "Yes, you have a slight fever."

"It's nothing, just—"

"I'll be right back." Ignoring the annoyance in his expression, she turned and left the bedroom.

Eli scowled at her departing back. Though he knew he

was running a fever, it wasn't serious, just his body's reaction to what he'd gone through the day before.

When Jade returned a few minutes later, she handed him a cup.

"I made you some tea," she said. "To lower your fever."

He accepted the cup, then frowned into the steaming liquid. "What's in it, another of your magic herbs?"

"I don't perform magic, Mr. Kinmont. I'm a healer, not a sorcerer. The tea is made with willow bark."

"Ah," he murmured, lifting the cup to his lips. After he took a swallow, he said, "For once I'll agree with one of your claims. This healing potion at least has some validity."

"What do you mean?"

"More than forty years ago, willow bark was found to contain salicin, which is responsible for its medicinal properties. Lowering fever. Reducing pain and inflammation."

Jade narrowed her gaze. "How do you know that?"

Eli shrugged. "I guess I . . . must've read it somewhere." Keeping his gaze averted from hers, he concentrated on the cup of tea clenched between his hands.

She crossed her arms over her chest and glared down at him. "That's not good enough. Ever since I found you in the mountains, you've been making statements that most folks know nothing about: stretched ligaments, vertigo, administering anesthetic. And now you tell me about the medicinal properties of willow bark."

Eli silently cursed his stupidity, not only for saying those things, but for thinking Jade would let such statements slide.

When he didn't reply, she said, "Where did you learn so much about healing?"

"I don't know what you're talking—"

"Don't take me for a fool. You know full well what I'm talking about. A man of your intelligence should have no trouble following this conversation." She took a deep breath, then lowered her voice to say, "I would like to know the truth."

"All right, dammit," he said, realizing she wasn't going to let the subject drop. "I went to medical school."

"You went to—?" Her eyes went wide. "You're a doctor!"

"Was. I was a doctor."

Jade blinked with surprise. "That's not true. You went to college to study medicine because you wanted to help the sick. You even took an oath."

He shot a surprised glance up at her. "What do you know about the Hippocratic Oath?"

"I may not be as well educated as you, but I've read what books my parents could find. I know medical students are required to take the oath before they graduate."

He scowled into his cup. "Meaning?"

"Taking the Hippocratic Oath is a lifetime commitment. You can't just ignore it and suddenly stop being a doctor."

"Well, I did. I stopped practicing medicine years ago."

"When you came to Texas?"

He finally met her gaze, his face grim. "That's right. I gave up being a doctor when I came to Texas six years ago."

Jade digested his statement for a moment, then said, "Where are you from?"

"What does it matter where I'm from?"

She shrugged. "It doesn't. You have a slight accent, similar to some of the soldiers at the fort, and I was just curious where you lived before you came to Texas."

He stared at her for a moment, mulling over whether he should make up an answer. Deciding there was no harm in telling her at least part of the truth, he said, "I was born and raised in Nashville, Tennessee."

"Do you have family there?"

Eli didn't immediately reply, a strange haunted look passing over his face before he jerked his gaze from hers. At last he said, "My mother and sisters. At least they were living there when I headed west."

"You haven't corresponded with them since you came

to Texas?" Jade couldn't keep the surprise out of her voice. She came from an extremely close-knit family and couldn't image six years passing without some sort of contact with them. "I don't understand how you could—"

"It's none of your affair," Eli replied before he could stop himself, turning a fierce glare on her. "I don't want to discuss my family. Got that?"

Jade nodded, his obvious distress forming a lump in her throat. She waited until he finished the willow bark tea before speaking again. In a low voice, she said, "Were you in The War?"

Eli squeezed his eyes closed, trying to block out the memories her question spawned. After a moment, he heaved a sigh, then opened his eyes. His voice a harsh whisper, he said, "Haven't you pried enough into my past? Leave it alone, dammit. Just leave it alone." He thrust the empty cup toward her.

The agonized look on his face and the torment in his voice answered her question more clearly than words could have, an answer that tore a gaping hole in her heart. Though he bore no physical scars, his experiences in The War had obviously been horrendous, leaving him filled with unimaginable pain and misery. She now knew his current injuries were minor compared to those on the inside, those gouged deep into his soul.

"If you can manage to put on your trousers, I'll be back in a minute to help you to the privy," she said, taking the cup from his hand. As she left the room, she prayed to the Spirits to show her a way to treat his deeply embedded wounds.

A little while later, she helped Eli to the privy and back, then got him resettled in bed. After she fetched his breakfast, she said, "I have to be at the post hospital before sick call, so I'll be leaving in a few minutes. Before I go, I'll bring you a pitcher of water and a chamber pot in case you need to—"

"You don't have to tell me what it's for," he said with more fierceness than he intended. "I'm not some back-woods bumpkin who's never used a chamber pot." He pinched the bridge of his nose, then said, "Look, don't worry about me. I'll get along fine." He waved his hand in a shooing motion. "So just run along. Wouldn't want the post surgeon's assistant to be late on my account."

Jade pressed her lips together, determined not to let him goad her into another show of temper. She exhaled carefully, then said, "I'll also bring you some biscuits and a jar of peach preserves, since I probably won't get back until the middle of the afternoon. Can I bring you anything else? More willow bark tea or—?"

"No. Just go."

Jade clamped her mouth shut, shot him a furious glare, then did as he asked.

Eli held his breath until he heard the door close, then let out a weary sigh. What was the matter with him? Ever since Jade Tucker had found him, he'd been not only curt but downright rude. Such behavior was not what he'd been taught as a youngster. His always genteel mother would tan his hide but good if she were to witness his deplorable lack of manners.

Damn. Why did Jade have to bring up his family? He didn't want to think about his mother and sisters, doing so was much too painful. Just as admitting he'd once been a doctor pained him. Yet somehow, one mahogany-haired, headstrong yarb woman had managed to keep poking into his past, prodding him with her questions, digging into memories he didn't want exposed, until he'd finally snapped and told her the truth. What was it about Jade Tucker that made him tell her things he hadn't shared with anyone in the past six years?

Eli refused to examine the possible answers to that question too carefully, for fear he might learn more than he wanted to know.

* * *

Halfway to the army post, Jade remembered she'd forgotten to put Zita outside. The dog had slipped through the door while she helped Eli back inside from his trip to the privy, and with the unsettling conversation she'd had with him still ringing in her head, she'd forgotten to check on the dog's whereabouts before she left. Normally that wasn't a problem, but since she hadn't thought to warn Eli that Zita wasn't especially fond of men, she had planned on keeping the two of them separated. Well, there wasn't time to go back to her house, so Zita and Eli would have to make the best of the situation.

Jade couldn't help smiling at the thought of her dog and her patient being cooped up all day in the same house. That exasperating man deserves everything Zita does to him, she decided in a moment of pique, then immediately withdrew such a heartless thought. Eli was recovering from his injuries, and he didn't need the antics of a dog who didn't trust men impeding his progress.

She entered the infirmary's dispensary and found the hospital steward, Sgt. Lamar Davidson, talking to two soldiers from the Ninth Cavalry—one of the all-black units dubbed Buffalo Soldiers as a term of respect by the Indian Nations who'd fought against them.

"Good morning, Sergeant Davidson. Did these men report for sick call?"

Davidson glanced over at her, thick black eyebrows pulled low over equally dark eyes, his thin lips pulled into a frown. "You just go about your business, Miz Tucker. I can handle these two."

"What are their symptoms?"

"They're complaining of the bellyache. Probably something they et didn't agree with 'em. Ain't nothing a dose of castor oil won't cure."

"You're not a doctor, Sergeant, so you shouldn't be diagnosing what's wrong with these men, much less prescribing a treatment. If you'll move aside, I'll examine them."

He straightened and turned a fierce glare in her direction. "I said, there's no need."

"I don't understand. What—?"

"The way I figure it, I've got more right to treat these two than the likes a you. Wouldn't you agree, men?"

Before the soldiers could reply, Jade said, "What do you mean? I've been trained to—"

Davidson let out a long sigh, his jaw clenched. "Never thought I'd have to spell it out for ya, but the fact is, I'm a man, Miz Tucker. Womenfolk got no business pretending they're doctors. Or working as a surgeon's assistant."

"I'm not pretending to be a doctor, Sergeant, but I have spent my entire life learning how to treat the sick and injured. Dr. Chadbourne thinks I'm qualified to be his assistant."

His lips curved into a grin, one lacking any humor. "Chadbourne may have fallen for such nonsense, but not me. And most of the men on this army post agree with my opinion." He looked at the two men standing in front of him. "Ain't that right?"

The two bobbed their heads in agreement, but refused to look at Jade.

Davidson's smile broadened. "Now, either get me a bottle of castor oil, Miz Tucker, or go see to something you are qualified to do. Like changing beds or sweeping floors."

Jade stared at the man who stood only a few inches taller than herself, shocked and confused by his venomous words. Sergeant Davidson had been on leave when Dr. Chadbourne hired her, returning to duty just a couple of weeks ago. Since the steward's return, she'd spoken to the man several times, and though he'd never gone out of his way to be friendly, he'd always been polite. Why had he waited until now to reveal his true feelings? Realizing her previous dealings with him had always been in the presence of Dr. Chadbourne, she found her answer.

Her father had warned her about the reaction she might get when folks learned she'd taken a job working for the post surgeon. Though he'd told her that some men might be outright belligerent, she brushed off his worries as those of a concerned parent. And when Eli mentioned something about soldiers taking exception to having a female assistant surgeon, she hadn't taken his warnings seriously either.

Were her father and Eli right? Was her stay at Fort Davis going to be filled with this kind of treatment?

She finally found her voice to say, "I'll be in Dr. Chadbourne's office." Not waiting for a reply, she turned on her heel and left the infirmary.

By the time Jade left the hospital and headed for home that afternoon, she'd once again discounted the warnings of both her father and Eli and come up with an explanation for her disturbing conversation with Sergeant Davidson. The steward's bias against women working at the infirmary was undoubtedly because he'd never had occasion to see how talented and dedicated a woman could be. Once he saw how she treated her patients and realized she had true healing skills, then surely he'd change his attitude. Yes, that was a plausible conclusion, she decided, provided she got an opportunity to treat one of the soldiers on the military post and prove her abilities.

She arrived at her house, determined to forget about what had happened earlier. She had a patient to tend and that's how she would expend her energies, not worrying about the upsetting incident with Sergeant Davidson.

Zita wasn't in the kitchen or the main room of her house, making Jade wonder if the dog had somehow managed to slip outside. Approaching the bedroom and looking through the open doorway, her eyes widened. Her dog—the one who had little use for men—lay stretched out on her back beside Eli, while he idly rubbed his fingers over her chest.

Jade stepped into the room. "I don't believe this," she said with a laugh.

Eli looked up, a strange warmth sweeping through his veins at the sight of her. Trying to stifle feelings he wanted no part of, he glanced back at the dog who half-dozed next to him. "She likes to have her chest rubbed," he said.

"I know." She shook her head. "This is amazing. Zita doesn't like men, especially strangers." Jade watched Eli's long fingers move over Zita's chest in a light caress, the sudden desire to have those hands touch her in such a sensual way nearly choking her. Jerking her gaze back to his face, she said, "She'd never get that close to you unless she trusted you. How did you manage that?"

Eli flashed her a smile. "Bribed her with a piece of biscuit covered with peach preserves."

"Ah," Jade replied with a chuckle. "I should have known. She'll do most anything for food."

He smiled at the memory of how Zita had stuck her head into the bedroom, wary of him in spite of his efforts to coax her into the room. She finally moved inside the bedroom door and sat down, refusing to get any closer. When he reached for the plate of biscuits, she lifted her head, ears perked and nose twitching. Thinking he'd hit on the key to making friends with Jade's dog, he held out a bit of biscuit slathered with preserves. That time, Zita didn't hesitate, but rose and trotted over to the bed. And in a matter of minutes, she hopped up on the bed and flopped down beside him.

"Watch what she does when I quit scratching her. It's the damndest thing I've ever seen," he said, demonstrating by withdrawing his hand.

Zita opened her eyes, then pawed at his hand. When he didn't respond, she wriggled closer then used one paw to pull his hand toward her chest, leaving no doubt about what she wanted. Eli chuckled. "Okay, girl, I got the hint."

Looking over at Jade, he said, "Smart dog, figuring out a way to get what she wants."

Jade stared at the man and dog for a moment, thinking about Eli's words and applying them to herself. Was she smart enough to figure out a way to get what she wanted? Her parents had raised her to believe she could do anything if she worked hard enough. She wanted to be the best healer possible, one people trusted. Was her lifelong dream in danger of being tossed aside and trampled? Would one man's snide remarks erase her plans for the future? An enormous lump formed in her throat. No, she couldn't—she wouldn't allow that to happen.

A few moments passed before she could find her voice. "I'd better check your ankle to see if I need to make another poultice."

Eli started to tell her not to bother, but couldn't form the words. He wanted Jade to touch him. The realization didn't sit well, but before he could do anything to stop it, she lifted the corner of the sheet and flipped it off his feet. As her hands pushed up the leg of his trousers, then touched his ankle, he bit back a groan. He could actually feel the delicate probe of her fingers in places far removed from his leg. *Dammit, this has got to stop! There's no place for Jade Tucker in my life. Not now. Not ever.* Squeezing his eyes closed, he endured her examination, determined to heed his own advice. Yet, when he lifted his eyelids and looked into her beautiful green eyes, he couldn't make his lungs work. This must be how a drowning man feels, he decided, unable to breathe while the water sucks him deeper and deeper into its depths.

Jade's voice finally freed him from his daydreams.

He blinked. "What?"

"Welcome back, Mr. Kinmont," she said, amusement making the silver flecks in her eyes more prominent.

The heat of a flush crept up his neck. He swallowed, then said, "Eli. Call me Eli."

She straightened, her brow slightly furrowed. "All right.

Eli. I'd appreciate an answer to my question. Are you in any pain?"

"Some, but it's more like a dull throb."

She nodded. "Your ankle is still pretty swollen, so I'll make another poultice. You should stay in bed a few more days, otherwise it will take longer for your ankle to heal."

"Yeah, I know," he said, draping one forearm over his eyes. "Badly stretched ligaments can take a long time to fully recover."

Jade wasn't sure whether his reaction stemmed from disappointment or anticipation. As she turned to leave, she couldn't stop the hope from building inside her that it was the latter.

Chapter 5

Jade had just finished wrapping the warm cloth around Eli's ankle, when Zita gave an excited yip, then jumped off the bed and raced into the other room.

"What's with her?" Eli said.

"She always lets me know when some—" A sharp knock echoed through the house. "When someone's coming to the door."

She made one last adjustment to the poultice, then said, "After I see who that is, I'll start supper."

Eli heard Jade open the front door, then strained to make out the voices filtering to him from the other room.

"What can I do for you, *Señora* Domingo?" Jade said, studying the petite woman she ushered into her house. Liana Domingo, not yet eighteen, had an olive complexion and long, jet black hair worn in a loose knot at her nape.

"I was hoping you could help me, *Señorita* Tucker," Liana said, her dark brown eyes looking unusually large in her round face, her swollen belly making her movements awkward.

"I'll try. But first you must tell me what's wrong."

"It is my back. There is an ache here." She pressed her hand to her lower back. "Each day, it is more and more difficult to finish my work. Naldo is afraid for me and the baby. And I worry, too, that something is wrong."

Jade stared at Liana for a moment. She'd met Naldo Domingo, Liana's husband who worked as a laborer for the army, and knew how much he cared for his wife. "You have no other symptoms? No bleeding. No cramps."

The young woman shook her head, then grasped Jade's hands. "Will I lose this baby, *Señorita* Tucker?"

"No," Jade replied with a smile. "You and the baby will be fine. But you are trying to do too much. If you recall, I told you there was no reason you couldn't continue working as a laundress. And you should also remember, I told you that when you got closer to the birth of your child, you would have to stop doing laundry for so many officers, maybe even leave your job. That time is now, Liana. I want you to promise me you'll do less, or even better, quit, *bueno?*"

"*Sí*, I remember. But Naldo and I are saving to build a larger house, a house we have dreamed of since we were first married. Without my wages, our dream will have to wait even longer."

"I know, *señora*, but isn't your health and the health of your baby more important right now?"

Liana flushed and dropped her gaze. "Of course. I just don't want Naldo to be disappointed."

"Naldo won't be disappointed. He only wants what's best for you."

"*Sí*, I know," Liana replied, lifting her head to reveal eyes shiny with tears. "I will tell the major and the lieutenants that they must find someone else to do their laundry."

"If they give you any trouble, tell them to talk to me, *bueno?*"

Liana bobbed her head once, then said, "What about my back? Is there nothing more I can do for the pain?"

"Your back shouldn't bother you as much once you stop

working so hard, but in case the ache continues, I have something which will help," Jade said, pulling a chair away from the table. "You just sit here and rest while I get it ready for you." She helped Liana lower herself onto the chair, then headed for the small room off the kitchen where she prepared and stored her healing plants.

Jade returned a few minutes later. Handing a small leather pouch to Liana, she said, "A tea made from the plant in this bag should ease the pain in your back."

Liana accepted the pouch, then rose. *"Muchas gracias, Señorita* Tucker. I am sorry if I sounded like a spoiled child a moment ago. Both Naldo and I are most grateful for all you have done for us."

"De nada. It has been my pleasure. Now I want you to go home and rest. Then the next time I see you should be at the birth of your child."

A frown marred Liana's smooth face. Placing a hand on her stomach, she said, *"Sí,* I hope that will be soon. Naldo's son or daughter is making it hard for me to get around. But I . . . I am also afraid."

Jade gave her an encouraging smile. "You're just nervous, which is natural since this is your first child. Rather than focusing on the fear of the unknown, you should concentrate on how it will be to finally see your baby, to hold him in your arms. And remember, I'll be there to make it as easy for you as I can."

Liana nodded. *"Sí,* you are right. I will try not to worry so much."

"We've talked about what to expect when your time comes, so send for me at the first sign."

The young woman nodded again, then moved toward the door. *"Buenas tardes*—good afternoon, *Señorita* Tucker," she said with a smile, then opened the door and stepped outside.

Jade returned her smile. *"Buenas tardes."*

* * *

After Liana Domingo's departure, Jade prepared supper, dished up two plates then headed for the bedroom. She set Eli's plate on the bedside table, then took a seat on the foot of the bed.

"Was that one of your patients?" he said, reaching for his fork.

"Yes, Liana Domingo. Her first child is due in a few weeks, maybe sooner if she doesn't follow my advice."

Though Eli told himself he had no interest in her patients, he couldn't stop himself from saying, "Why did she come to see you?"

"Backache."

"Early labor?"

Jade shook her head, swallowed a bite of food, then said, "I don't think so. I told her she should quit her job." At Eli's arched brows, she added, "She works as a laundress for several of the officers at the fort."

"So, what did you prescribe for *Señora* Domingo's aching back?"

Jade glanced over at Eli, wondering if his question came from sincere interest, or was merely an opening for another round of sarcastic barbs. "I told her to stop working so hard and to get more rest." She took another bite of food, then added, "What would you have prescribed?"

Eli ignored her question and said, "Rest, is that all? No special teas or root salves? Surely, there's something in your bag of herbal tricks to ease backache during the latter stages of a woman's confinement."

She tightened her grip on her fork, longing to stab the tines into his ankle. Several moments passed before the urge passed and her temper cooled. "Wild buckwheat," she finally said through stiff lips. "Tea made from wild buckwheat—a remedy used by the medicine men and women of many Indian Nations for hundreds of years— relieves back pain."

Eli made a sound, somewhere between a snort and a laugh, but didn't reply.

"You didn't answer my question," Jade said, glaring at him. "What would you have prescribed?"

His mouth thinned. "I told you, I'm not a doctor anymore, so I no longer prescribe treatments for patients."

"But you must remember what you—"

"I don't want to remember, dammit. Now, change the subject or get out of here."

The pain Eli saw flicker through Jade's beautiful eyes made him feel like a first-class cad, but he refused to apologize. Until she understood he was deadly serious, that the subject of his former life wasn't open to discussion, he'd be forced to continue such rude behavior.

Jade finished her supper in silence, wondering why she bothered talking to Eli Kinmont. All the obstinate man ever did was make cutting remarks about her healing abilities. Even so, she reminded herself, he was injured and—whether he would admit it or not—for the time being he needed her to take care of him.

She stole a quick glance in his direction. If only she could get him to take an interest in medicine again, then maybe—She abruptly went rigid, her surroundings fading away until she saw and heard only the scene unfolding before her mind's eye.

A lone rider directed his horse around the rocks strewn along a path leading down into a mountain meadow. The man wore a buckskin breechclout and knee-high moccasins, his thick black hair hanging past his wide shoulders onto his bare back.

Jade studied the trees and rocks around the rider and his white horse, recognizing the location, a meadow in the mountains not far from her house. An area she'd often traversed while gathering plants. As the man came closer, she got a better look at his face. Long narrow nose, prominent cheekbones, deep-set dark eyes. Night Wind!

Eli stared at Jade, his heart thundering in his ears. *What the hell's wrong with her?* She'd suddenly gone stone-still, her eyes open yet glazed as if she were totally unaware of her surroundings.

"Jade?"

No response.

"Jade, are you ill?" he said, louder this time.

When she still didn't respond, he nearly shouted, "Answer me, dammit. What's wrong?"

When even that didn't garner a response, he pushed himself away from the headboard and leaned toward her. Ignoring the sudden wave of dizziness, he managed to scoot toward her enough to wrap his fingers around her right arm. He gave her a gentle shake. "Jade? Can you hear me?"

Jade blinked. The mountain scene and Night Wind faded from her mind's eye, slowly replaced by the furnishings of her bedroom. She frowned, hoping the Spirits would speak to her again, to tell her why Night Wind was coming to see her. But no, they remained silent. She blinked again, realizing someone was talking to her. Carefully turning her head, she looked directly into the eyes of Eli. Her frown deepened. Was that concern she saw mirrored in those gorgeous blue pools? No, she must be—

"*Roja*, please, talk to me!"

Jade shifted her gaze from Eli's eyes to where his fingers gripped her arm, then back to his face. Shaking off the last vestiges of her trancelike state, she said, "Talk to you about what?"

He released her and eased back to his original half-reclining position against the headboard. Scowling at her, he said, "You scaring the devil out of me, that's what I want to talk about." When she didn't answer, his voice turned steely. "Are you going to tell me what the hell just happened to you?"

"You wouldn't believe me if I did."

"Try me."

She cleared her throat. "I had a vision."

"A vision!" he said, surprise evident in his voice. Then

the furrows in his brow smoothed and his eyes widened. "Are you referring to a Fata Morgana?"

"I'm not sure what that is."

"An illusion of the mind."

"My visions aren't illusions, they're real," she replied, looking at him warily.

"Real? How?"

"I see things in my visions before they actually happen."

"Do you have these foreseeing visions often?"

"Sometimes they come frequently. Other times, they're weeks or even months apart."

"I've heard about people with psychic powers, but I've never had occasion to meet someone who's experienced that kind of phenomenon." He folded his hands over his belly, then said, "Tell me about it. When did you start having visions?"

Jade had never discussed her psychic abilities with anyone except her family, and she wasn't sure she should do so with Eli. What if he had some ulterior motive and planned to use the information against her? Her mother had often warned her that not everyone would believe she had visions and to be careful whom she told. The reaction to such a revelation could range from amusement to being called crazy or worse.

She studied Eli's face, looking for a sign that he was more than just curious. He was quick to criticize her healing abilities, so would he also find fault when she revealed her other ability? She remembered her parents telling how her father had first mocked her mother's claims of having visions, calling them outrageous and impossible. Maybe Eli Kinmont would react the same way. Finding nothing in his expression to indicate he had anything other then genuine interest behind his questions, she finally said, "I experienced my first vision when I was just a child. The Spirits revealed I would have a baby brother." She smiled, remembering how shocked her parents had been by the declaration of their five-year-old daughter.

"The Spirits?"

"My *Nde* ancestors believe those who have visions are receiving direct communication from the Spirits—the *Nde* Gods. Those who have visions are usually held in high esteem, like the band's medicine man. But having visions can also bring the opposite reaction, one made by those who don't believe what the Spirits have said."

Something in her tone made Eli say, "Has that happened to you?"

"No, but it did to my mother. When she tried to warn a council of *Nde* leaders about the dangers their people would face, they accused her of being a witch. She tried to defend herself, telling them what the Spirits had revealed in her visions—about the Americans coming west, the soldiers building a fort here and how the *Nde* would be forced from their homeland—but they refused to believe her."

"Your mother has visions, too. Interesting," Eli said more to himself. Louder, he added, "What about the charges against her?"

"The leaders found her guilty of witchcraft and sentenced her to the punishment always given to a witch: death by fire." Ignoring the shocked expression on Eli's face, she said, "She was hung by her wrists over a fire. My father found her and cut her down before she was burned too severely, but she still carries scars on her feet from that day."

"No one came looking for her once they found out she'd escaped?"

"Mama said some of the *Nde* leaders were too superstitious, believing she must have extraordinary powers in order to survive their sentence. And several of the others couldn't be bothered, since they didn't consider her a threat to their bands. But Long Knife—the leader who had accused her of witchcraft—did try to find her, determined she wouldn't escape punishment a second time. He eventually gave up when protecting his band required all his time and energy.''

Eli thought over the story Jade had just related, then said, "So, tell me what it's like to have a vision. How do they come to you? Do you ever lose consciousness?''

Jade heard the excitement in his voice and bit her lip to hide a smile. "Sometimes I see and hear the vision, scenes so real it's like I'm actually there. Other times the Spirits give me only a picture, and others just sounds. I've learned to recognize when a vision is about to begin. I can't really explain it, but a strange sensation comes over me, then all sound begins to fade and everything around me slowly dims to blackness. I'm awake and yet I'm not, if that makes any sense.''

"Yes, I think I understand. What about the visions themselves? Have any of them predicted danger, like your mother's visions about the *Nde*?''

"Some of my visions have been warnings—though not as grim as my mother's—some have shown me what to do to treat a patient and others have been predictions, mostly telling me of a future event. Like the visions I had about the birth of my brother and then my sister a year later. Or the one about finding you.''

"Me!'' His eyebrows lifted. "You're not serious?''

She smiled. "Yes, I am. In fact, the Spirits gave me several visions about you.''

"What exactly did the Spirits tell you about me?'' he said, hoping his voice didn't betray his uneasiness.

"Only that I would find a man with a dun horse and a pair of burros in the mountains, and he would need my help.''

"That's all?''

"The Spirits don't reveal everything. They tell me only what I need to know.''

Eli slowly released his held breath. After a moment, he said, "One of my professors in France would have loved hearing this discussion. He was fascinated with the human brain and its potential."

"You went to school in France?"

Eli silently cursed his loose tongue, then said, "Yes."

"Is that were you got your medical degree?"

"No, I went to France to continue my studies after I earned my medical degree. The schools in Europe are far superior to any here in the United States, which is—"

His mouth clamped shut, he pinned her with his narrowed gaze. "Why is it our conversations always shift to me? I told you I don't want to talk about my past, and yet you keep bringing it up."

Jade lifted her chin and glared down her nose at him. "You're the one who brought up studying in France, not me. If you want to pretend your past doesn't exist by refusing to talk about it, then go right ahead. But sooner or later, you're going to have to face your past and come to grips with it. Continuing with your silly game of self-denial will only make that confrontation more difficult."

Eli exhaled with a huff. "So, now you're a psychologist as well as a yarb woman. Is there no end to your amazing abilities?"

"Such sarcasm is exactly what I was talking about." She sighed, her momentary anger slipping away. "I'm sorry for whatever happened to you, but refusing to talk about your past will not make the pain and bitterness go away."

When he didn't reply, Jade got off the bed, then picked up his empty plate. "I have to go out for a while. Do you want me to help you to the privy before I leave?"

Though Eli wished he could tell her he wasn't helpless, he knew his ankle was still too sore to support his weight. As much as the admission galled him, he needed her assistance. Realizing she was waiting for his answer, he managed to murmur an affirmative response.

After Eli and Jade made the trip outside and he returned to bed, he couldn't help wondering about Jade's destination. Before she left, he'd given in to temptation and hinted about her visiting a patient. The curt "no" he received in response squashed the urge to question her further. Where she went and who she saw were none of his business, just like his past was none of Jade's business.

Such logic, while absolutely accurate on the surface, had a major hidden flaw. If who Jade went to see was none of his business, why was his gut tied in a knot at the thought of Jade in the arms of another man?

Eli gave a snort of self-disgust, then rolled onto his left side, facing the wall. Though he told himself he had no right to feel anything for Jade Tucker, the burning ache in his belly told him a much different story.

Chapter 6

Jade waited beneath the leafy canopy of a stand of oak trees, her gaze focused on the path leading deeper into the mountains to the north. She didn't wait long. A huge white horse soon appeared at the end of the small mountain meadow, moving in an easy canter toward the grove of trees.

As the horse drew closer, Jade moved out into the open, stopping at the edge of the path. When the rider spotted her, he kicked his horse into a run. The animal raced across the meadow, his long strides smooth and fluid. Jade smiled at the picture the pair made, watching them come closer until the rider jerked back on the reins and brought the horse to a skidding halt directly in front of her.

The man stared down at Jade, his dark eyes inscrutable in the deepening shadows of dusk, the wind fluttering the ends of his long black hair. Easily controlling his horse's nervous prancing with his knees and a softly spoken command, he slid to the ground then moved to stand beside Jade.

''It is good to see you, *shila*—my sister. Once again, I

see the Spirits warned you of my visit." One corner of his mouth lifted in a faint smile.

Jade returned Night Wind's smile. "It's good to see you, too, my brother." Although Jade and Night Wind weren't siblings—his father was her uncle—the *Nde* language had no word for cousin. Instead, cousins referred to each other as brother and sister. "And, yes, the Spirits told me you were coming to see me, but they did not reveal why."

When her twenty-five-year-old cousin didn't respond but dropped his horse's reins to the ground then turned and started walking, she fell into step beside him. After a few minutes, his continued silence made her apprehension grow. "Has something happened to Night Hawk and Yellow Bird, or to Bright Star?"

"My parents are well, as is my sister. At least they were the last time I saw them," he replied, unable to keep the bitterness out of his voice. "They are not why I came."

Jade exhaled a relieved breath that nothing had happened to his family. "Then why are you here?"

He stared off into the distance for a moment. A muscle ticked in his jaw. "I came to see you because I heard something I could not believe."

"What did you hear?"

"I heard you are treating the blue-coats at the fort. Is this true?"

"I was hired by the post surgeon to be his assistant. Though I haven't actually treated any of the soldiers yet, I intend to."

Night Wind stopped abruptly and swung around to face her. "How can you do such a thing?"

Jade stared at her cousin, her brow furrowed. "What do you mean? I'm a healer, and I—"

"The blue-coats are enemy to our people!" he said in a fierce voice. "They are the ones who do not want us to live in these mountains, homeland to our *Nde* band. They are the ones who are trying to send us back to that miserable Bosque Redondo.

"The *Nde* will never go back there. The government agents of the White Eyes lied to our people. They said we would have the reservation to ourselves, then they forced us to share the land with the Navajo. The agents said they would give us food and blankets and clothes, but there were never enough of any of those things. Have you forgotten that's how our people were treated?"

"I haven't forgotten, Night Wind, but I can't turn my back on those who need my help. Plus this may be my only chance to work with a real doctor, to learn more about healing from someone who's gone to medical school. Surely you can understand that."

"What I understand is, if you treat the blue-coats, you are betraying our people." He folded his arms across his muscular chest, a harsh expression on his finely sculpted features, his dark gaze boring into hers. "Or do you no longer acknowledge the *Nde* blood you carry?"

She glared up at him. "I'm proud of my *Nde* blood, Night Wind. I love our people, and I don't want to see any more of them get hurt or worse, die. But as a healer, I must use the skills the Spirits have given me on anyone who needs them. For now that's working with Dr. Chadbourne at Fort Davis, and if that also means treating the soldiers there, then I will."

He made a snorting sound at her words, bringing Jade's chin up. "Night Wind, I swear I would never betray the *Nde* to the soldiers, but neither will I turn my back on someone who's sick or injured."

After a long silent moment, he drew in a deep breath then released it slowly. "My heart wants to believe you because we share the same blood, but my head tells me to trust no one working beside the blue-coats."

Jade's heart cramped at his words. She knew Night Wind had every right to be wary. The United States government and their Indian agents had broken every promise made to the *Nde*. Even so, her cousin's distrust of her stung. Though her Uncle Mateo had chosen the *Nde* way of life while her mother chose to live among the white man, Jade, Night Wind and his sister Bright Star had spent much of their childhood together and had always been close. Apparently their blood ties meant little to him now, which made his wariness all the more painful.

"If you won't take my word," she said, "then there's nothing more I can say to change your mind. I will pray to the Spirits to protect you." With that she turned and started across the grassy meadow, toward town.

Night Wind watched her walk away, her back stiff and head held high. If only the White Eyes had left his people alone. If only the White Eyes would stop trying to force his people off their ancestral home and back onto the reservation. Then everything would be different. The *Nde* would have a decent place to live, enough food to fill their bellies, and he wouldn't have caused the wounded look in Jade's eyes by accusing her of the worst crime a *Nde* could commit: betraying their people.

He didn't move until Jade was out of sight. Then he turned and walked back to where he'd left his mount. Gathering the reins in one hand, he vaulted into his saddle, wheeled the big horse around, then touched his heels to the white's sides. As he rode back to the north, Night Wind made a decision. He would stay in the area one more day, rather than following his original plan to leave as soon as he talked with Jade. Perhaps by staying close to the fort, he'd learn something useful about the blue-coats, information he could take back to his camp deeper in the mountains.

His decision made, he started looking for a place to spend the night. At first light, he would move to the lip of the high mountain ridge at the northern edge of the fort. From such a vantage point, he'd have a clear view of the entire canyon below and could watch the movements of the blue-coats.

* * *

Jade entered her house, lit a lamp then turned to look down at Zita. "How's our patient?" she said in a low voice. "Still grouchy, or did you sweeten his disposition with your antics?"

The dog sat up, ears perked and head cocked to one side.

Jade smiled. "Yes, I know you want some attention." She crouched down in front of Zita, chuckling when the dog waved a paw at her. "Okay, okay, I'll scratch. But just for a minute."

After Jade gave her pet the requisite amount of scratching, she rose and moved toward the bedroom. At the door, she paused. Before she could decide whether to go in, Eli spoke.

"You don't have to be quiet. I'm awake."

Jade took a step into the room. "I thought you'd be asleep."

"I tried, but guess I slept too much today. I was just about to light the lamp in here."

Jade heard the scratch of a match, then saw the tip flare to life. She watched the bright yellow flame move toward the lamp's wick. As a soft golden circle of light chased the darkness from the room and allowed her a view of Eli's face, her breath caught in her throat. The lamplight accented the planes and angles of his rugged features, the blond streaks in his hair gleaming.

She swallowed, then moved farther into the room, stopping a foot from the bed. "Can I get you anything?"

Eli blew out the match, then looked up at her. "No, I'm fine." He stared at her face, wondering at the shadows in her eyes, shadows that hadn't been there earlier. "What about you, do you need something?"

She blinked with surprise. "No, nothing."

He scooted over on the mattress, then patted a spot next to his hips. "Sit down and tell me what happened."

"I don't know—"

"Those beautiful eyes of yours don't lie, *roja*. They tell me you're upset. If you talk to me, maybe I can help."

She drew a deep breath then exhaled slowly, ignoring her body's response to both his calling her eyes beautiful and inviting her to sit beside him. After a moment, she finally said, "All right, I'll tell you."

Jade eased down onto the mattress, thinking about what she would say. She knew she had to be careful what she revealed, so she chose her words carefully. "I just came from seeing my cousin. He's upset because I'm working for Dr. Chadbourne."

"You have a cousin living in town?"

"No, he lives . . . to the north. He was on his way to see me, but I intercepted him in the mountains."

"Is that why you left in such a hurry? Your vision was about your cousin coming to see you?"

She nodded. "I recognized both my cousin and the mountain meadow in the vision the Spirits gave me, so I went there to wait for him. He told me he'd heard I was working at the fort hospital and wanted to know if the rumor was true."

"I take it he agrees that a yarb woman isn't qualified to work as the post surgeon's assistant?"

"No, that's not why he's upset." She drew a shaky breath. "He thinks I'm betraying my *Nde* blood by working for the army, enemy to the *Nde*. I told him that wasn't true, that I only wanted to learn more about healing from a real doctor and to treat those who need my help."

"But he didn't believe you."

She nodded, a sad smiled curving her lips. "I should have known he wouldn't understand. The *Nde* have been lied to so many times that now some of them don't trust even their own family." She sighed. "Knowing Night Wind doesn't trust me really hurts."

"Night Wind?"

Jade squeezed her eyes closed for a moment. She hadn't meant to reveal her cousin's name, but it had slipped out. "Yes, Night Wind is the son of my mother's older brother, Mateo Valdez, though when my uncle made the decision to live among the *Nde*, he took the name Night Hawk."

"They're the relatives you mentioned when we talked about the Bosque Redondo?"

"Yes. My mother, her sister and two brothers were raised to know both the *Nde* ways of their mother and the ways of the white man from their father. But eventually, each of them had to make a decision about which world they would live in, since trying to walk in both worlds became impossible. Of my mother, her sister and two brothers, only Uncle Mateo chose the *Nde* life-way. In '63, he and his family, his wife Yellow Bird, Night Wind and their daughter Bright Star, moved to Bosque Redondo with the other *Nde* bands."

"Where did they go when they left the reservation?"

"They . . ." She avoided his gaze, staring down at her tightly clasped hands. "They came back to Texas."

"Is Night Wind one of the warriors causing trouble with the freighters and stage line on the San Antonio-El Paso road?"

She swallowed hard, then said, "Why is everyone so quick to place blame on the *Nde*?"

Eli stared at her for a moment, then said, "You're right. I was wrong to make that assumption." Since she was already upset over her cousin's visit, he saw no need to press her on a subject she obviously didn't want to discuss. Instead he said, "Come here, *roja*. Let me hold you."

Her gaze snapped to his outstretched arms, then to his face. "What?"

"You're upset and I'm offering to comfort you." Seeing her eyes widen, he said, "I'm just going to hold you for a few minutes, that's all. Now, come here." He wiggled his fingers at her.

Jade knew she shouldn't accept his offer, but his arms looked so inviting. Before she could talk herself out of it, she moved closer, then leaned toward him and let herself be wrapped in his embrace.

She sighed with pleasure. The musky scent of his skin, the warmth of his naked chest beneath her cheek, the muscular arms holding her gently yet firmly, combined to make her head reel and her pulse increase.

After a few minutes, he said, "Better?" The softly whispered word tickled her ear and sent a shiver up her spine.

"Hmm, yes," she replied, scooting even closer.

Eli smiled, allowing his head to fall back against the headboard. He still wasn't certain what had possessed him to offer to comfort Jade, but he couldn't remember the last time he'd experienced such contentment. Certainly not since he'd made the journey to Texas after leaving— No, he refused to think about that now. Maybe someday he'd have to think about his past and come to terms with what he'd done, but not tonight. Not while he gave Jade what little solace he could.

Night Wind sat on the ground, his back resting against a large rock, gazing down at the fort below. He'd been sitting there since before daylight, and now the sun had risen halfway to its zenith in the eastern sky. He shifted positions, wondering why he didn't leave, why he persisted in watching the fort's activities when he'd seen nothing of interest taking place. There seemed to be few blue-coats at the fort, which meant most of them were out on patrol. That was another reason he should leave, but for some—

Movement behind one of the stone buildings far below halted his musings. Two women moved down the steps of the rear porch then stopped in the yard behind the house. The sun reflecting on the head of one of the women made Night Wind blink with surprise. Never had he seen such light-colored hair, a shade of gold so pale that the sun's rays made the hair appear almost white.

He narrowed his eyes, studying the woman. Other than her blue dress, she was too far away for him to make out any details. If only he was closer, then he might be able to hear the conversation between the two women.

"I'll be fine, Aunt Amelia, so stop fretting." Dee-Dee Luden looked at her mother's oldest sister. Amelia Fryman was short and slightly plump with an enormous bosom, soft gray eyes and light brown hair heavily sprinkled with silver. Dee-Dee offered her aunt a reassuring smile. "I can take care of myself."

"Deirdre, I—"

"Dee-Dee, remember. Both you and Uncle Phillip agreed to call me Dee-Dee."

"Sorry, dear. Dee-Dee, I wish you wouldn't do this. There are so many dangers here in the wilds of West Texas."

"We've had this conversation before, Aunt Amelia, and I'm not afraid of anything that might be in these mountains."

Amelia sighed, certain her headstrong niece wouldn't listen to any arguments she made. "All right, dear, but do be careful."

Dee-Dee laughed. "Don't worry, I'm always careful." She gave her aunt a quick hug, then turned and headed toward the rear of the canyon. She'd only arrived from New York two days before to begin a several-month visit with her aunt and uncle, but she already had the itch to explore the area where she'd be staying.

"Will you be back for dinner?"

Dee-Dee stopped and looked back at her aunt. "I'm not sure. But don't keep Uncle Phillip's dinner waiting. You two go ahead and eat."

"But you really . . ." Amelia gave up. Dee-Dee had already turned and started walking again. *Dear Lord, what am I to do with that girl?* Though Deirdre wasn't a young girl, even at twenty-five years of age, she was still a handful, definitely too much for a couple in their fifties. Too bad Deirdre had lost her husband at such a young age. What her niece needed was a man in her life. Amelia suddenly smiled, her spirits lifting. There were plenty of single men at Fort Davis.

She turned and hurried back to the house she and her husband had shared for the past nine months. Walking up the back steps, she started planning ways to make sure Deirdre was introduced to every eligible bachelor at the fort as soon as possible. Surely one of them would be willing to overlook her wild tendencies and find her suitable as a wife.

Dee-Dee moved carefully over the rocky path, completely enthralled with the scenery around her. She had never seen anything which came even close to the incredible beauty of Limpia Canyon and the Davis Mountains. The sky was a cloudless, brilliant shade of blue, the air so fresh, so absolutely pure.

She hadn't intended to walk so far, yet she found she couldn't stop until she saw what was beyond the next bend in the canyon, and then the next. Realizing she'd better head back before her aunt sent out half the troops at the fort to look for her, she took one last look at the mountains in front of her, then turned on her heel and nearly bumped into the solid wall of a man's chest. A naked chest.

Dee-Dee gave a squeak of surprise, then jumped back and lifted her gaze to her unexpected companion. "What are you—?" The rest of her words froze in her throat. The man standing less than a foot away was an Indian, a nearly naked, long-haired, sinfully handsome Indian. "Oh, my," she said in a low voice, taking in his knee-high moccasins, revealing loincloth made from some sort of animal skin and heavily muscled thighs.

Acting purely on instinct, she lifted one hand, intent on running her fingers over the smooth skin of his well-defined chest, on touching the small rawhide bag hanging from a thin leather thong tied around his neck. Realizing the impropriety of what she was about to do, she jerked her hand away from his chest and shifted her gaze back to his face.

The impact of such a fierce stare from his intense, dark eyes made her knees momentarily weak. "Who are you?" she said in the haughtiest voice she could muster. "And why did you sneak up on me like that?"

"I am Night Wind, and I did not sneak up on you." The woman was older than he'd first thought, but no less lovely. The light-colored hair he found so fascinating curled softly around her oval face, where a few wisps had escaped the thick braid trailing down her back. Her eyebrows were darker than her hair and slightly arched, her eyes a soft shade of blue and her mouth rose-colored and full. He drew a deep breath before he said, "I have been following you since you entered the narrow part of the canyon."

"Following me!" This time when she lifted her hand, she did touch him. But instead of a caress, she jabbed the tips of two fingers against the center of his bronze chest, making the rawhide bag bounce against his hard muscles. "What reason could you possibly have for following me? I'm on foot. I'm carrying nothing of value." She eyed him for a moment, then dropped her voice to a silky whisper. "Or were you planning to ravish me?"

Night Wind blinked, shocked to realize the heat of a flush crept up his neck and cheeks. He should be angry that a woman, especially a White Eyes, could embarrass him so easily. He should tell her he wanted nothing from her, that he preferred dark-eyed, dark-haired women, then walk away, but he knew he'd be lying. From the moment he'd first seen her from high on the edge of the canyon wall, he could think of nothing except getting a closer look. And now that he had, all he could think about was holding this feisty woman in his arms, staring into her light blue eyes and running his fingers through the soft golden strands of her hair.

He finally found his voice to say, "Are you offering yourself to me?"

Dee-Dee sucked in a sharp breath. Before she could give vent to her temper, she noticed the gleam in his dark eyes. Sensing this man wasn't all savage warrior, in spite of his harsh demeanor, she batted her eyelashes at him and said, "You, sir, are incredibly rude to ask that of a lady."

Night Wind threw back his head and laughed. "You are very brave to walk in these mountains alone, but also very foolish."

"Really?" Dee-Dee replied, stepping closer. Giving in to temptation, she ran one finger over his muscular chest. She'd never been so bold in her life, but some inner sense told her she wouldn't stir his anger by such behavior.

"If another *Nde* warrior had found you," Night Wind said in a voice he prayed wouldn't betray the desire her touch sparked, "he might not be as tolerant as I have been. You are lucky I am the one who followed you here."

"Yes," she said, smiling up at him. "I'm extremely lucky."

Chapter 7

Night Wind loped up the narrow mountain path, heading for the trees where he'd left his horse more than an hour earlier. Though he tried to put the pale-haired woman from his mind, she refused to be banished from his thoughts. Dee-Dee. An unusual name for the White Eyes, a woman unlike any he'd ever known, with the exception of Jade who possessed the same defiant streak, the same inner strength.

After Dee-Dee had literally bumped into him, she'd shown no fear, though other women would have screamed, cowered in fear, or collapsed on the ground in a faint. But not Dee-Dee Luden. She had actually played word games with him, her light blue eyes teasing and flirting, her small fingers trailing down his chest, leaving a blaze of heat in their wake. He grunted, determined to stop thinking about her.

Night Wind reached his horse and vaulted into the saddle with a flying leap. Picking up the reins, he urged the big white stallion out from under the trees, then turned the animal to head deeper into the mountains. With luck, he'd reach the *Nde* camp before nightfall.

As Night Wind's horse settled into a steady cantor, his thoughts again drifted back to Dee-Dee and the hour he'd spent walking and talking with her, and how her looks, her voice, her touch had affected him.

He pressed his lips together in annoyance. He couldn't be attracted to her, a White Eyes, enemy to his people. He prided himself on his dedication to the *Nde,* and his vow to see them returned to what was once their homeland. So allowing his attraction to the pale-haired woman to go any further would be a betrayal to all he stood for. In spite of his self-disgust over an attraction he couldn't seem to control and his inner arguments to forget about the woman, he knew deep down that he would give in to Dee-Dee's final request. He would see her again.

Night Wind kicked his horse into a run, calling himself every despicable name he could think of, first in the *Nde* language, then in Spanish and finally in English. Yet none of the names he came up with erased Dee-Dee's smiling face from his memory.

Jade sat behind Dr. Chadbourne's desk, her thoughts drifting from the medical book lying open in front of her. She'd been trying to read the same page for the past hour, yet each time she started reading, the words became a jumble in her head. Instead, her mind drifted to more interesting topics. Like Eli Kinmont.

She just couldn't stop thinking about the way Eli had held her the night before, how wonderful his skin had smelled, how secure she'd felt in his embrace. But mostly, she couldn't stop thinking about how her body had reacted to their closeness. As the memory coaxed the heat inside her belly back to life and revived the ache between her thighs, a low moaning sound vibrated in her throat. Slamming the book closed, she pushed away from the desk and rose.

Why did Eli Kinmont affect her in ways she'd never experienced? Why did he—? She stopped her pacing, her eyes going wide. Perhaps this was what her mother meant when she'd talked about finding the man destined to be her mate. Just thinking of Eli in that way sent shivers up her spine. She barely knew him, and yet in some ways she felt as though she'd always known him. Her brow furrowed. That's what her parents often told her and her siblings. Soon after Rafe Tucker and Karina Valdez met, both knew they'd found the other half of their soul. Though Rafe and Karina fought the notion at first, they finally realized the truth: they were meant to spend the remainder of their lives together.

Jade sighed, thinking of the love and happiness her parents shared. She used to daydream about one day having a love as special as Rafe and Karina Tucker's. But as Jade grew older, her dedication to improving her healing skills always took precedence in her life, leaving little time to spend searching for the one man who could give her a lifetime of love. Perhaps the Spirits had intervened, taking up the search and bringing Eli into her life.

"You're being ridiculous," she said, startled to realize she'd spoken the words aloud. Then she thought again of her parents, recalling how the Spirits had given her mother visions of her father before the two met. So, maybe . . . She shook her head, determined to stop thinking about Eli Kinmont and the possible purpose behind his entrance into her life.

Three days later, Eli awoke from a mid-morning nap and stretched, relieved to find his head no longer hurt. The cut along his hairline was still tender to the touch, but at least his vertigo had ended the day before, and now the annoying ache in his head had vanished as well.

Though his ankle would require more time to heal, at least the crutch Jade had brought him from the post infirmary gave him the mobility to move around inside her house and to the privy and back without her help.

The clicking of Zita's nails on the floor alerted him that he was about to have company. Turning his head toward the bedroom door, he watched the dog cross the threshold then stop. He smiled at the hopeful look on Zita's face. "It's okay," he said, patting the mattress beside his hip. "You can get up here."

The dog didn't hesitate. She bounded toward the bed, leaped up next to him then lay down. Rolling onto her side, she snagged his hand with one paw and pulled it toward her. Eli chuckled, then complied and started scratching.

As he absently moved his fingers over the soft hair on Zita's chest, his mind wandered to the dog's owner. Realizing the direction of his thoughts, he scowled. Why couldn't he stop thinking about his hostess? He shouldn't have trouble keeping his mind away from disturbing subjects. Hell, he'd successfully done just that for most of the past six years. Yet ever since Jade found him in the mountains, controlling his thoughts had become more and more difficult.

Why did I have to track that damn mountain lion? If I hadn't tried to outsmart the miserable cat, I wouldn't be in this fix. He exhaled on a long sigh, wishing he had something to occupy his time. Before Jade left that morning, he should have asked if she had something he could read. He pressed his lips together in a grimace. Bad idea! She probably would've handed him a medical journal. That was the *last* thing he wanted to read. He'd just have to find some other way to occupy his time.

When Jade returned to her house later that afternoon, she found Eli sitting up in bed, reading one of the medical journals Dr. Chadbourne received at the fort. As she stepped closer to the bed, her presence didn't seem to register with him. After a moment, she cleared her throat, then said, "Sorry to disturb your reading." She hoped her voice didn't betray the excitement she felt at seeing him so engrossed in the journal.

Eli blinked, then turned his gaze on her. A sudden frown passing across his features, he said, "You're not disturbing me. Now that my head's stopped hurting, I . . . uh . . . needed something to help pass the time. This is all I could find." He closed the journal then tossed it onto the bedside table.

"Oh, I see," she replied, biting her lip to halt the threatening smile. "I could bring other journals home, if you'd like to read them."

Eli's brows snapped together. "No!" His voice came out louder than he intended. Attempting a smile, he said, "Thanks, but they aren't my taste in reading material."

"Well, if you change your mind, let me know." She took a seat on the edge of the mattress. "When did your head stop hurting?"

"This morning," he replied in a strained voice, Jade's nearness doing odd things to his insides.

She nodded, her gaze moving to the cut along his hairline. "Good, let me have a look at your forehead."

Before Eli could offer a protest, she lifted her hand to his head and leaned toward him. With the heady spice of her scent surrounding him and her breasts just inches from his face, his mouth went dry. Breathing normally became impossible, and he thought he might suffocate before she finished her examination.

"The cut's healing nicely," she said, removing her hand and sitting back. "I don't see the need to—" Her gaze met and held his, whatever she'd been about to say slipping away like a puff of smoke. The heat in his blue eyes—a heat she knew had nothing to do with his injuries—chased all rational thoughts from her head.

She dropped her gaze to his mouth. A wild fluttering started inside her belly, her lips tingled with anticipation, a shiver of exhilaration raced across her skin. As she studied his flushed face, she ran the tip of her tongue over her lips to ease the tingling. Her eyes widened at Eli's reaction. The color of his eyes deepening to the blue black of the night sky, his nostrils flared and a low groan rumbled in his chest.

There was something about this man, an invisible force pulling her to him, an attraction she didn't completely understand, yet felt compelled to act on. Leaning closer, she shifted her gaze back to his mouth. "Eli, I . . ." Her words ended on a deep shuddering breath.

Eli watched her mouth come closer and knew with a certainty what she planned to do. But for some reason he was powerless to stop her. He knew this wasn't a good idea, in fact it was a damn poor one, and yet he still couldn't make himself move.

Jade leaned even closer, resting the fingertips of one hand on Eli's chest to brace herself. The catch in his breathing barely registered but the warmth of his smooth skin did, bringing back memories of the night before. Her cheek pressed to the solid wall of muscle, his arm wrapped around her. She drew another unsteady breath. Letting her eyes drift shut, she closed the last few inches separating them and pressed her lips to his.

She heard a moan, uncertain if the sound came from her throat or Eli's. Nothing had prepared her for the incredible rush of sensation storming her body. Unlike her mother, who'd been raised knowing nothing about kissing—the custom was not part of the *Nde* culture— Jade grew up seeing her parents frequently kissing, their enjoyment unmistakable. But everything she'd witnessed fell far short of reality. Her entire body was on fire, every nerve ending ablaze and straining for more.

As soon as Eli realized he couldn't stop Jade from kissing him, he'd vowed to remain unaffected, to let her satisfy her curiosity and be done with it. But when her mouth settled atop his and a whimper vibrated in her throat, his intentions were immediately forgotten.

He lifted one hand, threading his fingers through the heavy mass of her hair to cradle the back of her head. Holding her gently, he changed the angle of their melded lips so he could deepen the kiss. He moaned into her mouth, his chest burning where her fingers touched him, his pulse pounding against his eardrums so hard he could barely hear.

After a moment, his senses righted themselves enough for him to realize he had not only broken his vow to remain unaffected, but he was actually contributing to the pleasure created by their kiss. Grasping Jade by the shoulders, he eased his mouth from hers.

"Enough, *roja,*" he said in a raspy whisper, pushing her back to a sitting position.

Eli watched her struggle to cool her reaction to his kiss, remembering what it was like to be swamped by desire. If not for shutting down that part of his life, along with everything else about his past, he might also be struggling with needs left unsatisfied. Even so, kissing Jade had affected him more than he'd thought possible, certainly more than the prostitute in Presidio who'd wanted to show him a good time—a circumstance other men suffering from the same debility would have found encouraging. But he refused to let himself think along those lines. Instead, he searched for a reason for the confusing thoughts filling his head. Why was everything he'd worked so hard to maintain over the past six years suddenly in jeopardy? What would happen if the life he'd led since coming to West Texas fell apart?

He squeezed his eyes closed, uncertain whether he could deal with the aftermath. Opening his eyes, his gaze settled on the cause of his disturbing thoughts. Jade. If she hadn't found him and brought him to her house so she could treat his injuries. If her scent wasn't so damn intoxicating, filling his head with all kinds of notions better left alone.

If not for Jade Tucker, he wouldn't be faced with the possible collapse of his life. A hot burst of anger rushed through his veins, making him clench his hands into fists atop his thighs. He couldn't let some yarb woman with a mouth as sweet as honey ruin the life he'd made for himself.

He stared at her a moment longer, then said, "What the hell was that all about?"

Jade started at his voice then slowly met his gaze. She blinked at the fierce gleam in his eyes, at the harsh set of his jaw. "What do you mean?"

"You don't have to play games with me. I see what you're trying to do. Using your feminine wiles to get me to teach you what I know about doctoring."

Jade swallowed the sudden lump in her throat. "That's not true."

"Isn't it?" Before she could open her mouth to respond, he continued. "Didn't you just kiss me?" When she nodded, he said, "And wouldn't you like me to teach you what I learned in medical school?"

"Well, yes, but—"

"Then I've proven my point."

"You haven't proven anything, you pigheaded fool," Jade said, her temper springing to life. "Now listen here, your accusations are nothing more than the warped workings of a suspicious mind."

When he started to speak, she held up one hand. "Wait. I haven't finished." She drew a deep breath, then said, "I'll admit I'd welcome your teachings about doctoring, especially since Dr. Chadbourne is away from the fort again. But I assure you, I did not kiss you in order to convince you to become my teacher."

Eli crossed his hands over his chest and glared at her. "Can I talk now?"

Her lips pressed into a flat line, she gave him a curt nod.

"If your little speech is the truth, then why did you kiss me?"

"I don't know, damn you. I just . . ." Mortified by her outburst, her flare of temper abruptly receded. Avoiding his gaze, she lifted one shoulder in a shrug. "I just wanted to, that's all," she said, her voice calmer and much softer.

"Are you often struck with the urge to kiss your male patients?"

Jade's head snapped up. "Of course not! You're the first patient I've wanted to kiss."

Eli couldn't stop the burst of combined pride and relief from blossoming in his chest. Though he now knew she wasn't prone to such forward behavior, he figured he still had to say something to ward off any possible future advances.

After a moment to gather his thoughts, he cleared his throat, then said, "In case you're considering more than kisses from me, I have to warn you that you're barking up the wrong tree."

"Wrong tree? What are you talking about?"

"I can't . . ." He ran a hand through his hair, cursing under his breath. "That is, I'm not capable of doing the deed. Do you understand what I'm saying?"

"I don't think so."

"Dammit, I'm trying to tell you I'm impotent." He pinned her with a fierce gaze. "You do understand what that means, don't you?"

"Yes, of course." She stared at him thoughtfully for a moment. "That's what you meant by your affliction when I first brought you here, isn't—?"

"I don't want to talk about it. Let's just forget the last few minutes ever happened. Agreed?"

She managed a nod, though she longed to shout a protest. How could she forget something as wonderful as the kiss they'd shared? Or his surprising revelation? He talked like kissing her had been nothing more than a minor annoyance, not the heart-stopping, breath-stealing passionate blending of lips she'd experienced. In spite of agreeing to forget both the kiss and the disclosure of his impotency, she feared she never would, just as she feared she was dangerously close to losing her heart to this infuriating, yet equally desirable man.

The following day was Sunday, and although Jade normally wouldn't be required to report for work at the post infirmary, Dr. Chadbourne's absence changed her routine. Once she'd seen to any soldiers who reported for sick call, she planned to ride out to see Paloma Diaz and spend the rest of the day with her friend.

When she arrived at the infirmary, she was relieved to find Sergeant Davidson not in attendance. *He's probably passed out from swilling too much whiskey in Chihuahua. I hope he has a miserable hangover. He deserves every*—Though she instantly scolded herself for having such cruel thoughts, she also knew she had good reason for doing so. The hospital steward had a propensity for liquor, one he'd done little to hide. She'd smelled whiskey on his breath more than once in the days since Dr. Chadbourne's departure. And when the sergeant had been drinking, his behavior was even more reprehensible. He constantly made nasty comments to Jade about a woman's place as well as making some lewd suggestions about how she could better use her time.

Jade drew a deep breath and exhaled slowly, relieved she wouldn't have to put up with the hospital steward for one day. The sound of the infirmary door opening jerked her attention back to the present. Stealing herself, she turned around, fearful the man she'd been thinking about would ruin her day after all.

A soldier, a private from the Ninth Cavalry, stood just inside the door. He was of medium height, with a muscular build and broad shoulders. His dark face was long and narrow, his nose straight and slightly flat, and he wore a closely clipped moustache. Seeing Jade, he snatched his forage cap from his head and gave her a nod.

When the man made no offer to move, Jade gestured toward the cloth wrapped around his left hand. "Can I help you, private?"

"I—Where's Sergeant Davidson?"

"He's not here today. If you need medical care, I'm Jade Tucker, Dr. Chadbourne's assistant."

"Begging your pardon, Miz Tucker. But the sergeant said while Dr. Chadbourne's away we're supposed to see him, not the fool woman—" He cleared his throat. "Sorry, ma'am, but that's what we were told."

Jade curled her fingers into fists. "Yes, I'm sure you were. But I can assure you, private, I'm a fine healer. I wouldn't be here if Dr. Chadbourne didn't think so."

He thought about that for a minute, then said, "Reckon you're right."

"Now, what happened to your hand, Private . . . ?"

"Mitchell, ma'am. Isaac Mitchell." He moved farther into the infirmary. "I cut my hand on a piece of wire." He swallowed hard. "I think it's gonna need sewing up."

"Come into the dispensary and take a seat, Private Mitchell, so I can look at your hand."

"Yes, ma'am," he replied, doing as she'd directed.

Jade carefully removed the piece of cloth the man had haphazardly used as a bandage. The gash on his palm looked to be several inches long and had bled freely.

"Once I wash off the blood, I can tell more, Private. But I don't think you'll need stitches. Just sit here while I get what I need." She turned and crossed the room to fetch the necessary supplies.

A few minutes later, Private Mitchell rose to leave.

"I thank you, ma'am, for treating my hand. You did a fine job." He flashed her a smile. " 'Specially since you didn't have to do any sewing on this tough hide of mine."

Jade returned his smile. "You're welcome, Private. But

if you don't do what I told you and rest that hand, you may still end up with stitches."

Mitchell chuckled. "Yes, ma'am, I'll remember. And I'll do what I can to convince the others to stop listening to what Sergeant Davidson says about you."

"I'd appreciate that, Private Mitchell."

As the soldier left the dispensary, Jade hoped he'd not only do what he said, but that the other soldiers would believe him.

Jade finished cleaning up the supplies she'd used, then prepared to leave for the day. After making one last check to be sure everything was in order, she headed outside and pulled the door shut behind her. Retrieving Luna from beneath a small stand of oak trees where she'd tethered the horse after arriving at the infirmary, she swung into the saddle.

She kept the mare at a walk until they left the grounds of the fort. Then leaning over Luna's neck, she kicked the horse into a faster pace, anxious to get to Paloma's hut.

Chapter 8

Jade slipped off Luna's back a few yards from Paloma's small home, then picketed the mare beneath a cottonwood tree. She headed for the house, smiling as the goats bleated a greeting.

"*Maestra*, I've come to spend the day with you," Jade said, pushing open the door and stepping inside.

"Ah, *chica*, I am so glad to see you," Paloma replied. "I've been thinking about you and your Anglo patient." She waved toward the chair across from her. "Come. Sit. Tell me all about this man of yours."

Although Jade started to say "He isn't my man," she couldn't make herself deny what she'd already admitted to herself. Having spent most of the past few days with Eli, having experienced her body's reaction to his touch, then actually kissing him, she had to face reality. She wanted Paloma's words to be the truth. She wanted Eli to be her man. Clearing her throat, she finally said, "What do you want to know?"

"Tell me how he is. His injuries are healing well, *sí*?"

"*Sí*. The cut on his head is almost completely healed.

His ankle is much better; he's able to use a crutch to get around. But it will be several more days before he can put any weight on the leg.''

Paloma nodded. *"Bueno,* you have done well, *chica.* Now, tell me, what is this Anglo like?''

Jade thought for a moment, then said, "When I first found him, he was rude and overbearing at every opportunity, mocking first my healing skills, then my working with Dr. Chadbourne.''

"Such words made you angry, *sí?*"

Jade gave her friend a sheepish smile. "At first I thought his comments showed what a mean-spirited person he was, one who sees no joy in anything, who finds fault with everything. But now I'm sure he's not really like that. He has hurts I cannot see, hurts deep inside from something in his past, which make him act so spitefully toward me.''

"Why do you think this?''

"He's a doctor, *maestra.* He went to medical school, even studied in Europe. But something happened six years ago—he wouldn't tell me what—that made him give up being a doctor and move to this part of Texas.''

Paloma clapped her hands together, a broad smile creasing her face. "So this is the other reason your Spirits brought him into your life. He will teach you about Anglo medicine, *sí?*"

"I'm not counting on it. He says he's no longer a doctor, and he refuses to answer my questions. But yesterday, I found him reading one of Dr. Chadbourne's medical journals, so maybe whatever drew him to medicine in the first place still exists.''

"I think you may be right, *chica.* And if anyone can bring back his desire to be a doctor, you can.''

"I appreciate your confidence, *maestra.* But I don't know if I can.''

"Just do the best you can, isn't that what I've always taught you?''

Jade nodded, but didn't reply. She stared thoughtfully

at her friend for a moment, then said, "You said something about there being another reason the Spirits told me about Eli. What did you mean?"

"You truly do not know?" When Jade shook her head, she reached over and placed one gnarled hand atop the younger woman's. "*Chica,* the Spirits sent him to you because he's meant to be your *esposo*—husband."

"You're certain?" Jade replied, holding her breath for the answer.

Paloma gave Jade's hand a gentle squeeze. "*Sí,* now that I know this Anglo is also a doctor, I am sure of it." At Jade's skeptical look, she said, "You are attracted to this man?"

"Yes."

"And you desire him?"

A flush crept up Jade's face, the kiss she and Eli shared leaping to mind and making the heat spread over her entire body. Knowing Paloma would immediately see through a lie, she bobbed her head in a jerky nod.

"And he desires you as well?"

After swallowing the sudden lump in her throat, Jade said, "I wish I could be certain. I thought he did, that he also felt the wild tingling each time we touched. And I was sure he enjoyed our kiss yesterday, but . . ." Paloma's chuckle made her face burn even hotter. Determined to finish, she said, "But he told me not to consider more than kisses from him. He isn't capable of doing more because he's impotent."

"Ah, the giant is sleeping."

"The giant?"

"*Sí,* that part which makes him a man. His words meant he cannot be intimate with you, is that not so?"

"Yes."

"And you would like your relationship to be more than kissing?"

Another fiery blush rose to Jade's face. "Yes, but I don't

know how to treat his ... um ... problem. Is there a treatment I can use, *maestra?*"

Paloma gave her a sad smile. "I once knew an old *curandera* down in Mexico who claimed she could make a tea which would help that part of a man. I never saw her prepare or use the remedy, so I do not know if her claims are true. But even if you wanted to try giving such a tea to the Anglo, would he not question what you are giving him?"

"You're right. I doubt he'd drink it."

"I'm sorry, *chica,* but you must find a way to reawaken his sleeping giant on your own. Find the key to healing the Anglo's hidden hurts, and you will also find the key to making him your *esposo.*"

Jade nodded, her brow furrowed. In spite of her attraction to Eli, she wasn't altogether certain she wanted a husband.

"Don't look so worried. You must have faith in your abilities, as I do. You will find a way, *chica,* I know it."

She managed a small smile, then sighed. She longed to believe Paloma's intuitive powers were accurate—as they usually were—but this time, she didn't want to risk the possible results if her friend was wrong: giving up her life as a healing woman in addition to a broken heart.

On Jade's ride home later that afternoon, she replayed parts of her conversation with Paloma in her mind. Could her friend be correct, was her future really with Eli? And if she and Eli were to marry, would she be able to continue the work she loved? Her profound concern over the idea of marrying Eli vied with another emotion. Her newfound desire touched off a wildfire in her belly, one she instinctively knew only he could extinguish.

Such sensations were new to Jade, having spent little time in her twenty-one years doing anything other than learning about healing and then putting her lessons to use. And now that she'd experienced a woman's desire for a man and felt the first stirrings of love, she wasn't sure what to do. She wished her parents lived closer so she could talk to her mother. But since that wasn't possible, she'd have to figure out how to deal with her feelings for Eli on her own.

When she returned home, she found Eli sitting at the table in the main room of her house, his injured foot resting on the seat of another chair.

Though his recuperative progress stroked her healer's ego, a stronger emotion clutched at her heart: fear that he'd soon be well enough to leave. She would have to do something quickly. But what?

She approached him with a smile. "You must be feeling a lot better."

Eli returned her smile, hoping the thrill of seeing her wasn't obvious. "Getting around is a bit awkward, but I'm managing pretty well."

"Just don't push your recovery," she said, praying he wouldn't detect the true reason for her words. "You shouldn't risk reinjuring your ankle by putting weight on that foot too soon."

"Yes, I know, and I've been careful. But lying in that bed every day for almost a week was becoming downright tiresome, so I had to get up for a while."

She nodded. "Are you hungry? Should I fix supper?"

"No rush," he replied. "So, did you and *Señora* Diaz catch up on all your female chatter?"

She pulled out a chair and sat down across the table from him. "We had a nice visit," Jade said, wondering what he'd say if she told him that he had been the main topic of discussion.

After she and Eli chatted about inconsequential things for a few minutes, she said, "I was wondering whether you'd given any thought to writing to your mother."

He scowled at her. "Why would I?"

"Because she deserves to know you're still alive. She

hasn't heard from you since you came west, so she probably thinks you're dead.''

"Maybe she's better off believing that," Eli said, staring at the center of the table where he'd clenched his hands into tight fists.

Jade leaned forward and wrapped her fingers around his. "That's not true, Eli. No matter what you've done, a mother's love is unconditional."

He grunted, but didn't speak. She didn't understand. If he wrote to his family, he'd have to tell them things he hadn't told another living soul. Struggling for control, he squeezed his eyes closed for a second. No, he couldn't do it. The cost was too high.

After a long silence, Jade said, "I've been thinking about what you said yesterday, about why I . . . um . . . kissed you." Seeing his eyebrows arch, she added, "Your accusations are still false, but since you are a college-trained doctor and Dr. Chadbourne is away from the fort, I thought maybe you'd consider being my teacher."

Before he could reply, she added, "I know, you've already told me you don't want to return to medicine. But think about all your training, all the time you spent studying to be a doctor in medical school and in France. If you'd teach me, at least all of that wouldn't be going to waste."

Eli lifted his gaze to look into her eyes. He saw no deception lurking in the depths of those silver-flecked green orbs. He found only genuine honesty, something he knew she couldn't fake. At last he said, "Even if I wanted to be your tutor, what I learned in medical school is years out of date and would be of little value to you."

"That's not true, Eli. What you could teach me is far more advanced than what I already know."

He considered her words for a moment, then gave his head a shake. "Sorry, I can't. When Dr. Chadbourne gets back, he can teach you."

"If the coming months are anything like the past two,

he'll never have time. How am I supposed to learn about medicine if he's never here?''

"That's not my problem. Like I told you before, my life as a doctor is over. So, I'd appreciate it if you'd keep your nose out of my business.''

Though Jade longed to press him on the issue, she didn't want to rouse his temper again, so she remained silent. Her only hope was that something would eventually change his mind.

Later that night, Eli lay in bed contemplating his conversation with Jade. Why did she have to keep bringing up his past? She knew he didn't want to talk about his medical career or his family, yet she persisted in saying things which forced him to dredge up all the old painful memories.

He rolled onto his side, determined to go to sleep. But the image of his mother's face, then those of his two sisters, kept him awake. Realizing the images in his mind's eye were more than six years old, he wondered how they had changed. Had either of his sisters gotten married? Had one or both of them made him an uncle? The thought of his sisters being wives and mothers brought a sudden lump to his throat. He smiled at the picture of his mother's face, imagining her reaction when she learned she was going to be a grandmother. His smile abruptly faded. How was her health? Was she well, or had she taken ill, or even—? He couldn't make himself complete the thought; it was too painful.

He flopped over onto his back. Folding his hands beneath his head, he stared up at the ceiling. Maybe Jade was right. Maybe continuing to ignore his past wasn't a good idea. Maybe he should write to his mother. But if he did, would he be able to face his past? And more importantly, would he be able to come to grips with what he'd done? Unable to find answers to ease the torment eating at his insides, he finally drifted into a fitful sleep.

* * *

On the way to the post infirmary the following morning, Jade spotted a woman standing beneath a stand of oak trees not far from the hospital buildings. Detouring to the shady grove, she approached the woman. "Good morning. Is there something I can help you with?"

The woman didn't respond for a moment, then finally turned to face Jade. A few strands of her pale blond hair had escaped from her thick braid and fluttered in the breeze. "Thank you, but I was just thinking about someone I met up there." She waved one hand toward the back of the canyon.

"I see," Jade replied, her brow furrowed at the woman's words and the direction she indicated.

"Oh heavens, how rude of me," the woman said, moving closer to Jade and offering a smile. "I'm Deirdre Luden, but you must call me Dee-Dee. I recently arrived from New York to stay with my Aunt Amelia for a few months. Her husband is Captain Phillip Fryman."

Jade returned the smile. "Pleased to meet you, Dee-Dee. I'm Jade Tucker. I'm an assistant to the post surgeon. I've never met Captain Fryman, but I do know your aunt." She hesitated a moment, then said, "Dee-Dee, what were you doing in the canyon? The post commander doesn't want anyone, especially female civilians, wandering around the fort."

"Yes, I know," Dee-Dee replied with a sigh. "I intended to go for a short walk, but these mountains are so lovely that I got swept up in the beauty and kept walking. That's when I met him."

"Him? Are you talking about a soldier?"

Dee-Dee smiled. "No. At least not a soldier from the fort. Though I suspect he's just as fierce." She brushed a wisp of hair away from her face. In a soft voice, she said, "He was magnificent."

Jade tipped her head to one side, noting the woman's flushed face and dilated eyes. "Who was he?"

"His name is—" Dee-Dee snapped her mouth shut, belatedly realizing she shouldn't be telling anyone about Night Wind. After a moment, she said, "His name's not important." Looping her arm through Jade's, she turned them toward the hospital. "Jade . . . you don't mind if I call you Jade, do you?"

When Jade shook her head, Dee-Dee continued. "You must tell me all about your work in the infirmary. How exciting for a woman to be working in a man's field."

Once they were inside Dr. Chadbourne's office, Jade responded to Dee-Dee's request. "There have been women healers among my grandmother's people for generations. The Anglos are the ones who think only men can treat the sick and injured, which is pure nonsense. Women should be able to do whatever they choose."

Dee-Dee threw back her head and laughed. "I couldn't have said it better. We share a common outlook on the fairer sex, being a woman does not—as the male of our species would have everyone believe—make us less intelligent or less capable. I like you, Jade Tucker, and I think we'll get along famously while I'm here. Now, I want to hear all about this line of women healers you're from. Who are your grandmother's people, and how did they become so progressive in this male-dominated world?"

Jade had never met anyone like Dee-Dee Luden, but she had to admit she felt an instant kinship with the woman. "My grandmother's people are the *Nde,* called Mescalero Apache by the United States Government and anyone else who doesn't know our true name. She grew up in these mountains, home to the *Nde* for many generations."

"Indians! I would never have guessed you're Indian, not with your striking hair."

"My grandmother married a man whose ancestors came from Spain, and my mother married an Anglo, so my blood is a mix of several cultures. As for my hair, my father says I inherited the color from his mother."

"I've always been fascinated by other cultures," Dee-Dee said, her eyes sparkling with anticipation. "So, tell me more about the *Nde.*"

Jade told Dee-Dee how she'd been taught the *Nde* ways beginning when she was a small child, and how her aunt and uncle would travel from their *Nde* band to visit her parents' ranch several times a year. Then she lamented not having been able to experience more of the *Nde* lifeway. "When I was very young, we couldn't visit a *Nde* camp because of some trouble between my mother and the *Nde* leaders. Then when I was older, my relatives' bands agreed to go to the Bosque Redondo reservation in New Mexico Territory. And now the bands are scattered. Many chose not to return here to their homeland. Some bands moved down by the river, and others went east into Comanche territory. The few who came back here make their camps deep in the mountains, so the soldiers won't find them."

"Find them? Why are they hiding from the soldiers?"

"When the *Nde* left the reservation almost six years ago, they snuck away in the middle of the night. They never received any of the things promised them by the United States. Instead, they were exposed to the white man's diseases, forced to live in squalid conditions with no sanitation, shoddy clothes and worthless blankets. Their food rations were constantly cut until many faced starvation. The *Nde* knew the consequences of leaving without permission, but they preferred death to remaining at the Bosque Redondo."

Dee-Dee swallowed hard. "Is that why Uncle Phillip said the army considers the Indians around here at war with the U.S. Government? Why he gave the order to kill any who resist capture, just because they wanted better living conditions?"

Jade nodded. "Some of the *Nde* leaders want peace and are willing to talk to the authorities, but other leaders are too angry to agree to anything." She sighed. "I fear what's left of the *Nde* will one day disappear completely."

Dee-Dee inhaled sharply, the color draining from her face.

"Dee-Dee, are you all right?"

The woman managed a jerky nod. "I'll be fine in a minute."

"Are you sure? You're awfully pale. Would you like a glass of water?"

"No, I . . . I just had a terribly upsetting thought. The man I said I met, the man in the canyon? He's an Indian, and the possibility that he might be killed . . ." She dropped onto a nearby chair, a shudder racking her shoulders.

"An Indian? Did he tell you his name?"

Dee-Dee opened her mouth to respond, but the door swinging inward halted her reply.

"Miz Tucker, have you—?" Sergeant Davidson stepped into the office. "Well, well, who have we here?" he said, pulling his hat from his head and moving closer, his gaze glued to Dee-Dee. "Miz Tucker, I demand an immediate introduction to this lovely creature."

Jade frowned, wishing she could refuse his request. "Sergeant Davidson, this is Deirdre Luden, niece of Captain Fryman's wife and guest in their home while she's visiting Fort Davis." Turning to Dee-Dee, she said, "Sergeant Davidson is the hospital steward." She gave Dee-Dee a pointed look. "The man I mentioned earlier."

Dee-Dee blinked up at her, her cheeks slowly regaining their usual pink glow. "Yes, of course, I remember," she replied, offering her hand to the man and forcing her lips into what she hoped passed for a smile. She did indeed remember their conversation about the hospital steward, especially the horrible way he treated Jade.

Davidson bowed over her hand. "I hope Miz Tucker said nothing unseemly about me, Miss Luden."

"That's Mrs. Luden," she replied in a clipped voice.

Though she normally wouldn't have made the correction in quite so rude a manner, she hadn't been able to resist with this strutting popinjay. The shocked expression on his face nearly made her laugh. She cleared her throat, then added, "But I'm a widow." As soon as the words left her mouth, she wished she could call them back.

Davidson's dark scowl slowly changed back to a leer. "My condolences," he said, although his voice revealed no sympathy. He pressed another kiss to the backs of her knuckles, then gave her fingers a squeeze before releasing her hand. "I do hope we'll have the opportunity to get better acquainted during your stay."

Dee-Dee bit her tongue to hold in a shout of outrage. Somehow she managed to murmur an appropriate— though purposely noncommittal—response, then kept her mouth frozen in a forced smile until he turned and headed for the door. Glaring at his back, her lips pursed with distaste, she wiped her hand on her skirt. As soon as he stepped outside and shut the door behind him, the words she'd held back came out in a fierce whisper. "In a pig's eye."

Jade's mouth fell open, then she burst out laughing, certain she and this outrageous woman would become the best of friends.

Chapter 9

As Jade walked home from the infirmary later that day, her thoughts dwelled on what Dee-Dee had revealed after Sergeant Davidson's departure. The man Dee-Dee told her about—the Indian she met while walking in the canyon behind the fort—was Night Wind.

Jade shook her head, still finding it hard to believe. Why had her cousin still been in the area? When she spoke to him the day before he and Dee-Dee met, she assumed he was heading back to his camp. More surprising was how he'd actually walked and talked with Dee-Dee Luden, something she couldn't imagine Night Wind doing. When he and the other *Nde* moved to the Bosque Redondo, he was a seventeen-year-old who believed the United States Government would keep its promises. Two years later, he left the reservation emotionally scarred by the experience, no longer the happy, trusting boy she remembered from her girlhood. He lost the innocence of youth while on the reservation, his carefree attitude replaced with bitterness and distrust. And the most difficult change for Jade to accept was his hatred. He hated the soldiers in the U.S.

Army and anyone else associated with the government, and she suspected he hated all White Eyes as well—including women. That's why Dee-Dee's claim of having had a friendly conversation with Night Wind came as such a surprise.

Jade was certain Dee-Dee hadn't made up her story, so what could have brought about such a change in her cousin? Pondering that question, she turned off the main road of town onto the path leading to her house. She'd only gone a few yards when she pulled up short. Blinking with surprise at the sight meeting her gaze, thoughts of Night Wind and Dee-Dee fled.

She froze, watching Eli come down the path, his progress slow because of having to use the crutch. His head down, concentrating on the terrain in front of him, he hadn't yet spotted her. Keeping her gaze fixed on the man who was becoming more and more important to her, she hurried toward him.

As she drew closer, she noted his clenched jaw and the deep lines bracketing his mouth. "Eli," she said in a soft voice so she wouldn't startle him. "What are you doing? Your ankle isn't healed enough for you to be out walking."

He glanced up at her from beneath his hat brim. "I have an errand to take care of. It may take me a while, but I can make it." He tried to smile, but the twisting of his lips was more of a grimace. "I'll be fine."

"Yes, you will. In a few more days, but this is too soon to walk so far. Why didn't you tell me you needed something? I could have stopped on my way home from the fort."

"I didn't know when you left this morning. I spent the day thinking about something you said to me, and this afternoon I . . . uh . . . decided to write to my mother. I hope you don't mind, but I went through some of your things, looking for writing paper."

"Of course not," Jade replied, her heart beating faster. "You really wrote to your mother?"

He nodded. "You were right, I should have done it long before now."

"Oh, Eli." She put her hand on his forearm. "I'm glad you did. She'll be so happy to hear from you."

"I'm sure she will. I just hope the surprise isn't too much for her."

"Don't go second-guessing yourself. You did the right thing."

He looked up at the clear, azure blue sky, a muscle in his jaw ticking. "I sure as hell hope so."

Jade understood the uncertainty she heard in his voice and wished she could say something to reassure him. But she knew only time could do that. Moving her hand higher, she wrapped her fingers around the bulging muscle of his upper arm. "Come on, I'll help you get back into the house. Then I'll see about sending your letter."

Though Eli wanted to protest, he knew she was right. His strength was already flagging, so there was no way he could've made the walk to town and back. Giving Jade a nod, he turned and started toward the house, letting her support part of his weight with each awkward step.

Half an hour later, Jade returned from sending Eli's letter. As she approached the front of her house, the sound of voices coming from inside made her pause. She recognized the deep voice as Eli's, but she couldn't immediately place the female voice.

She hurried through the door where she found Eli talking with *Señora* Juanita Nunez, an elderly resident of Chihuahua and one of the first people Jade had met after moving to Fort Davis. Crossing the room to where the silver-haired woman sat on one end of the settee, she said, "*Señora*, I am sorry to keep you waiting. I see you've met my patient and houseguest, Eli Kinmont."

The woman offered Jade a smile, deepening the wrinkles in her dark brown face and revealing several missing teeth.

"Do not worry, *Señorita* Tucker, you had no way of knowing I would come to see you today. I was passing the time by talking to *Señor* Kinmont." She lowered her voice to add, "He is *muy guapo, sí*?"

Jade's face burning with a blush, she shot a quick glance toward the opposite end of the settee. If Eli heard the woman's comment, he gave no sign. In a whisper, she said, "*Sí*, he is very handsome." Louder, she added, "What can I do for you today?"

"It is Alfredo. He is in much pain."

"His rheumatism?" When *Señora* Nunez nodded, Jade thought for a moment, then said, "*Señor* Kinmont is a doctor, so perhaps you should ask him what he would recommend for your husband."

Eli sent an icy glare Jade's way, then said, "I don't want—"

"Don't worry, Eli," Jade said, giving him a sweet smile. "I know you're not trying to interfere with my patients. I'm just asking for your opinion on treating rheumatism."

Eli saw the mutinous set to Jade's jaw behind her smile and knew she wouldn't give up until he gave her an answer. He pinched the bridge of his nose, exhaled a weary breath, then said, "As I recall, the treatment which produced the best results was salicylate of soda. But even then, some who suffer from chronic rheumatism get little relief."

"That is not the case with *Señorita* Tucker's treatment," *Señora* Nunez said, turning her narrowed gaze on Eli. "What she does for Alfredo has always relieved his pain. You and those other doctors could learn from her, *señor.*"

Jade smiled at the irony of the woman's statement, then said to Eli, "The treatment I prescribe has been used by many ancestors of *Nde* healers and in my experience has been extremely effective in relieving the pain of rheumatism." Turning to *Señora* Nunez, she said, "I'll get what I need, then we can head for your house."

"That is not necessary, *señorita,* I can make the poultice for Alfredo."

Jade left the room, returning a few minutes later with a small cloth bag which she handed to the *señora*. "Are you sure you don't want me to go with you?"

"*Gracias, señorita,* but as I said, that is not necessary. I have watched how you made the poultice, so I know what to do."

"*Bueno,* but send for me if you need me for anything."

Señora Nunez nodded, then rose and crossed the room to the door.

Jade said goodby to the *señora,* then closed the door. When she swung back to face Eli, he said, "What did you give her?"

"Dried creosote bush."

"Good God, not the stuff in that awful smelling salve you used on my cut?"

"Yes. For treating rheumatism, the top part of the plant is heated then applied as a dry poultice to the area of pain. Like I said, it is an effective treat—"

Eli made a snorting sound. "You really think I'm going to believe that some old Indian remedy relieves the pain of rheumatism better than modern medicine can?"

She glared at him. "I don't know about the sal-something-or-other-soda you mentioned, but I do know my treatment works. You shouldn't criticize remedies you know nothing about. If you don't believe me, talk to Alfredo Nunez. He'll tell you how well the poultices relieve his pain." Her chin came up. "In this case, I think the methods of my *Nde* ancestors are more advanced than the white man's medicine."

Eli clamped his mouth shut, squelching the urge to jump to the defense of methods he'd been taught in medical school. Surprised he even wanted to defend something he'd given up, he finally said, "Well, I guess that ends your notion of being tutored by a doctor."

"That's not true," she replied, her momentary pique fading. "Even though this one issue proves not everything in modern medicine is more advanced than what I already know, there's much more I could learn from a medical doctor."

Though the words were on Eli's tongue to agree, he refused to say them. He had to stop thinking about medicine, a monumental task since he was staying in the house of a yarb woman. He reached for his crutch, then started to rise from the settee. "I think I'll go lie down for a while."

Jade hurried across the room. "Here, let me help you."

When she reached out to grasp his arm, he tried to jerk away. "That's not necessary. I can—" Poised halfway between sitting and standing on one foot, the movement threw his already precarious balance off even more. He tried to right himself by putting part of his weight on his injured leg, but immediately regretted his action. The pain in his ankle momentarily took his breath and made staying on his feet impossible.

As he started to pitch forward, Jade grabbed his arms and braced herself to break his fall if she couldn't steady him. Several tense seconds passed before his swaying stopped, allowing Jade to relax her tight muscles.

She lifted her gaze to meet his, then inhaled sharply. His dilated eyes, flared nostrils and slightly parted lips ignited a flame deep in her belly. The heat intensified, inching lower to nestle between her thighs. If she didn't get herself under control, she would be the one tumbling to the floor, taking Eli with her.

She cleared her throat. "Um . . . do you . . . want to sit down for a minute?" She winced inwardly, wondering if the high thready voice had actually come from her.

Eli slowly shook his head, never taking his gaze from her face.

"Then, um . . ." Jade licked her dry lips, bringing a rumble from Eli's chest. "I'll help you into—"

His mouth pressed to hers halted her words, making her forget everything except the taste of him. The kiss began as a soft and easy exploration of her lips, then quickly escalated into a fierce possession of not only her mouth, but of something much deeper as well. It was as if he had taken possession of the core of her being with his kiss. Moaning, she rose to her toes, then slid her hands up his arms and over his shoulders to lock behind his neck.

Eli's head spun, his senses in complete disarray. He shouldn't be kissing Jade, shouldn't be enjoying the kiss so much. Though his pulse pounded heavily against his eardrums and a tenseness gripped his belly, the lack of reaction in another part of his anatomy snapped him out of his momentary lapse. He tried to end the kiss, but Jade would have no part of it. Instead, she pressed more fully against his chest, tightening her hold on his neck.

When Eli lifted his hands to remove her arms, she tried to twist out of his reach, causing him to lose his balance. Just as he lowered his hands to grasp her waist, they started to fall. He managed to turn sideways so that he landed in a half-reclining sprawl on the settee, a gasping Jade lying atop him.

Jade opened her eyes, blinking several times to clear her spinning head. When her vision finally cleared, she found herself looking at the room from an odd angle. She struggled to sit up, but couldn't move. Hoping to free herself, she lowered one hand to tug at her skirt. The fabric was partially caught beneath Eli and kept her pinned against him.

"Eli," she said, her voice breathless from their kiss. "I can't get up. My skirt's caught."

Eli chuckled, surprised to realize he was thoroughly enjoying their positions. His hands had slipped from her waist when they fell and now cupped her bottom. Unable to resist, he squeezed the soft flesh, and was rewarded by her yelp of surprise then a new round of wiggling to free herself. For the first time in years, a short-lived flicker of desire flared in his groin.

"Easy, *roja*," he said with a laugh. "You'll tire yourself out."

She lifted her head from his chest and looked down at him. The silver in her eyes gleamed like shards of bright light, her cheeks were flushed a deep coral and her lips were swollen from his kiss. Caught again in the snare of her feminine allure, he moved his hands to the back of her head, then held her fast while he raised his head. *One more taste, I've got to have just one more taste of her mouth. Then I'll be satisfied.* But as soon as their lips touched, Eli knew he'd been wrong. Dead wrong. He'd never be able to get enough of Jade Tucker's sweet mouth.

He continued kissing her, nibbling on her mouth, laving the silky underside of her lips with his tongue until he thought his lungs would burst. Reluctantly he eased his mouth from hers. After giving himself time to catch his breath, he said, "When I lift my hips, pull your skirt out from under me."

Jade nodded mutely, barely able to hear him over the blood thundering in her ears. As he pushed his pelvis upward, the movement pressed one of his legs between her thighs. Incredible heat rushed through her body, making her throb where his leg touched her. If she reacted this strongly with the layers of clothes between them, what would it be like if they weren't wearing—? She bit her bottom lip, trying to hold in the groan her overactive imagination had spawned.

"Jade, what are you doing? I can't stay like this forever. Hurry up and free your skirt."

Eli's words snapped her back to reality. She had to make several attempts, but she finally tugged the fabric from beneath his body. Keeping her gaze averted, she braced her hands on his chest then got to her feet.

She cleared her throat, then forced herself to look at his face. His smile and the glow in his eyes eased her anxiety over his reaction. "Are you all right? I didn't hurt you, did I?"

Eli sat up. "Just my pride. Not being able to stand on my feet while kissing a beautiful woman is damn humiliating."

Jade laughed. "In that case, next time I suggest we lie down, then you won't have to worry about falling."

Though Eli laughed with her, he wasn't certain how to interpret her words. Did she mean what she'd said, or was she only teasing?

Two nights later he found out.

Jade had spent her normal hours working at the post infirmary, then returned home to find Eli reading another of the medical journals she'd borrowed from Dr. Chadbourne's library and purposely forgotten to take back. Watching him read, his face taut with concentration, her heart swelled with her growing feelings for this man—feelings she now knew had blossomed into love.

She had never considered falling in love. The future she'd started mapping out when she was only a child had never included a man in her life. But now that her heart had been stolen by a man who wouldn't face his past, a past that had caused him to suffer deep-seated pain, would he ever love her in return? Suddenly chilled, she rubbed her hands up and down her arms.

There had to be a way to rekindle his interest in medicine, just as she hoped there was a way to win his love. Deeply afraid both tasks might prove to be insurmountable, she forced herself to remember what she'd been taught as a child. Nothing worth having comes easily.

She thought about that all through supper, while washing dishes, and later when she went out to check on the horses and burros. By the time she finished her chores and returned to the house, she decided Eli was definitely worth having. However, there was one potentially fatal obstacle to her conclusion, she didn't know if she'd be able to convince him of that fact.

She drew a deep breath to try to slow her racing heart, then headed toward the bedroom door. It was time to take their relationship a step farther.

Eli sat fully clothed on the bed, his back against the headboard, his gaze focused on the medical journal he'd been reading earlier.

She stepped closer. "What's so interesting?"

He glanced up at her, then automatically scooted over to make room for her to sit on the edge of the bed as he'd done so many times. "Some of the treatments mentioned in these journals are no different than what I learned in medical school, but others are much more advanced. Like this essay on—" He frowned, then cleared his throat. "Never mind, it wasn't important."

"Eli, tell me about being a doctor," she said. Rather than sitting on the foot of the bed as she normally did, she sat down beside his hips. "Maybe if you talk about it, your memories will stop being so painful."

At first she thought he wasn't going to respond, then finally, he said, "I'd been in France for a year and a half when word reached us that the North and South were at war. The other American students and I immediately made plans to return. As soon as I arrived home, I was offered a commission as a field surgeon in the Army of Tennessee. I joined my regiment late in '61."

When he didn't continue, she said, "A few years ago, I overheard my father talking with a man who fought with one of the Texas brigades. Papa fought against Mexico with his company of Texas Rangers, so he knows what it's like to fight in a war, but he was appalled by the stories the man told him. Papa said what he experienced was nothing like the War Between the States." Her voice dropped to a whisper. "No one should have to endure the horrors both armies were forced to face."

"No," Eli said in a thick voice. "They shouldn't."

Jade waited for him to pick up his story, but he remained silent. Finally, she said, "With so many wounded, The War must have been especially hard on the doctors."

He dropped his head back against the headboard and

closed his eyes. A shudder rippled across his shoulders. "You can't imagine how difficult."

She lay one hand atop his. "The man my father talked to about The War said he had nightmares for months afterward, and that talking about what he'd been through helped him forget. Maybe if you—"

"I don't want to talk about it," he said, lifting his head and fixing a fierce gaze on her.

"But, you'd feel better if—"

"I said no. I've already told you more than I meant to, so be satisfied with that."

She nodded, swallowing any further protests. At least he'd shared a little more of his past. With the gentle persuasion of her love, she hoped he would eventually open up completely. Until then, she would have to be content with the sporadic crumbs of information he tossed in her direction.

Gloomy silence settling over them like a shroud, Jade said, "Let's talk about something cheerful."

When Eli didn't respond, she knew she had to take matters into her own hands.

Before he could react, she shifted her position and reached for his ribs.

"Hey, what are you—?" His outraged bellow ended with a sharply indrawn breath followed by a loud guffaw, and then another. Trying to control his reaction to her tickling fingers, he made a grab for her hands. Weakened and rendered nearly helpless by laughter, he needed several tries before he succeeded in capturing her wrists.

"What was that for?" he said in a breathless voice.

"I decided I had to do something to sweeten your mood, since you were being so . . . so peevish."

"Peevish, am I?"

She managed a nod, struggling to maintain a solemn expression.

"Is tickling me the only way you could think of to 'sweeten my mood,' as you call it?"

"No," she replied, her lips twitching with secret amusement. "Another way did come to mind."

His eyebrows lifted. "Really? And what might that be?"

As she stared into his flushed face, her voice turned silky. "Let go of my wrists and I'll show you."

Chapter 10

Eli's heart gave a lurch. There was no mistaking the fire blazing in the silver-flecked depths of Jade's eyes or the provocative smile curving her lips. *Damn, why didn't she listen to me?*

"Roja, this isn't a good idea. I told you there could be nothing physical between us. Have you forgotten that I—?"

"I haven't forgotten. But I don't see any reason why we can't do other . . . well, things to each other, do you?"

"Things?" he said, his voice cracking.

"You know, like kissing and touching. You do enjoy kissing me, don't you?"

He swallowed hard, his breathing suddenly erratic. "Yes, but I . . . I still think—"

"Stop thinking and let go of my wrists." When he didn't react, she said, "If you don't like what happens, tell me and we'll stop."

Eli felt as if he'd just received a speech prepared for a virgin bride, not an experienced man. The situation might have been amusing if it weren't for the reason she made the statement. His impotence. Looking into Jade's lovely face, seeing the passion just waiting to be set free, he realized he wanted to be the one to rouse that passion to feverish heights, to make her burn with desire. Even if he couldn't complete the act, at least he would see that her needs were satisfied—provided their kissing and touching escalated that far.

He took a deep breath, exhaled slowly, then carefully loosened his fingers.

Jade flashed Eli a triumphant smile, then shifted her position until she was close enough to feel his breath on her face, to feel the heat emanating from his body. Lowering her head, she pressed her nose into the opened neck of his shirt.

"I love how you smell," she whispered, nuzzling his neck while filling her lungs with his scent. She straightened, then reached for the buttons on his shirt.

His heart pounding a wild rhythm against his ribs, he held his breath in anticipation. He wanted—no, he needed her to touch him, certain her fingers on his naked flesh would give him incredible pleasure.

When she pushed open his unbuttoned shirt and lay her hands on his chest, he wasn't disappointed. In fact, her touch was like nothing he'd ever experienced. Light and delicate, yet strong and confident. Her fingers skimmed in gentle exploration over his skin, leaving a ribbon of fire in their wake. Remaining still while she satisfied her curiosity proved more difficult than he'd imagined, but somehow he managed to do so.

Jade had touched numerous men, since being a healing woman required physical contact with her patients. Yet treating those men, putting her hands on their naked skin had never affected her this way. She realized touching Eli was different because she'd never touched a man solely out of love.

Eli's skin was warm and smooth, his muscles firm and well defined. She found the patch of dark brown hair in the center of his chest especially intriguing, drawing first her gaze then her hands. As she threaded her fingers through the slightly curly hair, she sucked in a surprised breath, delighted by the soft texture. She longed to press her face into the silky mat, to nip his heated skin with her teeth, to run her tongue over his tiny, flat nipples.

The ideas swirling around in her head came as a shock. She knew about the sex act from her mother's teachings, but she didn't remember their discussions ever including what she'd just imagined doing. So, where had she learned such behavior? When no answer immediately came to mind, she didn't take time to further analyze the question. Her head was already too full, crowded with thoughts of doing all those exciting things to Eli, and more.

Eli endured her fiery touch for as long as he could, then he brushed Jade's hands away from his chest. Wrapping his arms around her waist, he pushed away from the headboard. When she opened her mouth to protest, he gave her a quick kiss, then whispered, "Shh, it's okay. I'm just getting us into a more comfortable position." Holding her firmly against him, he scooted away from the head of the bed until they were lying face to face on the mattress.

"Isn't this better?" he said, dropping another kiss on her mouth.

"It would be," she said, wiggling to free her legs from the bunched fabric of her skirt. "If we weren't wearing any clothes."

Eli cleared his throat, the heat of a flush creeping up his neck. "Yes, well, we'll do fine just like this. Now kiss me."

Jade complied, eagerly fitting her mouth to his, then wrapping an arm around his neck and grasping a handful of the thick hair at his nape.

Though their previous kisses had been wonderful, she soon realized they had been merely short forays into the world of kissing. This time, Eli didn't seem satisfied with only a gentle blending of their mouths. This time, his kisses were much deeper, more aggressive, more exciting. He suckled on her bottom lip, used the tip of his tongue to urge her lips apart then slipped his tongue into her mouth.

A bolt of intense heat zigzagged through her veins, making her body come alive with a need she'd never known. Her breasts ached and a dull throb began low in her belly. She clenched her knees together, hoping to ease the pressure building between her thighs. Her efforts failed; the throbbing not only remained, but grew more intense with each feverish kiss, each quest of his exploring tongue.

Eli lifted one hand to delve into her hair. The heavy waves felt like silk against his skin, curling around his hand in a teasing caress. A groan rumbling in his chest, he threaded his fingers deeper into the thick mahogany strands.

He savored the taste of Jade's mouth, the silky texture of her hair and the fullness of her breasts pressing against his chest. In the far reaches of his mind, he wondered if he would survive the onslaught of sensations roused by kissing her, touching her. Though his blood was ablaze and his head reeled with desire, only a flicker of heat sparked to life in his groin. Determined to forget about his own lack of response, he concentrated only on Jade and her needs. He carefully untangled his fingers from her hair, then moved his hand to her throat where her pulse beat frantically against the pad of his thumb. He trailed his fingers down to the gaping neckline of her blouse.

"I want to touch more of you," he said in a raspy whisper, brushing his fingertips over the exposed upper swell of her breasts.

Jade closed her eyes against the hot rush of desire his touch stirred. Certain she'd never be able to speak, she opened her eyes and gave him a jerky nod.

A brilliant smile appeared on his face, crinkling the corners of his eyes and deepening their color to a blue so dark it was almost black. With slow deliberate movements, he tugged her blouse from the waistband of her skirt then did the same with her chemise. When he had freed both garments, he pushed them upward to reveal her bosom. He stared at her full breasts with their coral tips for a moment, his breathing suddenly uneven.

"*Roja*, you are so beautiful, you take my breath away." He bent his head to taste one nipple, running his tongue over the hardened tip before pulling the bud into his mouth.

Jade gasped, arching her back to press closer to the source of the red-hot heat careening through her. She thrashed her head from side to side, the exquisite pull of his mouth on her breast intensifying the throbbing between her thighs.

He shifted to her other breast, his mouth and tongue artfully continuing his assault on her senses until she thought she'd surely lose her mind.

She groaned his name, her fingernails biting into his upper arm. "I . . . I can't take any more. Please . . ." Her plea ended with a sob.

"Shh, it's okay, *roja*. I'm here and I'll help you." He reached for her skirt, grasped a handful of fabric then pulled the hem up past her knees. Removing her moccasins with one hand proved to be a more difficult task, but he finally managed to tug them off her feet. He ran his fingers over one well-muscled calf, then slid his hand higher, easing under her bunched skirt. He moved slowly, not wanting to frighten her or to deny himself the opportunity to feel her heat, to touch her woman's center. When his fingers brushed the hot satiny skin of her inner thigh, she gasped and tried to scoot away from him.

"No, don't move," he said, before pressing his lips to hers in a gentle kiss. "I won't hurt you."

He waited until she relaxed, then continued moving his fingers upward. When he reached his intended target, he cupped the mound of her sex through her drawers then applied a small amount of pressure with the heel of his hand. Her body jerked in reaction and a moan vibrated in her chest.

"Easy now," he whispered, his fingers searching for and finding the opening in her undergarment. "You're so close. Just relax and let yourself go."

He stroked her intimately, savoring the heat, the dampness of her woman's flesh. Running a finger over the swollen bud nested in the moist folds, he bit his lip against the urge to shout his joy. She was truly exquisite, so sensitive and responsive to his touch. With slow, gentle movements, he began stroking her.

Jade had never thought having a man touch her in such an intimate way would affect her so strongly. Her mother had told her how wonderful the physical relationship could be between a man and a woman, an incredibly erotic journey that left them both sated then hungry for more. Jade had thought she understood, at least a little. But now she knew that wasn't true. Until she'd experienced the flame of desire Eli had sparked and continued to stoke higher, she hadn't realized how wonderful, or how erotic the journey could be. Catching the rhythm of his stroking fingers, she began lifting her hips to match his pace.

"Yes, that's it, *roja.*"

She heard his words, but they seemed to come from far away. The sound of her harsh breathing and the thundering of her heart drowned out nearly everything else. The heat kept building in the place he caressed with such expertise, spreading outward in ever-widening circles, until her every muscle, every nerve ending screamed for some unknown relief.

She wanted to savor the sensations coursing through her forever, to never let them reach a conclusion. Yet at the same time, she desperately needed to find a way to end the delicious torment racking her body.

Eli kept his gaze on Jade's flushed face, his heart swelling at the knowledge that he had been the one to bring that color to her cheeks. He had been the one to unleash her woman's desire and coax it to an even hotter level. And he would be the one to bring her to the climax her body sought.

Jade suddenly stiffened, crying out his name in a quavering sob. Her fingers clenched on his arm, she began bucking her hips against him, moving in a faster tempo.

He murmured unintelligible words to soothe her, stroking his fingers on her slick flesh in tandem with the frantic rhythm she set.

She continued moving, the heat and pressure between her thighs reaching their crescendo a few seconds later. Arching against him, she went perfectly still. After a moment, she dropped her hips back onto the bed, her fingers slipping away from his arm. Feeling like she was floating, her body weightless, she exhaled on a sigh.

Eli pressed a kiss to her forehead, easing his hand from beneath her skirt. "Are you all right?" he said, tugging her chemise and blouse back down to her waist.

She inhaled a deep breath, then turned her head to meet his gaze. Her eyes, the silver flecks even more noticeable against the passion-darkened green background, looked glazed and slightly disoriented. "I . . . yes, I think so."

He grinned. "You're incredible, *roja.*"

The corners of her mouth lifted in a weak answering smile. "No, you're the one who's incredible. Mama said it would . . . but I never imagined . . . I mean, I didn't know . . ." She ran her tongue over her dry lips. "If not for you, I wouldn't be feeling so exhausted or so . . . so satisfied."

He chuckled. "I can't take all the credit. Let's just say it was a team effort."

Jade nodded. "We make a good team." Yawning, she snuggled closer. In a matter of moments, her breathing slowed to the easy cadence of sleep.

Eli smiled down at her face, still glowing from her climax. Jade Tucker really was an incredible woman. Beautiful, sharp-tongued, passionate. Something cracked inside him, opening enough to allow a tiny bit of the pain and bitterness to seep out. During his years in Texas, he'd given no thought to writing his family back in Tennessee or making peace with his past, to settling down or living a normal life. And yet now, after meeting the woman sleeping so peacefully at his side, the woman who forced him to remember what he'd had before The War, he'd actually written his mother. Did that mean he was primed to do the other things?

He scowled at the ceiling, telling himself that sending a letter to his mother shouldn't be used as a marker to determine whether he'd lost control of his life. But the thought didn't pacify him much, just as another thought did nothing to ease his agitation. If he didn't do something soon, his plan to spend the rest of his life as a wandering, solitary trapper could well be in grave danger.

He flexed his injured ankle, wincing at the stab of pain shooting up his leg. *Dammit, I'm not fit to travel. But if I stay here, I might end up*—No, he wouldn't finish that thought.

Jade murmured something in her sleep, pulling him from his musings. Brushing the backs of his knuckles down the side of her face, he wondered if staying in Fort Davis would be so bad. For a moment, he allowed himself to contemplate starting a new life, returning to medicine, marrying again. He quickly shoved such foolish notions aside. The path he followed had been decided by his actions six years earlier, and there was no way he could alter that route now.

Jade awakened from a deep, dreamless sleep but didn't open her eyes. Before she rose to begin a new day, she wanted a few more minutes to savor the softness of the mattress, something she hadn't experienced since she found—Holding her breath, she opened her eyes then turned her head on the pillow. Her chest tightened at the sight of Eli lying beside her, still caught in the peacefulness of sleep. The previous night came back to her in a rush, her body warming at the memory.

She recalled his kisses, the feel of his mouth and tongue on her breasts, the way he caressed her until she exploded in a flood of sensation more intense than she'd thought possible. Then when the aftershocks faded, an incredible lethargy had settled over her, a relaxation so complete that she felt boneless, and then . . . then what? Her smile faltered. She squeezed her eyes shut for a moment, trying to remember. Had they actually spent the night together, sleeping side by side in her bed? Glancing down at her rumpled clothes, she had her answer.

How things had changed in the days since she'd found Eli Kinmont lying injured in the mountains and brought him to her home. She had experienced the awakening of her desire as a woman, the headiness of falling in love, and the night before, she'd experienced the euphoria of sexual fulfillment. All because of the man sleeping beside her. She swallowed to ease the welling of emotion in her throat.

So now what? Other than having increased her personal knowledge of the intimate relationship between a man and a woman, nothing had really changed. She wasn't so naive as to think Eli would awaken, then turn to her and declare his love. Though she had needed little time to realize she had fallen into the emotion's clutches, she knew his fall—if he fell at all—would not happen so easily. With the issues he already faced in his life, adding his falling in love with her to the list seemed a remote possibility at best.

She eased herself into a sitting position then swung her feet to the floor. Though Eli had been inordinately caring and tender the night before, awakening to find her lying beside him might bring about a drastic change. Unwilling to deal with another show of his temper, she decided escape from the room was her best choice.

After she took a quick sponge bath and changed into clean clothes, she poured herself a cup of coffee then stood looking out the kitchen window. A soft thumping on her home's wooden floors broke into her thoughts.

She turned to see Eli standing just inside the kitchen, his weight balanced between his good leg and his crutch. He was barefoot, his hair tousled from sleep, his shirt unbuttoned and hanging open. Her cheeks warmed at the memory of freeing the buttons of his shirt, of running her hands over the hard muscles of his—His voice penetrated the flood of memories. She lifted her gaze to his face. "Pardon?"

"I asked if you're all right?"

She took a sip of coffee. "I'm fine." After turning back to look out the window, she said, "Did you sleep well?"

Eli stared at her back, at the tenseness of her shoulders; his brow furrowed. "Uh . . . yes. What about you?"

Jade's heart did a strange flip-flop at the uncertainty she detected in his voice. Maybe he was beginning to care for her. She frowned. Why didn't the notion lighten her spirits? That's what she wanted, to have him care for her, to come to love her. Yet, the consequences of achieving what she wanted suddenly came into focus. She couldn't let love interfere with her plans to be a highly skilled healer whose abilities were always in demand. Even so, she couldn't just stop loving Eli or wanting him to show her more ways to find pleasure in his embrace.

"I slept very well," she finally said, swinging back to face him once more. Deciding to test his mood, she added, "You certainly know an excellent treatment to ensure a wonderful night's sleep."

He blinked at her, then a smile slowly broke across his face. "The oldest sleeping potion known to man," he said, humor sparkling in his eyes along with something else, something that sent hot and delicious shivers racing up her spine.

Jade laughed, the last of her anxiety slipping away. Moving to the stove, she picked up the coffeepot and poured a cup for Eli, then refilled her own. As they sat at the table,

drinking their coffee in silence, she decided improving
her healing skills had to remain her primary goal. In spite
of Paloma's claims that the Spirits had sent Eli to her for
two reasons—to teach her about Anglo medicine and to
become her husband—she had her doubts.

Though Eli knew about medicine, so far he'd refused
to teach her any of what he'd learned in medical school.
And although she had fallen in love with him, she wasn't
sure she wanted a husband. Her best course of action,
she decided, would be to reserve judgment on Paloma's
predictions until something happened to prove the woman
correct.

Chapter 11

Night Wind waited in the high mountain meadow, alternately filled with anticipation over seeing Dee-Dee Luden again and self-disgust for allowing a woman—especially a White Eyes—to bewitch him. Ten days had passed since he first saw the pale-haired beauty, ten of the longest days of his life. But being honest with himself, he knew he would have returned to Fort Davis sooner if he could have left his camp without stirring unnecessary curiosity among the others in his band.

He glanced around him carefully taking in his surroundings while searching for the beacon of Dee-Dee's light-colored hair. Perhaps she wouldn't come. Perhaps she'd changed her mind about making a habit of going to the meadow as part of her daily walk. He clenched his teeth together in frustration, his anger building at being played for a fool.

Just when he was ready to give up waiting, he spotted her moving between the trees along the edge of the far side of the meadow. His anger fled, replaced by a different kind of heat rushing through his body. Getting to his feet, he watched her move closer. When she stepped from the trees, she stopped and looked around. Spotting him, she smiled and waved, then lifted the hem of her skirt and hurried across the meadow.

"I was afraid I'd never see you again," she said when she reached him.

"I told you I would come back."

"I know, but I came here every afternoon and waited for hours. When you never came, I thought you didn't want to see me again."

Night Wind saw the pain in her eyes and longed to reach out and take her into his arms. But he kept his hands at his sides. "I always keep my word," he said.

"Yes." She smiled up at his stern expression. "I'm sure you do." Placing a hand on his arm, she said, "Let's sit down. There's so much I want to ask you."

Night Wind waited until Dee-Dee had taken a seat on a large rock, before lowering himself onto the ground beside her. "What is it you want to ask me?"

"I want to know everything about you," she said. "About your family, where you live, about your life."

He frowned. "Why do you want to know those things?"

"Because you're like no man I've ever known, and I want to learn all I can about you."

"You have known many men?"

"Well, of course, most of my colleagues are men." Seeing his eyebrows lift in question, she said, "I'm a teacher; a profession where I'm greatly outnumbered. Anyway, the majority of the men of my acquaintance are stuffy, old prigs with no sense of adventure, and with few exceptions, about as interesting as watching mud dry."

The corners of Night Wind's mouth twitched. "And you find me more interesting than mud drying?"

She turned her pale blue gaze on him and smiled. "Infinitely more interesting."

He laughed, surprised the lighthearted sound had come

from his mouth. He hadn't found anything amusing in a long time. "Where should I begin?"

"Start with where you learned to speak such good English."

"Many *Nde* speak more than one language; it has become a necessity over the generations. My father insisted my sister and I be able to speak with others on both sides of the river. So he taught us both English and Spanish when we were children."

"A wise decision," Dee-Dee said. "Tell me more about your family."

Night Wind thought a minute, then began speaking in a low voice. He told her about his Spanish grandfather marrying a *Nde* medicine woman, his father's decision to live among his *Nde* relatives and his own childhood in a close-knit *Nde* band. Before he realized what he was saying, he started telling her about living on the reservation then abruptly halted his story.

Dee-Dee leaned forward and placed a hand on his arm. "You don't like talking about it, do you?"

He didn't answer, just stared at her with his intense dark eyes, his lips pressed into a thin lip.

Her heart cramping at his pained expression, she said, "That must have been horrible for you and your band, and I understand—"

"How can you say you understand?" he said in a fierce whisper. "You, a White Eyes who has lived a pampered life, could not know what we suffered."

"You're right, Night Wind. Of course, I don't know what you and the others suffered. I only meant, I understand your not wanting to talk about the conditions on the reservation. Not wanting to relive those painful memories."

When he didn't respond, but continued to glare at her, she said, "Let's talk about something else."

After a moment's silence, Night Wind said, "Tell me about your life."

"Okay," Dee-Dee replied with a smile. "I was born and

raised in the city of New York, and have always lived there except for the year after I married—''

''Married?'' Night Wind's dark eyebrows snapped together. ''You have a husband?''

''I married Charles Luden when I was nineteen, and we moved away from the city. Charles was killed in an accident just before our first anniversary, then I returned to New York. After my year of mourning, I decided to attend college. When I announced my plans to my parents, they were extremely upset. They wanted me to find myself another husband and give them grandchildren. But I'd been married long enough to realize I would never be happy with only the running of a house to fill my time. I needed to be independent, to do something more stimulating with my life. I wanted to teach.''

''Is it not possible for you to be a wife, a mother and a teacher at the same time?''

Dee-Dee smiled. ''If only my family and the men I know in New York were as open-minded as you. They insist I must choose marriage and motherhood or teaching. My mother keeps saying, 'Deirdre, haven't you taught long enough? Isn't it time you give up this silly notion of independence and find yourself a husband?' '' Dee-Dee sighed. ''Mother is too old-fashioned. She doesn't understand that I don't want to be constantly under someone else's thumb. I want to make my own choices, to think for myself, to . . . to take a trip to West Texas if I decide that's what I want to do.''

When he remained silent, she said, ''Have I surprised you? Is my need for independence and wanting to direct my own future an idea that's too extreme for you to accept?''

Night Wind shook his head. ''I speak the language of the White Eyes, but I don't always understand what goes on in their minds. Why can't a woman choose to be a wife, a mother and also walk another path in life? Why are the White Eyes so opposed to such an idea? In my own family, this has happened. My father's sister is a skilled medicine woman, yet Silver Eagle is also a wife and mother. No one among our people has an objection to her being all those things at the same time."

"Apparently, the *Nde* are more advanced when it comes to allowing women the freedom to make choices."

"Perhaps in some ways, that is true."

"I wish everyone could be as open-minded."

Night Wind nodded, then after a long silence, he said, "Tell me about the place where you live."

Dee-Dee smiled. "New York is a wonderful city. Living there is fast-paced and always exciting. It's nothing like Texas, with all this open space and so few people." She went on to tell him more about the city and her life back East.

Though Night Wind was fascinated by her description of New York, her comments also made him realize the true extent of their differences. "Staying here must be a hardship for you," he said, unable to keep the bitterness out of his voice. "With none of the luxuries you are used to."

Her brow crinkled, she met his gaze. "Of course, I miss some of the things I'm accustomed to, piped-in water and a real bathtub, going to the theater, traveling by train rather than stagecoach. But even without those conveniences, I love it here. As soon as I arrived, I was captivated by Fort Davis. The fresh air, the incredible beauty of the . . ." Her gaze dropped to skim over the smooth expanse of his muscular chest and arms. ". . . the scenery. Even without the conveniences of the East, I'm enjoying my visit." She lifted her gaze to meet his once again. "Especially since I met you."

Night Wind's pulse pounded in his temples, a flash of intense heat shooting through his veins. He longed to wrap his arms around the woman sitting next to him, to hold her pressed to his heart, but he didn't move. He might desire Dee-Dee more than any woman he'd ever known, but she was still a White Eyes, part of a race he didn't trust.

Dee-Dee noticed the unmistakable glint of desire in his eyes, but when he didn't act on it or say anything, she glanced up at the sky to check the sun's position. "Drat, I've got to go," she said, getting to her feet. "Aunt Amelia will be in a real dither if I don't get back soon."

Night Wind rose to stand beside her. Watching the wind loosen a wisp of pale golden hair from her thick braid, he could no longer hold his temptation to touch her at bay. He tucked the silky strand behind her ear, his fingers lingering on her cheek for a moment longer.

She smiled up at him. "I enjoyed talking with you, Night Wind. I hope we can do this again."

He smiled in return, the deep dimples revealed by his first real smile catching her by surprise. She inhaled a deep breath, hoping to clear her senses, but her lungs filled with his scent instead, making her breathing more erratic.

She ran her tongue over her suddenly dry lips. "May I kiss you?" she whispered.

Night Wind blinked with surprise at her boldness. He opened his mouth to tell her kissing was not part of the *Nde* culture, but he couldn't form the words.

Dee-Dee moved closer, taking Night Wind's silence as an affirmative response. She placed her hands on his shoulders, rose up on her toes, then pressed her mouth to his.

Night Wind had never experienced anything coming even close to the wild jolt ricocheting through his body. Acting purely on instinct, he widened his stance, then wrapped his arms around Dee-Dee's waist and pulled her close. She moaned into his mouth, pushing her breasts firmly against his chest, their tightened tips burning him through her clothes. Shocked to realize he was fast approaching the point of losing control, he jerked his mouth from hers. "Enough, *shijei*," he said in a raspy whisper. "We must stop this."

She stared up at him with wide eyes, then eased her

hands from his shoulders and took a step back. When her breathing slowed, she said, "Has my forwardness made you angry?"

He gave his head a shake. "I am not angry. You must go now, before someone comes looking for you."

She nodded, then turned to leave. She'd gone a few steps before stopping and turning back to him. "What did you call me a moment ago?"

Night Wind had hoped she hadn't noticed his slip of the tongue, but obviously that wasn't the case. Knowing she wouldn't let him brush it off, he blew out a breath, then said, "I called you *shijei, Nde* for my heart."

Dee-Dee stared at him for a moment, then flashed a dazzling smile. "Will I see you tomorrow?"

Night Wind nodded before he could stop himself. He started to call her back, to tell her he couldn't see her again, but she had already turned and started running across the meadow.

He watched her until she disappeared in the trees. With a heavy sigh, he headed back to where he'd picketed his horse. Though he wondered at his inability to refuse to see Dee-Dee again, he didn't wonder at his reaction to his first kiss—a kiss still vivid in his mind, a memory which kept his blood heated nearly to the boiling point.

Four days had passed since the night Eli skillfully guided Jade to her first taste of fulfilled passion. Though neither had mentioned what had happened that night, for Jade the incident was far from forgotten and often filled her daydreams. As she finished saddling Eli's gelding early that morning, the memory replayed again in her head, making her body burn with rekindled need. Forcing herself to shake off her reaction, she retrieved her saddle from the shed then headed toward Luna.

Both Luna and Rex needed exercise since the small corral afforded them little room to burn off their excess energy. So Jade had given in to Eli's claims that, although he still couldn't walk with his full weight on his injured leg, he could now wear his boot and was capable of sitting a horse without doing his ankle any further damage. After she made sure her services weren't needed at the infirmary, she and Eli planned to take the horses out for a long ride.

She tightened the cinch, then unhooked the left stirrup from the saddle horn and dropped it back in place. Grabbing Luna's bridle, she led the mare from the corral to the house. She looped the reins over a post by the back door, then went inside.

"Eli?" she said, stepping into the kitchen. When he didn't answer, she went into the main room, then to the bedroom door. "Eli, I'm—" Finding him sitting on the edge of the bed and pulling on his shirt, the sight of his naked chest momentarily stole her breath.

He glanced up at her. "You're what?"

She cleared her throat, then said, "I'm leaving for the infirmary now. I've already saddled Rex, so as soon as I get back, we can leave."

He nodded. "While you're gone, I'll pack some food to take with us."

She mumbled a response, though she couldn't be certain what she'd said, then turned on her heel to leave. Over her shoulder, she said, "Hopefully, I won't be long."

Eli rose and made his way into the kitchen. Through the window, he watched Jade mount her mare then wheel the horse around toward the fort. When she was out of sight, he turned his attention to filling a cloth sack with enough food for half a dozen people. Maybe if he ate too much when they stopped to eat, he'd be able to keep his mind off of using the time for more exciting purposes, like giving Jade another lesson in making love. *Whoa, Kinmont, hold it right there. You're getting way ahead of yourself. This has nothing to do with love. What's between us is nothing more than sex.* His lips curved in a humorless smile. Okay, so it wasn't sex in the traditional sense, since his affliction had prevented him from actually performing the act a few nights ago. Even so, sex was a better description than making love for what had happened. His smile changed to a scowl. Wasn't it?

"Damn right," he said under his breath, pushing his unwanted and unwelcome thoughts of sex and love to the back of his mind.

Jade left Luna in her usual place beneath the oak trees near the fort's hospital, then hurried into the infirmary. A soldier sat on one of the chairs in the dispensary.

She approached the man and said, "Is there something I can do for you?"

He looked up at her and shook his head. "Sergeant Davidson is looking after me."

"Perhaps I should check you over as well."

"No, ma'am. I thank ya just the same, but the sergeant said he knew what to do."

Jade frowned, but didn't reply. Hearing sounds coming from another room, she left the dispensary. She found the hospital steward in the surgery rifling through the medical supplies.

"Can I help you find something, sergeant?"

He halted his actions long enough to glance over his shoulder. Resuming his rummaging, he said, "You can just skedaddle on home, Miz Tucker. Only one soldier reported to sick call, and I can handle his complaint."

"But—"

"I don't need no help. I just need to find—Ah, here it is." He picked up a brown bottle then turned to face Jade. "I said you can leave. Are you hard of hearing, or do you enjoy annoying me with your presence?"

"I've never done anything to you, Sergeant Davidson. Why do you insist on being so hateful towards me?"

"Because you don't belong here," he said, his thick eyebrows pulled together over eyes glittering with an emotion Jade didn't want to name. "I told ya before, you got no business pretending yer something you can't ever be. Women ain't cut out to be doctors or surgeons' assistants. That's work best left to men. Now, do more of yer reading in Dr. Chadbourne's office or go back home, I don't care which. Just get out of my sight. Have I made myself clear this time, Miz Tucker?"

"Yes, perfectly clear," she said, fighting the urge to vent her outrage at his haughty attitude. As she turned away from the infuriating man, she said, "Good day, sergeant." Without a backward glance, she left the surgery, then marched from the building.

Only when she stepped into the fresh morning air did she relax the stiffness of her spine. Sagging against the adobe wall of the infirmary, she tried to pull herself together before heading home. After several minutes, she pushed herself away from the wall and started toward the grove of trees where she'd left Luna. She'd only taken a few steps when someone called her name.

Jade stopped and turned toward the officers' quarters. Lifting a hand to shield her eyes from the sun, she watched Dee-Dee rush towards her.

"Jade, I'm glad I caught you, there's something I wanted to tell—" Dee-Dee tilted her head to one side, studying her friend's face. "What's wrong? Either you're ill, or you're ready to skin somebody alive."

"I'm fine," Jade replied with a chuckle. "And you're right about me wanting to skin someone."

Dee-Dee lowered her voice. "Is it Sergeant Davidson?"

Jade nodded. "He gave me another lecture on women not being qualified to treat patients."

"That's absurd. Women have been treating sick members of their families since the beginning of time," Dee-Dee said. "I've a mind to go in there and give him a good—"

Jade's hand on Dee-Dee's arm stopped the blond in her tracks. "No, don't. If you say anything to him, he'll know I told you what he said."

"Are you sure? He's been annoying me, too. Always showing up wherever I go, trying to get me to sneak off somewhere with him so he can—Well, never mind about that. Your latest run-in with him just gives me another reason to tell him what I think of his behavior and his biased attitude. When I get through with him, he'll think he got run over by the lightning express."

Jade laughed at the fierce expression on the other woman's face. "Yes, I'm sure he would. But, please don't say anything to him. I can handle the sergeant."

"All right," she replied after a moment. "I'll keep quiet."

"Thanks. Now what did you want to tell me?"

"That snake Davidson almost made me forget." A bright smile replaced Dee-Dee's frown. "I saw Night Wind again."

"What? When did you see him?"

"Yesterday, and I'm supposed to meet him again this afternoon."

"Dee-Dee," Jade began. "I didn't say anything before because I didn't think you'd see Night Wind again. But now I feel I have to tell you something. I . . . uh . . . I know Night Wind; he's my cousin."

Dee-Dee's eyes widened. "You and Night Wind are—" She shook her head. "Why didn't I put this together before? Night Wind told me his father's sister is a medicine woman. And you told me you learned about healing from your mother, who's a medicine woman. But I never made the connection. This is amazing. I can't wait to tell Night Wind."

"Dee-Dee, I told you this so I could also tell you to be careful. Night Wind has been through a great deal in the past few years. He's full of anger and hatred, and I wouldn't want to see you get hurt."

"Are you saying I should be afraid of Night Wind? That he might hurt me?"

"I'm not sure what I'm saying. Night Wind is a fierce warrior, and normally he would never hurt anyone he cares about. But he's never expressed interest in a white woman before, in fact he has always steered clear of them, so I don't know what to think. And because of the time he spent on the reservation and the government's repeated attempts to kill any *Nde* they can find, he's sworn vengeance on all Anglos." She took a deep breath and exhaled slowly. "Dee-Dee, I'm not sure what I'm trying to tell you, but I just wanted to make you aware of those things."

"I know he's suffered. He told me a little about living on the reservation, and I can see the pain in his eyes. But I really like him, Jade, and I trust him. I wouldn't see him again if I didn't."

Jade nodded. "I don't think Night Wind would risk coming so close to the fort if he didn't like you, too. But be careful, Dee-Dee. I don't want either one of you to get hurt."

When Dee-Dee didn't respond, Jade said, "Are you still going to meet him this afternoon?"

"Yes," she said in a whisper. "I don't think I can stay away."

Chapter 12

The sound of pounding horse hooves pulled Eli from his task of checking on his burros. He looked up to see Jade's mare galloping toward the corral. Frozen in place, he watched the woman and horse come closer. Leaning over her mare's neck, her mouth crimped in concentration and hair fluttering in a wild tangle of dark mahogany, she literally stole his breath.

When she spotted him, she reined Luna toward the corral, then pulled the mare to a halt and dismounted.

Eli forced air into his lungs, then said, "You weren't gone long." Giving one of the burros a final pat, he tucked his crutch under his arm, then headed toward the gate. "No soldiers reported for sick call?"

"One."

When Jade offered no more, he said, "Must not have been serious."

She shrugged. "I hope it wasn't."

Eli moved closer, wondering at her odd reply. Stopping in front of her, his gaze searched her face. She looked drawn and troubled, her eyes a duller green than usual.

He lifted one hand to stroke her cheek with the backs of his knuckles. "What is it, Jade? What happened?"

"I don't know what you mean. Nothing hap—"

"Don't tell me nothing happened. I wasn't born on crazy creek." Noting her confused expression, he smiled. "That's one of my mother's favorite sayings. She'd say that to one of my sisters or me whenever we tried giving her some lame excuse for getting home late or not doing something we were supposed to." He paused, then said, "I can tell something is troubling you, *roja,* so talk."

She closed her eyes for a moment, then shifted her gaze to the mountains beyond the corral. "I had a little problem with the hospital steward."

"Problem? What kind of problem?"

"Just a difference of opinion. I'm sure everything will work out."

He stared at her for a long moment before speaking again. "If there's something I can do, I want you to let me know. Okay?"

"I can fight my own battles," she said more sharply than she'd intended. Smiling to soften her response, she added, "But, if I need to bring in reinforcements, you'll be the first on my list."

Eli wasn't sure whether she meant what she said, or had simply made the statement to pacify him. Deciding not to press the issue, he said, "Well, we're a-burnin' daylight by standing here jawin'. How 'bout we take that ride now, Miss Tucker?"

Jade's eyes widened at the change in his speech. His teasing banter revealed a new side to the man—a side she found even more appealing than the brooding, often angry man she'd first met. Her smile turned into a grin. "What happened to that Southern drawl of yours?"

He grinned in return. "I've always had a good ear for languages. French came real easy for me while I studied in Paris. Then after I came to Texas, I learned to speak a pretty fair Spanish. And I've picked up some of the other lingo heard around these parts. So whaddaya say, should we make tracks?"

Eli watched her blink up at him, the distress in her eyes clearing to reveal those enticing shards of silver.

A burst of laughter bubbled up from her chest. "Yes, let's get out of here."

As she turned back to remount her horse, the sound of her throaty laugh continued to ring in his head, sending a rush of intense pleasure up his spine.

He found himself once again frozen in place. Staring at the mesmerizing woman now sitting astride her horse just a few feet away, he couldn't make himself move. How was it that Jade Tucker—a woman he'd known for a mere two weeks—had managed to put a chink in the invisible shell he'd built around himself? And why was this woman capable of doing what no one else had been able to do in the past six years? Not wanting to contemplate the answers too long for fear he'd discover something even more disturbing, he pushed those thoughts aside and concentrated on making his feet move.

After checking the cinch one final time, he gingerly stuck his left foot into the stirrup. Gritting his teeth, he shifted his weight onto his injured foot then lifted himself up while swinging his right leg over Rex's back.

As he eased down onto the saddle, he exhaled slowly, waiting for the dull throb in his ankle to subside. When the pain faded, he directed the gelding to follow Jade's pinto. He could see Zita trotting ahead of the mare, her curly tail bobbing from side to side and long ears flapping in the warm spring breeze.

He sucked in a deep breath of fresh air, relishing his return to the wild beauty of the surrounding mountains. If only he were totally healed and returning to the life he'd led before Jade had rescued him. As much as he looked forward to that day, the anticipation of leaving no longer held its previous appeal. He frowned, wondering what was different. The years he'd spent in West Texas had taught him to live off the land, to enjoy the outdoors, to crave the privacy of making his living as a trapper. So why did the thought of returning to the solitary life he'd chosen turn his blood cold?

His gaze landed on the woman riding in front of him, giving him his answer.

His frown deepened. When he came to Texas, he'd vowed not to let anyone get close to him or to reveal anything about his past, and he sure as hell hadn't planned on letting himself care about a woman. His light mood spoiled by the direction of his thoughts, he stared at the passing scenery, the incredible beauty he'd always enjoyed barely registering. He had to get back on the path he'd laid out for himself when he left the Confederate Army.

He closed his eyes against the sudden rush of unwanted memories. Just thinking of the army made him relive the sounds, the sights, the smells of those abhorrent years. Battles raging in the distance, the incessant echo of gunfire; the endless groans and shrieks of pain, the maniacal ravings and piteous cries. Countless wounded being hauled by ambulance to the field hospital, their bodies sporting gaping holes or limbs shattered by a minié ball. The acrid scent of spent gunpowder hanging heavy in the air; the stench of blood and gore filling his nostrils.

Though what he'd been called upon to do in The War bore absolutely no resemblance to his reasons for going to medical school, working as a field surgeon contributed heavily to his decision to leave the army.

He squeezed his eyes closed even tighter, hoping to clear his senses and calm his roiling stomach. After a moment he let his eyelids drift open, then took a deep cleansing breath. Exhaling slowly, he wondered if he would ever be free of the painful memories from his past. Probably not, he decided with a grimace, not when the shame of what he'd done constantly ate at him. Not when those memories included desertion.

Several hours later, Jade pulled Luna to a halt at the

mouth of a shallow canyon then turned to look at Eli. He'd been extremely quiet during their ride, absently nodding in response to something she said, if he responded at all. Most of the time, he appeared to be unaware of their surroundings or of her presence. Her heart ached at the torment reflected on his face. If only the Spirits would tell her how she could help this man, the man who had captured her heart.

She tried to hide her concern by forcing her lips to curve into what she hoped was a bright smile. "This is one of my favorite places in the mountains. I thought beneath those trees—" she nodded toward a stand of cottonwoods at the edge of a small creek, "—would be a nice spot to have our dinner. What do you think?"

"Doesn't matter," he replied, his voice lacking any enthusiasm. "Wherever you decide is fine." Not waiting for her to respond, he nudged Rex forward.

Jade watched him dismount, loosen his horse's cinch, then reach up to untie the rolled blanket from behind his saddle. "Where do you want this?"

She glanced around the canyon. "There, on that patch of grass," she said, pointing to a shady place beneath the trees.

Eli nodded, then turned. As he started toward the place she'd indicated, she held her breath. He'd elected not to bring his crutch, so walking without the extra support could be difficult. She watched him carefully. Though his progress was slow, thankfully putting his full weight, even briefly, on his injured leg didn't appear to cause him a great deal of pain. When he reached his destination without incident, she finally allowed herself to breathe normally.

By the time he'd managed to spread the blanket then lower himself onto one side, Jade joined him with their food. Zita bounded toward Eli, stopping a few feet away. She tipped her head to one side, dark eyes looking at him expectantly, tail beating the air in a furious rhythm.

Eli smiled for the first time since leaving Jade's house.

"Come on," he said, patting the blanket beside him. "There's room for you, too."

Giving an excited yip, Zita darted forward. The dog stretched out on the blanket next to Eli, then pawed at his hand. "I know. I know. Scratch you," he said with a chuckle, rubbing his fingers over the dog's chest.

Jade glanced at her dog then up at Eli. "If you don't want to be bothered with Zita, make her move."

"She's no bother," he replied, smiling at the now-dozing dog. "I enjoy having her around, and . . ." He lifted his gaze to meet Jade's, his expression sobering. "I'll really miss her when I leave."

Though Jade knew he was talking about Zita, she couldn't help thinking there was an underlying message in his words. Was he trying to tell her he would be leaving soon? His ankle wouldn't be completely healed for at least several more weeks. But maybe he wouldn't stay that long. Maybe he had already decided to leave. Ignoring the pain such thoughts caused, she turned her attention to setting out the food for their meal.

Once they'd eaten their fill, Eli stretched out on his back with a contented sigh. Jade gave part of the left-over food to Zita, then stuck the rest back in the cloth bag. When everything was put away, she drew her knees up to her chest and wrapped her arms around her legs. She loved this small isolated canyon. The reddish brown walls of solid rock gleamed like polished jewels in the sun; the warm wind rustled the treetops and bent the grass and wildflowers in a gentle swaying dance. The spectacular display of nature's handiwork never failed to relax and rejuvenate her tired senses. Spending time in this mountain canyon was a true balm to her spirit.

She brushed a tendril of hair off her face, then turned toward her companion. "Eli?"

"Hmm?"

"When did you decide you wanted to become a doctor?"

He opened his eyes to stare up at the canopy of branches

high overhead. "I was about ten, I guess. It was right after my father took sick and died. On the day of his funeral, I remember telling Mama that I wanted to become a doctor so other folks wouldn't have to die."

"If you could go back to that day, would you make the same choice?"

"Yes," he replied without hesitation.

"Even knowing you'd end up serving in a war?"

He heaved a weary sigh. "Probably. Becoming a doctor was all I ever wanted to do. I had my future all laid out. After I returned from studying in France, I planned to give the people of Nashville the best medical care they ever had." He gave a derisive snort. "What an innocent fool I was. Even after I accepted a commission with the Army of Tennessee, I still thought I could accomplish my goals when the war ended. In the aftermath of the first battle, the reality of the situation hit me hard. My plans became another casualty of war, dying an agonizing death like the thousands of men who fell during battle. Instead of becoming a great doctor—" He clenched his hands into fists on the blanket, his voice turning harsh. "I became a butcher."

Jade shifted on the blanket, moving close enough to curl her fingers around one of his fists. "Stop punishing yourself, Eli. You did what you had to do."

He turned his torture-filled gaze on her. "I know that, but it doesn't stop the god-awful memories. All those men who lost an arm or a leg . . ." A muscle in his jaw ticked. "Sometimes without anesthesia. And it sure as hell doesn't change my disgust with the surgeons who had a fondness for the knife. The ones who were too quick to amputate."

He jerked his hand out from under hers, then sat up and stared off into the distance. "Can you imagine what it must've been like for the men who survived losing a limb to return to their former lives?" Not waiting for Jade to answer, he said, "I can't. Nothing would be the same for those men. Nothing."

"Eli, the soldiers knew the risks of war. So stop torturing yourself."

"Sure they knew they might die. We all knew that. But that still doesn't justify what happened to thousands of soldiers. Death would have been less cruel."

"How can you say that? In spite of losing an arm or a leg, those men survived. They—"

"Dammit, don't you understand? I studied medicine to become a doctor, not to learn how to maim my patients."

"Yes, of course, I understand," she replied, an enormous lump wedged in her throat. "You wanted to help the sick and injured. But you must remember, you *did* help the soldiers. Not in a way you would've preferred, but you still gave them the benefit of your medical training."

"What I had to do during those years isn't something I learned in medical school. Hell, most of the surgeons in the army had never seen an operation before they enlisted, let alone performed one."

"No one is prepared for war," Jade said in a quiet voice. "Men have to do things they wouldn't normally do."

"Amen to that. But it never got any easier." Eli hadn't planned on telling Jade any more, yet once he started talking, the words kept coming. "After each battle, it was always the same. When the hours of fighting finally ended, the field hospital became overwhelmed with patients. Darkness often fell before we finished treating the wounded, forcing us to continue performing operations by torchlight. Our medical supplies were paltry at best. The surgical instruments we had to use were inferior, and there was never enough chloroform or morphine. And for the men who somehow survived surgery, we couldn't even give them the decent food they needed to recover."

Tears burned the backs of Jade's eyes, but she blinked them away. She couldn't cry; she had to be strong for Eli. He'd carried the heavy burden of guilt for too many years, and now he needed her support to help ease his pain. She opened her mouth to speak, but his voice halted her words.

"I took it as long as I could. God knows I tried. I prayed for His help every night, pleading with Him to end the damn war so I wouldn't have to do another amputation. I guess my prayers were too selfish, because the fighting never stopped."

He drew a deep, shuddering breath. "When I left the army, I also decided I had to leave everything about my life behind, especially being a doctor. I thought time and distance would help me deal with the memories of those hellish years, so I headed west." He shook his head. "What a fool I was to think losing myself in the wilds of West Texas would make me forget."

"No matter where you went when The War ended," Jade said, "you should have talked about your experiences. Memories don't go away just because you don't speak of them. Talking about what happened in the past would have kept your painful memories from haunting you all these years."

Eli didn't correct her assumption that he'd stayed with the army until the end of The War. He'd already told her more than he intended, and he refused to reveal his shameful departure from the army for her scrutiny. Suddenly angry at himself for telling her anything at all, he said, "When did you become an expert on the workings of the human mind?"

Jade started at his sharp tone. "I'm not an expert. But my mother taught me, and I've observed this myself, that people must not keep a painful experience locked inside. They must talk about whatever bothers them, otherwise they will fall sick."

He glared down at her. "Are you saying I twisted my ankle because I never talked about The War?"

She shrugged. "Is that so hard to imagine? Perhaps your concentration wasn't as good as usual because of the pain you kept in here." She placed her hand over his chest. "The *Nde* believe a person enjoys good health when there is harmony between all things. Harmony with nature, community and the spirit realm. There must also be harmony between a person's body and their mind." She offered him a smile. "Now that you've begun talking about The War, you'll be able to free yourself of your inner pain and regain your harmony."

Eli stared at her for a long time. If only he could believe regaining his harmony, as she called it, was as simple as she made it sound. But he doubted any amount of talking about his war experience would ever make him whole again. At last he said, "I appreciate your vote of confidence, but I—" Her sudden gasp halted his words. The look on her face made his blood run cold. Reaching towards her, he gripped her upper arms. "*Roja*, what's wrong?"

When she didn't reply, he gave her a gentle shake. "Talk to me. Was it another vision? Tell me what you saw."

She managed a jerky nod, then moistened her lips with the tip of her tongue. "I didn't see anything. This time the Spirits gave me only sounds. I heard someone in great pain, heard their cry for help." Shrugging off his hands, she struggled to her feet. "We have to get back to town. Someone needs me."

Eli didn't question her statement, but rose and quickly started rolling up the blanket. By the time he finished the chore, Jade had already tightened the cinch of her saddle and swung onto her mare's back. Seeing the apprehension on her face, he said, "Go on. I'll catch up."

She looked at him for several seconds, then nodded before wheeling Luna around and heading toward the mouth of the canyon. Moving as fast as he could, he made his way to Rex. He secured the blanket behind his saddle, checked the cinch around the gelding's belly, then carefully mounted. Once he sat astride Rex, he glanced around to make sure they hadn't left anything behind. Finding everything in order, he touched his heels to his gelding's flanks, calling to Zita.

"Come on, girl, let's catch up with Jade."

Chapter 13

When Jade and Eli arrived in Fort Davis, she found Naldo Domingo pacing in front of her house. She pulled Luna to a halt by the corral then quickly dismounted. As she hurried toward the slim man, she could see the tension in his well-muscled shoulders and arms, in the pinched expression on his round face.

"*Señorita* Tucker," he said, removing his hat to reveal a shock of thick black hair. "I am relieved you have returned. When I did not find you at the fort hospital, I came here to wait. I am so glad to see you. I did not want to go home alone."

"What's happened?" she replied. "Is it Liana?"

"*Sí.* She say the baby is coming and to fetch you." His Adam's apple bobbed several times. "She is in great pain. You must hurry, *por favor*—please, *señorita.*"

"We should have time, *señor.* First babies are usually in no hurry to be born. Just give me a couple of minutes to gather a few things, *bueno*?"

Naldo nodded, then dropped his hat back onto his head. "I will unsaddle your horse while you get what you need."

"*Gracias.* And please make sure she has water and hay. Eli can tell you where to put my saddle," she said, then turned and entered her house.

Jade just finished packing a buckskin bag with the supplies she would need to deliver Liana Domingo's baby, when Eli came into the house.

She looked over at where he stood just inside the door. "Will you come with me?"

His brow furrowed. "You've delivered babies before, haven't you?"

"Yes, a few, but I need someone to assist me. I don't have time to get Paloma, and since you're a doctor, you're the logical one to be there." Seeing his expression darken, she added, "Please, Eli, for Liana's sake."

Eli silently cursed his reaction to her words. She always managed to tug at something deep inside him, prodding places he hadn't allowed anyone to touch in years. He realized with a start that he was beginning to care for this yarb woman, something he hadn't anticipated happening. He hadn't cared about anyone in years, so what was different now? Deciding he shouldn't dig too deeply for answers, he exhaled on a sigh. "All right, but you go on ahead. I'll only slow you down. Tell me where the Domingos live, and I'll get there as soon as I can."

Jade flashed him a smile, then picked up her bag. "They live in Chihuahua. The last house on the south end of the main road. Liana planted wildflowers in front of the house, so you can't miss it."

"I'll find it, now go before the father-to-be comes in here and drags you out."

Jade started to move past him, then impulsively stopped, rose on her toes and pressed a kiss on his mouth. He started at her boldness, but didn't pull away. She deepened the kiss for a moment, wishing for more time, then withdrew. Seeing the flash of desire in his eyes, she bit her lip to hold in a shout of joy.

"See you soon," she whispered before leaving him alone in the house.

Eli stared at the door, still dazed by the unexpected kiss. Jade Tucker was like no other woman he'd ever known. For the first time in six years, he cursed his decision to cut himself off from everything in his past life. Whether that choice had caused his impotency, he didn't know. But regardless of the cause, his sexual urges were part of his former life and he'd never bemoaned making the sacrifice. Until now. Now that he knew what a passionate woman Jade could be, he regretted the loss of his virility. Not that he was an expert on a woman's passion. There had only been a handful of women in his past—several before he started medical school, one in France and then Nora— hardly a sufficient number to make him an authority on female sexuality.

Even as a husband, he'd had scant little time to practice the physical side of marriage. He and Nora met before his final year of medical school when her family moved to Nashville. They kept company until he left for Europe, and though there had been no formal engagement, both families assumed they would marry some day. Then war had broken out, completely destroying the timetable he'd carefully laid out for his future.

As soon as Eli returned from France, he asked Nora to marry him. Because of his imminent departure to the army, the wedding was held two days later, and after a one-night honeymoon, he left to join his regiment. He was rarely granted leave, and after Nora started working in the Confederate Army hospitals, they seldom saw each other. On the rare occasions they were able to meet for a day or two, he was usually too exhausted to do anything of a conjugal nature. Instead, he spent the majority of their time together trying to catch up on his sleep. Nora, bless her heart, never complained and was the reason he'd stayed with the army as long as he had.

But as the years passed, the horrors he endured never

lessened but continued to eat away at him. In spite of her protests, he began to give serious thought to taking a French leave—a polite name for an unauthorized furlough which became desertion if the soldier didn't return. He tried to stick it out, but when word reached him of Nora's death, his decision was sealed.

Eli rubbed a hand over his face. He hadn't thought of Nora in a long time. His guilt over her death was another memory too painful to examine, one he'd kept locked away with the others. Thinking about her again, he was surprised to realize the pain of her loss had eased to a dull ache.

He shook his head to chase the memories from his mind. He didn't want to think of the past; he had to find something else to occupy his thoughts. As so easily happened in the last few weeks, an image of Jade popped into his head. Her devil-may-care smile and the mischievous gleam in her eyes made him forget everything except what an enticing picture she made. Deciding the direction of his thoughts wasn't much better than his best-forgotten memories of the war and Nora, he went to fetch his crutch so he could head for Chihuahua.

Jade stepped into the Domingo house just as Liana let out another scream. She offered an encouraging smile to Naldo. "Try not to worry. Soon your baby will be here."

Naldo swallowed hard. "Do women always have so much pain?" he said in a low voice.

"I'm afraid bringing a baby into the world can be a painful experience, especially if the woman is afraid. This is Liana's first child, so naturally she doesn't know how to handle what's happening to her. I'll try to change that, *bueno*?"

At Naldo's nod, she headed for the home's single bedroom. "After I check on your wife, I'll let you know what's happening."

Liana Domingo looked up at Jade's entrance, her face damp with sweat. "*Señorita, gracias a Dios*—thank heaven, you are finally here."

Jade approached the bed, then set the buckskin bag containing her medical supplies on the small bedside table. "I told you I would be here for the birth of your child. When did the pains start?"

"Early this morning. At first they were only twinges, but then they kept getting stronger and stronger. I was so afraid you would not get here in time."

Jade brushed the woman's hair away from her face. "I know. This is new to you, so being afraid is normal." She gave her a smile of encouragement. "I think Naldo is nearly as frightened as you."

Liana's flushed face darkened even more. "I did not mean to frighten my husband, but I—" She gasped. "*¡Dios, mío!* Here comes another one."

"You can help control the pain by taking slow deep breaths until it passes," Jade said in a soothing voice, watching Liana's belly contract. When the contraction receded, she said, "Good. You did just fine, Liana. Now, I want you to get up and walk."

"Oh, no, *señorita*," she said, her eyes wide. "I do not think I can do that."

"Yes, you can." When the woman made no move to do as she'd requested, Jade slipped an arm beneath Liana's shoulders and helped her into a sitting position. "Remember, I told you the birth would go much easier if you walked around. And you must eat and drink to keep up your strength. Have you eaten today?"

"No, not since last night," she replied, allowing Jade to help her to her feet.

"You walk around the room while I speak to Naldo, then I'll fix you something to eat."

* * *

By late afternoon Jade became concerned that Liana's labor wasn't progressing quickly enough. She wiped a wet cloth over the woman's face, then went to find Eli. He'd agreed to wait outside until she needed his help.

"How's she doing?" he said from where he sat in the meager shade provided by a small tree next to the Domingo house.

"I thought she would have given birth by now, but everything seems to have slowed down."

"Is the baby in the correct position?"

She nodded. "At least I thought it was."

"You should be able to feel the baby's head."

"How can I be sure?"

"While the patient exhales, check the baby's position with your thumb and first two fingers of each hand. Gently push just above the pelvic bone with one hand and at the top of the womb with the other."

Jade stared at him, imagining what he'd described. "Will you show me how?"

"I don't know if—"

"Please, Eli." She dropped her voice to a whisper. "Both Liana and her baby could be in danger."

"What if she doesn't want me to examine her? Some women don't want men in the room while they give birth, let alone touching them."

"I already told her you would be assisting me when the baby came, and she didn't object."

He sighed. "Okay, fine."

Jade smiled, then offered her hand to help him to his feet.

Once the two of them went into the Domingo bedroom, Eli moved to the side of the bed. Offering Liana a gentle smile, he said, "*Señora* Domingo, when I tell you to, I want you to exhale completely then hold your breath while

Señorita Tucker and I check the position of your baby. Can you do that?"

She nodded. "I will do whatever you say if it will bring this baby into the world."

At Eli's signal, Liana exhaled. As he made his examination, he explained the procedure to Jade. "By placing your hands like this, you should be able to tell how the baby is positioned. The head will feel hard and round, the buttocks wider and larger."

Once he withdrew his hands, he said, "You did fine, *señora*. Now let's try it one more time so *Señorita* Tucker can do the exam."

Jade followed Eli's instructions and carefully placed her hands on Liana's stomach. After several seconds, she looked up and smiled. "The head is down." At his nod, she removed her hands. "Liana, your baby is in the proper position, but is just being stubborn. Come on, let's walk again. Give me your hand and I'll help you up."

Liana struggled to a sitting position and then onto her feet. As she walked beside Jade, she gave a sharp gasp then abruptly stopped. *"Señorita!* Something happened."

Jade glanced down at the puddle on the floor, then smiled over at Eli. "Everything is fine, Liana. Your water broke, a sign your baby will be coming soon. You sit down and relax while I make you some tea, then I'll bring a basin of warm water and give you a quick bath."

Eli followed Jade into the Domingo kitchen. "What are you giving her?"

"A tea made from the *yerba buena* plant, to ease the final stage of her delivery."

Eli lifted his eyebrows but made no comment. As she started back to her patient, he said, "What do you want me to do?"

"I'll need you to help support Liana while she delivers the baby."

He stopped halfway across the main room of the house.

In a low voice, he said, "Support her? I think you'd better explain that."

She halted and turned back to look at him. "Giving birth is much easier if the woman is in a squatting position."

"You're not serious?"

"Of course I am. Allowing gravity to play a roll in the birth process makes more sense than working against it by keeping a woman flat on her back."

Eli closed his gaping mouth with a snap, too shocked by her words to reply. He watched her head for the bedroom, then after a moment he followed her.

By the time Jade finished bathing Liana, the woman's contractions were coming closer and closer.

"Finish your tea and use the chamber pot," Jade said, spreading several layers of sheets on the floor beside the bed. "Then we'll see about bringing that baby into the world."

Jade looked over at Eli. "I want you to stand behind Liana and help her stay in a squatting position. You may need to put your hands under her arms to support her, or wrap your arms around her chest." She stared at him for several seconds, making sure he understood her instructions. At his nod, she made a final check of her supplies: sharp knife, string, clean cloths and a blanket for the baby—all within reach.

Once Liana was in position, Jade gave her an encouraging smile. "It won't be long now, Liana. When the next pain comes, I want you to breathe through it, and if you feel the urge to push, push hard with your stomach muscles, *bueno?*"

Liana nodded. When the pain began, she did as Jade had instructed. By the time the contraction faded, she was panting hard. And before she could catch her breath, another pain hit her. She sucked in a lungful of air and pushed again, crying out when the pain increased.

Jade encouraged her with soothing words and wiped her damp face with a cool cloth. Constantly monitoring Liana's progress, Jade finally said, "You can stop pushing. The baby is coming. From now on, just breathe deeply with each pain."

She had barely spoken the words, when the contraction hit. "Take a deep breath. That's it. Now exhale slowly. You're going great, Liana. Almost done. One more time. Perfect, now relax for a few minutes."

Jade deftly cradled the baby as it eased into her waiting hands. She looked up at a limp and exhausted Liana and smiled. "You have a son, Liana. A beautiful, healthy son." As if to prove her point, the baby let out a piercing yowl. "You'll be able to hold him soon. First we need to get both of you cleaned up."

A few minutes later, Jade helped Liana into a clean gown, then laid the baby in her arms. When Liana spoke, tears streamed down her face. *"Gracias, Señorita* Tucker. And to you *Señor* Kinmont. I cannot thank you enough for all you have done."

Jade smiled. "You're welcome, Liana, but you did the hardest part."

Eli turned toward the door. "I'll go get Naldo. He'll be anxious to see his son."

While Jade disposed of the afterbirth, the new parents examined their son, unwrapping his blanket to check fingers and toes, stroking his dark hair and laughing at the baby's cooing.

Several hours later, Jade and Eli bid the new family goodbye, then left to walk back to Jade's house in the deepening shadows of evening.

Eli limped along next to Jade, his thoughts on what he'd witnessed over the past few hours. He'd watched Jade deliver Liana's baby, done as well as the few births he'd witnessed during his medical training. In fact, the techniques she used to help Liana relax and the instructions she gave to make the birth as easy as possible were superior to anything he'd learned. And now that he'd seen the results, having a woman give birth in a squatting position made more sense than what he'd been taught.

The entire experience had touched him more than he thought possible. Before he stepped from the bedroom to fetch Naldo, he'd caught a glimpse of Liana cuddling her son, love shining on her face as she kissed the baby's black silky hair. And then he'd seen the look of wonder on Naldo's face when the man learned he had a healthy son, his dark eyes bright with unshed tears of joy and love. Eli knew those images would remain with him forever.

What had just taken place at the Domingos was part of why he'd decided to become a doctor—to help bring new life into the world, to see the happiness on the faces of new parents. Realizing the direction his thoughts had taken, he shoved them aside.

After walking a little farther, he said, "What kind of herb remedy was in that bottle you left with Liana?"

"It's made from the leaves of the manzanita tree. I told her to add a little to her bathwater, then sit in the tub for an hour once or twice a day for the next week. The plant will make her recovery from childbirth much easier."

Eli bit the inside of his cheek to hold in a snort of disbelief. At last, he said, "She didn't seem to suffer any ill effects from the birth. No tearing or heavy bleeding."

"Everything went well. That's another reason why using the squatting position is so much better—it helps prevent those kinds of problems. Besides, Liana is young and strong. And even though her labor was long, she should recover quickly."

"You know, some doctors advocate using chloroform during delivery for women who don't want to experience the pain."

Jade looked over at Eli and frowned. "I suppose there are times when using chloroform would be beneficial. But giving birth is such a natural and joyous process that I'd hate for my patients to miss the experience unless it was absolutely necessary. I think the techniques Paloma taught me, those used by midwives for generations to calm their patients and help them manage the pain, are a much better way to deliver babies.''

"After watching you with Liana, I'd have to agree."

Jade smiled at him, then said, "Chloroform is also used during surgery, isn't it?"

"Yes, that and other opiates."

"I've seen bottles of chloroform in the hospital's storeroom, but I don't know anything about using it."

"Administering chloroform is relatively simple, for both surgeries and childbirth."

"Will . . ." She swallowed. "Will you teach me how to administer chloroform?"

Eli glanced over at her. The hope on her face tugged at his heart. He didn't want to agree, yet he found he also didn't want to deny her the knowledge she craved. "I guess there'd be no harm in me teaching you."

Jade stopped, then turned to give him a hug, nearly making him lose his balance. "Thank you, Eli."

"I haven't taught you anything yet," he said in a gruff voice.

She gave him a bright smile, determined not to let his grumpy reply spoil her happiness. She'd just safely delivered a healthy baby and Eli had agreed to teach her about chloroform. Finally, she would learn something about modern medicine, something that would increase her healing abilities. And maybe having Eli teach her would revive his interest in being a doctor.

Her happiness slipped a notch. If his love of medicine was rekindled and he decided to be a doctor again, he wouldn't want to stay in West Texas. He'd want to go back East, back to Nashville to fulfill his dreams. Her happiness slipped even lower.

Jade gave herself a mental shake. She'd spent her entire life learning to be a healer. All she had ever wanted was to help people with her healing abilities and to continue improving her skills. So Eli heading east, or in any other direction he chose, shouldn't matter. After all, then things would go back to the way they were before she met him. That's what she wanted, wasn't it? To let nothing interfere with her work as a healing woman? So why did the thought of getting her wish cause such emptiness inside?

She glanced over at the man walking beside her and the answer was clear. She loved him. Determined not to think about what the future held, she drew a steadying breath. There was no point in dwelling on what she couldn't change. She would enjoy her time with Eli for as long as he stayed in Fort Davis. Then when he left . . . She repressed a shudder, not willing to allow her mind to venture into that uncharted territory.

Once they reached Jade's house, she announced her plans to take a long hot bath right after supper and immediately put water on to heat.

After they finished eating, Jade cleared the table then hauled the bathtub into the kitchen. Getting to his feet, Eli said, "I'll fill the tub for you, then I . . . uh . . . think I'll check on the horses."

Jade wanted to tell him he didn't have to leave the house, but she squelched the words. Instead she said, "If you'd like to take a bath after I finish, I'll put more water on to heat."

As he finished pouring the kettle of hot water into the tub, the thought crossed his mind to tell her they could share the tub. Wondering where such a tantalizing, yet totally unacceptable idea had come from, the heat of a blush crept up his neck and cheeks. Hoping Jade would attribute his flush to the steam rising from the hot water, he finally met her gaze. "Sure, let me know when you're finished."

Jade would have enjoyed her usually long luxurious soak, but she cut her bath short so Eli could have his turn in the tub. After scrubbing herself and giving her hair a thorough washing, she rose and reached for several lengths of toweling. She wrapped her hair in one piece and used the other to dry herself.

A few minutes later, she opened the back door and called for Eli to empty the tub.

By the time Eli had finished his bath and emptied the tub a second time, he found Jade sitting on the edge of her bed brushing her hair, clad in only her chemise and drawers.

The sight of her caused his heart to increase to a frantic rhythm. He squeezed his eyes closed against the beautiful picture she presented. When he allowed his eyelids to lift, he found her staring at him, a mysterious look—one he suspected meant she was up to something—on her lovely face.

He swallowed, and though he didn't want to speak, he forced himself to say, "Why are you looking at me like that?"

"Like what?"

He blew out his breath in a rush. "Don't pretend you don't know what I'm talking about." When she didn't offer to respond, he said, "Come on, out with it. What's going through that mind of yours?"

She laid her hairbrush on the bedside table, then lifted her gaze to meet his once again. "Besides teaching me how to use chloroform, I also want you to teach me how to arouse a man."

Chapter 14

Eli shook his head, certain he'd heard wrong. "Say that again."

"I said, I want you to teach me how to arouse a—"

"That's enough! Have you—" He drew a deep breath, then exhaled slowly. "Have you forgotten what I told you? About my affliction, that I can't—"

"No, I haven't forgotten. But if you teach me what men like, then maybe that will change." At his skeptical expression, she added, "What can it hurt to try?"

When he didn't respond, but continued to stare at her, she shifted positions, scooting to the other side of the mattress then stretching out on her side. "Come to bed," she said in a low voice.

"I . . . I don't think that's a good idea," he said, shaking his head and taking a step back.

"Of course it is." She patted the mattress. "Come to bed."

"You've had a busy day. Don't you think you should get some sleep?"

"I'm not sleepy. In fact, I'm all wound-up. I guess it's the excitement of delivering Liana's baby."

"That's probably it. Bringing a new life into the world can be exhilarating," Eli replied. "But if you close your eyes and relax, I'm sure you'll realize how tired you are."

Jade chuckled. "I don't think so. Now stop making excuses and come here." Seeing the panic replace the skepticism on his face, she gave him an encouraging smile. "I'm not looking for any promises, Eli. I know you'll be leaving soon. But in the meantime, I think we should . . . well, enjoy each other. Even though you aren't capable of—I think your exact words were—doing the deed, you still enjoy kissing me, don't you?"

She held her breath while she waited for his reply, silently praying she wasn't making a mistake.

"Yes," he replied in a croaking whisper. "But I still don't think—"

"Then stop thinking, and come here."

He squeezed his eyes closed for a second. *This shouldn't be happening. I should turn around right now and get the hell out of this bedroom as fast as I can.* Even though he knew that's what he should do, he couldn't make himself carry out the order. Something drew him to the woman lying on the bed, something he was powerless to stop.

Eli thought the past six years had taught him restraint, but when it came to Jade Tucker, the self-discipline he so carefully cultivated had apparently sprung a leak—one growing bigger by the second. As he opened his eyes and started across the room, he no longer cared whether the leak could be patched. All he wanted to do was sample her sweet mouth, to run his hands over her silken skin.

He lowered himself onto the mattress next to her, then leaned closer and cupped her chin with one palm. *"Roja,* what have you done to me?" he whispered. When she opened her mouth to reply, he pressed his thumb against her lips. "Shh, it doesn't matter."

As he stared down at her, her scent wrapped around

him like an invisible cloak, a combination of the spicy tang of her wildflower soap and the heady natural musk of pure woman. The blood pounded in his ears, shutting out all other sound. He was aware of only the woman lying beside him and his need to kiss her.

As if reading his thoughts, she murmured, "Kiss me, Eli."

He groaned, then lowered his mouth to press against hers. He tried to keep the kiss gentle, but when her hands came up to lock around his neck and her back arched to press her breasts against his chest, his gentleness gave way to a surprising wildness, a hungry fierceness he hadn't known he possessed.

His tongue teased her lips until she opened for his explorations, allowing him to feast on the warm interior of her mouth. He buried one hand in her hair, groaning at the feel of the still-damp strands wrapped around his fingers. Pulling his mouth from hers, he shifted his attention to her neck then nibbled his way down to the indentation at the base of her throat. He pressed his lips to the hollow, laved the soft flesh with his tongue, felt the heavy pounding of her pulse.

Why this woman had come into his life now, after he'd elected to live a solitary existence for the past six years, still bewildered him. At first he'd thought Jade's finding him and treating his injuries was an ironic fluke—a yarb woman using her primitive skills to treat a man formally trained as a doctor. She claimed to have had visions predicting they would meet, which to her way of thinking meant coincidence played no part in her finding him in the mountains. Or if he were a believer in fate, he might be inclined to think they were predestined to meet. Refusing to allow his mind to dig any further into the notions of visions or coincidence or fate, he moved his head even lower.

He nuzzled the upper swell of her breasts with his nose and lips, then pushed aside the fabric of her chemise to reveal one coral nipple. With a groan, he settled his mouth over the peak and suckled gently. She gasped, one hand gripping his shoulder, her nails digging through the fabric of his shirt.

"Eli?" she said, half sobbing. "Tell me how to touch you. Please. I want to make you burn like I—"

The warmth of his mouth pulling harder on her breast took away her ability to speak.

When he released her hardened nipple, he lifted his head to look down at her. "Touch me any way you want."

"But—"

"It's okay, I swear." One corner of his mouth quirked upward. "As long as you don't tickle."

Her breathing erratic, she said, "Then take off your shirt. I promise I won't tickle."

He sat up and did as she requested, then lay down on his back.

Jade stared at his muscular chest with its patch of dark hair, wanting to touch him everywhere at once. Finally, she tentatively lifted one hand and touched him with her fingertips, savoring the texture of warm smooth skin stretched over hard, well-sculpted muscle, then the small nubbins of his male nipples.

"If I do something you don't like," she said in a hushed voice, shifting her gaze from his chest to his face. "You'll tell me, won't you?"

He chuckled. "As long as you don't tickle, I doubt that's possible." Meeting her gaze, he saw the uncertainty in her eyes, their color darkened to a much deeper green, the silver flecks even more pronounced. Lifting a hand to grasp a lock of her hair, he rubbed the silky strand back and forth between his thumb and forefinger. "If I don't like something, I swear I'll tell you," he said, tucking the hair behind her ear.

She stared down into his blue eyes, the urge to reveal her love for him nearly overwhelming. Swallowing the words, she moved her gaze back to his chest, hoping she could at least show him what was in her heart.

Her hands explored his chest, his shoulders, his arms and fingers, delighting in each new place she touched. Then she followed a similar path with her lips and tongue until the cadence of his breathing changed to a series of rasping pants. When she reached for the buttons of his trousers, his hand clamped around her wrist.

"Uh-uh. That's not a good idea," he said in a low voice.

"But how can I learn what men like, if you won't let me touch more of—?"

"Not this time, *roja.*"

She could tell by the tone of his voice and the harsh set to his jaw that he wasn't going to be swayed. Yet his words hadn't ruled out that there might be another time. With a sigh, she said, "Okay."

When he released her wrist, she slowly withdrew her hand, purposely moving downward to rub over the fly of his trousers. He sucked in a sharp breath, his hips bucking up at the contact.

"Oh, sorry," she said, keeping her gaze averted for fear he'd see the flare of hope in her eyes. Hope that with time, he'd recover from his impotence.

Eli blinked up at the ceiling, still in shock by what had just happened. Even through several layers of fabric, Jade's hand brushing his manhood had sent an intense bolt of sensation coursing through his body. For the first time in more than six years, he'd experienced a rush of blood to his groin, a wild tingling that told him he hadn't lost all sensation in that part of his anatomy. He'd almost forgotten what those first stirrings of desire were like.

He frowned. What if the sensations never increased beyond what he'd just experienced—a tantalizing glimpse of what he'd missed for so long, yet remaining forever forbidden to him? That would be infinitely crueler than feeling nothing.

Jade's movements roused him from the painful contemplation of his future. He turned to look at her, then blinked. Stunned, he watched her fingers pluck at the ribbons of her chemise.

"Wait," he said in a raspy voice, reaching toward her. "Let me do that." Cursing his shaking hands, he managed to loosen the ribbon ties, push the straps off her shoulders then shove the garment down to her hips. Seeing her naked from the waist up for the first time, his breath hissed through his teeth. *God, she's even more beautiful than I thought.* Struck with the sudden wish to have her completely naked, he clamped his jaw shut against giving voice to his wishes.

He reached up to caress one breast, the crested nipple instantly puckering even tighter at his touch. Pulling her down onto her back beside him, he bent his head and took one hardened tip into his mouth while working the other with his fingers. She writhed on the mattress, her soft moans surrounding him, urging him for more.

As he suckled first one nipple, then the other, Jade was quickly spinning out of control. The heat of his mouth sent an equally hot surge of incredible pleasure shooting through her body, settling low in her belly and causing a throbbing between her thighs.

"Eli, Eli," she said in a low moan. "I can't . . . I can't take much more."

He released a nipple long enough to say, "Yes, you can." He shifted to her other breast.

"No! No, I can't." When he didn't respond, she grabbed one of his wrists and pushed his hand down to her thighs. "Please, Eli," she whispered, lifting her hips in silent pleading.

He moved his fingers over her feminine mound, then slipped lower to find the opening in her drawers. She was incredibly hot and slick. When he opened the petals of her flesh and found the swollen bud, she gasped and bucked up against his hand. He stifled a groan, then began moving his fingers in a gentle rhythm.

Jade soon matched the tempo he set, then quickly

increased the motion of her hips. The heat and the throbbing intensified until all she could think about was ending the pleasure-torment. She had to find relief before she went mad.

Just when she thought she couldn't bear a second more, her breath caught in her throat, her body going rigid. After a moment, her back arched, then her hips pushed against Eli's hand in a faster and faster rhythm. Then the release she sought swept over her, in one crashing wave of mind-numbing spasms after another. Crying out his name, she lifted her hips one last time, then sank back on the mattress with a long sigh.

Eli carefully removed his hand, then slipped one arm beneath her shoulders and pulled her against his chest. Her ragged breathing the only sound in the room, he stroked her hair then kissed the top of her head. After a while, he said, "Are you all right?"

"Mmm, yes," she said, rubbing her cheek against his chest. "Except every bit of my strength has drained away. I can barely move. Does sex make a man feel as weak as a newborn?"

Eli smiled. Though her question should have shocked him, he found her frankness refreshing. "Probably weaker. That's undoubtedly when a man's the most vulnerable physically."

"I can see why," she replied around a yawn. "I think I can go to sleep now."

His smile broadened. "Don't fall asleep yet, *roja*. You're not wearing your nightgown."

She roused herself up onto one elbow. "I'd rather sleep like this," she said, pulling her chemise up over her head, then tossing it aside. She looked down at his trousers. "Wouldn't you be more comfortable without those?"

Eli swallowed hard. Though the idea of a half-naked Jade sleeping beside him definitely had its merits, he wasn't sure they should spend another night together in her bed.

Jade sensed his hesitation and said, "If you're shy, I won't look while you take them off."

Another smile stole across his face. "You've already seen more of me than just about anyone else I've known, so there's no reason for me to be shy."

"Then stop talking and start doing."

He chuckled. "Yes, ma'am," he said, reaching for the waistband of his trousers. After he freed the buttons, he lifted his hips, pushed the buckskin down to his knees, then sat up to pull the garment over his feet.

He returned to a prone position, tugging the top sheet with him, then pulled Jade back into his arms. "I shucked my trousers. Is there anything else I can do?" he said, rubbing his cheek against her silky hair.

She wanted to say, "Love me the way I love you," but she swallowed the words. Instead she shook her head then pressed a kiss to his chest. " 'Night, Eli."

The touch of her lips and her softly spoken good night tightened something in his chest, something dangerously close to his heart. Refusing to examine what such an occurrence could mean, he whispered, "Sleep well, *roja.*"

She murmured something indecipherable, then almost instantly her breathing slowed, settling into the gentle pattern of deep sleep.

Eli lay awake, his fingers idly rubbing a strand of Jade's hair. Though he was physically tired, his mind refused to shut down for the night. He didn't want to think about what he'd experienced that day, what he'd agreed to do or what he was beginning to feel for Jade, but he didn't have any choice—his brain insisted on making him relive the events of the day.

A long time passed before he finally joined Jade in the oblivion of slumber.

When Jade returned from the fort hospital the following afternoon, she immediately sought out Eli. She found him checking the hooves of his gelding. Before she could say anything, he spoke.

"Is there a blacksmith in town? I need to get Rex reshod."

"Yes, Max Anderson's place is at the north end of Main Street."

"Good. I planned on getting him reshod when I got back to Presidio, but his shoes don't look like they'll last that long."

Fear twisted Jade's insides. Hoping he wasn't planning on leaving so soon, she summoned the strength to say, "Can we start my lesson now?"

Eli dropped the gelding's hoof and straightened. Turning to face her, he said, "Let me wash up first."

She nodded, then started toward her house.

A few minutes later, he pulled out a chair at the table and sat down across from her. Though he wished he hadn't offered to hold this lesson, the sparkle of excitement in her eyes chased away the last of his misgivings.

He rested his forearms on the table, his hands curling into loose fists. In a low voice, he began speaking. "Chloroform is safe as long as it's used properly. First, try to make sure the patient has an empty stomach, although that's sometimes difficult to control. To administer the chloroform, pour a few drops onto a sponge, a handkerchief or a piece of cloth, then hold it over the patient's mouth and nose. Once they're in a deep sleep, remove the sponge or cloth. That's extremely important. Don't let the patient breathe more of the chloroform than necessary." He paused for a moment. "Do you understand?"

At her nod, he said, "As soon as the patient is under the anesthetic, quickly proceed with whatever medical procedure you're to perform. The least amount of time they're asleep, the better."

She nodded again, then said, "Is that how you gave chloroform during The War?"

His mouth tightened. "Yes, when we had it. One of

our surgeons finally invented an inhaler which used less chloroform and helped conserve our supply. I don't know what the army uses now. Maybe a different inhaler or some other type of device, but the way I described will work fine as long as you follow my instructions."

Jade thought about what he'd told her for a moment, then said, "When the procedure is finished, how do I wake the patient?"

"As soon as the chloroform wears off, they'll wake up on their own. But if they don't show signs of rousing when you think they should, pass a vial containing liquor of ammonia under their nose." He frowned. "At least that's what we did six years ago. When Dr. Chadbourne returns to the fort, you should ask him what he recommends as an antidote to chloroform."

"I will." She chewed on her bottom lip, mulling over her next words. Drawing a deep breath, she finally said, "Will you teach me more of what you learned in medical school?"

He shifted his gaze from the table to her face. Instead of the reaction such a question would have stirred just a few weeks earlier, he was surprisingly calm. Though guilt and self-disgust remained a deep wound in his soul, the idea of talking about medicine no longer made him want to lash out in anger. But if he were to become Jade's teacher, she deserved to hear the entire story. And maybe once she knew the truth, she'd change her mind about wanting him to teach her. Deciding to let her make that choice, he cleared his throat.

"I'll teach you what I can under two conditions. The first one is, I'd like you to teach me about the plants and herbs you use." Seeing her eyebrows lift, he said, "I know, I've been quick to make some pretty snide remarks. I had my reasons, but I've also seen what you've accomplished with your remedies. I'd be a fool to ignore such fine results."

"I'd be happy to teach you," Jade replied. "What's the second condition?"

"I . . . uh . . . I have something I need to tell you. And after you hear me out, if you want to withdraw your request, I'll understand."

She reached across the table and wrapped her hands around his. "Whatever you have to tell me, it can't be that bad."

When he met her gaze, the haunted look in his eyes sent a shaft of pain through her heart. Wishing she could reassure him by declaring her love, she settled for giving his hands an encouraging squeeze and offering him a smile. "Tell me, Eli," she said in a soft voice.

"Like I told you, I was commissioned into the Army of Tennessee as a field surgeon late in '61. I had more experience than most of the others, since my training in France included performing several surgeries. Except for a few doctors who served in the Crimean War, no one had ever treated a gunshot wound or performed an amputation. But none of the surgeons had witnessed the destruction a minié ball could do to an arm or a leg."

He shuddered visibly, then after drawing a deep breath, he continued. "I also told you how bad the conditions were, but I didn't tell you that the carnage and the suffering of the men I was supposed to save finally became too much for me. I thought nothing could be worse than Chickamauga. With both sides losing so many men, the days after that battle were pure hell. But conditions just kept getting worse. I constantly thought about leaving my regiment, but Nora convinced me I had to stay."

Jade's head came up at the mention of a woman, but she remained silent, holding in her questions until Eli purged himself of his painful memories.

"Then late in '64, our troops lost the battle for Atlanta and marched to Tennessee. God, you couldn't believe what the soldiers looked like. Gaunt, their clothes in rags, hunger glistening in their eyes." He closed his eyes, the muscles in his jaw working in his effort to control the emotions churning inside him.

"Go on, Eli," Jade said. "Finish it."

His eyelids lifted. Though he looked directly at her, she could tell he didn't see her but something from his past.

"The battle for Nashville lasted two days. When it finally ended, the Army of Tennessee was in even worse shape. Many of the soldiers had lost their weapons, most didn't have blankets and half didn't have shoes. They wore old cloth or gunny sacks tied around their feet.

"I knew the Confederacy had to be on its last legs and kept telling myself the hell would be over soon. Then word reached me of Nora's death, and I—I couldn't take anymore of the gore, the constant amputations, the bitter sobs of the wounded, the death rattle as another soldier breathed his last. Late the next night, I checked my patients one final time, then I left camp. A few months later I ended up in West Texas, and I've been here ever since."

He blinked several times, Jade's face coming into focus. "So, if you don't want a despicable man like me teaching you, I'll understand."

Her heart aching over what he'd told her, she swallowed the lump in her throat. "Why wouldn't I want you to teach me?"

"Because I'm a deserter, that's why," he said in a heated voice. "I'm ashamed to say it, but it's true. So, like I said, I'll understand if you—"

He tried to pull his hands out from under hers, but she tightened her grip. "Eli, you're not despicable, and you're certainly not the only man who deserted during The War."

"No, but I was a surgeon, for God's sake! My job was to help the wounded, not sneak off in the night."

"Stop torturing yourself. You finally reached the point where you couldn't stand what was happening, and you reacted in the only way you knew how. There's nothing terrible about that, and there's no reason for you to be ashamed."

His back stiffened. "Well, there is to me. It's my fault Nora died. She wouldn't have been working in the army hospitals in the first place if it weren't for me. I should have tried to talk her out of volunteering. I should have stayed with my regiment and not deserted like a coward." His jaw worked while he tried to compose himself. "I'm guilty as hell on both counts."

She stared at him for a few moments. At last she said, "I think you're wrong. Based on what you went through, no one would see your desertion as cowardly and shameful. I certainly don't. As for Nora, you can't blame yourself for her death. Just like you wanted to become a doctor, she was obviously doing what she wanted to do." She gave his hands another squeeze. "You've got to let go of your guilt over Nora's death, and then you have to forgive yourself for deserting."

Eli looked into Jade's eyes, searching for and finding the honesty of her words. Though what she said made sense, he didn't think what she suggested was possible.

Chapter 15

Over the next several days, Jade and Eli spent an hour or two each evening sharing their knowledge of healing. Though Jade longed to ask him about Nora, she kept her questions to herself. Instead she concentrated on listening to his explanations about each facet of medicine he explained, and then trying to remember everything he said. That wasn't an easy task when another set of lessons—lessons she learned while lying in his arms—also swirled in her head.

Since the night of the Domingo baby's birth, Eli had not hesitated to share Jade's bed. Nor had he balked at continuing her lessons of an intimate nature. As soon as they got into bed each night, he pulled her close, kissing, caressing and guiding her on the mind-boggling journey to ecstasy. In fact, he seemed as eager to escort her up the slope of fulfillment as she was to experience the pleasure of her release.

If only she knew whether their one-sided physical relationship had done anything to reverse Eli's impotence. He never mentioned his condition, and she feared bringing up the subject would stir his anger. For the time being, she would have to be content with his willingness to continue sharing his knowledge of healing.

That evening, Jade began their lesson by saying, "The *Nde* believe many sicknesses can be cured by a plant which has similar characteristics. For instance, if a person is bitten by a rattlesnake, they would be treated with snakeroot, which resembles an undulating snake. Or, if a person vomits yellow bile, they would be given a remedy made from a plant with yellow roots."

Eli frowned. "The doctrine of signatures."

Jade looked over at him. "I've never heard the term. Is it well-known among doctors?"

"I suppose some believe such foolishness. Probably the same ones who believe in native remedies—that cures for the diseases of one area grow in that same area's soil. But I'd venture to say, most doctors agree with my opinion. The philosophy of like curing like is pure nonsense."

"How do you know?" she said, glaring at him. "Have you tried treating patients using that idea?"

He snorted. "Don't be ridiculous. Of course I haven't tried it."

She pressed her lips into a thin line. "Well, maybe you should have. I'll admit, such treatments don't always produce the best results, but the *Nde* have survived for many generations by following the teachings of our ancestors."

Eli lifted his hands in surrender. "Fine."

"I thought you asked me to teach you about the healing plants and herbs I use because you were beginning to believe in their effectiveness. I must have been wrong. Why else would you start finding fault again?"

He rubbed the back of his neck. "Look, I'm sorry. I do believe in your plant remedies, at least some of them, but . . . It's just that, I keep thinking about The War and a book the medical officers received from the Surgeon General. It contained instructions on how to prepare the medicines we needed from plants growing in the Southern states. What drivel."

"Why do you say that?"

"We weren't in the army to be chemists. But some of the other surgeons in my regiment went on foraging trips to collect the plants, then followed the book's instructions on how to prepare the medicines. I'll admit the concoctions they came up with to replace opium and chloroform were satisfactory. But the others . . ." He blew his breath out in a long sigh. "Who knows how many patients we lost because they were given one of the poor substitutes the Surgeon General suggested. The whole idea was ludicrous from the start."

"He was only trying to help the wounded."

He looked down at where Zita sat beside his chair, her dark quizzical eyes staring up at him. Stroking the dog's head, he said, "That's the hell of it. I know he had the book distributed for the good of the Confederate troops, but such gallant intentions didn't change anything. Nothing could have changed the outcome. There were already too many obstacles for the South to overcome."

Jade heard the pain and bitterness in Eli's voice and wished she could help him lighten the burden of his memories. But at least his revealing a little more of his past gave her a better understanding of the inner torment she'd sensed from the beginning. Now that he had spoken of The War, perhaps she should ask the burning question she'd held inside for the past few days.

She considered the idea for a long moment, then finally decided to plunge ahead. "Eli, who's Nora?"

His shoulders tensed, then slowly relaxed. "She was . . ." He swallowed, then lifted his head to meet Jade's gaze. "She was my wife."

Though Jade had suspected the response he gave, the reality struck a more painful blow than she'd anticipated. Knowing her next words would be difficult to say, she still made herself speak them. "Tell me about her."

Eli shifted his gaze from Jade's face to stare out the window at the purple-tinged sky. "Nora and her family moved to Nashville the summer before I started my final year of medical school, and the two of us soon became great friends. I suppose our families figured we'd get married one day, but Nora and I weren't sure that's what we wanted."

"But you did get married."

"Yes. When I returned from France, I guess I started thinking about my own mortality and the possibility of dying in the war, so I proposed." A shadow crossed his face. "If I hadn't, she'd still be alive."

"You can't know that for sure." When he didn't respond, she said, "What happened after you got married?"

"I left the next afternoon to join my regiment, and she went back to her parents' home. We wrote to each other whenever we could, though mail delivery was erratic. In one of my letters a year or so later, I wrote that word had filtered down to our regiment about the lack of help in the army's general hospitals." He rubbed a hand over his jaw, then exhaled heavily. "I never should have told her that. Next time I heard from her, she was already on her way to volunteer as a nurse.

"I wrote back right away and tried to convince her to go back home, but her reply insisted she was needed. I couldn't argue with her; the army hospitals needed every able-bodied person they could find to care for the wounded. I was proud of her dedication, but I was also afraid. Afraid the grueling schedule of taking the train to whichever hospital had received the latest casualties, or moving an entire hospital to another location when the Union Army got too close, would be too much for her."

Eli fell silent, chastising himself again for not forcing Nora to give up working as a nurse.

Jade longed to smooth the furrows in his brow. Uncertain of how he'd respond, she didn't touch him. "Nora was obviously dedicated to helping the wounded, just like you were."

"Maybe, but she never would have volunteered in the first place if I hadn't mentioned the shortage of help in the hospitals."

"There's no way you could know that. She might have made that decision even if you hadn't said anything to her."

"I suppose. She had the kindest heart of anyone I'd ever known."

When he fell silent again, Jade said, "What happened to her?"

"Influenza. The illness swept through the hospital in Griffin, Georgia where Nora was working, killing most of the patients as well as the civilians caring for them. When I heard all the nurses at the hospital had died in the epidemic, I knew I couldn't stay in the army any longer." He turned his head to look at Jade. "You know the rest of the story."

She nodded, tears clogging her throat for the pain Eli had suffered. His boyhood dream of becoming a doctor and helping people had turned into a horrendous nightmare that may have altered him forever.

"Eli," she said in a choked voice. "You can't keep blaming yourself for Nora's death. She volunteered to work in the hospitals, so she must have known the risks."

"She did. Every time I wrote, I never failed to remind her of what could happen."

"Then she obviously continued as a volunteer because she considered her work more important than any danger to her own health."

Eli's eyebrows pulled together in a frown. "I still should have been able to find a way to convince her to return home. But she wouldn't listen to me."

"You can't always make people do what you think is best. Sometimes you have to let them make their own decisions."

His frown deepened. "You always think you have the answer, don't you?" he said, his voice rising in volume. "Well, let me tell you something, Jade Tucker, you don't."

Before Jade could reply, he pushed away from the table, got to his feet, then turned toward the bedroom. She watched him limp across the room, her heart heavy. The only thing her efforts to help had accomplished was rousing his anger.

Dee-Dee hurried from her uncle's house, resisting the urge to break into a run. More than a week had passed since she'd last seen Night Wind and she knew he would be waiting today. As she walked past the hospital buildings, someone opened the door of the infirmary and stepped outside. Glancing toward the person, Dee-Dee frowned. Sergeant Davidson stood on the stoop of the adobe building. Hoping she could get past the hospital before he spotted her, she picked up her pace.

She thought she'd made it when his voice reached her.

"Mrs. Luden, hold up there."

Dee-Dee stopped, then turned toward the man. She'd managed to avoid him since he'd made his interest known, but this time she had no choice. She would have to speak to him.

When the sergeant reached her side, he pulled his hat from his head and gave her a leering smile. "Where you off to in such a hurry?"

Dee-Dee fought the urge to shudder, his lecherous expression making her skin crawl. "I'm going for my daily constitutional."

His smile faded. "Yer what?"

"A constitutional is a walk taken for one's health."

"That so?" He rocked back on his heels, staring down his nose at her with his piercing black eyes. "Ya know it ain't safe for a woman, 'specially one as lovely as you, to be taking constitutionals in these mountains by herself."

"Do tell," she said, tamping down her temper. "Well, for your information, Sergeant, I've taken a walk every day since I arrived at Fort Davis, and I've yet to have any trouble."

Davidson leaned closer, his whiskey-laced breath hot on her face. "Then I'd say you've been damn lucky. The situation could change at any time." He wrapped his hand around her elbow. "How 'bout I keep you company today?"

"I don't think so," she replied, shaking off his hand. "I enjoy taking my walks alone. Now, if you'll excuse me." Not giving him a chance to reply, she turned and walked away, praying he wouldn't press the issue any further.

Davidson watched her for several minutes, idly slapping his hat against his thigh and wondering what she found so enjoyable about her daily treks into the mountains. The answer that came to mind made him scowl. Could she be meeting one of the other soldiers? God knew practically every eligible bachelor on the fort had fawned over her like a lovesick pup at a recent gathering hosted by her aunt and uncle. Hell, any one of those men would gladly have agreed to a secret rendezvous. As she disappeared around the bend in the canyon, his gut churned with anger. "Dammit, Dee-Dee," he whispered. "Who are you meeting?"

Dee-Dee forced herself to maintain an easy, unhurried tempo until she rounded the first bend in the canyon. Once she was certain Sergeant Davidson could no longer see her, she lifted the hem of her skirt and increased her pace to a near run.

She arrived at the meadow flushed and out of breath. Disappointed Night Wind wasn't waiting for her, she selected a shady spot beneath an oak tree then sat down to wait. Her arms wrapped around her up-drawn knees, she stared at the patch of wildflowers a few feet away and let her thoughts drift.

A voice directly behind startled her from her musings. "What were you thinking about," Night Wind said, moving to her side, "to make your face so flushed?"

"You wouldn't want to know," Dee-Dee replied, marveling at how he'd approached her without making a sound.

"How do you know that?" With graceful movements, he lowered himself to a cross-legged position beside her. "I want to know everything about you."

She stared into his dark eyes, her heart hammering painfully in her chest. Reaching for the small medicine bag hanging around his neck, she lifted the small buckskin pouch into her hand. The backs of her fingers brushed the hard sleek muscles of his chest, sending a wild tingling through her body. Her voice breathless, she said, "I was thinking about kissing you."

His eyes sparkling, he grinned, deep dimples digging into his cheeks. "Since the last time we met, I have spent much time thinking of the same thing."

When Dee-Dee didn't respond, he leaned toward her. Cupping her face with his hands, he pressed his mouth to hers in a brief kiss. "You must teach me more about this fascinating custom of kissing. I never thought I'd want to do anything that is a White Eyes tradition." His mouth gently touched hers again. "But this time, I will make an exception."

"You're already good at kissing, so you won't need many lessons," she said, before running her tongue over his upper lip, then the bottom one.

He started, his breath momentarily wedged in his throat. A groan rumbling deep in his chest, he repeated her actions then lifted his head. "How was that?"

"Hmm, you're definitely a quick learner," Dee-Dee told him, her voice a husky whisper. "At this rate, you'll soon be an expert. Then you can teach the *Nde* maidens how to kiss."

Night Wind's eyebrows snapped together. "I did not ask you to teach me about kissing so I could show the women of my people."

"Then why did you?"

Night Wind dropped his hands to his sides, the corners of his mouth turned down. "I do not know." He shifted his position, turning to stare across the meadow. "When I'm with you, I no longer recognize myself."

"I understand," Dee-Dee replied. "I feel that way, too."

After the awkward moment passed, Dee-Dee asked him more questions about his life, and soon their usual easy camaraderie returned.

"I know your cousin," she told him a while later. "She works at the fort hospital, but of course you knew that. I'm sure Jade and I would be great friends if I weren't going back to New York."

An intense pain struck Night Wind in the chest, making his ability to draw a breath nearly impossible. When he could breathe without pain, he said, "Like her mother Silver Eagle, a *Nde* medicine woman, Jade is a skilled healer. She told me—" He swung around to look behind them, his gaze narrowed.

"What is it, Night Wind?"

He placed a finger over her lips. After giving the area another visual search, he moved his gaze back to her. "I thought I heard something in the rocks behind us." He shrugged. "I guess it was only the wind."

Dee-Dee glanced over her shoulder, not liking the thought of someone spying on them. Hoping Night Wind was correct, she said, "What were you saying about Jade?"

"She told me she came to work with the blue-coats to learn about the medicine of the White Eyes. You have seen this happen?"

"Not exactly. Most of the soldiers haven't accepted her working at the fort hospital. Some have been extremely rude."

Night Wind's expression changed, his features turning harsh and forbidding. "I will go to—"

Dee-Dee grabbed one of his forearms. "No. Jade can handle this." Seeing the doubt reflected on his face, she added, "I swear to you, Night Wind, if I thought Jade needed your help, I'd tell you."

After a moment, he relaxed. "I believe you."

"Good, now help me to my feet. I need to get back."

Night Wind did as she asked, but didn't release his grip on her arms. He pressed a gentle kiss on her mouth, then said, "I'm not sure when I can see you again. My band needs fresh meat, so I must go with some of the others to hunt."

"Of course, I understand."

"You'll still be at the fort when I return, won't you?"

"I won't be leaving for another month, so I'll be here."

He nodded. "Good. I'll get word to you somehow when I return."

Dee-Dee stared up at him with wide eyes. "Please be careful, Night Wind. I couldn't bear it if something happened to you."

"Do not worry, *shijei*, I'm always careful."

After one more long, lingering kiss, Night Wind stepped back, then gave her a gentle push. She started toward the fort, glanced over her shoulder once, lifted her hand in a wave then continued walking.

Night Wind inhaled slowly, trying to ease the ache in his chest. He'd never experienced anything close to the range of emotions tumbling through him, all created by the pale-haired Dee-Dee Luden. With sudden clarity he realized what her returning to the East would cost him; his heart would be leaving with her. He couldn't believe he had come to love a White Eyes, yet he knew it was true. Why the Spirits had allowed him to give his heart to an enemy of his people totally baffled him. But a bigger concern was, now that he'd admitted his feelings, how would he survive after Dee-Dee left? He closed his eyes for a moment, offering a prayer to his personal spirit for the strength to withstand whatever the future held.

The following day, Dee-Dee started on her daily walk—a ritual she maintained whether or not she was to meet Night Wind—when the clomping of boots behind her caught her attention. Stopping, she swung around to find Sergeant Davidson bearing down on her. She groaned inwardly, wishing she could persuade the sergeant that she wasn't interested. The man had a thick skull when it came to subtle hints, so she decided she'd have to be more blunt.

She opened her mouth to speak, but he spoke first, cutting off her words.

"Gonna meet yer Injun friend, Mrs. Luden?" he said, anger and disgust all too evident in his voice in spite of the soft tone he used.

Dee-Dee frowned. Was he bluffing, or did he actually know something? "What are you talking about?"

He stepped closer, grabbing her upper arm with one hand and hauling her closer. "Don't play dumb with me. I saw the two of you. Cozy as bedbugs under that tree." He squeezed her arm tighter, his fingers biting into her flesh. "So, did ya spread yer legs for that red heathen?"

"How dare you cast aspersions on my name," she said in an even voice, though she longed to scream at the top of her lungs.

"I dare anything I damn please," he replied, his dark eyes glittering with rage. "For the past couple a weeks, I've been tryin' to charm you, treating you like the lady I thought you was, so I might get me a kiss or two." He gave a bark of demented laughter. "Well, you surely did play me for a fool, didn't ya? Leading me on, when all the while you were lettin' a damn savage under yer skirts."

Dee-Dee's face burned with a flush of outrage. "I never led you on, Sergeant. And who I see and what I do are none of your concern." She tried to twist out of his grasp. "Kindly let go of my arm."

"I don't think so, I think you and me should—"

"You and I aren't going to do anything, Sergeant. Now, let go of me or I'll . . . I'll tell the post commander about you being drunk while you're on duty."

His gaze narrowed. "You ain't got nothing to tell Colonel Shafter."

"Don't I?" she replied, keeping her gaze fixed on his. "Every time I've seen you at the hospital, I've smelled liquor on your breath, and I'm sure I could find others who would agree with me. I hardly think drunkenness on duty conforms to the army's idea of proper conduct for its soldiers."

He wavered for a moment, his expression changing to confusion. "The army is my life, and one smart-mouthed slut ain't gonna take that away from me."

Dee-Dee curled her fingers into fists, resisting the urge to drag her nails down his face. Drawing a deep, calming breath, she managed to control her sudden thirst for violence before she spoke. "If you let go of me and promise not to mention this conversation to anyone," she said, pleased with the normalcy of her voice, "I promise I won't talk to Colonel Shafter." She paused to let her words sink in, then said, "Do we have a deal, Sergeant?"

He stared down at her for what seemed an eternity, a muscle ticking in his jaw. With a snarled curse, he jerked his hand away from her arm so fast he nearly made her stumble. Giving her a curt nod, he said, "Deal. Now get the hell outta my sight."

Dee-Dee didn't give him a chance to change his mind, but turned and hurried away.

She didn't slow her pace until she was well away from the man who had her heart pounding with fear. *Dear God, what am I going to do?* If Sergeant Davidson had followed her and saw her with Night Wind, perhaps someone else would do the same, or perhaps the sergeant wouldn't keep his word. She wasn't worried about herself, whatever names people wanted to call her didn't matter—they were only words. But she did worry about Night Wind. If something happened to him because of her, she'd never be able to forgive herself.

She stopped beneath a stand of cottonwood trees at the edge of the post garden to figure out what she should do. Night Wind said he would send word when he returned, which probably meant he'd contact his cousin. Deciding Jade needed to know about her confrontation with Sergeant Davidson, Dee-Dee forgot about her daily walk in the mountains and headed toward town.

Chapter 16

The next morning, Jade arrived at the post hospital still thinking about her visit from Dee-Dee the previous afternoon. Concern for Night Wind's safety had always nagged at Jade, but now she had even more reason to be afraid for her cousin; someone knew about his visits to the Fort Davis area.

Though the episode with Sergeant Davidson had obviously shaken Dee-Dee badly, she had stoically maintained her composure while repeating her conversation with the hospital steward. Her voice remained steady, never breaking until she spoke of her concern for Night Wind's safety—concern which mirrored Jade's.

Jade had no problem interpreting the look on the woman's face when she spoke of Night Wind; Dee-Dee loved her cousin. Was it possible he returned her feelings? As crazy as the idea appeared at first glance, Jade didn't dismiss the notion. Dee-Dee was a caring, brave and intelligent woman, just the kind of woman her cousin would be drawn to—in spite of being a White Eyes—just the kind of woman he needed. And there was no doubt Night Wind was already attracted to the lovely widow. If he weren't, he wouldn't risk so much by continuing their secret meetings.

She sighed, wishing she could have given Dee-Dee more comforting advice. Other than assuring her Night Wind was capable of taking care of himself and wouldn't take any unnecessary chances, there had been nothing more she could say.

As Jade approached the hospital buildings, she tried to concentrate on something else. Her lessons with Eli came to mind, bringing a smile to her lips. She'd learned so much in the days since he'd become her teacher, knowledge she hoped to put to use in her work as a healer. Her smile broadened. Her lessons in another area had continued as well. She was still amazed that a simple touch or a brief glance from Eli could make her body crave what she had never known only a short time before. Just thinking about what he did to her made her skin warm with a flush, made the place between her thighs throb with anticipation.

Her mind filled with heated memories, she opened the door to Dr. Chadbourne's office and stepped inside. When her eyes adjusted to the dim interior, her smile faded, the memories scattering like a puff of smoke in the wind.

Sergeant Davidson sat in the doctor's chair, booted feet resting on the corner of the desk, legs crossed at the ankles. As she moved closer, he dropped his feet to the floor but remained seated.

Jade struggled to hide her disgust with the man, forcing herself to say, "Good morning, Sergeant."

"Indeed it is, Miss Tucker," he said. His teeth flashed in what she assumed was meant to be a smile, but the way his lips curled revealed not even the slightest bit of good humor. Rather, his artificial smile masked something dark and sinister.

As she took a step closer to the desk, his intense gaze raked over her, touching her in a way that made a cold shiver race up her spine. Hoping her expression didn't reveal her reaction to his perusal, she said, "What are you doing here?"

"I'm the hospital steward. I got every right to be in the post surgeon's office any time I want. 'Specially while I'm waiting on you."

Jade tipped her head to one side, studying the smirk on his face. "Is there something you wanted to say to me, Sergeant?"

"Damn right, there is." His voice turned harsh. "I wanted to tell ya to turn yerself around and head right on outta here. Yer services ain't needed at the hospital anymore. Not for anything. Now git and don't let me see you around here again."

"What do you mean I'm not needed here for anything?"

He heaved a frustrated sigh. "I told ya before, there ain't no room here for a female who thinks she can doctor folks. And this time I'm tellin' ye, there for sure ain't no room for an Injun woman on this post, even one with the blood of a medicine woman. I reckon ya didn't tell Doc Chadbourne about that, did ye? Otherwise, he never would've hired ya."

Jade's hands clenched into fists in the folds of her full skirt. Obviously, Davidson had not only witnessed Dee-Dee and Night Wind's rendezvous, but he'd also gotten close enough to hear at least part of their conversation. Though she'd already drawn her own conclusion, she felt compelled to be sure. "Where did you hear I have Indian blood?"

He leaned back until the front legs of his chair came off the floor, then laced his fingers over his stomach. "Let's just say, my . . . uh . . . source ain't wrong about this."

Jade eased her breath out a tiny bit at a time, thankful he'd at least kept his promise to Dee-Dee. Though with his propensity for whiskey, there was always the risk that too much liquor would loosen his tongue.

At last, she lifted her chin and said, "You may think Dr. Chadbourne wouldn't have hired me had he known about my heritage, but I think the doctor is more charitable than you're giving him credit. Therefore, he'll have to be the one to end my employment.''

"Maybe," he replied, loosening his hands and bringing the front legs of the chair down to the floor with a resounding thump. "But until he returns." He pointed a finger at her. "I don't wanna see your face around here for any reason. If I do, I might havta have a talk with the colonel. I reckon he'd be real interested to learn there's an Injun buck on the loose close to the fort. Now, have I made myself clear?''

Her chin climbed a notch higher. "Yes, perfectly clear, Sergeant. You won't see me until Dr. Chadbourne returns." Biting her lip to hold in a scream of protest or hot tears of outrage—she wasn't sure which—she squared her shoulders, then turned and exited the office.

Jade thought of not going home, of finding someplace away from Eli where she could lick her wounds and feel sorry for herself in private. Someplace where the pain and humiliation of Sergeant Davidson's dismissal wouldn't hurt so much. But she realized she didn't want to be alone; she wanted—she needed to be with Eli. Lifting the hem of her skirt, she picked up her pace.

When she reached her home, she gave a cursory glance toward the corral to make sure he wasn't with the horses before hurrying to the house.

She threw open the back door and headed for the main room. "Eli, where . . . ?" Seeing him in the doorway of the bedroom, she exhaled a relieved breath, then ran toward him.

Eli snagged Jade around her waist, bracing himself against the door frame to support their combined weight. Surprised by her quick return from the fort, he was more stunned by her throwing herself into his arms.

"Easy, *roja*," he said with a chuckle. "My balance still isn't back to normal. We could end up on the floor if—" A muffled sob vibrating against his chest halted his teasing.

He held her away from himself, his gaze moving slowly over her flushed face, her tightly closed eyes. He lifted a hand to smooth the furrows in her forehead with his fingertips. "What happened?"

When she opened her eyes, revealing the pain swirling in their green depths, he bit back a curse. "Out with it. Did someone hurt you?"

She shook her head. "Not . . . not like you mean. No one hurt me physically." She paused to gather her thoughts. "My father used to tell my sister, brother and me that we might face prejudice someday, but I always thought he was being overly protective, that no one would care about our being a quarter *Nde*. Even you warned me that my welcome at the fort might change if someone learned the truth." She drew a shaky breath. "You and Papa were right."

When she didn't go on, he turned her toward the bed. "Come on, let's sit down."

Once they were seated on the edge of the mattress, Jade's hands resting between Eli's, he said, "Okay, now start from the beginning and tell me what happened."

Her voice quavering slightly, she said, "When I got to the hospital, Sergeant Davidson was waiting for me. We've had our differences before, but—" At Eli's lifted eyebrows, she said, "He said being a doctor was man's work and I had no business treating patients. I always ignored his snide remarks, but this time . . ." She swallowed. "This time, he told me to leave and not come back, that there was no room on the fort for a woman with Indian blood." In a halting voice, she told him about the rest of her conversation with the hospital steward.

When she finished, Eli swore under his breath, then said, "How did Davidson find out about your mixed blood?"

"I think he overheard Dee-Dee Luden talking to Night Wind."

"Who's Dee-Dee Luden?"

"She came from New York to visit her aunt and uncle.

Her uncle is a captain with the Ninth Cavalry, so she's staying with them in their officer's quarters."

Eli mulled over her answer for a moment, then said, "I can't believe your cousin talked to a white woman. I thought he had no use for any White Eyes."

"He doesn't. At least he didn't. I haven't spoken with him since he met Dee-Dee, so I can't be certain he still feels that way. But he's obviously changed his mind where Dee-Dee is concerned, otherwise he wouldn't continue seeing her."

"So how did Sergeant Davidson find out about Night Wind and this Dee-Dee?"

"The sergeant has been interested in Dee-Dee ever since he found me talking to her and demanded an introduction. She's tried everything to discourage him, but he isn't one to give up easily. When she refused his request to accompany her on her daily walk two days ago, he followed her. Then yesterday, he confronted her about her secret meetings with a red heathen, and made all sorts of rude insinuations."

"The miserable son-of-a-bitch," Eli said under his breath. Louder, he added, "Do you think he'll tell his superiors about seeing Night Wind?"

"He promised Dee-Dee he wouldn't after she threatened to tell the post commander about his drunkenness while on duty. The sergeant wouldn't tell me how he found out I'm part *Nde*, even when I made a point of asking him directly. Then the last thing he said was, if he saw me on the fort, he'd tell Colonel Shafter about an Injun being on the loose near the fort. For now he's keeping his promise, but I don't know for how long."

"You're right to be concerned. Too much whiskey and broken promises go hand in hand."

Jade nodded. "That's why I don't trust him to remain silent."

Eli released her hands then wrapped one arm around her shoulders and pulled her against his chest. Tucking her head beneath his chin, he idly ran one palm up and down her back, massaging the tight muscles, the silky strands of her hair teasing the backs of his hand. After a few minutes, a moan rumbled in her throat, the last of the stiffness leaving her body.

"What are you going to do?" he said.

She sighed, her warm breath tickling his neck. "I can't go back to the post hospital since my being there might make Sergeant Davidson break his word. Until Dr. Chadbourne gets back I guess I'll just take care of the patients I have in town."

Eli heard the pain in her voice, his heart cramping with sympathy. He shifted positions. "You've had a rough morning. Why don't you rest for a while?"

As he pushed her onto her back, she stared up into his face. "I'll lie down, but only if you'll stay with me."

He gave her a crooked smile. "If I do, you may not get much rest."

Her eyes brightened, their usual silver-flecked sparkle restored. Smiling, she reached up to press a fingertip into the cleft in his chin. "Really?" Her fingers moved up to run over his lips. "I wasn't tired anyway."

A groan rumbled in his chest. "In that case, we're vastly overdressed." His eyebrows arched. "Wouldn't you agree?"

A delighted giggle bubbled up and escaped her smiling lips. "Absolutely." She sat up and began pulling off her clothes.

Eli watched her until she returned to a prone position, clad in only her underclothes. The blood pounding in his ears, he jerked off his shirt and boots then placed one knee on the bed. "*Roja,* you really have bewitched me," he said, shifting to stretch out beside her.

"Not any more than you've bewitched me," she replied, looping her arms around his neck and pulling him close.

Eli couldn't reply, not with Jade's mouth mere inches away, her eyes glowing with an emotion he refused to name. With a soft growl, he captured her lips in a heated kiss, his hands skimming down her back, over her hips, then around to her inner thighs.

Jade moaned into his mouth, changing her position to give him better access to the place burning for his touch. He cupped her through the fabric of her drawers, bringing her hips off the bed to press closer to his hand, silently pleading for the magic of his intimate touch.

He obliged, finding her through the opening in her drawers, the pad of his thumb rubbing her sensitive bud with slow deliberate strokes. "Ah, *roja*, you are incredible," he whispered against her neck. "I'll never tire of touching you."

"And I'll never tire of having you touch me," she replied, her voice breathless. Releasing her grip on his neck, her hands slipped from his shoulders, her heels dug into the mattress. The heat continued to build, rushing through her body to settle between her thighs. The throbbing pressure increased beneath his fingers, sending her breathing into a series of harsh pants. The now-familiar beginnings of her release made her hands curl into fists in the bedclothes and her head roll from side to side on the pillow.

"Eli! Please, Eli."

The pleading in her hoarse cry told him she was nearing her peak. Removing his hand, he rose onto his knees, then reached for the waistband of her drawers and tugged at the ribbon tie.

She roused enough to say, "What are you doing?"

"Shh, it's okay. Lift your hips," he said. When she complied, he pulled the garment down over her thighs, calves and feet, then tossed it to the floor.

She lifted her head to stare at him through eyes glazed with a mixture of passion and confusion. He shifted his position again, this time nudging her legs apart then kneeling between her opened thighs. She watched him lower his head, her brow furrowed. When she realized his target, she gave a soft gasp and tried to scoot away.

"No, don't," he said, gripping her legs to halt her movements.

"But—"

"Let me, *roja*. Let me taste you. I've never wanted to do this before, but with you I . . ." His words drifted away, his concentration focused on what he was about to do. He parted her with his fingers, then ran his tongue along the rim of her feminine center.

She stiffened for a second, her breath lodged in her throat. When he didn't stop, but continued to lave her with his tongue, her muscles slowly relaxed, the heat, the throbbing, the pressure all returning with a surprising intensity. His soft groan mixed with her moan of pleasure.

Eli had never experienced anything more erotic than loving Jade with his mouth. Once again the stirrings of desire flickered in his groin, still not a full-fledged fire, but definitely hotter than any he'd known in the past six years. Forgetting about his body's tepid response, he concentrated on her, teasing the distended bud with the tip of his tongue, then suckling the kernel of flesh. His head reeled with the sweet scent of her and the knowledge that he was taking her closer to her climax.

Jade couldn't take much more. The heat between her thighs kept building, the pressure almost unbearable, yet she continued climbing the invisible road leading to that allusive treasure waiting at the summit. Fighting to hold in a scream, her fingers tightened their grip on the bedclothes, her hips lifting and retreating in a faster and faster rhythm. Just when she thought she would surely die if she didn't find relief, she sucked in a sharp breath then arched her back to press herself more firmly against Eli's mouth. She froze for an instant, then with a ragged cry, the first convulsion hit her, then another and another. As wave after wave of her mind-shattering release washed over her, she sobbed his name again and again. When the last spasm passed, she exhaled on a long sigh then went limp. The harsh rasp of her breathing was the only sound in the room.

Eli carefully eased his mouth away from her, then placed a soft kiss on the inside of her thigh. Moving to her side, he sat watching her, his heart swelling until he thought it might burst. Rubbing one hand over his chest as if to ease the sensation, his eyes suddenly widened. *My God, it can't be!*

The conclusion he'd drawn came as a shock. Yet, thinking back over the past weeks, he realized he shouldn't be surprised. The seeds had been planted soon after they met. And with the gentle nurturing of such an incredible woman as Jade, it was only natural for those seeds to take root and sprout. Giving his head a shake, he realized he'd never stood a chance. From the moment they met, he'd been doomed. She might not have set out to snare him, and he sure as hell hadn't planned on giving his heart away. Yet that's exactly what happened—he'd fallen in love with Jade Tucker.

He swung his legs over the edge of the mattress, sitting with his back to her. Elbows braced on his knees, his head bent, he stared at the floor between his feet. Now what did he do? He couldn't tell Jade how he felt because that wouldn't be fair to her. A declaration of love would only create complications and expectations—expectations he wasn't prepared to face since he still planned to return to his life as a trapper.

He rubbed the back of his neck and released a weary sigh. The only solution was not telling Jade how he felt. Though he knew he'd arrived at a logical conclusion and decided on the best course of action, he didn't like himself for having made the right decision. One corner of his mouth lifted in a derisive smile. Well, that, too, came as no surprise. He hadn't liked himself much since he deserted the Confederate Army.

* * *

Jade spent the next week trying to forget Sergeant Davidson's hateful words by keeping herself busy. She visited her patients in town or gathered healing herbs and plants from the mountains or the nearby desert. Once she collected the plants, she taught Eli about the various ways to prepare them. The roots of some plants had to be carefully sliced and dried, the seeds of others ground into a paste and added to animal fat to make salves, and another group steeped in water to make decoctions, some to be used as a wash for burns and others as a tonic for assorted ailments.

While Jade explained the preparation of each plant, she silently wondered about Eli. Ever since the day she'd told him about the hospital steward ordering her to stay away from the fort, she sensed there was something different about him. At first, she feared he had decided to leave, but when each day passed and he still hadn't broached the subject, her fears began to ease. Even so, she still sensed a change, though he'd neither said nor done anything to give her any insight. She could only wait helplessly until he chose to reveal the cause.

Several days later, Jade paid a visit to Liana Domingo and her three-week-old son. Pleased Liana had regained her strength and the baby was growing rapidly, Jade bid them goodbye. On the walk back to her house, she abruptly halted. Closing her eyes, she waited for the Spirits to speak to her in a vision. An image of a man's hands holding a folded piece of paper appeared in her mind's eye. The image faded before the hands unfolded the paper and revealed what was on the inside. She waited, but no other images appeared, only blackness.

She opened her eyes, wondering what the Spirits were trying to tell her about the paper and its contents. A sensation of something ominous settled over her, touching her like the prickle of ice shards against her spine. She shuddered violently.

As she continued walking, she couldn't shake the feeling that the brief vision had something to do with Eli. Was this somehow connected to the change she'd sensed in him? She knew she couldn't just dismiss such a possibility. Over the years, she had learned to implicitly trust what the Spirits revealed to her in visions. She'd also learned to trust her own feelings about visions, and though the idea pained her, she couldn't dismiss her latest premonition.

Chapter 17

Several times over the next few days, Jade experienced that same vision. And like the first one, as soon as the man's hands started to unfold the piece of paper, the image disappeared. Though the Spirits had their reasons for all things, frustration ate at Jade each time the vision ended without her learning what she knew had to be the key to its meaning—what was written on the paper.

For a reason she didn't understand, she was unwilling to discuss her disturbing visions with Eli and decided to seek Paloma's counsel. After telling Eli she would be gone for most of the afternoon, she mounted Luna then turned the mare south.

Paloma was working in her small fenced garden and looked up at Jade's approach. A smile adding more creases to her deeply lined face, she hurried from the garden and closed the gate behind her.

"*Chica,* what a pleasant surprise." She stared at Jade through squinted eyes for a moment, then waved her toward the door of her hut. "Come in, come in, and tell me why you are here on a Saturday."

"You mean, you weren't expecting me today? You always know when I'm going to visit."

Paloma smiled again. "Even I can be wrong occasionally."

Jade chuckled, then dismounted and followed the older woman inside.

Once they were settled in the single room of Paloma's tiny home, the woman poured them each a cup of tea. Taking a seat, she turned to Jade. "How are *Señora* Domingo and her baby? They are doing well, *sí?*"

Jade nodded. "I saw them just a few days ago, and they're fine. Liana has fully recovered from the birth and her son is a happy and healthy baby."

"What of *Señor* Kinmont? There is a problem with the two of you?"

Jade took a sip of tea, then said, "Last time I was here, I told you he finally agreed to teach me about Anglo medicine, in exchange for me teaching him about the plants and herbs I use, didn't I?" At Paloma's nod, she continued. "We're still holding lessons, and as for our personal relationship, it's—" She cleared her throat. "Well, there have been no additional problems between us. He still hasn't recovered his ability for intimacy, but that hasn't stopped him from . . ." Her cheeks burned with a deep flush. "From seeing to my . . . um . . . needs."

Paloma chuckled. "Don't be embarrassed, *chica*. A man who knows how to pleasure a woman is indeed a rare find, but even more so when he cannot take his own pleasure. Do not let him get away. He will make a fine *esposo.*"

Jade stared into her cup of tea. "I've thought a lot about that, *maestra,* and I don't think I want Eli to be my husband."

"What do you mean?"

She lifted her head and met Paloma's gaze. "I love Eli, but I also love helping people with my healing skills. If we were to marry and Eli decided he wants to return to being a doctor, he wouldn't want to stay here. He'd want to go back East, to fulfill his dream of being a doctor in his hometown. As his wife, I would go with him, but I would no longer be able to use my healing abilities.''

"Why do you say that? Your services might still be needed.''

Jade shook her head. "There are many doctors in the East. No one would want a part-*Nde* healing woman treating them.''

"You can't be sure of that, *chica*.''

"I am sure. I feel it here,'' she replied, placing her hand over her heart. "I have spent my entire life learning how to care for the sick and injured. I couldn't stand not being able to do what I love.''

After a moment, Paloma said, "What if he doesn't want to become a doctor again? Then you could be together, *sí*?''

"I've thought about that, too. If Eli isn't interested in returning to medicine, then he'll go back to being a trapper. I could travel with him, and we'd be close to my family. But I still would have to give up being a healer. When someone needed me, there would be no way to send word. Even if we made sure someone knew where we would be at all times, I still couldn't be summoned in time to help whoever had fallen ill or suffered an injury.'' She heaved a sigh. "There's no way Eli and I can be together.''

"If you have already made up your mind about this, why did you come here, *chica*?''

"I wanted to tell you about a vision the Spirits have sent me. I've had the same vision several times, and I was hoping you could help me figure out what it means.''

Paloma nodded. "I will help you if I can.''

In a calm voice, Jade told her friend what the Spirits had allowed her to see. When she finished, she added, "I don't know what the Spirits are trying to tell me, except that ever since the first time I experienced that vision, I've had an odd feeling. Like there's an enormous black thundercloud hanging over me, waiting to split open at the first flash of lightning and pelt me with rain and hail. I just don't know when the storm will hit."

The old woman remained pensive for a moment, then spoke. "I think you are right. There is something important written on the paper. But unless your Spirits give you another vision which allows you to see those words, or the vision becomes reality, you will have to be patient."

"Yes, I know. But this sense of foreboding is extremely unsettling."

"Do not worry so much, *chica*. You cannot change what your Spirits have destined to be."

"I suppose you're right," Jade replied in a low voice. Trying to push her worries aside, she summoned a smile. "Let's talk of something else. Tell me about your goats. Has Cano gotten into your garden again?"

Paloma laughed at Jade's question about Trella's off-spring, a young buck named for his gray coloring. "Cano is a clever one," she said. "But I think I have finally broken him of his habit of escaping from the pen so he can eat the vegetables in my garden."

The two women talked of many things, wiling away the afternoon as they'd done so often in the past. By the time Jade announced it was time for her to return to town, she had put the disturbing vision from her mind.

She rose, gave the old woman a kiss on the cheek, then headed for the door. "I will visit again soon, *maestra*."

"*Sí, sí*, come whenever you can. And bring that Anglo doctor of yours next time. I would like to meet the man who makes your heart sing, *bueno*?"

"Perhaps I'll do that. *Adiós*."

"*Vaya con Dios, chica*."

Jade mounted Luna, waved at Paloma, then urged the mare into a trot. As she rode toward Fort Davis, her thoughts dwelled on Paloma's words about Eli. "The man who makes your heart sing." Yes, he certainly did that, along with the rest of her body. But even if he wanted to make their relationship permanent—something he'd never hinted at—she didn't see how they could have a future together. Then the song he'd created would be silenced forever.

Late the following night, Jade and Eli were roused from sleep by Zita's barking and someone pounding on the front door.

Jade pulled on a dressing gown, then left the bedroom, closing the door behind her. After quieting Zita, she answered the incessant knocking. On the other side of the door stood Private Mitchell.

As the soldier removed his cap, he said, "Miz Tucker, you have to come quick. There was a fight at one of the saloons in Chihuahua. Guns were fired, and two soldiers got hurt real bad."

"Hasn't Dr. Chadbourne returned?"

"No, ma'am. He sent word a couple of days ago that he was fixing to leave Fort Stockton. But we don't expect him to arrive before late tomorrow."

"I'd like to help, Private, you know that. But Sergeant Davidson and I—"

"I know the sergeant's got no use for your medical skill, Miz Tucker," Mitchell replied, his jaw tight. "But this time he should be grateful you're around. He's one of the men who got shot."

Jade stared into the man's dark face for a long moment. Finally she said, "Come in for a minute while I gather my supplies and get dressed."

"I think it would be best if I waited out here, ma'am."

"Don't be silly. The wind's nippy tonight, so come in and warm yourself while I get my things together."

Private Mitchell stepped over the threshold, looking extremely uncomfortable. He closed the door behind him, but didn't move any farther into the room.

Jade excused herself, then quickly filled a buckskin bag with supplies before heading for the bedroom.

As soon as she slipped inside, she heard the scratch of a match flaring to life, then a circle of yellow light flickered across the room from the bedside table.

Eli extinguished the match, then dropped back onto the mattress. "Who was that?"

"Private Mitchell from the fort. I'm needed at the post infirmary. Dr. Chadbourne won't be back until late tomorrow, so the private came to get me."

"What happened?" he said, watching her pull on her clothes and moccasins.

"There was a fight at a saloon in Chihuahua and two soldiers got hurt. One of them is Sergeant Davidson."

Eli's eyes widened. "You don't really think he'll let you treat him, do you?"

"I don't know. But Private Mitchell said both men are hurt pretty bad, so the sergeant may be in no condition to object. I've got to go; the private's waiting for me." She moved to the side of the bed, then bent to press a brief kiss on his lips. "Go back to sleep. I'll see you as soon as I can."

"Be careful," he said around a yawn.

She smiled, taking the time to brush a lock of gold-streaked, light brown hair off his brow. "Sleep well," she murmured, then turned down the lamp before hurrying from the room.

At the infirmary, Jade realized Private Mitchell hadn't been exaggerating when he said the injured men were seriously hurt. Both were unconscious, their uniform blouses covered with blood, though their wounds had stopped bleeding by the time Jade began her examination. The sergeant had a lump on the back of his head and a gunshot wound in the upper left side of his chest. The other man, a tall wiry corporal named Anthony Milan, had been hit by two bullets, one in his left side just above his waist and the second on the right side of his neck.

Jade worked quickly, cleaning the wounds to gauge the condition of each man. Corporal Milan's neck wound looked much worse than it was, turning out to be only a deep graze which accounted for the heavy bleeding. Even the wound in his side wasn't as serious as she'd originally thought. The bullet had gone through cleanly, and with a few stitches he would be fine.

Sergeant Davidson's condition concerned her. Though she'd cleaned his wound and stopped the renewed bleeding, she knew the bullet needed to come out. Her mother had taught her about treating both gunshot and arrow wounds, but she'd never been called on to remove a bullet. She was going to need help.

She turned to Private Mitchell, who had offered to stay and help after escorting her to the infirmary. "Private, I've got to leave for a few minutes. Will you stay here and watch Sergeant Davidson until I return?"

His dark eyes went round. "Don't the sergeant and the corporal need you here?"

"Corporal Milan will be fine. I gave him something to help him sleep. Sergeant Davidson needs to have the bullet in his chest removed, so I'm going to get someone to help me. I'll be back as soon as I can."

"What should I do if he wakes up?"

"From the lump on his head, I don't think he'll wake up right away. But if he does, make him lie still so he doesn't reopen the wound in his chest. And he can have a couple sips of water, but no more."

The private nodded, then stepped aside to let Jade pass.

Jade left the infirmary, then broke into a run. The sky was still dark, though the first pink smudges of dawn appeared on the eastern horizon. She arrived at her house a few minutes later and entered the back door, pushing it shut with a bang.

Once inside her bedroom, she found Eli sitting up in bed, apparently awakened by her arrival. She grabbed his clothes from a chair and tossed them onto the bed. "Get dressed, Eli. And please hurry, I need you at the infirmary right away."

He frowned. "What are you talking about? I don't want to go to the—"

"You have to. Sergeant Davidson was shot in the chest and the bullet has to come out. I don't know how, so I came to get you."

Eli stared at her long and hard. "You want me to help save the man who's responsible for making your life miserable these past few weeks?"

"Yes." Seeing his eyebrows arch, she said, "Eli, he's been shot! I've spent my whole life learning how to treat people who are sick or injured, like Sergeant Davidson. But I don't know the proper way to remove a bullet, and you do." When he didn't move, she added, "Are you going to help, or not?"

He exhaled on a long sigh. "Okay, but you're the one who's going to remove the bullet. I'm only going to the infirmary so I can give you instructions on how to do the procedure."

Jade released the breath she'd been holding. "Fine. Just put on your clothes so we can leave."

Back at the Fort Davis infirmary, Eli concurred with Jade's assessment. Davidson would likely die if the bullet wasn't removed. "Where's the surgery?" he said to Jade.

"The room next door."

He looked at Private Mitchell who stood nearby. "Has he come to at all?"

"Once. He roused a little and asked for water. I gave him a couple of sips like Miz Tucker told me, then he went back to sleep."

"Good, then he's not suffering from a severe concussion. Private, would you help me move him?"

The private nodded, then helped Eli carry the sergeant into the surgery. Once the patient was settled on the table in the center of the room, Eli looked over the surgical instruments. Turning back to Jade, he handed her a bottle. "Give the sergeant some chloroform to make sure he doesn't wake up while you're operating, then we'll begin."

She drew a deep fortifying breath to slow her pounding heart, then took the bottle. Pouring a few drops onto a clean cloth, she looked to Eli for his approval. When he nodded, she set down the bottle then held the cloth over Sergeant Davidson's mouth and nose.

After several seconds, Eli said, "That's long enough. He's under." When Jade removed the cloth and laid it aside, he said, "Using your finger, I want you to gently probe the wound to see if you can locate the bullet."

Jade did as he instructed. After a moment, she looked up at him with anguished eyes. "I can't feel it."

"It's all right. I figured the bullet went deeper, but it was worth a try." Turning to the case of surgical instruments, he picked up a flexible wire with a small ball of porcelain fastened to the end. He swung back to face Jade, holding the instrument toward her. "Here, use this."

"What is it?"

"A bullet probe. Hold it lightly in your fingers and drop the tip into the wound. Maintain gentle pressure, but don't push. The probe will follow the path of the bullet almost of its own accord. Understand?"

Jade nodded, then placed the tip of the probe into the wound, and using only minimal pressure, let it ease deeper. When the probe would go no farther, she pushed it gently and felt the resistance of something hard. Smiling up at Eli, she said, "I think I found it."

He offered a brief smile in return, then reached for another instrument. "Withdraw the probe, then use these forceps to extract the bullet."

Jade wiped her brow, then removed the probe and took the forceps from Eli's hand. After several tries, she finally managed to grab onto the bullet with the tip of the forceps, then carefully made the extraction from the wound. Seeing the piece of lead caught between the beaks of the forceps, a giddiness swept over her. *I just performed my first surgery!* In reality, she knew it wasn't true surgery, but the procedure was still closer than anything she'd ever done. The experience left her feeling exhilarated and—

Eli's voice ended her silent celebration, snapping her back to the present. "The bleeding isn't bad," he said, looking closely at the wound. "So apparently no major arteries were severed. All that's left to do is clean and dress the wound. And you should put in a couple of stitches. But you'd better hurry, just in case the chloroform wears off before you're finished."

Jade nodded, laying the forceps aside.

Eli watched her tending Davidson, quietly admiring her skill, her gentle touch and natural ability for treating patients, and thinking she would make a damn fine doctor. Once she finished binding the sergeant's wound, he said, "You don't need my help any longer, so I'll be leaving."

Jade's gaze swung up to meet his, her pulse pounding. Though he was speaking of the present situation, she couldn't help wondering if he would be repeating those words soon. Only the next time, he would be referring to their personal relationship. Swallowing her fear, she walked with him to the door of the infirmary.

"I want to thank you for helping me. I learned a lot tonight." She glanced outside. "I mean, today." She rose up on her toes to touch her lips to his. "I'll be home later. I want to check on the corporal again, and I'd like to wait until the sergeant wakes up before I leave."

"If he doesn't come out of his chloroform-induced sleep in a few minutes, use liquor of ammonia to bring him around. I saw several vials in the surgery. And be sure to give the instruments you used a thorough cleaning."

She nodded.

"Don't stay too long," he said in a soft whisper, running the backs of his knuckles down her cheek. "You didn't get much sleep."

Gooseflesh popped up on her arms, not from a chill, but from his touch and his tone of voice. "I'll be home as soon as I can."

Once Eli left, Jade hurried back to the ward where Eli and Private Mitchell had carried Sergeant Davidson after she finished binding his wound. Just when she thought she was going to have to fetch the liquor of ammonia, the man stirred.

She moved to the side of his bed. "Don't try to get up, Sergeant. You've been—"

"What the hell are you doing here?" He jerked his head toward her, his dark eyes glazed with a mixture of pain and anger.

"You were shot and I treated your wound."

"Shot?" His thick eyebrows snapped together, then slowly relaxed. "Oh, yeah, some Mex bastard made a comment I didn't take kindly to. Milan musta jumped in when the shooting started. How bad is he?"

"The corporal's wounds aren't serious," she replied. "He's sleeping right over there." She nodded to the opposite side of the ward. "With a few days' rest, he'll be just fine."

He tried to raise his head, then sank back on the pillow. "Damn, guess I had too much whiskey. My head feels like it's gonna burst. Where was I hit?"

"Your chest. I removed the bullet and stitched up the wound."

When Davidson grunted in response, Private Mitchell moved into the room from where he'd been standing in the doorway. "You're lucky you had Miz Tucker take care of you, Sergeant. If not for her, you'd be fighting off the fires of hell right about now."

"That right? And what would you know about it, Private?"

"I know because I watched her take the bullet outta your tough hide. No doctor could've done a better job."

"Humph, you don't know nothing," Davidson said, closing his eyes. "Why don't the both of you get the hell outta here? I'm tired."

Jade and the private exchanged a look of disgust. After

she checked on Corporal Milan, she followed Private Mitchell from the ward.

"Don't pay him any mind, Miz Tucker," Mitchell said a few minutes later. "Sergeant Davidson probably just don't know how to thank you."

Jade managed a weak smile. "I'm sure he knows how, Private. He just doesn't want to. The sergeant is probably lying in there trying to figure out when to get even with me for disobeying his order to stay away from the fort."

"Begging your pardon, ma'am. But do you honestly believe, after you saved his life, that he'd actually do something like that?"

She met his troubled gaze. "Yes, Private, I'm afraid I do."

Chapter 18

Jade wouldn't leave the infirmary until Mrs. Fryman—who'd agreed to watch over the two injured men—arrived to take her place. She spent a few minutes giving instructions to Dee-Dee's aunt, then bid the woman goodbye with a promise to return after she'd taken a nap.

When Jade returned several hours later, Mrs. Fryman told her the men had slept nearly the entire time she was gone, although the sergeant was flushed and slightly feverish.

"I'll make a tea for his fever." Jade picked up her bag of supplies. "Could you stay until I brew the tea?"

"I'm planning on staying all day."

"That isn't necessary, Mrs. Fryman."

"I know, dear, but someone should be here with you. Taking care of two sick men can be exhausting work, especially if they're anything like my Phillip. Always complaining about how awful he feels, and carrying on like he might slip through death's door at any minute, when all that's wrong with him is a simple catarrh." She heaved a sigh. "Men!"

Jade chuckled. "I know men can be terrible patients, but really, Mrs. Fryman, I don't mind being here alone."

"Well, you might not mind being alone, but I won't allow it. Now, go make the sergeant's tea."

"Yes, ma'am," Jade replied, turning toward the hospital's kitchen at the rear of the building.

By early evening, Corporal Milan was able to take some broth, and the tea Jade made Sergeant Davidson drink— over his less-than-civil protests—had begun to reduce his fever.

As Mrs. Fryman prepared to leave for the day, she said, "I'll send my husband over with a supper tray."

"Thank you, but you've already done plenty."

"Don't be silly. Cooking for one more is no problem. Besides, that way I know you're getting a decent meal."

"Well, if you're sure."

"Absolutely, dear." She took her hat from the rack by the door. "Are you planning on staying here tonight?"

Jade nodded. "I'm concerned the sergeant may become feverish again, so I think it would be best if I spent the night."

"I can come back later, if you'd like."

"That won't be necessary. But you could do one other thing for me. Would you ask Private Mitchell to come to the infirmary? I have a message I'd like him to deliver."

"Certainly, dear. I'll stop by the barracks on my way home."

After Jade gave Private Mitchell a message for Eli, she busied herself in the infirmary until Captain Fryman arrived with her supper.

Later, she checked her patients again, making sure they were comfortable and their wounds hadn't reopened. After giving Sergeant Davidson another dose of tea to ward off the return of his fever, she lay down fully clothed on one of the empty beds in the ward. Exhausted after the long night and even-longer day, she immediately fell asleep.

She rose twice during the night to check on the men under her care, each time finding no change before returning to her bed in the ward.

Someone shaking her arm woke her with a start. "What—?" She blinked up at the man staring down at her, his face just visible in the weak morning light. "Dr. Chadbourne?"

"Yes, Miss Tucker. I've finally returned."

She sat up, running her hands through her hair to smooth the unruly mass. "Did you just get back?"

"Not long ago. I stopped to see my wife, then came here when she told me what happened in Chihuahua." He glanced over at the sleeping men. "How are they?"

Jade quietly told him about the wounds the men had sustained and what she'd done to treat them.

After she finished, the doctor said, "You did a fine job, Miss Tucker. As good as I could've done. I hope those men realize they owe you a huge debt of gratitude."

Jade rose from the bed. "Dr. Chadbourne," she said in a whisper. "I need to talk to you. In private."

"Surely. Just let me check on these two, then we'll go to my office."

In Dr. Chadbourne's office, Jade told him about her confrontation with Sergeant Davidson, omitting Dee-Dee and Night Wind from her narrative. When she finished, she added, "I told the sergeant that since you hired me, you'd have to be the one to tell me my services are no longer needed in the infirmary." She paused, then said, "If that's how you feel, I won't come back."

The doctor sat in his chair, elbows on his desk, fingers steepled under his chin. "I agree you probably should have told me about your mixed blood when you applied to be my assistant. But to be frank, even if I'd known, I'm not sure what I would've done. Being a doctor, I try to hold myself above prejudice. That isn't always an easy task, considering I've seen what Indians did to soldiers. Such villainy is hard to forget."

"Did it ever occur to you that maybe those Indians had reason to do what they did?"

He removed his spectacles and rubbed his eyes. "Point taken, Miss Tucker. Anyway, I'd like to think I could have put aside such prejudicial feelings and not let them interfere with my decision to hire an assistant."

He replaced his spectacles, then rose from his chair and came around the desk. Turning her toward the door, he said, "For the time being, why don't you go home? Now that I've returned you're entitled to a well-deserved break from your duties. In a few days, we'll talk more about your returning to work."

"I should warn you, Sergeant Davidson never liked me working as your assistant, but now that he knows about my ancestry, he'll be even more adamant about not wanting me here."

"The sergeant's got nothing to say about who I choose to work in the post hospital. So I don't want you worrying about him."

She stopped and looked up at him. "You should also know he threatened me. If I show up here, he plans to go to the colonel with what he knows. I can't allow that to happen."

The doctor's jaw tightened. "Leave Sergeant Davidson to me. I'll talk some sense into him."

Jade nodded, not altogether certain anyone could change the sergeant's biased attitude. Opening the office door and stepping outside, she said, "Thank you for saying I can continue working here. But I'm not sure I'll be back."

Dr. Chadbourne gave her a weak smile. "I understand. Let me know what you decide."

As Jade started to close the door, he said, "I want to tell you again, Miss Tucker. You're to be highly commended for the excellent job you did taking care of those two men.

And I also want you to know, I appreciate all you did while I was away."

She whispered a thank you, then pulled the door shut behind her. On the walk home, Dr. Chadbourne's words of praise continued to ring in her head, bringing back the exhilaration she'd experienced after removing the bullet from Sergeant Davidson. Basking in her restored high spirits, she smiled, the sergeant's threat temporarily forgotten.

Dee-Dee braced the tray she held on one hip while she opened the infirmary door. Stepping inside the building, she called to Jade. When she received no response, she started searching the rooms.

In the ward, her call was answered by a male voice. "She ain't here."

Dee-Dee froze with recognition. Steeling herself to face the man who made her blood boil, she moved closer to the bed of Sgt. Lamar Davidson. "Do you know where she is? My aunt sent me with her breakfast."

"She left with Doc Chadbourne. I heard him say they were goin' to his office."

"I didn't know the doctor had returned."

"He just got back this morning. Now that he's here." He glanced over to make sure Corporal Milan was still asleep. "That part-Injun assistant of his can clear out for good."

Dee-Dee's hands clenched harder on the tray she held, trying valiantly to keep her temper under control.

Davidson glared up at her. "Speakin' a clearing out, why don't you get outta here, too. I got no use for Injun lovers; the sight of 'em makes me sick."

"How dare you speak to me like that?" Dee-Dee said in a fierce whisper.

"I dare anything I damn well please," he replied, his voice rising sharply. "Just git. Why don't ya go see that red-skinned buck yer so fond of?"

A flush of outrage burned Dee-Dee's face. Though she longed to make a scathing retort, she managed to bite back the words. Turning on her heel, she started to walk away, only to pull up short. "Oh, sorry, Dr. Chadbourne. I didn't see you there."

"Mrs. Luden, isn't it?"

"Yes. It's nice to see you again." Glancing up to see his furrowed brow and two bright splotches of color on his cheeks, she said, "If you'll excuse me, I was just leaving." She stepped around him, set the tray on a table near the door then bolted from the room.

Dr. Chadbourne watched her leave, then swung his gaze back to Davidson. "What was that about?"

The sergeant lifted a shoulder in a shrug, wincing at the movement. "We had a little run-in a few days ago."

"Really? About what?"

"Nothing important."

"Does it have something to do with Mrs. Luden and an Indian?"

Davidson's eyes widened for an instant, then his lips thinned. "Where'd you get that idea?"

"I heard you tell her to go see a red-skinned buck."

"So what if I did?"

"How do you know Mrs. Luden has been seeing an Indian?"

" 'Cuz I saw her with my own—Never mind, I ain't gonna say no more."

The doctor stared down at him for a long moment. When the sergeant refused to continue, he said, "I'll take care of the situation, and I want you to stay out of it. That's an order, Sergeant."

"Yes, sir."

Dr. Chadbourne turned and walked away, wondering what he should do with the information he'd just learned.

*   *   *

As Jade approached her house, she spotted Eli leaning against the corral fence. The smile she couldn't seem to wipe off her face broadened. When she was within earshot, she called his name. He looked up, then turned toward her, an odd look on his face.

She came to a halt a few feet from him, her gaze moving over his face then down to his chest and—Her smile disappeared. Standing rooted to the spot, blackness crept into the edges of her sight, blocking out everything except Eli's hands and what they held. "Oh, my God," she whispered. "This is just like my vision." At least she had one answer about her disturbing vision: the man's hands were Eli's. Now she had to find out what was written on the paper.

Her legs unsteady and her heart pounding against her eardrums, she moved closer. "Eli, what is it?"

He swallowed, then said, "I received a letter. From my mother."

The pounding of her heart started to ease. "That's wonderful. I'm so glad she—" Noticing he didn't share her joy, she said, "Is something wrong?"

He flicked a glance toward the mountains, then drew a deep breath and exhaled slowly. "Nora's alive."

Jade swayed on her feet. Of all the things Eli might have said, those words had never crossed her mind. Unable to think of anything to say, she just stood there, in shocked silence.

When Eli held the letter toward her, she shook her head.

"Please, Jade. I want you to read it."

She hesitated for a moment, then finally reached out with ice-cold fingers and took the piece of paper. Whispering a prayer for the strength to do this, she forced her eyes to focus on the neatly penned script. "My dearest Son," the letter began. "You can't imagine how elated I was to receive your letter . . ." The words swam on the page, forcing Jade to blink back her tears. She read the rest of the lines quickly, looking for the name she feared finding. As she got closer to the end of the letter, she began to hope that maybe she had misunderstood Eli, or maybe he'd misread his mother's words, or maybe—No, there it was. "Your sisters, and even dear Nora, finally gave up hoping for your return after all these years. But I continued to keep the faith that you were alive and would come back to us one day. At last my prayers have been answered. I anxiously await your return, dear Eli. Please hurry home."

She refolded the letter, then squeezed her eyes closed, the pain ripping at her insides nearly unbearable. "When . . ." Opening her eyes, she swallowed hard, then forced herself to finish the sentence. "When are you leaving?"

He took the letter from Jade then tucked the paper back in its envelope. "I haven't decided if I'm going."

Somehow she managed to summon the strength to speak. "But you have to. Your mother and sisters haven't seen you in more than six years. And your . . ." Her mouth was so dry she could barely say the word. "Your wife is alive."

He turned away, rubbing a hand over the back of his neck. "I know, but I'm not sure I can—"

"Not sure you can what?"

He swung back to face her. "I'm not sure I can leave you."

His words came as such a surprise that Jade's knees nearly gave way. "What . . . what do you mean?"

He closed the distance between them and grabbed her by the shoulders. "I love you, Jade, surely you knew that."

She shook her head. "How would I know how you felt? You never—" Her cheeks warmed at the thought of how they spent their nights. Certain he had read her mind, she said, "I mean, you never *told* me how you felt."

He sighed. "You're right. Believe me, I do love you, more than I thought possible."

She stared into his eyes and found only truth reflected in their deep blue depths. Her heart cramped with love, but she didn't voice her feelings. To admit she loved him, to say the words aloud while knowing he would be leaving soon, would only make his departure all the more painful for both of them.

A moan rumbling in his chest, he pulled her into his arms. Rocking her against him, he rested his chin on the top of her head. "God help me, *roja*," he whispered, his voice breaking. "But I don't know what to do. All I know is that I love you and I don't want to lose you."

"What about Nora? Don't you love her?"

"I thought I did, once. But what I felt for Nora is nothing like my feelings for you. You're the one I love, Jade."

Tears again filled her eyes. "Eli, I wish I knew what to say."

He held her for a long time, his thoughts a jumbled mess. He knew he had to go to Nashville to see his mother, his sisters and Nora, but he didn't want to risk losing Jade. So what should he do? There had to be an answer. There just had to be.

After a few minutes, Eli inhaled a sharp breath, then loosened his embrace. Holding Jade at arms' length, he flashed a bright smile. "I've got it. Come with me."

She blinked up at him. "What?"

"Come to Nashville with me."

"No, I couldn't."

"Yes, you can. It's the perfect answer. I love you and I don't want to lose you. If you go with me, we'll be together."

"Are you forgetting you have a wife waiting for you in Nashville?"

"Of course not. I haven't figured out all the details yet, but there has to be a way for us to be together. And the best way to accomplish that is for both of us to go to Nashville."

"I don't know, Eli. I still don't think it's a good idea."

"There are hospitals in Nashville, *roja*, excellent hospitals. And I'd take you to see one of them."

Her brow furrowing, she frowned. "That's not fair."

His smile broadened to a grin. "I know. But I'll do whatever is necessary, as long as you'll agree to go with me."

When she didn't respond, his expression sobered. "Promise me you'll think about it?"

She stared at him for several seconds, then finally exhaled a weary sigh and nodded.

Eli smiled again, then draped one arm around her shoulders. Sensing her need for silence, he didn't say anything while they walked into her house. Even Zita's greeting was more subdued than usual. Apparently the dog sensed the heavy emotions hanging in the air.

Late that afternoon, Eli sat in the main room of Jade's house reading an article in a medical journal, while she worked in her storeroom. Though she'd originally planned to spend the afternoon giving Eli more instruction regarding the plants she used, she decided to skip that day's lesson and prepare the ocotillo root herself. She wanted some time alone.

She had just finished pounding a piece of root into a fine powder, when she heard a knock on the front door. Wiping her hands on a piece of toweling, she headed for the main room. Her eyes widened in surprise at finding Dee-Dee Luden talking to Eli.

"Dee-Dee? Are you all right?"

"Oh, Jade," Dee-Dee said, her face pale and stained with tears. "You have to help me."

"Of course. Did Eli introduce himself?" At her nod, Jade took the woman's hand and pulled her toward the settee. "Come, sit down and tell me what's wrong."

Once Dee-Dee was seated, she said, "I need you to get word to Night Wind. I'm leaving Fort Davis, and I want to see him before I go."

"Leaving?" Her gaze narrowed. "Did Sergeant Davidson break his promise to you?"

Dee-Dee shook her head. "That isn't what happened. Aunt Amelia sent me to the infirmary this morning with your breakfast tray, but you weren't there. Sergeant Davidson told me you were talking to Dr. Chadbourne, then before I left, he had to add more of his vile comments about Night Wind. When I turned to leave, I nearly ran into the doctor. Now I remember noticing the odd expression on his flushed face, but at the time, I was too upset to realize why. He'd been in the ward long enough to overhear most of what the sergeant said to me. I don't know whether he got Sergeant Davidson to tell him more after I left, but in any event, a short time later the doctor went to my uncle's office. Then the two of them went to see Aunt Amelia."

Jade squeezed Dee-Dee's hand. "And they're making you leave Fort Davis?"

She nodded. "For my own good, they said," she replied, sniffing back more tears. "Anyway, they would have put me on this afternoon's stage, but I told them I couldn't possibly be packed in time.

"I know they consider me too progressive for a woman, but since they're family, I'd hoped they would be more supportive. Aunt Amelia tried to see my side. When I told her I thought I was in love with Night Wind, she was sympathetic. But she's too passive in her marriage and would never go against Uncle Phillip's orders 'to get myself on the next eastbound stage.' He was furious that I would even talk to an Indian, let alone think of them as human beings. He's such a nearsighted bigot—spouting more of the military's drivel about force being the only thing Indians understand. If he wasn't my uncle, I'd tell him—" She drew a deep, calming breath. "Well, that doesn't matter now. What does matter is seeing Night Wind before I leave."

Dee-Dee stared at Jade, the tears she'd been holding back finally trickling down her face. "Please tell me you have a way of sending word to Night Wind."

"I . . . I'm not sure, Dee-Dee. If we had more time, I could look for him. His band stays in these mountains, but they move their camp from one valley to another. I know where some of their favored campsites are located, but it could take weeks to find the right—" Dee-Dee's stricken expression brought a lump to Jade's throat. Swallowing hard, she said, "There has to be another way. You've seen him several times. How did you arrange those meetings?"

"We always met in the same place: a beautiful little meadow in the mountains behind the fort. A couple of times we agreed to meet there on a certain day, but usually Night Wind would find me. I'd go to the meadow on my daily walk, and suddenly he appeared. If I could, I'd still go there every day, but my aunt and uncle are treating me like I'm under arrest. I managed to slip away today, but I'm not sure I can continue eluding them."

Jade thought a moment, then said, "Tell me again what Night Wind said last time you saw him."

"That was three weeks ago. He said his band needed fresh meat, he was leaving with some of the others to hunt and he didn't know when he'd be back. And, like I told you after my confrontation with Sergeant Davidson, Night Wind also said he'd try to send word when he returned. I thought he meant he'd contact you, and yet you haven't heard from him."

"Even if his hunting party traveled a great distance, he should've returned by now," Jade murmured. Seeing the pain and desperation on Dee-Dee's face, she said, "Don't worry, I'm sure he's fine. And the next stage won't be through here until Friday, so I'll figure out something."

Dee-Dee rubbed the back of her hand over her cheeks to wipe away her tears, then managed a watery smile. "Thank you, Jade. You're a true friend."

For the remainder of the day, Jade's thoughts alternated between trying to come up with a way to help Dee-

Dee and trying to decide what to do about Eli's request to accompany him to Tennessee. Unfortunately, answers to both dilemmas eluded her. Determined to put the unsolved problems from her mind and get a good night's sleep—if that was possible, given the day she'd had—she waited until Eli went out to the privy then retrieved a stack of blankets and a pillow from her bedroom.

She would no longer share her bed with Eli. Instead, she planned to make up a pallet in the main room, as she'd done when she first brought him to her house.

When Eli returned from outside and realized her intent, a muscle worked in his jaw. "You don't have to do that," he said, struggling to keep his voice calm. "We can still share the same bed."

"No, we can't," she replied, keeping her back to him. "You're a married man."

"I won't touch you. I give you my word."

Jade gulped down a sob. "I know you'd keep your word, but that still wouldn't make it right." She shook out another blanket and let it settle on top of the others she'd already spread on the floor.

"Then let me sleep out here."

She shook her head. "You're still my patient and since your ankle isn't completely healed, I insist you take the bed."

Eli curled his hands into fists, frustration over her obvious excuse eating at his insides. She knew his limp was barely discernable, so there was no reason for her saying he should use the bed. Forcing himself to relax, he tried to see the situation from her viewpoint. His mother's letter had to have been both shocking and upsetting to Jade. He could understand that. Hell, the letter had shocked him, too. After all, he'd suddenly learned he wasn't a widower as he'd believed for the past six years. But ever since his conversation with Jade by the corral, she'd refused to discuss the topic any further. In fact, the only thing she said had been a curt, "I don't want to talk about it," whenever he tried to broach the subject.

Though he longed to try again to get her to talk, he decided it would be best to wait until the shock wore off and she could think rationally about his suggestion. Resigned to wait, he murmured good night and hoped like hell for better results in the morning.

Chapter 19

Eli rose the following morning, more tired than when he went to bed. He'd spent the night tossing and turning, his conversation with Jade from the previous day repeating over and over in his head.

Sometime during the night a painful realization struck. When he told Jade he loved her, she hadn't repeated the words. Was he wrong to think she loved him, too? He would've wagered every animal pelt he'd ever sold that she did. But if his instincts were correct, why hadn't she told him?

Still certain he hadn't read her wrong, in spite of her silence, he pushed his disappointment aside. She had other things on her mind—like the sudden resurrection of her lover's wife—so it was no wonder she hadn't said the words. Taking heart from that conclusion, he'd managed to fall into a fitful sleep, only to be awakened by a gut-wrenching dream of a bleak future without Jade by his side.

He pulled on his clothes, then moved on stocking feet into the main room so he wouldn't waken Jade.

She wasn't on her pallet, the blankets barely disturbed.

He found her standing in front of the kitchen window, staring out at the mountains.

He watched her for a moment, the dejected slump of her shoulders tearing at his heart. Taking another step into the room, he said, "Did you even try to sleep?"

Jade glanced over her shoulder, then quickly shifted her gaze back to the window. Seeing him that way—with sleep-tousled hair and a day's growth of dark stubble shadowing his jaw—was too painful. Would seeing him first thing in the morning soon come to an end? She wrapped her arms around herself, chilled to the bone at the thought.

Eli moved closer and reached out to touch her shoulder. "Jade, I—"

A sharp knock sounded on the front door. Eli frowned at the interruption, withdrawing his hand.

Jade exhaled a compressed breath, then turned and headed into the main room. As she walked toward the front door, she wondered what calamity awaited her on the opposite side. What else could happen to turn her world any more upside-down than it already was?

When she opened the door, she found out. With a synchronized "Good morning," a couple flashed a pair of bright smiles at her. Too stunned to speak, Jade's mouth gaped open. What were her parents doing on her doorstep?

Rafe Tucker chuckled, then glanced down at his wife. "Looks like our daughter isn't as thrilled to see us as we thought she'd be."

Jade snapped out of her momentary lapse and said, "Of course I am, Papa. You just surprised me." She took a step back. "Please come in."

Rafe allowed Karina to enter first, then each kissed their daughter's cheek. "We didn't mean to startle you," Rafe said, once Jade had closed the door behind them. "But we—" Spotting a man standing across the room, his jaw tightened. "Who the hell's this?"

"Rafe," Karina Tucker said, placing a hand on her husband's forearm. "I'm sure Jade will introduce us, so just be patient." She turned back to look at her daughter. "Forgive your father, sweetheart, he sometimes forgets you aren't five any longer."

Jade's cheeks warming with a flush, she said, "Mama, Papa, I'd like you to meet Eli Kinmont. He's a patient of mine. Eli, these are my parents, Rafe and Karina Tucker."

Eli shook Rafe's hand, staring into eyes as green as Jade's though they lacked the silver flecks. "Pleased to meet you, sir," he said, silently appraising the older man. Though Eli guessed Rafe to be past fifty, the man was solidly built, his grip firm, and only a few strands of gray showed in his tawny hair.

When Eli turned to take Karina's offered hand, he found himself looking into the source of the flecks in Jade's eyes—the incredible pure silver of her mother's eyes. Unlike Jade, Karina Tucker's *Nde* heritage was apparent in her coloring, darker skin tone and jet black hair, and in the clothes she wore, buckskin trousers and shirt. His eyebrows lifted at the latter, but he didn't comment on the woman's unusual style of dress.

Karina returned Eli's murmured greeting, then said, "I hope my daughter has taken good care of you, Mr. Kinmont."

"Please, call me Eli, and yes." He sent a warm glance Jade's way. "I've been in excellent hands."

"She's a talented healer," Karina said with a smile, wondering at the look the Anglo directed at Jade. Turning to her daughter, she said, "I apologize for showing up unannounced, Jade. We really should have let you know we were coming. But your father decided at the last minute to help our men bring a herd of cattle to the fort, and then I decided to come with him. By then it was too late for a message to get here ahead of us. We'll be staying with the Murphys, but we wanted to stop and see you first."

"You don't have to apologize, Mama. I'm thrilled to see

you. It's just that you never make the trip with Papa, so seeing both of you came as a double shock.''

"I know, sweetheart. We got word a few weeks ago that Long Knife was killed. I never wanted him dead, but I can't say I'm grieving deeply over his death.''

"The past has finally been put to rest,'' Rafe said, wrapping an arm around his wife and pulling her against his chest.

Jade glanced at Eli and saw the confused look on his face. "I think I told you about Long Knife. He's the *Nde* leader who accused Mama of being a witch.'' At his nod, she added, "Even though he hadn't tried to find her for many years, she never traveled in areas of the mountains she knew his band favored.''

She turned back to her mother. "What about the rest of Long Knife's band? Now that he's dead, will some of the others try to carry out his threat to kill you?''

Karina smiled. "No. Thankfully, the others knew Long Knife's hatred of me was personal, and not something they needed to continue.'' Glancing over to her husband, she said, "Why don't you let the Murphys know we've arrived? While you're gone, Jade and I can catch up on what she's been doing.''

Rafe nodded. "I also need to go to the fort. I have to meet with the commissary officer about the cattle. I might not get back until after dinner.'' He kissed Jade's cheek again, then pressed a longer kiss on his wife's mouth. "I'll see you later, honey,'' he whispered. Looking over at his daughter, he said, "Will you be here this afternoon, or should I meet you two at the post hospital?''

"No, don't go there,'' Jade replied more fiercely than she intended. "I . . . uh . . . I won't be going to the infirmary today.'' Hoping her parents didn't think her response odd, she said, "Take your time, Papa. Mama and I will be here whenever you get through.''

Rafe nodded, then turned toward the door. As he started to step outside, he swung back to Eli. "If you'd like to get away from all the female chatter that'll be going on in here soon, you're welcome to come with me."

Eli shifted his gaze from Rafe to Jade. The look she gave him, though not panicked, was definitely wary. Sending her a glance he hoped offered the reassurance she needed, he said, "Thank you, sir, I'd like that. Just let me fetch my boots and hat."

"Fine, I'll wait outside."

When Eli returned to the main room, Jade and her mother had already gone into the kitchen. Disappointed he wouldn't have an opportunity for a moment alone with Jade, he settled his hat on his head then crossed the room and stepped through the front door.

After the men left, Karina watched her daughter pour two cups of coffee. Accepting one of the cups, she smiled. "Jade, I haven't told you the real reason I wanted to make this trip. I didn't tell your father either, because I didn't want to upset him."

Jade's gaze jerked from contemplating the contents of her cup to her mother's face. "What is it?"

"I had a vision—actually just a partial vision—about you and a man. Unfortunately, the Spirits didn't reveal much, but I got the impression that the man means something special to you." When Jade didn't comment, Karina continued. "The vision struck me as odd. I mean, I know you've never been interested in a man because he might interfere with your being a healer."

There was still no response from Jade.

"Jade," Karina said in a low voice, "I'm certain the man in my vision was Eli."

Jade's fingers tightened on her cup. After a moment, she said, "The Spirits didn't reveal anything else? Something to tell you what the future will bring?"

Karina tipped her head to one side, wondering at the hopeful tone in her daughter's voice. "Sorry, sweetheart. Like I said, the vision was extremely brief."

"So were mine." Seeing her mother's eyebrows arch

with surprise, she said, "I had visions about Eli, too. The Spirits showed me an injured man lying in the mountains. But they revealed nothing more, nothing about whether our futures would be linked."

Karina set her cup on the table, then placed her hand on Jade's arm. "You care for Eli, don't you?"

Jade squeezed her eyes closed for a second. "I haven't told him, but, yes, I love him," she replied in a whisper.

"Are you afraid he doesn't return your love?"

"He told me he loves me, and I believe him, only . . ." She sniffed, hoping to hold back the threatening tears.

"Only, there is still a problem?"

At Jade's nod, Karina said, "Is there some way I can help you, sweetheart?"

"I don't think so, Mama. I don't think anyone can." Taking a deep breath to work up the nerve, she said, "Eli's married."

Karina swallowed hard. "I hope your father doesn't find out. There's no telling what he'd—"

"Mama, it isn't what you think! Eli thought his wife died six years ago. Then yesterday, he found out she's still alive. That's when he told me he loves me and doesn't want to lose me."

"Come on, let's sit down," Karina said, taking the cup from Jade's hands and setting it beside hers on the table. "Then you can tell me the whole story."

Jade allowed her mother to escort her back into the main room. Once they were seated on the settee, her mother encouraged her to begin. After gathering her thoughts, she began speaking in halting sentences. Then once she got past the initial awkwardness, the words came easier, until the entire story poured out. She held nothing back, ignoring her burning cheeks when she told about their one-sided intimate relationship and ending with the letter Eli received the day before.

After Jade finished, Karina brushed the tears from her

daughter's cheeks, then said, "He wants you to go to Tennessee with him, but what do you want to do?"

Jade sniffed. "I don't know. I'd like to go with him. But I'm afraid if I do, I'll only be making things worse."

"Considering the circumstances, sweetheart, you have to admit, things couldn't get much worse."

"Mama, this isn't funny!"

"I know, Jade. I didn't mean to sound like I was making fun of the situation. So, why don't you tell me what you meant."

"All I've ever wanted to be is a healer. I've spent my entire life learning how to care for people. First from you, then from Paloma. And the last few weeks, Eli has been teaching me about Anglo medicine. But if I go to Tennessee with him, my skills will no longer be needed. I couldn't bear to give up being a healer, even for—" She drew a deep breath. "Even for the man I love."

Karina remained silent for a few minutes, mulling over Jade's words. She certainly understood her daughter's priorities. When she was Jade's age, she, too, had wanted only one thing from life—to be the best medicine woman possible. Nothing had been more important than helping those who were sick or injured. Then she met Rafe Tucker.

At last Karina said, "Making the trip to Tennessee would allow you to see parts of this country that you've never seen, something your father and I hope to do one day."

"But I love it here," she said, pressing her lips into a flat line.

"Yes, I know, sweetheart," Karina said, smiling at Jade's mutinous expression. "We love West Texas, too, and we couldn't imagine living anywhere else. But that doesn't mean we wouldn't enjoy visiting other places. Besides, once you get to Tennessee, you might find you like it as much as Texas."

"How can you say that?" Jade said, horrified at the idea.

"Because, you will never know for sure if you don't make the trip."

When Jade didn't look convinced, Karina decided to borrow the tactic Jade said Eli had used: dangling a carrot in front of her daughter's nose. "Don't forget, if you go, you'll get to see a city hospital. I hope you realize how lucky that makes you. And how many times do you think you'll get another chance at such a wonderful opportunity?"

"None," Jade replied in a low voice. Then her chin came up, an intense stare directed at her mother. "But that isn't reason enough for me to go with Eli."

"Perhaps, sweetheart. But you're the only one who can decide."

Jade slumped against the back of the settee. "Yes, I know," she said in a pained whisper, more confused than ever. Now that Dr. Chadbourne had returned and her services were no longer needed at the fort, there was nothing keeping her in Fort Davis. And she had to admit, the prospect of seeing other parts of the United States would be exciting. Then there was the even greater excitement bubbling inside her over the notion of seeing the inside of a real hospital. Going to Tennessee would also mean more time with Eli; an additional precious few weeks or months before she'd have to bid him a final goodbye, then return to Texas—her heart breaking over a love that could never be.

Rafe and Eli returned to find the women working in Jade's storeroom. Karina accepted Rafe's kiss, then said, "Everything all right with the cattle?"

"Fine," he replied with a smile, tunneling his fingers into her hair, something he never tired of doing. "So, what have you two been doing, besides playing with your plants?"

"We're not playing, Papa," Jade said, glancing in his direction. "You know what we're—" Spotting him wink at Eli, she swung around to face her father. "Papa, what are you up to?"

"Nothing, sweetheart," Rafe replied, still fingering his wife's hair. "I was just confirming a comment I made to Eli on the way back here. I told him I bet we'd find you two elbow deep in making some sort of concoction from roots or twigs or leaves."

"Don't forget the berries," Eli said with a smile.

Rafe met Eli's amused look with a grin. "Right. Or berries. Never thought anyone could find a use for darn near every plant that grows in Texas, but I think these two may have succeeded."

Eli's smile broadened. "From what I've seen," he said, watching Jade return to her work, "you're probably right."

Rafe lifted a lock of his wife's thick hair and pressed his lips to the silky strand before releasing it. "Karina, did you tell Jade we saw Night Wind?"

Jade's head came up, her pulse pounding in her temples. She'd forgotten about Night Wind. Her mouth suddenly dry, she said, "When did you see him?"

"The day before we left to come here," Rafe replied. "He and a few others from his band were returning from Mexico, and he made a brief stop at the ranch."

"Then he should be back at his camp by now."

Karina studied Jade's expression. "Night Wind said he saw you a few weeks ago." When Jade nodded but remained silent, Karina said, "Has something happened to your cousin?"

"No, nothing's happened to him." Jade dropped her gaze back to the table covered with an assortment of plants in various stages of preparation for her remedies.

"Then what is it? As soon as we mentioned Night Wind's name, your expression changed."

Jade drew a deep breath then released it slowly. "Night Wind met a woman a month or so ago, a woman visiting her aunt and uncle at the fort, and he's been secretly meeting her ever since. Dee-Dee, that's the woman's name, came here yesterday to tell me she'll be leaving on Friday and asked if I could get word to Night Wind. She wants to see him before she goes."

Karina frowned. "This Dee-Dee is a White Eyes?"

Jade nodded. "I was surprised when I found out, too. But I know Night Wind wouldn't keep seeing Dee-Dee unless he cared about her."

"I agree," Karina replied. "So you are going to help this woman?"

"Yes, I just don't know how. I thought of looking for his band's camp." She sighed. "But if they've moved deeper into the mountains, that could take more days than I've got."

"Do you know a trail he uses frequently?" Karina said. "Someplace where you could leave a signal for him?"

Jade's face brightened. "Dee-Dee told me where she and Night Wind meet: a meadow not far from here." Frowning, she added, "I should have thought of that sooner."

"Don't be upset with yourself, sweetheart," Karina said, giving her a knowing look. "Remember, you've had a lot on your mind these last two days."

Rafe looked back and forth between his wife and his daughter. "What're you two talking about? Is there something wrong?" He finally pinned his narrowed gaze on Jade. "What've you had on your mind?"

Karina turned and placed a hand on her husband's chest. "We'll talk later," she told him, emphasizing the last word.

He scowled, then finally gave her a nod.

Jade turned back to her worktable. "As soon as I finish here, I'll go to the meadow." She paused for a moment. "Mama, would you come with me? It's been a long time since you taught me the *Nde* way of using stones to leave messages. If you're with me, you can make sure I don't make a mistake."

"Of course, I'll go with you." Glancing at her husband, she said, "Did you take our horses to the Murphys?"

When Rafe nodded then offered to fetch her horse, Eli spoke from where he lounged against the door frame. "You're welcome to use my gelding, Mrs. Tucker. Rex hasn't been ridden much lately, but he's generally well behaved."

Karina smiled. "Thank you, Eli. I'm sure I won't have a problem. And I insist you call me Karina. Mrs. Tucker is much too formal."

Eli nodded, then pushed away from the door frame. "I'll go saddle the horses."

A few minutes later, Jade and her mother mounted their horses then headed into the mountains. When they reached the meadow, Jade pointed to the stand of oak trees Dee-Dee said was the place she and Night Wind met.

They dismounted near the trees, then searched the area for a few small stones. When they'd gathered enough for their purpose, Karina watched Jade arrange them to form a message which Night Wind would understand. To anyone else, the stones would simply appear to be lying in a random pattern of nature.

Jade arranged a few of the stones so they pointed in the same direction. Then she placed another stone on end, leaning it against one of the others. She stood up, studied her handiwork for a moment, then looked at her mother.

"You did well," Karina said. "The first stones point toward town, and the stone on end is the symbol for requesting assistance. If Night Wind comes to this place, he will know you were the one to leave the message, and he will come to you."

"I just hope he comes here before Friday afternoon."

Karina pulled Jade into her arms for a hug. "I hope so, too, sweetheart."

As they rode back toward town, Jade wished there was

more she could do for Night Wind and Dee-Dee, but she knew she'd done all she could. The situation was out of her control. Her thoughts shifted from Night Wind and Dee-Dee to the decision hanging over her own head. Would she, too, soon have to say goodbye to the man she loved? Her heart ached at the thought. Then she realized that, at least for a while, she still had control over her own destiny.

She sat up straighter in her saddle, what she had to do suddenly clear. Though she feared she might live to regret her decision, she was determined to carry it through. Looking over at her mother, she said, "Mama, I've made a decision. I'm going with Eli."

Karina smiled to herself, wondering if she'd ever tell her daughter about the other vision she'd had in the past weeks: the one where she saw Jade embarking on a long journey. Deciding to keep that to herself for the time being, she said, "I'll pray to the Spirits to protect you on your trip." She also planned to ask for the safekeeping of her daughter's heart.

Chapter 20

Rafe and Karina left later that afternoon to have supper with the Murphys, promising to return sometime the following morning.

While Jade and Eli ate their own meal, they avoided the questions about their future, keeping their conversation on less disturbing topics.

Eli pushed aside his empty plate, then said, "Where did your parents meet?"

"San Antonio."

Eli's eyebrows rose. "Really?"

"Mama went to San Antonio to deliver her sister's baby and Papa was living there at the time. They met when they ended up on the same freight caravan heading for Presidio del Norte. Mama was coming home, and Papa was planning to look for lost gold in these mountains."

"And they fell in love on the trip west?"

"Not at first. Papa didn't have any use for marriage, and Mama didn't want anything to interfere with her being a medicine woman." She frowned, realizing her views on her own life mirrored her mother's more closely than she'd thought.

"But obviously they worked everything out."

"Yes," Jade replied absently. "Eventually, they did." She fell silent, caught up in thoughts of what her own future might hold.

"Jade. Jade, did you hear me?"

She blinked, Eli's concerned face coming into focus. "Sorry, I was just thinking." Before he could repeat whatever her woolgathering had missed, she said, "I'll go with you."

His eyes widened at her announcement, then narrowed again. "Are you sure?" He swallowed. "What about working at the post infirmary?"

She gave him a weak smile. "I'm not Dr. Chadbourne's assistant any longer."

"What?" he said with a scowl. "When did this happen?" His scowl deepened. "Is it that bastard Davidson? Why didn't you say something?"

Her smile broadened at his rapid-fire questions. "Yesterday. It wasn't entirely Sergeant Davidson's doing. And I didn't say anything because you already had enough on your mind."

"Tell me what happened."

She told him about Dr. Chadbourne returning from Fort Stockton and her private conversation with him. "I decided to tell him I'm part *Nde* before he heard it elsewhere, so I could find out if he shared Sergeant Davidson's opinion. Dr. Chadbourne admitted he wasn't sure how he would've reacted had I told him earlier, but he wasn't against my continuing as his assistant. At first I was relieved, but then I realized working at the infirmary would never be the same. It would only be a matter of time before word got out, and then who knows how long I'd be allowed to work there. Besides, with me no longer around as a reminder, I'm hoping Sergeant Davidson will forget about telling the colonel about Night Wind."

"I thought being an assistant to the post surgeon meant more to you than that. I never figured you'd run scared from a blackguard like Davidson."

She stiffened, her chin coming up. "You know working for Dr. Chadbourne did mean a lot to me. And I'm not running scared. I'm not going back to the infirmary because the safety of Night Wind and the others in his band are more important."

He stared at her long and hard, pride over her dedication to family filling his heart. He finally said, "Is that why you decided to go with me, because you no longer have a job with the army?" He held his breath, waiting for her answer and praying love had prompted her decision.

She hesitated before responding. "That was part of it. And part of my decision was your offer to take me to a hospital in Nashville. But mostly I wanted to be with you."

Eli waited a moment longer. When an admission of love didn't come, he released his breath slowly. For now, Jade's wanting to be with him would have to do. "Just as long as you're absolutely certain you want to go with me."

"I'm certain, but . . ." She paused to get her thoughts in order. "I also want you to know that no matter what happens in Tennessee, regardless of whether or not there's a future for us," her voice dropped to a pained whisper, "I don't want to give up being a healer."

"Why would you have to? Even with all the doctors in Nashville, I imagine there are still some folks who don't trust modern medicine. They'll want your services."

"You don't really believe that, Eli. You couldn't, not after you told me how the soldiers would react when they found out about my mixed blood. Be honest, the people of Nashville will be no different. They won't want a yarb woman, as you call me, touching them or their families." Her voice turned bitter. "Especially one who's part red savage."

Eli stared at the table, his stomach knotting. Jade's statement was something he hadn't considered. Dammit, why was everything so complicated all of a sudden? Lifting his gaze to meet hers, he said, "You have my word that I'll do whatever I can to make sure no one treats you with anything other than respect. And I know my mother and sisters will do the same."

Jade's throat closed at his gallant offer of protection, her love for him nearly choking her. "Thank you for saying that," she finally managed to say. She didn't add that she doubted his efforts would be enough to prevent the kind of prejudice she had recently experienced. Though a tiny part of her continued to cling to the belief that somehow she and Eli could have a future together, she also refused to give herself false hope.

Since Jade was no longer reporting to the post infirmary each morning, she divided her time between seeing several patients from Chihuahua, visiting with her parents and preparing for her trip. Rafe and Karina planned to leave at week's end, taking Zita, the horses and Eli's pack burros to their ranch. Jade and Eli would be boarding the east-bound stage the following Monday.

On Thursday afternoon, Karina watched her daughter sort through her packets of plant remedies from the door-way of Jade's storeroom. "You haven't heard from Night Wind?"

Jade poured seeds of the jimson weed—used to prevent miscarriage—into a small leather pouch. "No. I'm so afraid Dee-Dee will have to leave without speaking to him. I know how I would feel if I left without getting to talk to Eli."

Karina gave her a sad smile. "I have prayed for Night Wind to find the message you left him, so let's hope the Spirits will grant our wish."

Jade nodded. Hearing male laughter outside, she suddenly smiled. "Papa and Eli seem to be getting along."

"Yes. Both your father and I like Eli. The Spirits have sent you a fine man."

Her smile fading, Jade turned back to the task of choosing which medicines to pack. "What if you misunderstood the Spirits' message in your vision, and what if Paloma was wrong when she said Eli would become my husband? Maybe I was only supposed to find him and heal his injuries. Maybe he wasn't meant to be more in my life than a patient." Her breath caught on a half-sob. "Maybe I won't be forced to choose between my love for him and being a healer."

Karina's heart cramped at the sadness in her daughter's voice, and the pain reflected on her face. "Sweetheart, I wish I could tell you something more comforting, but for now, I'm afraid only the Spirits know the answers."

Jade nodded, swallowing the lump of tears in her throat. She continued her work of sorting through her medicines, praying she wouldn't go to Tennessee only to return with a broken heart.

Just as darkness began to settle over the town, Jade and Eli approached her house on foot. They had accepted an invitation to have supper with her parents and the Murphys, then enjoyed a leisurely walk back home. When they were a few feet from the front door, Jade suddenly stopped. Turning to look toward the mountains, she cocked her head to one side then held perfectly still.

"What is it?" Eli said in a whisper. "A vision."

She shook her head. "I just had the feeling that someone's—"

"Your senses are as sharp as ever, *shila*," a voice said from somewhere near the house.

Jade whirled around. "Night Wind!"

"*Au*—yes." The shadows cast by the house separated, one section moving closer and taking the shape of a man.

Jade picked up the hem of her skirt and hurried toward him. "I'm so glad you came."

"You left a signal for me. Why would I not come here?"

"I knew you would, but I was afraid you wouldn't see the stones until it was too late."

"What do you mean, too late? And why did you leave a signal in that place?"

"Come inside and I'll tell you." Taking his hand, she turned and led him toward the front door.

After Jade lit a lamp, Eli and Night Wind stood eyeing each other warily. Not wanting to deal with a battle of male egos, Jade made the introductions then said, "You two have nothing to fear from each other. Eli is friend to the *Nde,*" she said to Night Wind. "So you can wipe that warrior expression off your face."

Night Wind blinked at her words, but didn't reply.

Jade turned to Eli and said, "And you can stop looking like you might have to defend your life. I've told Night Wind I trust you, so he won't slit your throat." Seeing the stiffness in Eli's shoulders begin to ease, she couldn't resist adding. "Unless I tell him to."

Eli's eyes widened, then catching the hint of a smile teasing her lips, he chuckled. "Okay, I got your point." Holding out his hand to Night Wind, he said, "Jade has an odd way of saying things, but I think she wants us to get along."

Night Wind's gaze moved back and forth between Jade and Eli. A smile tipping up the corners of his mouth, he clasped Eli's outstretched hand in the way of the white man. "She is right. As long as you do nothing to break her trust in you, I will trust you as well."

Jade smiled at the two men, then said, "Eli, would you put a pot of coffee on to boil? This may be a long night."

Eli nodded, then excused himself and headed for the kitchen.

Night Wind widened his stance, then folded his arms across the buckskin shirt he wore to ward off the cool night air. "How did you know I would be in that mountain meadow?"

"Dee-Dee told me."

His dark gaze narrowed. "Tell me why you left the signal of stones."

Jade braced herself for his reaction to her words. "Night Wind, the doctor at the fort found out Dee-Dee has been seeing an Indian and he went to her aunt and uncle. They're making her leave Fort Davis on tomorrow's stage."

Anger, shock and finally pain flickered in his dark eyes, in the harsh set of his mouth. He did not speak, but nodded for her to continue.

"When Dee-Dee came to tell me what happened, she said she wanted to see you before she left and asked if I could get in touch with you. That's why I left the message where she said the two of you always met."

"Where is she?"

"She's still staying with her aunt and uncle."

Night Wind unfolded his arms, then started to turn. "I will go to her."

Jade grabbed his forearm. "No, you can't risk going to the fort. You could be captured or shot."

As he stared down at her, a muscle twitched in his jaw. "I want to see her."

"I know." She released his arm. "You stay here and I'll go to her uncle's house. Maybe there's a way she can sneak out."

After a moment, he exhaled his breath in a deep sigh. "Go."

Jade grabbed a shawl from a peg by the door, explained where she was going to Eli, then hurried from the house.

She ran most of the way to the fort, stopping a short distance from the Fryman house to catch her breath. A minute later, she squared her shoulders, marched up the front steps and knocked on the door.

Amelia Fryman answered her knock and thankfully didn't question her request to speak to Dee-Dee at such an hour. "I'm so glad you came by, Jade." In a softer voice, she added, "Dee-Dee has been like a lost soul these last few days. I certainly hope Phillip and I haven't broken her spirit." Snapping out of her moment of introspection, she said, "Would you like to come in, dear?"

"No, thank you. I don't want to disturb you and the captain. So, if you don't mind, could you send Dee-Dee out here?"

Jade held her breath until the woman said, "Certainly, if that's what you want. I'll go tell her you're here."

Only a minute or two passed before Dee-Dee stepped onto the porch and closed the door behind her. "Aunt Amelia said you came to say goodbye."

Jade waved her to the far side of the porch, away from the door and windows. "I came to tell you Night Wind is at my house."

Dee-Dee gasped. "Oh, thank God, I was so afraid I'd never see him again." She glanced back at the door. "But how can I get away at this time of night?"

"Does your bedroom have a window?"

Dee-Dee nodded, then said, "But, what does—Ah, I understand. In a little while, I'll tell my aunt and uncle I'm going to bed early. Which they won't question because of the tiring trip ahead of me. Then a few minutes later, I'll climb through my bedroom window."

Jade chuckled. "Exactly what I was going to suggest. Now you'd better get back inside. How long before you can slip away?"

"I'll wait fifteen minutes before pleading exhaustion, then maybe another fifteen before I go out the window."

Jade looked around, then said, "Okay, I'll wait for you

over there." She pointed to a stand of oaks. "And you'd better wear a shawl over your hair so you aren't recognized." Pulling her own shawl back up onto her head, she smiled. "So, aren't you getting sleepy?"

"What? Oh, yes. Yes, I am." She faked a yawn. "Guess I'd better be turning in soon." Moving back to stand near the door in case her aunt was listening on the other side, she said, "Thank you for coming by, Jade. I've enjoyed your friendship during my stay at Fort Davis."

Jade smiled. "Goodbye, Dee-Dee. Have a safe trip." Adding a whispered, "Thirty minutes," she went down the steps and headed toward town, planning to double back to the stand of oak trees.

Night Wind paced the length of the main room in Jade's house, his agitation growing. "She has been gone too long."

Eli checked his pocket watch. "It's been less than forty minutes. If anyone can get Dee-Dee away from the fort, Jade will find a way."

Night Wind seemed mollified for the time being, but continued his restless pacing. When another ten minutes passed, he murmured something Eli didn't understand, then started toward the door.

"Where are you going?" Eli said, rising from the settee.

"I cannot stand being inside a White Eye's house any longer," he replied. "The walls are closing in on me." Before his fingers closed around the doorknob, the door swung open. Taking a step back, he found himself staring into the face he'd dreamed of for the past three weeks.

"Night Wind," Dee-Dee said in a breathless whisper. She lifted one hand to touch his cheek. "I feared I might never see you again."

He placed his fingers over hers, then turned his head to press a kiss on the cool skin of her palm. "I am here now, *shijei*." Not releasing her hand, he lowered their laced fingers and held them against his chest. "My horse is not far from here. Let's ride to someplace where we can talk."

She nodded, swallowing hard. Tears started to fill her eyes, but she resolutely blinked them away. She would not spend her last moments with Night Wind crying; there would be time to cry an ocean of tears on the trip back to New York.

"You're welcome to stay here," Jade said. "Eli and I can go for a walk so you can talk in private."

Night Wind never took his gaze off of Dee-Dee. "Thank you, *shila*, but we would prefer to go into the mountains. Is that not so, Dee-Dee?"

"Yes, the mountains," she replied, knowing she would forever associate the mountains with this man—a man who possessed the same wild spirit, unique beauty and unwavering strength.

Dee-Dee turned to look at Jade. "Thank you for all you've done. And I do hope you'll write to me."

After the two women shared a quick hug, Night Wind pulled Dee-Dee back to his side. As the couple walked away, Jade joined Eli in the open doorway. She watched until well after their shadowy forms melted into the night. Finally, she sighed, then took a step back and closed the door.

Night Wind held Dee-Dee across his thighs until they reached a small clearing in the mountains. Lifting her off his lap, he shifted her position so she could slide to the ground. He dismounted then untied a blanket from behind his saddle.

After spreading the blanket on a rock-free patch of earth, he sat down and patted the spot beside him. "Come, sit, *shijei*. Tell me what happened."

Dee-Dee eased down next to him. After composing her thoughts, she began speaking. She told him about Dr. Chadbourne's visit to the Fryman home, and their confronting her with the doctor's allegations. She concluded by saying, "When I admitted Dr. Chadbourne's information was correct, Uncle Phillip insisted it would be best for me to cut my visit short, so I'll be leaving on tomorrow's stage."

"Did you not try to convince them to let you stay?"

"I might have been able to convince Aunt Amelia, but as for Uncle Phillip, well, I doubt there's anything I could've said that would have changed his mind. Besides, after I thought about their decision, I came to the conclusion that they were right." Feeling him stiffen beside her, she said, "Night Wind, the only reason I agreed to leave now was because I didn't want anything to happen to you."

"I am not afraid of your uncle, or any of the other blue-coats."

"I know you're not. Your bravery is one of the things I love about you, but if I stayed, I'd continue meeting you whenever possible. And that would mean greater danger for you." She turned to stare into his face, his features barely visible in the pale silver light provided by the rising moon. "Night Wind, I couldn't live with myself if you were to suffer injury or even death because of my selfishly wanting to see you for a few more weeks. Please tell me you understand that."

He didn't respond for a moment, then he finally exhaled with a sigh. "I would give my life to protect you. So, yes, I understand."

Dee-Dee released her held-breath, willing the fear-induced pounding of her heart to slow. "Then you're not angry with me?"

"No, I am not angry," he said, shifting their positions until she sat between his legs, her back resting against his chest. He nuzzled her hair, inhaling deeply to fill his lungs with her scent. "Did you mean what you said a moment ago?"

"I meant everything I said."

"Then you do love me?"

Dee-Dee's vision blurred, a lump wedged in her throat. "Yes," she finally replied in a raspy whisper.

He wrapped his arms around her in a fierce hug. "You have stolen my heart as well." He fell silent for a moment, then said, "Come away with me, Dee-Dee. Tonight."

She drew a ragged breath before answering him. "You know that isn't possible." Feeling his muscles go rigid against her back, she said, "In your heart, you know there's no future for us. Our worlds are too different. You would undoubtedly hate New York, and though I love the mountains, I'm not sure I could be happy living here." She sighed. "It's so unfair, my meeting a man like you and falling in love, only to face the rest of my life without you. I wish that weren't the case, but that's how it must be. You know I'm speaking the truth, don't you, Night Wind?"

Several minutes passed before he spoke. "Some of your words are not true. If the ways of the *Nde* weren't still being threatened by the White Eyes, we could be together. Other men among my people have taken wives who were not *Nde*, women from different ways of life. They have all lived happy, long lives together, as I know we would." He blew out a long breath. "But with so much uncertainty about what lies ahead for my people, you are right to say there can be no future for us."

Dee-Dee closed her eyes against the pain ripping through her chest. She'd come to West Texas not only to visit her aunt and uncle, but also for the excitement and the adventure of traveling to such a wild and remote area. Who would have guessed the outcome of her trip would be a lifetime of heartache?

She willed her mind away from that painful thought. "I'm so relieved Jade was able to get word to you. If I hadn't gotten a chance to see you, this would have been the longest night of my life."

He chuckled, the husky sound igniting a firestorm of desire low in her belly. "If you would like, this can still be the longest night of your life," he said, trailing soft kisses down the side of her neck, then to the underside of her jaw. "What do you think, *shijei?*"

She shivered, not from a chill, but from a fiery need singing in her veins. Turning in his arms, she brought her mouth closer to his. "Yes, Night Wind," she whispered against his lips. "Make this night last forever."

Chapter 21

As the stagecoach pulled away from Fort Davis Friday afternoon, Dee-Dee was the only passenger. Grateful to be traveling alone, at least on the first leg of her journey, she sat next to the window, her gaze glued to the mountains she had resigned herself to never seeing again. She should be exhausted, since she'd gotten only a few hours' sleep the night before, but strangely she wasn't.

She smiled, remembering again the hours she'd spent with Night Wind. He truly had made her last night in West Texas a memorable one. They had kissed and touched until she thought she would lose her mind if Night Wind didn't make her his completely. Dee-Dee shifted on the seat, her tired muscles protesting the movement. Yet in spite of her fatigue, recalling the moment Night Wind claimed her as his own fired another round of delicious heat shooting through her body. In vivid clarity, she remembered how his initial gentle lovemaking had given way to faster, more powerful thrusts until she'd convulsed in spasm after spasm of the most incredible release she'd ever known. A heartbeat later, his climax followed hers.

As he thrust into her one final time, his head thrown back, muscles corded with strain, chest heaving with exertion, he cried out her name. Those moments would remain a treasured memory until her dying breath.

Though the thought of spending the rest of her life without Night Wind should have brought more tears, she remained dry-eyed. The last of her tears had been shed after saying her final goodbye to Night Wind. Just before dawn, he'd made love to her again then insisted on escorting her back to the fort. Her arguments that going to the military post would be too dangerous were ignored. His only concession was to take her only as far as the trees where she'd met Jade earlier. After one final kiss, she somehow managed to wrench herself away from Night Wind then run to her uncle's quarters and slip back through her bedroom window.

From inside her room, she waited and watched from her window, her heart pounding with fear. But when no shout of alarm came after several long minutes, she allowed herself to breathe easier. She changed into her nightdress, then sank onto her bed, curled into a ball and cried herself to sleep.

Dee-Dee was brought back to the present by a swirl of wind buffeting the stagecoach and whipping the rolled curtain at the window. The wind tugged at her hat, pulling a lock of her hair free of its pins. Reaching up to smooth the hair back into place, her fingers encountered the strand's ragged ends. She bit her lip to hold in a sob.

Before she and Night Wind left the mountains to return to the fort, he asked for a piece of her hair to put in the medicine pouch he wore around his neck. She hadn't hesitated to grant his request. After using his knife to cut off two inches from a thick strand, he reverently kissed the hair before tucking it inside the buckskin pouch. "Now I can carry a part of you with me always," he'd told her. "Just as you will always be in my heart."

Since Night Wind had explained that each *Nde* kept

items of special, personal significance in his medicine pouch, the meaning of his actions touched her more deeply than she would have thought possible and made leaving him even more painful.

Though she'd thought she had no tears left, she was wrong. Hot, scalding tears filled her eyes and quickly overflowed. Her gaze still riveted on the beautiful mountains, she prayed for Night Wind's safety, her tears running unchecked in tribute to lost love.

Night Wind sat in the rocks high in the mountains, watching the floor of the valley far below. He'd been sitting in the same spot since just after dawn and finally his long wait was about to end. The stagecoach with an escort of soldiers from the fort came into view, working their way in his direction on the winding road. As the coach moved directly below him, he caught a flash of pale golden hair in the window. A pain like none he'd ever experienced ripped through his chest.

When he could no longer see the stagecoach, he got to his feet. Clutching his medicine pouch in one hand, he lifted his face to the sky. His eyes glazed with a sheen of tears, the surrounding rocks rang with his howling cries of anguish.

Jade and Eli bid Rafe and Karina goodbye early Saturday morning, then watched them ride out of town from the yard in front of her house.

"I'll miss Zita," Jade said. "I'm sure she sensed something was going on, but she still didn't understand why I made her go with Mama and Papa."

Eli nodded. "I'll miss her, too." He glanced around at the reddish brown mountains, then at the incredible deep blue of the sky. Frowning, he realized he was going to miss a lot more than Jade's dog once they left for Tennessee.

"It's going to be lonely around here now that everyone has gone," Jade said. "First Dee-Dee and Night Wind, now Zita and my parents."

Eli was quiet for a minute, then said, "Do you have any idea where Night Wind might go?"

Jade sighed, thinking about her cousin's surprise visit the night before. Looking haggard, his eyes haunted and his usual vitality subdued, Night Wind wanted her to know he was going away for a while and asked if she'd send word to his parents. "I don't know," Jade finally said. "Mexico, maybe."

Eli slipped an arm around her waist and pulled her against him. For the first time since he'd received his mother's letter, she didn't protest his touch or their closeness. "He's hurting, but he's young and resilient, so he'll bounce back. Right now, he just needs some time alone to heal his wounds."

Though Jade nodded, she wasn't so sure any amount of time would heal both a heart and a spirit broken as severely as Night Wind's. Offering a quick prayer for both her cousin's recovery and that her fate wouldn't be the same as his, she stepped away from Eli and headed for the front door.

Saturday passed quickly, with Jade spending the remainder of the day making final visits to the people she had treated in town. Then on Sunday, she borrowed a horse and rode out to see Paloma.

As usual the old woman didn't seem surprised at her arrival. "What news do you bring me, *chica?*" she said once they were seated in her hut.

"I don't know where to begin, *maestra,*" Jade replied. "So much has happened since I was last here."

"*Sí.* Why don't you begin with what is troubling you."

Jade smiled. "How do you always know when something's bothering me?"

Paloma gave a cackle of laughter. "The way you walk. The look in your eyes. Your voice. All those things tell me if you are well or if something troubles you. Now, talk to me, *chica,* and maybe you will feel better."

This time Jade's smile was bittersweet. "I doubt it, but I'll tell you anyway." She cleared her throat then began talking, telling her teacher and friend everything that had happened since her previous visit. As she'd done with her mother, she spared nothing and told all there was to tell. She ended her recitation with, "I told Eli I don't want to give up being a healer, but what if I have to make a choice? What if I have to choose between my love for him and remaining a healer?" She swallowed hard. "I don't know if I could make that decision."

Paloma was silent for several minutes. Finally she said, "I was so certain this Anglo would be your *esposo,* but now I do not know if there is a future for the two of you. You are right to go with him, *chica.* That is the only way to find out. Do not worry about making a decision. If the time comes when you must choose, you will have the strength to make the choice which is best for you."

The old woman shrugged. "And as you said, if you two are not meant to be together, at least you will have traveled to new and interesting places and visited a real Anglo hospital. Now, I want you to stop thinking such troubling thoughts. Remember, *Señor* Kinmont said he wants you to go with him because you are the one he loves." She pinned her narrowed gaze on Jade's face. "You do not doubt his word, do you?"

Jade stared at where she held her hands clasped in her lap. "No, I believe he loves me. Now. But he's also still married to Nora, and I'm afraid when we get to Tennessee, he'll see her and realize . . ." Her voice cracked. ". . . she's the one he really loves, the one he wants to be with for the rest of his life."

"Do not feel sorry for yourself," Paloma said in a stern whisper. "It is true you are faced with enormous problems, but do not give up hope. One must never give up hope, *bueno?*"

Jade drew a shaky breath, then nodded. "I will try, *maestra.*"

The following morning, Jade woke with a jumble of conflicting emotions roiling inside her: Excitement over her coming trip, sadness to be leaving everything she knew and fear about what would happen once she arrived in Tennessee. Trying to concentrate on only the positive, she rose, bathed and dressed.

After Eli headed to the post trader to sell the animal pelts he'd collected before his accident in the mountains, she washed their breakfast dishes then gave her house a final cleaning. When her chores were finished, she packed her meager wardrobe and the buckskin bag containing her herbal remedies into a leather satchel.

The morning passed quickly, and before she was aware of the passage of time, Eli said they had to leave.

She checked each room of her home again to make sure she hadn't overlooked anything, then picked up her satchel and joined Eli outside. Closing the door behind her, she didn't move for a moment. Her gaze sweeping the area, she tried to commit everything about the surrounding scenery to memory. Would this be the last time she'd stand in front of the house her father had built for her? Or the last time she'd look at the mountains she loved so much?

Eli understood Jade's hesitation and gave her as much time as he could. Finally, in a gentle voice, he said, "Come on, Jade. The stage will be arriving soon."

His voice pulled her back to the present. Nodding, she turned and fell into step beside him. As they walked to the stagecoach station, she tried to focus her thoughts on what lay ahead. She loved the man walking next to her, so she had to make the trip with him. If she changed her mind now, she would always wonder whether the outcome would've been different if she had gone. But could she actually board the stage not knowing if or when she might return? That thought brought her chin up. The blood of many generations of proud *Nde* ran through her veins. She would not be a coward; she would be strong.

Half an hour later, Eli helped her up into the stagecoach, then climbed in and sat down beside her. One other passenger boarded the stagecoach, a portly, middle-aged whiskey drummer with a bulbous nose and a curling black moustache. Once all the luggage had been stowed, the coach dipped as the driver and guard climbed up and took their seats.

Jade heard the stamping of horses' hooves and the jingle of their harnesses, the driver shouting to the army escort, then for the team to "giddap there." With the groaning of wood and the creaking of leather, the coach lurched forward. Grabbing the edge of the seat with both hands, she tried to calm the wild pounding of her heart. Her long journey—a journey to begin a new phase of her life—had finally begun.

Traveling by stagecoach proved to be both grueling and exhausting for Jade and Eli. The days took on a weary sameness, that thankfully ended with their arrival at Indianola more than two weeks later. From the Texas port city, they bought passage on a steamship bound for New Orleans.

At first Jade was apprehensive about traveling via ship. But after getting used to the gentle rocking motion, she found the salt air invigorating, the tranquility of the Gulf of Mexico taking the edge off her nervousness.

In New Orleans, they learned the next northbound train on the Nashville and Decatur Railroad wasn't scheduled to depart for several days, so Eli made arrangements for them to stay in a suite of rooms in a nearby hotel. Since they had no choice except to wait before beginning the final leg of their trip, Eli made use of the time by ordering himself some new clothes.

Compared to his buckskin trousers and loose-fitting cotton shirts, the tighter-fitting dress shirts and cumbersome suits were decidedly uncomfortable. Trying to ignore the pinching of his buttoned wing collar, he examined his image in the tailor shop's mirror. The sack coat and matching trousers fit well enough, he supposed, though he didn't care for the coat's wider and longer lapels. A lot more than the style of men's clothes had changed in the past six years, he mused, already having witnessed some of those changes in New Orleans. So far, he'd seen little to make him want to stay in a city. He frowned at the direction of his thoughts, then turned away from the mirror. After paying the tailor, he picked up two packages—one containing his old clothes, the other the rest of his new wardrobe—then headed back to the hotel.

When Eli entered the sitting room of their suite, Jade blinked with surprise at his new appearance. Gone was the rugged trapper she'd first met, the man who lived a hard, solitary life in the wilderness of West Texas. Instead, a sophisticated Southern gentleman stood before her—a man who lived a genteel life in a modern eastern city. Pushing aside the significance of her observations, she finally said, "I barely recognize you."

"Yes, I know," he replied, looking down at himself. "Quite a change."

When Jade didn't say any more, he said, "There's still time to get you some new dresses before we board our train tomorrow." She'd already turned down his offer once, but he thought he'd ask again. "We won't be able to hire a seamstress, but I'm sure we could find a ready-made that would—"

"I told you, I don't want any new clothes," she said more sharply than she intended. "Thank you again for the offer, but I'll wear what I brought with me." Seeing his frown, her chin came up. "Aren't my clothes good enough for you to be seen with me, is that why you keep hounding me to buy a new dress?"

"Of course not. I'd be proud to be seen with you no matter what you were wearing." His frown deepened. "And I wasn't hounding you. I just thought you might like to have something new. Most women would jump at the chance to get a new dress."

"I'm not most women."

He studied her in silence for a moment. "No, you're not."

Jade wasn't sure how he'd meant his response. Unable to bear his stare for fear she'd see her shortcomings reflected on his face, she dropped her gaze.

After another long pause, he finally said, "I'm sorry I brought up the subject. It won't happen again." With that he turned on his heel and headed toward the door to his bedroom.

"Eli, wait." He stopped but kept his back to her. "I'm sorry. I really do appreciate your offer, but I just can't accept."

He slowly turned and met her gaze. As he silently scrutinized her face, the hardness in his jaw slowly relaxed. "How about taking a walk along the levee after supper?"

She gave him a tremulous smile. "Yes, I'd like that."

After dining in one of New Orleans' best restaurants, they strolled arm in arm along the levee, enjoying the breeze off the river before returning to their hotel. For Jade, only one thing could have made their evening more enjoyable, something she couldn't allow to happen: spending the night in Eli's arms. She'd made her position clear on that issue after learning his wife was still alive, and not once had he hinted at reverting to their previous sleeping arrangements. Yet sometimes the heated look in his eyes told her he wouldn't push her away if she went to him at night.

His whispered good night pulled Jade out of her musings. She turned to see him enter his room, then heard the soft click of the door closing. She longed to follow him, to beg him to stoke the desire he roused so easily in her, to guide her to that magic moment of completion. With a shuddering sigh, she halted her torturous thoughts and turned toward the opposite side of the sitting room, toward her own bedroom. In spite of Eli's professions of love, he was still a married man, and therefore she refused to share his bed.

A few days later, Jade and Eli neared the completion of their journey on the Nashville and Decatur Railroad. As they waited for the train to pull into the depot, Jade could sense the anticipation in Eli. Anticipation filled her as well. But she felt certain the reasons for her damp palms, fluttering stomach and quickened pulse bore no resemblance to his.

Before she had time to fully compose herself, she and Eli had gotten off the train, climbed into a hackney coach and arrived in front of an elegant two-story brick home.

Jade looked up at the house and swallowed. "This is where you lived?"

He nodded. "My mother, sisters and I moved here a few years after my father passed away. It's been the family home ever since." He paid the hackney driver, jumped to the ground then assisted Jade from the carriage.

"Come on," he said, picking up their luggage and starting toward the front door. "I want you to meet my mother."

When Jade made no move to follow him, he retraced his steps. Seeing the panic on her face, he touched her cheek with the back of his hand. "Don't worry, *roja*," he said with a smile. "My mother won't bite." Giving her chin a gentle tap with a knuckle, he added, "Her fine Southern upbringing would never allow such vulgar behavior."

In spite of her jangled nerves, she returned his smile. "I wasn't worried your mother might bite me. I was—"

Realizing she had nearly voiced the fears she was trying hard to control, she cleared her throat. "It wasn't important." Giving him a gentle push toward the house, she said, "Get a move on. I know you're anxious to see her."

Eli opened the front door and stepped inside the foyer. As he straightened from setting their luggage on the floor, a petite woman, wearing a long white apron over her black dress, a white cap sitting atop her carrot-colored hair, appeared on the opposite end of the long foyer. "Here now, what are ye doing?" She bustled toward them. "Coming inta this house like ye owns the place?"

"Where's Clarissa?" Eli said, his eyebrows pulled together in a frown.

"Mrs. Billington passed on three years ago. Did ye know her?"

"Yes," Eli replied, saddened to hear he would no longer be able to tease the housekeeper he'd known since his boyhood. "Did you take her place?"

"Aye. Mrs. Kinmont hired me a month after Mrs. Billington's passing. That's enough prattle about me. Now, answer my question, if ye please." She placed her hands on her well-rounded hips. "What are the two of ye doing sneaking inta this house?"

Eli bit back a chuckle at the woman's no-nonsense tone. "Yes, ma'am. I'm Eli Kinmont, Mrs. Kinmont's son."

"Great heavenly days, she'll be so glad to see ye! Yer all she's talked of for weeks now." Lifting the hem of her skirt, she started to turn. "I'll go tell her yer here."

"No, wait, Miss . . . ?"

She stopped and turned back to face Eli. "McCormick. Maire McCormick."

"If you don't mind, Miss McCormick, I'd like to surprise my mother."

A wide smile appeared on the woman's face. "Aye, that's a lovely idea. Ye'll find Mrs. Kinmont in the back parlor."

Eli nodded, then turned to take Jade's hand. When she pulled away from him, his eyebrows lifted in question.

Jade didn't reply until the housekeeper disappeared into another room. "Maybe I should wait here," she said, suddenly uncertain about the reception she'd receive from Mrs. Kinmont.

"Don't be silly. I want you to meet Mama."

"But maybe she won't want to meet me," she replied in a low voice.

"Why would she—?" His eyes widened. "Ah, I see. You're concerned about what Mama will think of her married son returning with another woman in tow?" When Jade nodded, he said, "Don't worry, *roja*, she'll understand."

Jade wasn't so certain, but since she'd already spent more than three weeks traveling to Eli's home, she wasn't ready to give up yet. She took a deep breath, then lifted her gaze to his. "Okay, let's go."

He flashed her a dazzling smile. Holding her hand firmly in his, he started across the foyer.

Eli found his mother exactly where the housekeeper indicated, working at her small desk in the back parlor. He studied her from the doorway for a moment. She looked much like she had the last time he'd seen her, though her dark blond hair had more silver and her face a few more lines than he remembered.

When Jade pulled her hand from his, he opened his mouth to protest, but her whispered, "You two should have a moment alone," halted his objection.

He looked back at his mother, then stepped into the room. "Hello, Mama."

Olivia Kinmont's head jerked up. Her startled expression instantly changed to unmistakable joy. "Eli!" Pulling off her spectacles and tossing them aside, she rose and moved around her desk to meet him in the center of the room. She stared up at him, her eyes filling with tears. Lifting a trembling hand to touch his cheek, she said, "I can't believe you're finally here." After giving him a fierce hug, she took a step back. "Let me get a better look at you."

She studied him for a long moment. "You look wonderful, son. The best I've ever seen you."

"And you're looking fine, as well, Mama."

"As slick as a puppy's belly," she replied with a smile.

He chuckled. "Indeed." He gave her casual chignon a gentle pat. "But I believe I detect a bit more silver among the gold."

"Yes," she replied, batting his hand away. "And I've earned every one of my gray hairs these last six years."

His amusement fled. "I'm sorry I worried you, Mama."

Her eyes, so similar in color to the dark blue of his, shone with love. "Well, you're home now. That's all that matters. Your sisters aren't going to believe you're actually here. Which reminds me, why didn't you send word you were coming?" She gave him a playful swat on the arm. "Then I could've sent someone to meet you."

"I know, but I wasn't sure when we'd arrive."

Her thin eyebrows arched. "We?"

Eli moved back to the door and pulled Jade into the room. "Mama, I'd like you to meet Jade Tucker. She's an herbalist and midwife from Texas." He turned to Jade and gave her an encouraging smile. "Jade, this is my mother, Olivia Kinmont."

After Jade exchanged an awkward, though cordial greeting with Eli's mother, Mrs. Kinmont said, "Did you come here because of your interest in healing? The University of Nashville has a fine Medical College. The students there work closely with the doctors at St. Vincent's Hospital."

Jade cast a quick glance at Eli, then said, "I'm anxious to see the workings of a modern hospital. Your son has kindly offered to arrange for me to take a tour."

Olivia's gaze moved back and forth between Jade and her son, her brow furrowing. Based on the looks the two exchanged, she knew there had to be more than a hospital tour between them. Wondering if the situation could get any more complicated than it already was, she said, "I think we'd better sit down and have a talk."

Eli motioned for Jade to take a seat on a small brocade sofa, then sat down beside her. His mother returned to her chair behind her desk.

Olivia stared pensively at her son for a moment before speaking. "Eli, I didn't tell Nora about your letter until two weeks ago." Seeing his surprised expression, she said, "Believe me, dear, I had good reason. Telling her sooner could have caused . . . well, dire consequences."

"What do you mean, 'dire consequences'?"

She exhaled with a sigh. "When your letter arrived, I was afraid the stress of learning you were alive would cause Nora's baby to come too soon. Being a doctor, you know an early birth could have resulted in the death of the baby, or Nora, or even both of them. I couldn't bear to have that on my conscience, so I waited until after her lying-in before telling her about your letter. Even then I was concerned that—"

"Stop," Eli said, shaking his head. "Mama, you're not making any sense. Are you telling me Nora had a baby?"

Olivia nodded, then rubbed her temples with her fingertips. "Gracious me, I'm making a horrible muddle of this." She took a deep breath, then met her son's confused gaze. "Eli, a year ago this past March, Nora married Harrison Rawlings."

Chapter 22

Eli slumped against the back of the sofa, stunned by his mother's announcement. The possibility of Nora marrying had never occurred to him. He scowled. Now that he thought about the situation, he wouldn't have expected Nora to spend the rest of her life alone, pining away for him. In fact, he was glad she'd found someone else—not just because it should simplify his own circumstances, but also because he truly did want Nora to be happy. Still, there had to be legal ramifications to all of this. His mother's voice pulled him from his musings.

"Nora was understandably concerned about marrying again, so she and Harrison consulted with a lawyer before going ahead with their wedding. They were assured their marriage would be legal. I don't know the particulars, but I believe it had something to do with there being good reason to believe you were dead."

Eli clenched his hands into fists atop his thighs and blew out a weary breath. "Great, now I show up, alive and well."

Jade curled her fingers over one of his tight fists. "Don't blame yourself, Eli. You didn't know."

He turned to stare into her silver-flecked eyes. "But I could have. You know that. You were the one who couldn't believe I hadn't written to my family since I left the army. The one who made me realize I should let them know I was alive." Squeezing his eyes closed for a moment, he whispered, "If I'd only written sooner, this wouldn't be happening."

"Eli," Olivia said. "I won't pretend to know what your return means from a legal standpoint. But if you've come back thinking you and Nora can just go on with your lives as if these past six years never happened, you'd better think again. Nora and Harrison are deeply in love. And now with the baby, Harrison will stop at nothing to keep his wife and son."

Jade waited for Eli to respond, every muscle tense, her heart pounding so hard against her eardrums she could barely hear.

"The first thing I have to do is talk to Nora," he said, pushing to his feet. "If you'll tell me where she lives, I'll go see her right now."

"I'll tell you, son. But it won't do any good. Harrison and Nora are in Murfreesboro visiting some of his family. They won't be back until the end of next week."

Eli rubbed the back of his neck, trying to ward off the beginnings of a headache. "Then I'll make sure I see her as soon as they return."

Jade squeezed her eyes closed for a moment, trying to calm her racing heart. Eli's response had given her no clue as to his intentions, and the end of the next week seemed an eternity away.

Olivia noticed the misery in Jade's expression and knew her instincts had been correct. There was something between this lovely young woman and her son, at least on Jade's part. Glancing up at Eli, she wondered if he was aware of Jade's feelings. Knowing her son had to sort out his life on his own, she decided to keep her observations to herself—at least for the time being.

"Eli," Olivia said, rising from her chair. "Why don't you show Jade to Emma's old room while I send word to your sisters. Then I need to talk to Cook about tonight's menu." She flashed a brilliant smile. "I can't wait to have the entire family back together again. We'll talk more later, dear."

Eli kissed his mother's cheek before she left the room, then turned to Jade. Noting her pensive expression, he said, "Are you all right?"

Jade's gaze met his. "Yes," she said, "I'm fine."

"Come with me and I'll take you upstairs. Since you didn't get to see much of Nashville on the ride from the depot, how about if I show you more of the city later this afternoon?"

She managed a smile. "I'd like that."

After taking a quick sponge bath and unpacking her belongings, Jade left her room and headed back downstairs. She could hear muffled voices coming from behind the closed door of the back parlor, so she reversed direction. There were a number of rooms off the hallway, so whenever she found an open door, she stepped inside to explore. With each elegantly furnished room, her spirits sank a little lower.

Eli's return to such affluence would remind him of everything he'd missed during the past six years, and in the process, make her small adobe home in Texas less and less appealing. Sighing, she knew he would soon forget about Fort Davis, forget about being a trapper in the Davis Mountains, and most painful of all, he'd forget about her.

She had just returned to the foyer, intending to go back upstairs, when she heard the door of the back parlor open. Turning to look down the hall, she saw Eli and Olivia in the doorway. After a moment, Eli turned toward the front of the house and Olivia went in the opposite direction.

As Eli came closer, Jade could see the hard set to his jaw, the way the corners of his mouth turned down. Spotting her in the foyer, his grim expression softened.

"Ready for our carriage ride?" he said, coming to a halt beside her.

She nodded, then before he turned away, she placed a hand on his forearm. "Is everything okay?"

He looked startled by her question. "I . . . uh . . . thought I should tell Mama about leaving the army."

"And?"

"She cried." The muscles of his jaw worked. "I wish I could have saved her that pain, but like she said, that's in the past now."

"And she doesn't think you're a coward, does she?"

He smiled, though it didn't quite reach his eyes. "No. She said almost the exact same things you told me. About my not being the only soldier to desert, and doing what I thought was best under the circumstances." He stared down at her for a long time, but before he said anything more, she spoke.

"If we're going for a carriage ride, we should get going."

Eli nodded, then motioned toward the door. "Right this way."

Eli declined the use of his mother's driver, electing to take the carriage out himself. Though the air was extremely hot and heavy—not the cool, dry air in the mountains of West Texas—Jade still enjoyed sitting beside Eli and listening to him explain the many sites of Nashville. His six-year absence had brought numerous changes in the city, so many of the buildings were new to him as well. Before they started back, he took her past the University of Nashville and St. Vincent's Hospital.

When Eli slowed the carriage in front of the hospital, he saw Jade's eyes light up. "I'll ask Mama who's in charge of St. Vincent's, then I'll make arrangements to take you on a tour."

Jade nodded, her gaze still fastened on the three-story brick building.

A few minutes later, they returned to the Kinmont home

to find several other carriages in the yard. Jade drew an unsteady breath, knowing Eli's sisters must have arrived.

Eli jumped from the carriage, then turned to Jade. As he placed his hands around her waist and lifted her down, he longed to pull her into his arms but forced himself to release her once her feet touched the ground. Watching her fuss with her hair, which she'd pulled up into a loose knot at the back of her head, he smiled then whispered, "You look beautiful."

She started, then looked up at him. Remembering the women she'd seen at the train depot and on the streets of Nashville, she said, "You don't have to say that, Eli. I saw how the women here dress, how they arrange their hair, and I know I don't compare with them."

Before Eli could respond, she brushed past him and headed for the house. His eyebrows pulled together, he stared after her. *That's where you're wrong,* roja. *You not only compare, you outshine them all.*

He entered the front door a few seconds after Jade, just in time to see her hurrying up the staircase. He paused at the foot of the stairs, wondering if he should go after her, if he should try to convince her how—

A feminine squeal of delight—a sound he would recognize anywhere—brought his wonderings to a halt.

He turned, a smile on his face. In the door to the front parlor stood his youngest sister Emma, eyes glittering and a huge grin on her pixieish face. Noting her mussed blond hair and rumpled skirt, he said, "Well, I see some things never change. Still disheveled as ever. Right, brat?"

Emma's grin slipped for a moment. "Don't call me that, Eli. I'm a wife and a mother now."

"That's what Mama said. I can't imagine you in either role; you'll always be brat to me."

With another squeal, Emma raced across the foyer and threw herself into Eli's arms. He hugged her close for a second, then held her away from him to look into blue eyes a few shades lighter than his. "I missed you, Emma," he said.

"I missed you, too," she said, her fingers smoothing the lapel of his coat. "Mama told us what happened to you, Eli. I wish there hadn't been any old war, then you wouldn't have joined the army or gone through all those miserable years alone."

He stroked a hand through her wild tangle of hair. "It's okay, brat. I'm here now." After a moment he said, "Will you forgive me for not letting you know I was all right?"

Before she could reply, a voice answered from the door of the parlor. "Emma might forgive you, but I'm not so sure I will."

Eli shifted his gaze to look into the solemn face of his sister Caroline, four years younger than himself and two years older than Emma. "Hello, Caro," he said, releasing his hold on Emma. "Aren't you going to give me a hug?"

She didn't move for a moment, then finally crossed the foyer and stopped in front of him. "I meant what I said, Eli, I'm not sure I can forgive you for what you put us through."

Eli could see the pain and anger reflected in Caroline's hazel eyes, in the harsh line of her mouth. The opposite of their younger sister, Caroline was a picture of female elegance, always perfectly dressed, every hair neatly in place. "I won't ask you to forgive me, Caro, but I hope someday you'll at least understand."

She continued to stare up at him for several long seconds, then finally the stiffness of her posture relaxed slightly. "Oh, all right, give me a hug."

Eli pulled her into his arms, then lifted her off her feet and swung her in circles. As he whirled past Emma, he grinned at her and she grinned back. They both knew what was coming.

"Eli, for heaven's sake," Caroline said. "I'm not a child. Now put me down. You're wrinkling my dress."

He complied, letting her regain her footing before

removing his arms. "Still worried about appearances, I see."

"And what's wrong with acting like a lady?" she said in a sharp voice, checking to make sure the hairpins hadn't slipped from the intricate arrangement of her light brown hair. "That's certainly better than behaving like some ill-bred hoyden."

"You just had to throw in that last remark, didn't you, Caroline?" Emma said, hands fisted on her hips.

Caroline turned a cool gaze on her sister. "If the cap fits, Emma dear."

"Why you!" Emma launched herself at her older sister, and nearly succeeded in landing a punch before Eli stepped between the two.

"Settle down, brat," he said, grabbing her from behind and pinning her arms to her sides. "I thought by now you would've gotten over letting Caro's goading get you all riled up."

After a moment, she exhaled heavily then went limp against him. "I have, mostly. But sometimes she still makes me so huffy-mad."

He chuckled, then said, "I'm going to let you go, then all three of us are going into the parlor and act like adults. Is that understood?"

He waited until both sisters agreed before releasing Emma. He straightened his coat and tie, then offered an arm to each sister. As if nothing untoward had just taken place, the three of them entered the parlor.

After he greeted his mother and was introduced to his brothers-in-law, Olivia said, "Where's Jade?"

"Upstairs. She'll be down soon."

The words had barely left Eli's mouth when he glanced up to see Jade standing in the doorway. Looking like a rabbit cornered by a coyote, she took a tentative step over the threshold. Eli excused himself and went to rescue Jade. The relief on her face wrenched his heart, the need to kiss her nearly overwhelming. Giving her an encouraging smile, he tucked her arm through his, then led her into the room.

He stopped a few feet from the others and waited for the room to grow quiet. "Everyone," he said. "This is Jade Tucker."

Eli noticed Caroline's eyebrows lift at Jade's clothes—a matching cream-colored skirt and blouse in the simple style she preferred. But otherwise, his family greeted Jade as warmly as they would have any other guest.

Once the introductions had been completed, Olivia said, "Jade is an herbalist and midwife. Eli says she's a fine healer."

"Are you planning to open a practice in Nashville?" Emma said.

Jade looked at Eli's youngest sister. "I haven't decided."

"Well, I hope you do," Emma replied, then dropped her voice to a whisper. "Some of the doctors in town have such antiquated ideas about female problems."

Jade bit the inside of her cheek to hold in a chuckle, feeling an immediate camaraderie with Emma. "I'll think about it."

"Good," Emma said. "I know there are others besides myself who would make use of your services."

As the evening wore on, Jade's initial nervousness eased and she was able to enjoy the time with Eli's family. While every one of them was openly friendly, always included her in their conversations and never made her feel out of place, she knew the truth. She didn't belong in a big city. She didn't fit into such an opulent lifestyle. But Eli did.

During the following week, Eli took Jade to see more of the city's sites. They visited the Horticultural Gardens, City Park and the Race Course. Sometimes they would just go for a carriage ride through more of the mansion-lined streets of the suburban areas on the south side of town, along the Cumberland River, or where Jade enjoyed most, into the Tennessee countryside with its beautiful bluegrass meadows. Away from the city and its oppressive buildings and crowded streets, the air was cleaner, the openness easing her feeling of being hemmed in.

Jade sat beside Eli on one such carriage ride, her thoughts drifting to a conversation she'd had with Olivia Kinmont that morning. Eli had gone to pay a call on Dr. Briggs, the man in charge of St. Vincent's, and Jade had offered to help his mother weed her flower garden while the air was still relatively cool.

After they worked side by side for a time, Olivia had said, "It just occurred to me that I've never thanked you for convincing Eli to write me. I should have told you before now, but we've all been so busy since he came home."

Home. A lump formed in Jade's throat. Yes, Eli had come home. Ignoring the pain that thought caused, she said, "Thanks aren't necessary, Mrs. Kinmont. I made the suggestion, but he's the one who decided to write you."

"Regardless, I'm grateful for your help."

When Jade nodded but didn't say any more, Olivia looked over at her from beneath the wide brim of her hat. "May I ask you something, Jade?"

"Yes, of course."

"Do you love my son?" At Jade's startled expression, she said, "I know you must be thinking I'm just a nosy old biddy, but I see how you look at Eli, and I just wondered if my impression was right."

Jade swallowed hard, but couldn't get any words through her tight throat.

Olivia removed one of her gloves then laid her hand atop Jade's. "That's okay, dear. I shouldn't have asked. But in case Eli hasn't told you, I'm certain he loves you." Pursing her mouth in a thoughtful moue, she said more to herself, "I don't recall ever seeing him look at Nora that way."

"But surely he loved her?" Jade said in a neutral voice.

"Oh, I'm sure he did," Olivia replied, pulling her glove back on. "But not the way I suspect he loves you."

As the women finished weeding the flower bed, they lapsed into silence, Jade's mind whirling with Olivia's comments. Knowing Olivia thought Eli loved her more than he loved Nora was a definite balm to her aching heart. Still, the knowledge didn't entirely erase her uneasiness about the future.

That night Jade didn't sleep well. She tossed and turned, her too few periods of sound sleep interrupted by disjointed dreams—images of Dee-Dee's tear-streaked face, Night Wind's haunted eyes and Eli sitting beside a dark-haired woman she didn't recognize. She finally gave up on sleeping and rose to stare out the window at the blue black sky. As Saturday's rising sun cast its golden pink net over the city, she was still standing at the window.

Would this be the day she'd learn Eli's intentions? Nora and her husband had returned to Nashville the night before, and Eli was planning to meet with them later that morning. A sudden chill sent a shiver up her spine. Hoping that wasn't a bad omen, she released a shuddering breath, then turned to prepare herself to face the day.

Since Nora and her husband lived only a few blocks from the Kinmont home, Eli chose to make the trip on foot. He was shown to the parlor by Nora's housekeeper and informed Mrs. Rawlings would join him shortly.

The sound of footsteps in the hall ended his contemplation of a photograph of Nora and a tall blond man. Replacing the picture on the mantel, he turned to find Nora staring at him. As she moved closer, he saw the panic she was trying to hold at bay in her brown eyes and the lines around her full mouth.

"Hello, Nora."

"Hello, Eli," she replied, taking a seat in one of the pair of chairs bracketing the fireplace.

He eased down onto the other chair, then cast a quick

glance towards the door. "Will your . . . uh . . . husband be joining us?"

She shook her head, the movement bouncing the black curls left to dangle onto her neck from her upswept hairstyle. "Harrison thought it best if you and I talked in private."

Eli nodded, more nervous than he thought he'd be. Before he could decide how to begin, Nora broke the silence.

"Why, Eli? After all these years, why did you decide to come back now?"

He managed a crooked smile. "I met someone."

"Ah, a woman." The panic in her eyes began to recede.

"Yes. She badgered me about letting my family know I was alive, and finally I decided she was right."

"Do you love her?"

"I hope this won't hurt you, but I love Jade more than I thought possible."

She gave him a bright smile. "You don't know how happy that makes me. I was so afraid you'd want us to resume our marriage, and then I'd have to tell you that I love Harrison more than I thought possible."

Eli chuckled, then quickly sobered. "What a mess I've made of our lives. But I swear, I never meant for this to happen."

"What did happen, Eli? Where have you been all this time?"

He began by reminding her of his threats to leave the Confederate Army when conditions continued to deteriorate, then said, "What finally cinched my decision was getting word that you had died in an influenza epidemic. I just couldn't stay with my regiment any longer."

"I was afraid something like that had happened. By the time I found out my name was listed among the dead, nearly a month had passed since you were notified. I immediately wrote you, but I never got a response." She sighed.

"I always wondered if you'd received my letter before your disappearance."

"I left the army the day after I heard about the epidemic. But I don't understand why your name was included with the others. I thought you were still in Griffin."

"I was. I'd been working in a Griffin hospital ever since Atlanta fell in July of '64. But several days before the illness struck, I left to accompany some of our patients to a hospital in Macon. I expected to be gone no more than a week, but unfortunately, or as it turns out, fortunately, my return to Griffin was delayed by the arrival of more wounded from other hospitals. I was needed, so I stayed. As to why I was included as one of the deceased, I don't know the answer. But I suspect no one removed my name from the roster at the hospital in Griffin, either because the staff was too busy, or else they just didn't bother since I was due back within a week."

Eli nodded. "I guess that makes sense."

When Eli didn't say any more, Nora said, "Tell me about after you left the army."

He took a deep breath, exhaled slowly then began speaking. After summarizing the past six years, concluding with his stay in Fort Davis, Texas, he finished by saying, "So, I convinced Jade to come to Nashville with me, and here we are."

"And then Olivia told you I'd married Harrison."

"Yes," he replied, smiling for the first time. "I have to admit, that did come as a shock. Though after I thought about the situation, I realized I wasn't as shocked as I should've been." He paused for a moment. "Actually, relieved is a better word to describe my reaction."

Nora's eyebrows lifted. "Really?"

"After I found out you were alive and I made the decision to come back to Nashville, I decided something else." He cleared his throat, then said, "I decided to file a petition for divorce."

Nora sat back in her chair, gazing into the cold fireplace.

After a long silence, she said, "You and I should never have gotten married."

Eli blinked. "What?"

"With The War going on and our future in doubt, we reacted like most young people would, I suppose. Arranging a hurried wedding before the groom leaves to join the army, maybe never to return." Shifting her gaze to meet his, her lips curved in a sad smile. "I loved you Eli; I'll always love you. As a friend. But our getting married was a mistake."

He ran a finger around the inside of his tight collar, wishing for the more comfortable shirts he'd worn as a trapper. "You're right. Until I fell in love with Jade, I didn't really know what the word meant."

"That's how I feel about Harrison."

He leaned forward, bracing his forearms on his thighs. "So now what happens?"

"We'll need to speak to a lawyer. Before Harrison and I were married, we decided to consult with his cousin, Dillon Maxwell, who's had a law practice in town since The War. Dillon told us I would be free to remarry provided you've been absent from our marriage for five years, or I had good reason to believe you were dead. At the time of our meeting, it hadn't been quite five years since your disappearance, but Dillon thought you could be presumed dead since no one had heard from you in all that time.

"Obviously, I was relieved by what Dillon told us, even though I wasn't certain I believed he was correct to assume you were dead. But what I did believe was, if you hadn't returned or written in five years, you never intended to. So, to my way of thinking, whether you were alive or dead didn't make any difference." She drew a deep breath. "As it turns out, it may make a big difference."

Eli watched her eyes darken with pain. "I'm sorry, Nora. In spite of what I did, I truly never meant to cause you so much pain and trouble."

She managed a smile. "I know."

He rose and moved to stand next to her chair. Laying a hand on her shoulder, he gave her a gentle squeeze. "Try not to worry. Everything will work out."

She nodded. "I'll contact Dillon's office first thing Monday morning to make arrangements for us to meet with him."

"I already have a commitment for Monday morning, but any time in the afternoon would be fine."

"I'm sure Dillon can accommodate us. Once I set up an appointment, I'll send a messenger to Olivia's house."

"Fine." He gave her shoulder another squeeze, then turned and walked from the room.

Chapter 23

Promptly at a quarter to eight Monday morning, Eli and Jade headed for St. Vincent's Hospital on South College Street. They were to meet Dr. Terrence Henley who'd agreed to take them on a tour of the facility.

"Thank you, Dr. Henley," Eli said after introducing himself and Jade to the slender man with a hawkish nose and a small dark beard. "We certainly appreciate your taking time from your busy schedule to show us around."

"Always happy to oblige an alumnus of the Medical College."

Eli looked sharply at the man who couldn't have been out of medical school for more than a year or two. "How did you know I graduated from the university?"

"When Dr. Briggs asked me to conduct a tour for y'all, he mentioned you were a student here before the war."

Eli's eyebrows rose. "That's true. I graduated in '60. Dr. Briggs was one of my instructors, but I'm surprised he remembered me."

"He said you were one of the best students he's ever had."

A dull flush crept up Eli's cheeks. "That's kind of him to say."

Dr. Henley stared at Eli for a moment, then said, "Dr. Briggs also said you were a field surgeon for the Confederacy, but he lost track of you later in The War."

"I've been in Texas since I left the army."

"Ah, that would explain it," Dr. Henley said with a nod. His gaze flickered over to Jade then back to Eli. "So I assume the tour is for the young lady's benefit, since you've obviously seen the inside of a hospital many times."

"Yes. Back when I was attending the university, our clinical instruction was done at St. John's Hospital. And when I was in France, I studied at one of the larger hospitals in Paris. But Miss Tucker is from a remote part of Texas and has never seen a modern hospital, which is why I wanted her to see St. Vincent's."

The doctor smiled at Jade. "We can take care of that directly. Is there a part of the hospital you'd like to see first, Miss Tucker?"

"Wherever you'd like to start would be fine," she replied. "I'm anxious to see everything."

Dr. Henley chuckled. "Well now, I believe that can be arranged. We don't have any surgeries scheduled this morning, so how about if we begin there?"

When Jade nodded, he said, "If y'all will follow me, we'll get started."

Jade viewed each floor of the hospital with a wide, fascinated gaze, trying to commit everything she saw to memory. The surgery and patient wards were similar to those in the infirmary at Fort Davis, though the rooms at St. Vincent's were larger and more modern, the equipment more plentiful. Jade even found the doctors' offices interesting, the bookcases filled with medical textbooks and journals. She looked at the textbooks with longing. If only she had even part of the knowledge contained in those volumes. Combined with what she'd already been taught about healing, such knowledge would make her better able to help her patients. Casting one more look at the bookcases, she turned and followed after Eli and Dr. Henley.

At the conclusion of their tour several hours later, Eli and Jade expressed their thanks and started to leave when Dr. Henley said, "You know, Dr. Kinmont, the hospital is always looking for good doctors, especially competent surgeons. If you'd like, I'll speak to Dr. Briggs. Perhaps he'd even want you to help out with some of the classes at the Medical College."

Eli found being addressed as doctor strange after the past six years. Yet surprisingly, he also found the title comfortable, no longer cringing when he thought of himself as a doctor. "I appreciate that, Dr. Henley, but I . . . uh . . . haven't decided what I want to do yet."

"Well, even if you don't come to work at St. Vincent's, Nashville will be lucky to have another fine doctor like yourself practicing medicine here."

"Yes, well, thanks again, for both the tour and the offer. I'll be in touch." Eli shook the young man's hand again, nodded goodbye, then turned to escort Jade outside.

On the ride back to his mother's house, Eli was quiet, apparently lost in thought. Jade finally broke the silence by saying, "Why didn't you tell Dr. Henley you were interested in working at St. Vincent's?"

He didn't respond immediately, then finally said, "I'm not sure that's what I want to do."

"Why wouldn't you? I thought you were interested in medicine again."

"I am, but—"

"Then you should accept a position at the hospital. Now that you're back home, you'll need to find work. And working at St. Vincent's would be a wonderful opportunity for you. An opportunity to fulfill your dream to help the people of Nashville."

Eli frowned. Why was Jade so adamant about pushing him to accept Dr. Henley's suggestion? "Thanks to you, I've discovered I still love medicine and want to resume being a doctor. But like I told Dr. Henley, I haven't decided what I want to do."

"You're an experienced surgeon, surely the hospital could use you."

His lips curved in a sour smile. "Yes, thanks to The War I've had plenty of experience being a surgeon. But I doubt there's much need for a doctor in Nashville who knows how to treat gunshot wounds or amputate arms and legs."

"Maybe not, but I would think what you learned doing those surgeries could be applied to other types of operations."

"I suppose," he said, scowling. "Even so, I still don't know if I want to concentrate on being a surgeon or open a private practice."

Jade sighed, slumping against the back of the carriage seat. "Well, Dr. Henley was right. Whatever you decide, Nashville is lucky to have you."

Eli grunted, but didn't reply. Casting a quick glance in her direction, he wondered again at the reason for her comments.

As Eli and Jade entered his mother's house, Olivia came down the stairs to meet them. "A message arrived from Nora an hour ago," she said, indicating an envelope laying on a table in the foyer.

Eli tore open the envelope, read Nora's short note, then said, "I'm to meet her at the lawyer's office at one-thirty." He checked his pocket watch. Eleven-thirty. "Mama, is there any chance Cook can be persuaded to serve dinner earlier than usual? I'll need to leave here by one."

Olivia smiled. "Cook isn't as hard to get along with as you seem to think." She turned toward the back of the house. "I'll go talk to her right now."

After a hurried meal, Eli rose from the table, brushed a quick kiss on his mother's cheek then pressed a more leisurely, thorough kiss on Jade's surprised mouth. Forcing himself to break the contact, he straightened. "I'll be back as soon as I can," he said in a rough voice. He ran his fingertips along Jade's jaw, then turned and left the dining room.

Once Eli had departed, Jade decided to go outside, hoping the fresh air would clear her mind. Though she had enjoyed her stay in Nashville and especially the company of Eli's mother and sisters, the crowded city continually pressed in on her, making her long more and more for the openness of Texas. She'd made the trip to Tennessee because of her love for Eli. And although that love continued to grow stronger, she wasn't sure how long she could remain. At some point a difficult decision would have to be made.

As she wandered through Olivia's flower garden behind the Kinmont house, she drew a deep breath, filling her lungs with a heady combination of floral scents. Sighing, she sat down on one of the benches situated along the garden path. What would Eli say when he returned from the lawyer's office? Is that when he'd finally announce his plans for his future in Nashville? She sighed again. Once she knew what Eli had decided, she would have to start thinking seriously about her own—Her thoughts suddenly came to a halt. As the darkness encroached, blotting out the bright colors of the flowerbeds, she gripped the seat of the bench, waiting for the Spirits to speak to her in a vision.

The sounds came first: a woman moaning and making panting noises; a female voice whispering soothing words; the murmur of another voice—male or female, she couldn't tell—offering words of encouragement. Then the blackness lifted, revealing a room. With a start, Jade recognized the bedroom in her Fort Davis house. Studying the scene more closely, she noticed the sheets covering the floor beside the bed, and nearby, a pile of clean cloths, a knife, string and a blanket. She smiled. The room had been prepared for the birth of a child.

Her gaze snapped back to the woman who was assuming a squatting position on the sheet-covered floor. Recognizing herself as the woman about to deliver a child, Jade's breath lodged in her throat. She exhaled slowly, then shifted her gaze to the face of the other woman. There was no mistaking the silver eyes and long black braid of her mother. She smiled again, then turned her attention to the third person in the room, hoping to bring the face of that shadowy form into focus. Perhaps her friend and teacher, Paloma Diaz, was there to help deliver her child, but the shadows never lifted so she couldn't be certain.

Before she had time to further contemplate that unknown person's identity, the scene abruptly changed. Jade saw herself sitting against the headboard of her bed, a baby cradled in the crook of her arm. Her breath caught in a soft gasp. A daughter. There was nothing in her vision to tell her the sex of the child, yet she knew. She would have a daughter.

She swallowed her elation, then let her gaze move away from the baby and her tuft of chestnut-colored hair. Someone was sitting on the edge of the mattress, that mysterious person again, still cloaked in shadows. Jade strained to see something that would give her a clue to the person's identity. But just as quickly as the vision began, the images disappeared, leaving only blackness in their wake.

She blinked at the sudden brightness of the sun, the flower garden slowly coming back into focus. Clenching her hands in frustration that she wouldn't be allowed to see more, she released her breath in a long sigh. She knew the Spirits always had a purpose for everything they revealed to her. Sometimes their messages were obvious. Others were more subtle, often using symbolism to hint at the underlying meaning. The vision she'd just experienced fell somewhere in the middle of the spectrum—she'd clearly seen the images the Spirits had sent her and knew one day she'd have a daughter, but she didn't yet understand the significance of allowing her a brief glance into her own future or why the identity of one of the people in the vision had been withheld. Rising from the bench, she retraced her steps to the house. She needed time to think.

In her room, she stretched out on her bed then replayed the vision over and over in her mind, searching for clues. After analyzing everything the Spirits had shown her, she finally deciphered their message. Rising from her bed, she left the bedroom in search of Olivia.

Eli slapped the reins against the back of the horse hitched to his mother's carriage, urging the animal to a faster pace. Feeling lighthearted, his spirits higher than they'd been in recent memory, he couldn't wait to see Jade. The guilt he'd carried with him for six years—the guilt which had begun to ease after she prodded him into writing his mother, the guilt which had eased even more after his arrival in Nashville—had nearly disappeared. Though he'd taken Jade's advice and forgiven himself for deserting the Confederate Army, he would never look favorably upon his conduct. But at least the memory no longer filled him with the bitter bile of self-condemnation. Free from the burden of his guilt-ridden past, he could now concentrate on his future. A future he intended to live out as a doctor while happily married to Jade.

Eli arrived at his mother's house, turned the carriage over to the young man Olivia employed to care for the horses, then rushed through the rear door of the house. Calling for Jade, he started down the hallway.

Olivia appeared in the doorway of the back parlor. "What happened? Is something wrong?"

"No, Mama, everything's fine." He glanced down the hall. "Nora's lawyer is going to do some additional checking, but he thinks nothing more has to be done. Nora will remain married to Harrison and I'm free to—" He cast another glance down the hall then stared down at his mother. "Mama, where's Jade?"

Olivia's gaze skittered away from his. "I believe she's waiting for you in the library."

Eli eyed his mother, wondering at the odd expression on her face. He finally nodded, then said, "If you'll excuse me. I need to talk to her."

"Surely, son," she replied, giving his arm a gentle pat. "You go on."

Eli moved down the hallway to the library. He opened the door and looked into the room. Jade sat in one of the matching leather chairs flanking the fireplace, a book, one of his textbooks from medical school, lay opened in her lap. For a moment, he remained rooted in place, content to watch her. His heart near-to-bursting with love, he stepped into the room and closed the door behind him.

She looked up at his approach and met his gaze. He smiled, then said, "This was always my favorite room in the house."

"I can see why," she replied. "I'd spend every available minute in here reading." Waiting for him to speak, she closed the textbook with great care. When he remained silent, she finally said, "What happened at your meeting?"

He moved across the carpeted floor, then crouched in front of her chair. "The lawyer told us that even though the section of Tennessee legal code which allowed Nora to remarry doesn't specify what happens if the missing or supposedly dead spouse turns up alive, he doesn't think there will be a problem. It's his opinion that under the state statutes, my marriage to Nora will be viewed as null and void and that no charges will be filed. He's going to do some additional research to be certain. But even if there's a snag, he assured us that, given the circumstances, a judge would be more than willing to grant us a divorce."

Jade managed a smile. "I'm sure Nora was relieved."

"Yes," he said, returning her smile. "She was afraid of being arrested as a bigamist, so learning that isn't going to happen was an enormous relief." His expression sobered. "Jade, now that the issue of my first marriage is out of the way, there's something I want to say."

Jade nodded, realizing what she had to say would have to wait a little longer.

He took her hands in his. Rubbing the backs of her fingers with his thumbs, he said, "I love you, Jade, and I want to spend the rest of my life with you. Please say you'll be my wife."

Tears burned the backs of Jade's eyes and formed a lump in her throat. She needed several minutes to compose herself enough to speak. "I have something I want to tell you, too, and it won't be easy after . . ." She swallowed hard. "After what you just said." Pulling free of his grip, she curled her hands into tight fists atop the book in her lap, then forced herself to meet his confused gaze. "Eli, I can't marry you. I'm going back to Texas."

He stared at her for a long moment, taking in her stiff posture, her white-knuckled hands. "What? But I thought you loved me." Before she could say anything, he rushed on. "I know you never told me, but the way you looked at me, the way you responded to my kisses, my touch. I thought you loved me. Am I wrong?" His gaze landed on something he hadn't noticed before: the leather satchel sitting beside her chair. The significance of the satchel couldn't be denied. "My God, you're serious! You're really leaving."

His earlier joy shattered, he got to his feet. Rubbing the back of his neck, he paced across the room then returned to stand in front of her. "I think I deserve to know why," he said, folding his arms across his chest. "Does your decision have anything to do with the way some of Mother's guests treated you last night?"

Jade shook her head, vividly remembering the evening before. Olivia Kinmont had hosted a small party so a few of her friends could welcome Eli back into Nashville society. Everything had gone well until one of the men overheard

Jade talking to one of the women about being a healer. Though Jade had received sympathetic looks from nearly all the female guests and even from most of the men, the rest had a grand time tossing out insults and derogatory comments, all of which they thought hilariously funny. Even Eli's efforts to halt the rude behavior had done little good. Jade had managed to smile through the entire humiliating episode, but inside her temper raged against such ignorance.

"My decision has nothing to do with last night," she said at last. "You and Papa warned me that not everyone would look favorably on the life I've chosen for myself. And after my experience with Sergeant Davidson, I'm learning not to let comments like the ones I heard last night bother me."

Eli dropped his arms to his sides, then sank into the chair opposite Jade's. "So if that isn't the reason you're leaving, what is?"

She took a deep breath, then said, "I don't belong here." When he opened his mouth to say something, she held up one hand to stop him. "It's true, Eli. Your mother has been a wonderful hostess. I'll always be grateful to her and your sisters for making me feel welcome, and for treating me like I fit in when it was so obvious that I didn't."

"You're being ridiculous."

"No, I'm not. I could never fit into Nashville society. Life here is much too hurried, too sophisticated for someone like me. I'm used to simple clothes, a simple, relaxed way of life in the mountains of Texas. But you were born and raised here. You belong here, Eli. Your future is in Nashville." Recalling the message from the Spirits in her recent vision, she added, "And my future is in Texas."

Eli remained silent for a moment. "But you never let on. All this time, I thought you liked Nashville, that you were willing to live here."

"I do like Nashville, as a place to visit, and I've already explained why I can't live here. I've truly enjoyed the time

I've spent with you and your family. I told your mother, but I want you to know, too, how much I appreciate everything all of you have done for me, especially you, Eli. Thank you again for showing me the wonderful sights of the city, for the rides to see the beautiful countryside, and most of all, for arranging the tour of St. Vincent's. Actually seeing a city hospital is something I never thought I'd experience, and I'll never forget that day.''

Eli sat in stunned silence, now understanding the anguished look on his mother's face. Pity. Her expression had conveyed pity because she knew about Jade's plan to leave. As the realization sank in that his worst fear was coming to pass—he was losing Jade—a crushing pain squeezed his chest. Hanging onto his pride, he reacted in the only way left to him. With a flare of temper, he said, "So, the truth finally comes out. You lied to me in Fort Davis. Your only reason for agreeing to come here was so you could see a damn hospital!"

"That's not true," she replied, his sharply spoken accusation cutting her to the quick. "I told you before we left Texas that your offer to take me through a hospital was one of the reasons I decided to come with you. And if you'll recall, I also said I wanted to make the trip so I could be with you." She paused to regain her composure. "I didn't lie, but I also didn't tell you the main reason."

He glared at her, his eyes darkened to a deep stormy blue. "Then how about enlightening me now?" Before she could form a reply, he said, "And while you're at it, why don't you answer the question I asked a few minutes ago—am I wrong to think you love me?"

Jade stared at him for a long tense moment, trying to decide how to phrase her response. Finally, she released her breath with a shuddering sigh, then said, "The main reason I came here was because I'd fallen in love with you." She gulped down another lump of tears. "So, no, you're not wrong, Eli. I do love you, but I'm still leaving on this evening's train."

Chapter 24

Eli couldn't believe how one sentence could fill him with such sweet joy, and at the same time splinter his heart into a thousand pieces. Even the simple act of drawing a breath became an effort.

"You've been here less than two weeks. Hardly enough time to recover from our trip." His voice sounded hollow to his own ears, exactly the way his chest felt. "Wouldn't you like to extend your visit for a few more days? I . . . uh . . . I'll stay away from you, if that's a problem."

Jade's lips curved in a sad smile. Unwilling to tell him that delaying her departure would only make leaving him more painful, she said, "Thank you. But I think it would be best if I leave today."

He nodded absently, then said, "What time does your train leave?"

"Five-thirty."

He slowly got to his feet. "I'll take you to the depot, unless you'd prefer to have someone else."

"No, I'd like you to take me."

"Well, then, if you'll excuse me. I . . . uh . . . have some things to take care of. I'll see that a carriage is ready at quarter to five.''

Jade watched him walk from the library, her eyes and nose stinging with another round of hot tears. Though she knew her decision was the correct one, since the Spirits had sent her a vision revealing her future was in Texas, saying goodbye to Eli would be the hardest thing she'd ever done.

The long train ride to New Orleans was pure misery for Jade. She ate little and barely slept, her thoughts alternating between getting home and Eli. Though she knew going back to Texas was the right choice, such knowledge didn't ease her pain. Before making the trip to Tennessee, she'd prayed she wouldn't return home with a broken heart, but those prayers had been ignored. She'd also told both her mother and Paloma she feared her trip to Nashville would force her to choose between her love for Eli and being a healer. As it turned out, her fears hadn't been completely unfounded—she had been forced to choose. But the Spirits had taken the decision out of her hands. The corners of her mouth lifted in a weak smile. At least her vocation hadn't been an issue in deciding whether she stayed in Tennessee.

As the train traveled on, her thoughts returned to her last moments with Eli at the depot. He'd tried to appear unaffected by her leaving, stoically refusing to let her see how much she'd hurt him. But she knew. The pain in his eyes, the harsh set to his square jaw, his rigid posture told her the truth.

Somehow through the entire awkward scene she'd managed to control her emotions, though she'd nearly burst into tears when he pressed a soft kiss on her lips as a final farewell.

She drew a deep shaky breath, forcing herself to think of something less painful. She turned her thoughts to the vision of her giving birth, remembering the baby lying in her arms and wishing—A sob caught in her throat. If only she were returning to Texas carrying a child—Eli's child. But that wasn't possible. Because of his condition, they had never done what was necessary for her to conceive.

The Spirits had clearly revealed her having a child, so perhaps Eli's impotency was another reason they weren't meant to have a future together. But such an affliction would never have stopped her from loving him, or accepting his proposal to become his wife. He was the key to her happiness, not the prospect of bearing his children. Now of course, after the Spirits had revealed what her future held, the point was moot. Inhaling a long quivering breath, she stared out the window, barely noticing the passing scenery.

Eli went through the weeks following Jade's departure by rote. He'd accepted a position at St. Vincent's, not because the work was truly what he wanted to do—he had yet to discover the answer to that question—but to keep himself busy. Though he found great joy in getting back to practicing medicine and treating patients, there was still something missing.

For his mother's sake, he made an effort to return to the social life expected of him. But he soon found the constant round of parties, lectures, the theater and meetings of various philanthropic associations all enormously tiresome. The crowded rooms were suffocating, the formal attire much too restricting, the summer heat stifling.

Eli returned early from another such evening with a raging headache, no doubt brought on by the overpowering scents of perfume and the prattle of boring conversation. As he stripped off his clothes, he thought again of how he longed for the less complicated life he'd led before returning to Nashville, for the cool, fresh air of the moun-

tains in Texas. Texas. The word instantly filled his mind
with thoughts of Jade.

In the first few days after she boarded the train for
New Orleans, he'd tried everything possible to keep from
thinking of her. His efforts had met with minimal success,
since anything and everything reminded him of her. And
after he started working at the hospital, she was his constant, if invisible, companion, always looking over his shoulder when he examined a patient, whispering suggestions
in his ear for the appropriate herbal treatment.

He stared at his image in the mirror above his dresser,
frowning at his haggard face. Hell, what did he expect?
He hadn't gotten a decent's night sleep in almost a month.
Turning away from the mirror with a grunt, he climbed
into bed and hoped sleep would come easier that night.

Sometime later, he awoke from a sound sleep with a
start. He blinked, trying to figure out what had awakened
him. Ah, yes, he'd been dreaming of Jade. Not an unusual
occurrence, but this dream was different from the others.
This had been especially erotic, the two of them lying
naked in the bed in her Fort Davis house. Gentle kisses
and soft caresses had led to hotter, wilder kissing and
touching, and then to his shifting their positions so that
she straddled his hips. Just as she lowered herself to take
his turgid length into her waiting warmth, he'd awoken.

He scrubbed his face with one hand. *Damn, it was so real.*
As he rolled onto his side, the air left his lungs in a rush.
"Jesus," he whispered aloud, shocked to discover his
dream hadn't been entirely in his mind. Jade wasn't with
him, but he *was* aroused, fully aroused with a throbbing,
painful erection.

He scowled. *God, why now?* Staring at the darkened window in his room, waiting for the ache in his groin to ease,
he mulled over what might have brought about the reversal
of his impotency. By making a mental list of what had
changed in his life from the time he'd discovered his afflic-

tion to the present, he finally hit on what had to be the key. Guilt.

Guilt could be a powerful and destructive emotion. The past six years were proof of that. Considering the amount of guilt he'd heaped on himself after receiving word of Nora's death and then his desertion, and the strength of his determination to put everything about his former life behind him, it was no wonder a part of him had shut down. And now that he'd successfully faced and come to grips with his past, the burden of his guilt had eased, allowing his body to once again function normally. As strange as the notion sounded, the conclusion he'd reached was the only one that made any sense.

Struck by the irony of the situation, a wry smile curved his lips. All during the time he'd spent with Jade in Fort Davis, he hadn't been able to make love to her. And now that he was no longer impotent, he was in Tennessee and she was back in Texas.

He flopped onto his back, thoughts of making love to Jade sending another surge of blood to his manhood. He was instantly hard and throbbing for release. Gritting his teeth against the urge to shout his outrage at the turn his life has taken, he willed himself to relax.

A long time passed before he won the battle and finally drifted back to sleep. Even then, erotic dreams continued to disturb his slumber, so that he awoke in the morning groggy and exhausted.

Two days later, Olivia Kinmont returned from an afternoon of shopping to find Eli looking through the books in the library. A large wooden shipping crate sat in the middle of the room.

Her eyebrows knitted in a frown, she said, "Eli, what in tarnation are you doing?"

"Packing," he replied, not looking up from his task.

"Packing? Where are you sending all these ..." She

moved next to the crate and peered inside. "... medical books?"

"Texas."

Olivia's frown deepened. "Eli, I think you'd better tell me what's going on here."

He placed a copy of *Gray's Anatomy* in the crate, then turned to face his mother. "Mama, I'm taking my old medical books, along with some new ones I bought this morning, with me to Texas."

Olivia pressed one hand to her bosom. "Are you planning on returning to Nashville?"

"Not if Jade will have me."

She was silent for a moment, then stepped around the crate to stand in front of him. "Son, I know you and Jade love each other, so I'll pray everything works out for the two of you."

"Then you're not upset that I'm leaving?"

She swatted his arm. " 'Course, I'm upset," she said, though there was no heat in her words. "You've only been back a couple of months after being gone for more than six years, and now you're set to leave again." She gave him a weak smile. "But I understand. I could tell you haven't been happy since Jade left. And if your happiness means going to Texas to be with her, then I know that's what you must do."

"Thank you, Mama." A pang of anxiety gripped his insides. "I just hope I can convince her to accept my proposal this time."

"She may have given you the mitten once, but in my estimation, she won't refuse you a second time."

"I hope you're right," he replied, rubbing the back of his neck.

" 'Course I'm right. As soon as I met Jade, I knew she was a smart gal, a real huckleberry above a persimmon."

Eli chuckled. "Yes, she truly is a cut above any woman I've ever met." Wrapping his arms around her and pulling her close, he said, "Mama, I'm going to miss you and all your sayings."

"I'll miss you, too, son," she replied, returning his hug. "You-all will come back for a visit every now and again, won't you?"

"You know we will," he said, silently hoping he wasn't jinxing himself by including Jade. "And I hope you'll consider coming to Texas."

She stepped out of his embrace and stared up at him for a long moment. "I might just do that."

Jade rose from the chair in Paloma's small hut. "I should start back to town."

The old woman nodded, then said, *"Chica,* I wish I had never told you the Anglo doctor would become your *esposo.* If I had kept silent, perhaps you would not have fallen in love and not gone with him. Perhaps I could have saved you from the—"

Jade placed one hand atop Paloma's gnarled fingers. "Stop fretting, *maestra,* what you told me about Eli didn't make any difference. I would have fallen in love with him anyway, and it was my decision to go with him to Tennessee."

"Sí, but I hate to see so much sadness in your eyes."

"I'll be fine," she said, giving the woman's hand a gentle squeeze. "I just need a little more time."

Paloma stared up at her for a moment, then said, "What about the vision? You have had the same one?"

"Sí, a few days ago. It was just like the others. I can clearly see myself and my mother. But the other person remains in the shadows."

"You still think I am that mysterious person?"

Jade nodded. "You and my mother are the two people I would want with me."

"I know you would, *chica.* But my eyesight continues to

get worse, and I am old and tired. I might not be here to attend the birth of your child.''

''Have you been ill, *maestra*? You should have told—''

''There is nothing to tell; I have no illness. I meant that you should not count on my assistance, *bueno*?''

Jade swallowed, then bent to kiss one of Paloma's wrinkled cheeks. Straightening, she said, ''I'll come back soon.''

On the ride back to town, Jade wondered if she'd told Paloma the truth. Would she really be fine after a little more time passed? She'd been home for almost a month, and the pain in her heart had yet to lessen.

Since her return, she'd tried to stay busy—treating her patients, collecting and preparing plants and herbs, or visiting Paloma whenever she could—yet nothing kept Eli from her thoughts for more than a few minutes at a time. Even her parents' visit to bring back Luna and Zita a week after she'd arrived in Fort Davis hadn't lifted the shroud of despondency hanging over her. Though she was glad to see them, their sympathetic looks kept her on edge. Even more disturbing was having to witness the loving relationship between her mother and father—a constant reminder of what she'd lost. Thank goodness they hadn't been offended when she asked them to leave after three days.

She heaved a weary sigh. Perhaps it was time to consider leaving Fort Davis. Maybe she should move some place that didn't remind her of Eli at every turn. Looking at the Davis Mountains reminded her of the day she'd found him lying on a trail in those mountains. Examining a patient then preparing a remedy made her wonder what Eli would've prescribed. Getting into bed at night made her remember how they'd shared her bed, how he used his hands and his mouth to rouse her passion then guide her to completion.

Luna came to a halt, jerking Jade's thoughts back to the present. She blinked several times, then looked at her surroundings. Her mare had stopped next to the corral behind her house. Startled to realize she'd arrived home without recalling most of the trip from Paloma's, she slipped off Luna's back. After unsaddling the mare and turning her loose in the corral, she headed for the rear door of her house.

She entered the kitchen, then went into the storeroom where she deposited her bag of healing supplies. As she returned to the kitchen, she glanced into the main room and caught a glimpse of something sitting in the center of the floor. Moving closer to the doorway, she stared at the wooden crate through narrowed eyes. *Where did that come—?*

"Hello, *roja*."

Jade nearly jumped out of her skin. Passing through the doorway into the main room, her gaze quickly found Eli lounging on the settee, a contented Zita lying beside him. Jade closed her eyes for a moment, certain she had to be dreaming. When she let her eyelids drift open, she exhaled slowly. Uncertain what his return to Fort Davis meant and not wanting to find out just yet, she remained silent while her gaze drank in everything about him.

He was dressed in clothes similar to those he wore the first time she saw him: an open-neck cotton shirt, tight buckskin trousers and worn boots. A battered felt hat sat on the table next to the settee. His gold-streaked brown hair just brushed the collar of his shirt and the stubble of his beard darkened his jaw.

When her pulse slowed enough for her to hear over the wild beating of her heart, she said, "What are you doing here? And what's this?" She pointed at the wooden crate.

"I'm here because you're here. And the box is full of medical books."

She frowned. "I don't understand."

"After you left Nashville, I was determined to forget you. I started working at St. Vincent's and tried to get on with my life. I did enjoy being a doctor again, but I wasn't happy. I found city living tiresome and suffocating. I missed the open skies, a simpler style of life, everything I enjoyed before I went back to Tennessee. I finally realized the true source of my happiness wasn't in Nashville. It was here in Texas."

He rose and moved to stand in front of her. Skimming the backs of his knuckles down her cheek, he said, "You are the source of my happiness, Jade—only you." His fingers beneath her jaw, he lifted her chin until their gazes met. "I brought the medical books with me because I intend to set up a medical practice here in Fort Davis, if you'll agree to be my partner. I also came here to ask you again—" He took a shuddering breath then exhaled slowly. "Actually I'll beg if need be. Jade, will you be my wife?" He brushed the pad of his thumb over her bottom lip. "Please say yes, *roja.*"

Jade swallowed around the lump of tears wedged in her throat. "You want us to be partners in a medical practice?"

He smiled down at her. "Yes, I want us to be professional partners. But more importantly, I want us to be partners in life."

"And you want to live here?"

"Here, or anywhere you choose, as long as we're together."

She stared up at him for several agonizing seconds, then her mouth curved into a smile. "Yes, I accept both proposals."

Eli thought his heart would burst with joy. Giving a whoop of relieved laughter, he wrapped his arms around her waist and hauled her flush against him. After a long, sizzling kiss, he whispered, "I love you, Jade. I'll love you until the day I die."

Jade wriggled closer, reveling in the feel of his arms around her, of his heart pounding in the same frantic rhythm as hers, of the hardness of his muscular chest, his thighs and—She sucked in a sharp breath, then tentatively pushed her hips forward again. Leaning back in the circle of his arms, she looked up into his amused face.

When he didn't speak, she said, "Eli?"

"What?" he replied, his expression unchanged.

"Is there something you want to tell me?"

He chuckled. "Why would you say that?"

When her eyebrows rose in anticipation, he said, "I don't understand exactly what happened, but I think my being impotent had something to do with the guilt eating at me. Once I stopped feeling guilty, well . . ." He pushed his straining erection against her belly. "You can see the results."

A mischievous smile appeared on her flushed face. Rotating her hips, she said, "Actually I can't."

Before he could reply, she pressed a finger to his lips. "I can't see the results." Her smile broadened to a grin. "But I'd like to."

His grin matching hers, he nipped playfully at her finger. "Careful, *roja*. Keep rubbing against me like that and I may fulfill your wish."

Her eyes sparkling, she said, "Really?" Keeping her gaze glued to his, she thrust her hips forward to press against the hard ridge beneath the fly of his trousers.

He gave a bark of laughter, then bent to sweep her into his arms. "I warned you," he whispered. "You asked for it, and now you're going to get it."

Chapter 25

Eli strode into Jade's bedroom, lowered her onto the bed then dropped down beside her on the mattress.

"I nearly went crazy after you left Nashville," he murmured, closing the distance between them. "I threw myself into working at the hospital and attended every damn affair in the city, just to keep from thinking of you." He nibbled on the corner of her mouth. "Nothing helped though. You were always in my mind." He pulled her bottom lip into his mouth and suckled gently. "And in my heart, which is where . . ." He ran the tip of his tongue over her lips. "You'll always be."

She smiled. In a slightly breathless voice, she said, "You'll always be in my heart, too, Eli. Now, stop talking and start doing."

He lifted his head, laughter rumbling in his chest. "You're really something, *roja,*" he said, staring down into her silver-flecked green eyes. "Tell me this isn't a dream. Tell me you've really agreed to marry me."

"No, this isn't a dream," she replied, moving her hands

to the buttons on his shirt. "And yes, I've agreed to marry you."

When Jade opened his shirt and ran her fingers over his chest, he moaned. His memories of her touch didn't do justice to the reality of the liquid fire of her hands, lightly brushing over his skin and igniting each place she touched.

"Eli, hurry," she murmured, her mouth seeking his for a long, mind-drugging kiss.

She tasted of sweetness and wanton heat, sending his already tenuous hold on his control a little closer to total anarchy. Then she broke the kiss, pushing him away and struggling to sit up so she could remove her clothes.

In a matter of moments he'd managed to shrug out of his shirt, then pull off his boots and trousers. When he turned back to the bed, Jade lay naked in the center of the mattress, skin flushed with desire, hair spread on the pillow in a glorious mahogany tangle. His beautiful Texas Jade took his breath away.

He watched her gaze move from his face, to his chest, then lower. Resisting the urge to join her on the bed, he waited for her to finish her perusal, his pulse beating heavily in his temples. When her gaze found the proof of his recently revived masculinity, he saw her eyes widen and her lips part, with surprise or shock he couldn't be sure.

"Now that you've seen . . ." He touched himself, making his hardened manhood jerk at the contact. ". . . this, do you want to stop?"

Jade swallowed, then shifted her gaze to meet his. Rolling her head back and forth on the pillow, she held out her arms to him. "I want us to make love."

Eli's breath left in a rush of relief. If she'd asked him to stop, he would have found the strength somehow, but thankfully he wouldn't have to put his restraint to the test.

He placed a knee on the mattress, stretched out beside her then let her arms enfold him. "It's been a long time, so I—'' He swallowed, surprised by his level of nervousness. ''I don't know if—''

''Shh,'' she whispered, pressing a line of kisses down his neck. ''I love you, so stop worrying.''

Her words instantly easing his raging case of nerves, he braced his weight on his forearms and captured her face in his hands. ''I love you, too, *roja*,'' he said in a raspy voice before settling his mouth over hers. Then words were no longer necessary, their bodies taking over any needed communication.

He kissed her until she was breathless, caressed her breasts until her nipples were crested into tight peaks and wet from his mouth, and stroked the silky flesh between her thighs until she writhed beside him, sobbing her need.

Though she returned his kisses and caresses, he wouldn't allow her to touch him intimately.

''That isn't fair,'' she said in a gasping whisper. ''I want you to feel the way you make me feel.''

''I do.''

''But—''

Her protest ended when his lips captured hers. He deepened the kiss, intent on exploring the inside of her mouth with his tongue. He suddenly sucked in a surprised breath and jerked his mouth from hers. ''Dammit, *roja*, stop that!'' he said in a choked voice.

The next time her fingers tickled his ribs, she wrenched a laugh from him, then another and another. Weak from laughter, he needed several attempts before he finally managed to grab her hands and still her torturous fingers.

''Is this how—?'' He had to pause to drag more air into his burning lungs. ''Is this how you're going to react whenever you don't get what you want?''

She stared up at him, her lips swollen from his kisses, her eyes filled with green fire. She flashed him a saucy smile. ''If I have to.''

He chuckled. ''Well, at least you're honest.'' Sobering, he said, ''Believe me, I'd love for you to touch me, and next time you can touch me all you want. But not now. I'm already near the brink and just one touch from you could send me over the edge. Do you understand what I'm saying?''

After a moment, she heaved a sigh then nodded.

He smoothed her hair away from her face, then delved his fingers into the thick waves. "Jade, I want you to listen to me this time. I don't know if I'll be able to save you from any pain. I swear, I don't want to hurt you, but I might behave like a rutting boar.''

She lifted a hand and cupped the side of his face. "I told you to stop worrying. Pain or no pain, I'll be fine."

He turned his head to press a kiss on the palm of her hand. Swallowing the lump of emotion in his throat, he took the time to assure himself that her body was ready to receive him before shifting to his knees between her thighs.

He tried to make their joining as gentle as possible, carefully probing her feminine center before easing forward. As he pushed deeper, stretching her to accommodate him, she inhaled sharply. He froze, gritting his teeth against the urge to bury himself to the hilt.

"No, don't stop," she said in a rasping whisper. "I want you, Eli. I want all of you."

Her soft plea put an end to his determination to take her slowly. Pulling her legs up around his waist, he rocked his hips forward, easing into her a little more. She was incredibly warm and slick, her inner muscles pulling him ever deeper. With a savage growl, he withdrew nearly all the way, then plunged forward.

She gasped, went rigid for a split second, then slowly relaxed. When he was certain her pain had receded, he began moving his hips, withdrawing slightly then sheathing himself once more in her welcoming warmth. He set a slow, easy tempo for his strokes until she grew accustomed to his intimate intrusion. When her hips caught the rhythm, he increased the pace.

As she continued to match him thrust for thrust, her

mouth sought his for a fiery kiss, her fingernails dug into his back. Her passionate response whittled away at the fragile hold he had on his control, until he knew his release was only moments away. Hoping to take her with him on that phenomenal journey, he braced his weight on one forearm and slipped his other hand between their bodies.

When he touched just above where their bodies became one, she cried out. "Easy, *roja,*" he murmured in a gruff voice. "I can't wait much longer, and I don't want to leave you behind." He rubbed her damp flesh with his fingers, nudging her swollen bud with gentle strokes.

Jade arched her back, bucking against his hand, grinding her pelvis against his. She couldn't get close enough. The heat Eli had ignited between her thighs continued to build, growing hotter and hotter until she thought the flames would consume her. She thrashed her head from side to side, craving an end to the torment, yet wanting it to go on forever.

Then suddenly she was there. Sobbing his name, her climax overtook her in one astounding spasm after another.

At the first contraction of her inner muscles, the last thread of Eli's control snapped. His thrusts became harder, faster, his breathing a series of ragged gasps. Pushing into her as far as he could one last time, he went still. Head thrown back, a high keening cry escaping his throat, his release erupted in one throbbing spurt after another.

Several minutes passed before Eli could move. His muscles quivering with weakness and his lungs still gasping for breath, he finally summoned the strength to roll onto his back beside Jade.

They dozed for a while, letting their bodies recover. When Jade awoke, she rolled onto her stomach. Bracing herself on her elbows, she stared down at Eli's relaxed features.

"Eli?"

"Hmm?" he replied, his eyes still closed.

"I've been thinking about what you said about your guilt being the reason for your impotency. And I think you're right."

His eyebrows arched. "Do you?"

"Yes. I talked to Paloma about it and she—"

"What?" His eyes snapped open. "You talked to her about my being impotent?"

She tipped her head to one side. "Of course. She's been a healer for many years, and I wanted her opinion on how to treat—"

"Oh, God," he said with a moan, running a hand over his face. "Dare I ask what she said to do?"

Jade smiled. "Actually, she didn't know of a cure, not from plants anyway. She told me the key was to first find a way to heal your inner hurts. After what you told me, I think your guilt was the inner hurt she was talking about."

He stared at her for a moment. "Interesting."

"I agree." She leaned forward to press a soft kiss on his slack mouth, then shifted her weight onto one elbow so she could run the opposite hand through the hair on his chest. Tracing lazy circles with her fingers, she moved her hand down over his rib cage, around his navel and onto his flat belly. "As usual, Paloma was right," she said, moving her fingers even lower. "Healing your inner hurt was the key to awakening the sleeping giant."

Laughter rumbled in his chest. "Sleeping giant," he said. "How amusing, though not exactly accurate."

"I don't know," she replied, giving the body part in question a gentle thump before carefully wrapping her fingers around him and giving him a squeeze. Immediately his flaccid manhood jerked in her hand, swelling and throbbing within the circle of her fingers while she watched in fascination. "Looks like a giant to me."

She glanced up at his face, a triumphant smile curving her lips. He stared back at her with wide eyes, their color darkened to a deep midnight blue.

"I hope our daughter has your eyes," she said. "I know

she'll have hair something like mine, only lighter, but I couldn't see her eyes."

Eli forgot his growing desire for a moment. "What are you talking about? How do you know—?" His eyes widened even more. "You had a vision?"

She nodded, releasing her intimate grip of him. "The Spirits first sent me the vision while I was in Nashville. That's the reason I decided to leave. The vision clearly showed me having a child here, in this house, and I later realized the Spirits were trying to tell me my future was in Texas, not Tennessee."

"Why didn't you tell me about the vision when I asked you why you were leaving?"

"Since there was no way I could have been carrying your child when I left Nashville, I didn't want to hurt you by telling you I would bear a child by another man."

Eli lifted a hand and rubbed his thumb over her bottom lip. "Thank you. I would've had a hard time accepting that."

She nodded. "It was hard for me to accept, too. I didn't want a child by anyone but you."

"But if your vision didn't reveal who fathered the child, how do you know it'll be me?"

A bright smile lit up her face. "I've had the vision several times since I came back to Texas, and each was exactly like the first. My mother was there with me, along with a mysterious third person. I couldn't figure out why the Spirits wouldn't let me see the face of that person, but I always assumed it was Paloma since she's a midwife. A few minutes ago, while I was half asleep, the Spirits sent me that same vision. Only this time, I could see the faces of both people assisting the birth of my child. My mother was one and . . ." Her smile broadened. "The other person was you."

A look of absolute panic crossed his face. "I'm going to help deliver my own child! I don't think that's a—"

"Shh, don't worry. My mother has helped deliver many

babies, and she'll be there with us. Everything will be fine. The Spirits have said so." When he didn't look convinced, she added, "I've seen our daughter, Eli, she's beautiful."

The tenseness in his face drained away, his tight muscles relaxing. "A daughter," he whispered in awe. Then louder he said, "We're going to have a daughter!"

"Yes," Jade replied with a laugh. "But the Spirits didn't tell me when, so . . ." She moved her hand back to his manhood and gave the partially hardened flesh a squeeze. "Wake up, sleeping giant, we have work to do."

Eli's laugh soon changed to a groan, and a short time later, to a shout of elation.

Epilogue

Fort Davis, Texas, six years later

The door of the small building housing the medical offices of Eli and Jade Kinmont burst open. "Papa, Papa," Sheridan Kinmont said, skipping into the office, her thick chestnut braids bouncing with each step. "Mama says Gramma 'Livia's coming to see us."

Eli looked up from his desk and smiled. The sight of his five-year-old daughter, with her rosy cheeks and deep indigo eyes, made his heart cramp with love.

Sheridan's personality was a true paradox. At times she could be a perfect little lady, never causing a bit of trouble. And at other times, she turned into a mischievous, saucy-mouthed rascal who never failed to earn some sort of punishment from either himself or her mother.

He smoothed the collar of her dress, then said, "Did a letter come from your grandmother?"

Sheridan shot him an exasperated look. "No, Papa. Mama *saw* Gramma, you know, in here." She patted the top of her head.

"Ah, I see. Well, did your mother say when—"

"Soon, I think," Jade said from the doorway. "My vision showed her riding in a stagecoach." Closing the door, she crossed the room and stopped next to Eli's chair. She bent to press a kiss on his mouth, then said, "It'll be nice to see Olivia again."

"Yes," he said, caressing her slightly rounded belly. Their second child would be born that winter. "I just hope the trip isn't too much for Mama this time."

"She wouldn't come if she thought it would be."

"That's true," Eli replied. "If only the railroad would come this far west, then traveling here would be much easier for her."

"The railroad's probably still years away."

Eli nodded, his gaze shifting to Sheridan. She'd moved to stand in front of the cabinet containing the bottles of medicine he'd ordered from back East as well as an assortment of tonics and salves Jade had prepared. He watched her point at the bottles, her mouth moving silently.

Jade followed his gaze and smiled. "She's trying to memorize the names of all our medicines."

"Really?" he said, pulling her down onto his lap and nuzzling the side of her neck.

"She's already told me the next thing she wants to learn is what each medicine is used for."

He slipped a hand under Jade's skirts, easing higher until his fingers touched her inner thighs. "Do you think she wants to be a doctor?"

"I don't know," she said, her voice growing husky. "But if she tells us that's what she wants, are you going to try to talk her out of it?"

Eli chuckled. "Not me, *roja*. Even at five, our daughter definitely has a mind of her own. I almost pity the man who falls in love with Sheridan. He's going to have his hands full."

Jade smiled. "But she'll be worth whatever trouble she causes him."

Eli chuckled again, murmuring his agreement against her throat.

"Any chance you can close the office early?" she said, tipping her head to one side to give him better access.

He lifted his head to stare into her eyes. Noting the silver flecks were more pronounced against a darker-than-usual green background, he said, "What did you have in mind?"

Her voice dropped to a throaty whisper. "I thought maybe I'd do a little giant hunting."

Eli threw back his head and laughed. "No need to do any hunting," he replied in an equally low voice. "The giant's right here." He flexed his hips to bump his growing erection against her bottom. "Ready and willing whenever you are."

Jade ran her fingers through the hair at his nape, then leaned closer to his ear. "How about now?"

"I think that can be arranged." After pressing a quick kiss on her sweet mouth, he removed his hand from beneath her skirts then helped her to her feet. Turning to their daughter, he said, "Sheridan, come on. Your Mama wants to go home."

"But I wanna stay here, Papa."

"Not today, honey. Mama wants to lie down for a while."

Eli watched her shoulders lift in an exaggerated sigh. Turning away from the cabinet, she stomped toward the door.

"It's not fair," she said, her mouth puckered in a pout. "Grownups always get to do what they want."

"You'll be a grownup before you know it, Sheridan," Jade said. "Then you can do whatever you want."

As the girl opened the door, she stuck her chin in the air and said, "And I will, too."

Jade and Eli exchanged a look and groaned, certain their daughter had never spoken truer words.

Author's Note

I hope you found *Texas Jade,* the second book in my Texas Healing Women Trilogy, an enjoyable read. Writing Eli and Jade's story was truly a wonderful experience for me, an experience made even more satisfying because of the book's setting—a place I consider one of the most beautiful in this country. If you ever have the opportunity to go to the Davis Mountains, I sincerely hope you'll jump at the chance to see this remote area of Texas. The scenery there is truly spectacular, the small towns charming, the people open and friendly. The trips I made to far West Texas will always be cherished memories, memories I hope I can add to with future visits.

Although the U.S. Army did employ civilian doctors, especially in the years following the Civil War when there was a shortage of army physicians to staff the numerous frontier military forts, my research revealed that women were not hired to work as doctors—or as a surgeon's assistant like Jade Tucker. During the earlier 1870s, generally the only positions open to women at a military hospital were cook, matron or laundress.

As I revealed in my first Texas Healing Women book, *Texas Silver* and reiterated in *Texas Jade,* the Mescalero Apache did not use that name, but called themselves *Nde*— The People. Only after being forced onto a reservation did they reluctantly accept the name the American government insisted on calling them. The Mescalero were actually on two different reservations. In 1863 they were sent to the Bosque Redondo reservation along the upper Pecos River in eastern New Mexico. The living conditions these proud people had to endure were deplorable and only continued to grow worse. Two years later, the Mescalero rebelled, evading their guards to slip away during the night and return to their homelands to the south. Blamed for every depredation committed in their old territory, they were hunted relentlessly by the U.S. Army. Few in Washington, D.C. or the Indian Agency thought Indians were anything other than filthy savages who had to become civilized overnight or suffer the consequences—a punishment of death. In 1873, an Executive Order of President Ulysses S. Grant established the Mescalero Apache Indian Reservation. The remaining Mescalero—about four hundred of their former thousands—were forced onto this newly created resesrvation in south central New Mexico that same year. Later, they were joined by the surviving members of the Chiricahua and Lipan bands, where the descendants of all three bands live today.

Texas Indigo, the final book in my Texas Healing Women Trilogy, will be the story of Sheridan Kinmont, daughter of Eli and Jade, who continues her maternal family's legacy of healers.

After Sheridan receives her medical degree from an Eastern college, she accepts a position as the doctor for a mining company in far West Texas. But when she meets the mining company's general manager, Shay Bannigan, she wonders if accepting the job was a mistake. Sheridan joined not only the ranks of the college educated physician in the East, she also joined the woman's suffrage movement. Though she refuses to allow herself to be put under any man's thumb—especially the infuriating Shay Bannigan—his sinful good looks and heated kisses are simply too much to resist. Shay doesn't think women have any business being doctors and has no qualms about speaking his mind. Even so, he's irresistibly drawn to the paradoxical Sheridan, the epitome of a lady one minute and a sharp-tongued, hot-blooded temptress the next. He soon realizes his life's creed to "love 'em and leave 'em" could be in real jeopardy. Watch for the release of *Texas Indigo* in the summer of 1999.

I love hearing from readers and invite you to write me with your comments about *Texas Jade*. I always respond, plus I'll send you a bookmark and my current newsletter. Please write to: Arlene Hodapp aka Holly Harte, P.O. Box 384, Paw Paw, MI 48079-0384.

—Holly Harte

BOOK YOUR PLACE ON OUR WEBSITE AND MAKE THE READING CONNECTION!

We've created a customized website just for our very special readers, where you can get the inside scoop on everything that's going on with Zebra, Pinnacle and Kensington books.

When you come online, you'll have the exciting opportunity to:

- View covers of upcoming books
- Read sample chapters
- Learn about our future publishing schedule (listed by publication month *and author*)
- Find out when your favorite authors will be visiting a city near you
- Search for and order backlist books from our online catalog
- Check out author bios and background information
- Send e-mail to your favorite authors
- Meet the Kensington staff online
- Join us in weekly chats with authors, readers and other guests
- Get writing guidelines
- AND MUCH MORE!

Visit our website at
http://www.zebrabooks.com